To my darling Ben and Ali, you are why the world makes sense.

GOOD GIRLS

AMANDA BROOKFIELD

First published in Great Britain in 2019 by Boldwood Books Ltd.

Copyright © Amanda Brookfield, 2019

Cover Design by The Brewster Project

A CIP catalogue record for this book is available from the British Library.

Paperback ISBN 978-1-83889-313-2

Ebook ISBN 978-1-83889-311-8

Kindle ISBN 978-1-83889-312-5

Audio CD ISBN 978-1-83889-314-9

MP3 CD ISBN 978-1-83889-407-8

Digital audio download ISBN 978-1-83889-310-1

Boldwood Books Ltd
23 Bowerdean Street
London SW6 3TN
www.boldwoodbooks.com

'I am no bird. No net ensnares me. I am a free human being with an independent will.'

— JANE EYRE

PART I

PART I

1

Eleanor decided to take a taxi from the station, even though she knew it would cost ten precious pounds and mean a wait. Being so rural, only a handful of cars served the area, but she didn't want to be a bother to Howard, her brother-in-law. She texted both him and Kat to say she would be there within the hour and stayed as warm as she could in the small arched station entrance. It was a cold, dank morning, not raining for once but with air like icy metal against her skin.

The taxi driver who pulled up some twenty minutes later exuded an attitude of reluctance that made Eleanor disinclined to make conversation. When they hit a tail-back, thanks to a loop round the old Roman bridge, still not fixed from the heavy flooding over the New Year, he thumped his steering wheel. 'A bloody joke. We can land men on the moon and still it takes three weeks to fix a few old stones.'

Eleanor murmured agreement, but found that she didn't mind much. The fields on either side of the road were still visibly waterlogged. After the grimy mêlée of south London, it was a visual feast – ethereal, shimmering silver bands engraved with the black reflections of leafless trees and smudgy January clouds.

The usual criss-cross of feelings was stirring at being back in such proximity to the landscape of her childhood. Just twenty miles away, her father was a resident in a small care home called The Bressingham, which he had once included in his rounds as a parish priest, days long since lost to him through the fog of dementia. Howard and Kat's substantial Georgian house was ten miles in the opposite direction, on the fringes of a town called Fairfield. They had moved from Holland Park seven years before, a year after the birth of their third child, Evie. At the time, Eleanor had been surprised to get the change of address card. She had always regarded her little sister and husband as life-long townies, Kat with her posh quirky dress-making commissions to private clients and Howard with his big-banker job. It was because they saw the house in a magazine and fell in love with it, Kat had explained at one of their rare subsequent encounters, in the manner of one long used to plucking things she wanted out of life, like fruits off a tree.

But recently life had not been so cooperative. A small tumour had been removed from Kat's bowel and she was in bed recovering. Howard had reported the event earlier in the week, by email, and when Eleanor had got on the phone, as he must have known she would, he had said that the operation had gone well and that Kat was adamant that she didn't need sisterly visits. No further treatment was required. She would be up and about in a matter of days. Their regular babysitter, Hannah, was increasing her hours to plug gaps with the children and he was taking a week off from his daily commute into the City.

'But I am her sister,' Eleanor had insisted, hurt, in spite of knowing better. 'I'd just like to see her. Surely she can understand that.' Howard had said he would get back to her, but then Kat had phoned back herself, saying why didn't Eleanor pop down on Saturday afternoon.

'Nice,' said the driver, following Eleanor's instructions to turn between the laburnums that masked the handsome red-brick walls and gleaming white sash windows and pulling up behind the two family cars, both black, one a tank-sized station wagon, the other an estate. He fiddled with his satnav while Eleanor dug into her purse for the right money.

I am not the rich one, she wanted to cry, seeing the visible sag of disappointment on his sheeny unshaven face at the sight of her twenty-pence tip; *I am merely the visiting elder sister who rents a flat by a Clapham railway line, who tutors slow or lazy kids to pay her bills and who has recently agreed to write an old actor's memoirs for a sum that will barely see off her overdraft.*

Howard answered the door, taking long enough to compound Eleanor's apprehensions about having pushed for the visit. He was in a Barbour and carrying three brightly coloured backpacks, clearly on the way out of the house. 'Good of you to come.' Brandishing the backpacks, he kissed her perfunctorily on both cheeks. 'Brownies, go-carting and a riding lesson – pick-ups in that order. Then two birthday parties and a bowling alley. God help me. See you later maybe. She's upstairs,' he added, somewhat unnecessarily.

'The Big Sister arrives,' Kat called out, before Eleanor had even crossed the landing. 'Could you tug that curtain wider?' she added as Eleanor entered the bedroom. 'I want as much light as possible.'

'So, how are you?' Eleanor asked, adjusting the offending drape en route to kissing Kat's cheek, knowing it was no moment to take offence at the Big Sister thing, in spite of the reflex of deep, instinctive certainty that Kat had said it to annoy. At thirty-eight she *was* the big sister, by three years. She was also almost six foot, with the heavy-limbed, dark-haired, brown-eyed features that were such echoes of their father, while Kat, as had been pointed out as far back as either of them could remember, had inherited an uncanny replication of their mother's striking looks, from the lithe elfin frame and flinty-blue feline eyes, to the extraordinary eye-catching tumble of white-blonde curls. 'You look so well,' Eleanor exclaimed, happiness at the truth of this observation making her voice bounce, while inwardly she marvelled at her sibling's insouciant beauty, utterly undiminished by the recent surgery. Her skin was like porcelain, faintly freckled; her hair in flames across the pillow.

'Well, thank you, and thank goodness, because I feel extremely well,' Kat retorted. 'So please don't start telling me off again for not having kept you better informed. As I said on the phone, the fucking thing was small and isolated. They have removed it – snip-snip,' she merrily scissored two fingers in the air. 'So I am not going to need any further treatment, which is a relief frankly, since I would hate to lose this lot.' She yanked at one of the flames. 'Shallow, I know, but there it is.'

'It's not shallow,' Eleanor assured her quietly, experiencing one of the sharp twists of longing for the distant days when they had been little enough and innocent enough to take each other's affections for granted. They had been like strangers for years now in comparison, shouting across an invisible abyss.

She took off her cardigan, hanging it round the back of the bedroom chair before she sat down. The room was hot and smelt faintly medicinal. Several vases of flowers, lilies, roses and carnations sat on the mantelpiece, between get well cards. Above them hung a huge plasma television screen; enough to put her off reading, Eleanor decided, let alone any other pleasurable nocturnal activities.

'So how did you know something was wrong? If you don't mind my asking.'

Kat pulled a face. '*Changes*, which I have no wish to go into. Blood in the stool,' she went on breezily nonetheless, '– as the doctors so delicately like to call it – being one of the many highlights, together with "going" too much, or not at all. Little wonder I was in no hurry to discuss it with our GP. But then Howard said I was an idiot and he was right. I like my husband.' She grinned, leaning down to retrieve a pillow from the floor and slapping Eleanor's hand away when she leapt out of the chair to try to help. 'Sorry, but I just don't want a fuss. Everybody is fussing and it's driving me fucking nuts.'

Eleanor leant against the wall by the bed while Kat settled herself. Spotting their father's old Bible on the bedside table, she picked it up, absently riffling through its pages. 'And how are the children?'

Kat's face lit up, as if a bulb had been turned on inside her. 'Fantastic, thanks. Little monsters all. Annoying. Demanding. Wonderful. Luke has gone geeky and has a quiff and a last word for everything. Sophie is in love with horses, I think she would literally marry one if she could. And Evie... well, Evie is just Evie.' She sighed dreamily. 'On her own planet, as every seven-year-old should be.'

'Her asthma?' Eleanor ventured, painfully aware of how little she really knew of her sister's family life, the result of years of learned wariness, the age-old sense of being kept at arm's length.

'Oh, that's all gone. She grew out of it. Thank God.' Kat picked up a glossy swatch of her hair and scrutinised the ends. 'So, will you be visiting Dad? Kill two birds with one stone. So to speak.' Her sharp blue eyes flicked from Eleanor's face to the Bible in her hands, dancing but steely.

'I've come to see you, not him,' Eleanor replied levelly, putting the book down. As she did so an old empty envelope dropped out of its back pages. Scrawled across it in the big spider writing that Eleanor immediately recognised as having once flowed from their father's gold-tipped desk fountain pen was a note to their mother: *Darling Connie*, it said, *came home for a 10-min lunch. I love you. Vx.*

'Hey, look at this.' She held the note out to Kat.

Her sister nodded. 'Yes, it's been there, like, for ever.'

'Has it? Oh, okay.' Eleanor gently replaced the envelope, giving the book a pat as she closed it shut. A part of her waited to see if Kat said anything about their mother, whilst knowing she wouldn't, because she never did. 'It's nice though, isn't it?' she prompted. 'Given what happened... well, it can make one forget the good things.'

'Oh, I never forget good things,' said Kat briskly. 'By the way, you could borrow my car, if you did want to visit Dad.'

'I've told you, I don't want to. Thank you. Not this time.'

'It's up to you.'

Eleanor couldn't help laughing. 'Are you trying to get rid of me, or something?'

'Of course not. I'm glad you came. Thank you for coming, Eleanor.'

'Don't be silly. I had to. I wanted to. I'm just so pleased the bloody thing was harmless.' Eleanor returned to the window, folding her arms and gripping her elbows. 'I do go and see him from time to time, you know.'

'I know you do.'

'Not as much as you, but...' Kat had been the favoured child, at least when they were little. And if it hadn't been Kat in the spotlight, it had been their mother. Or God. When it came to the focus of Vincent's attention, it was invariably Eleanor who had come last.

'It's fine, Ellie.'

'It's like visiting a corpse.'

'Yes, it is.'

'So. What can I do now I'm here?' Eleanor asked brightly, wanting to wrest both of them back to the reason for her visit. 'Tea? A biscuit? Or is there something you'd like me to do? Hoovering? Shopping? I'd so like to be useful.'

'There's nothing, thanks. Hannah, our babysitter, and Howard are doing a brilliant job of keeping the show on the road.' Kat lay back against her pillows, her expression growing distant.

'Hey, guess what, I have just been commissioned to write another memoir,' Eleanor blurted. 'This time it's that actor, Trevor Downs? He's really old now but...' She broke off, feeling foolish, as Kat's eyes fell shut. Her sister's skin looked starkly pale suddenly beside the white January sunlight, now spooling into the room through breaks in the cloud and falling into misty pools on the silky grey carpet. There were marbled veins at her temples that Eleanor had never noticed before, threading under her cheekbones like the blue in a soft, pearly cheese. It made her want to stroke Kat's face, show the protective tenderness which always hovered but which never seemed able to come out.

She moved towards the bed but stopped as Kat puckered her lips, seemingly in preparation to speak, but then her mouth fell still again, the lips slack and slightly open.

Eleanor turned back to the window, feeling at a loss. The garden spread beneath her was ridiculously huge and orderly, comprising not just terraces of well-tended lawns and flower beds, but an all-weather tennis court and the smart black rectangle of a covered swimming pool. Kat had been such a wild child that there was something about this tidy state of adult affluence that Eleanor still found hard to buy into.

Yet she was hardly in a position to be critical, she mused, the cul-de-sac of her decade in Oxford coming back at her: the pitiful hanging on because of Igor, the Russian academic who had asked her to write his life story and then swept her into an affair before returning to his wife in Moscow; the subsequent abandoned and useless efforts at fiction; the ad-hoc tutoring to pay bills. Not to mention a social life which, in the three years since moving to London, had somehow deteriorated into a state of lurching oscillation between abject indolence and a sexual promiscuity that she couldn't have confessed to anyone, least of all her self-contained, snugly nested little sister. A recent nadir had been reached in the form of opening her flat door to the husband of her oldest and best friend from university, dear Megan.

Eleanor dug her fingernails into her forearms as the shame flared. Billy had been in London for a stag do. They had said drunken farewells through a taxi window after a chance encounter in a nightclub. Megan had been many miles away, safely ensconced with their three boys in their Welsh home. 'No,' Eleanor had said. But when Billy had reached for the zip on her dress, she had turned, lifting her heavy tumble of hair to make his task easier.

Eleanor had tiptoed as far as the bedroom doorway when Kat's eyes flew open. 'Actually, there is *something* I want, Ellie... something to show you... I don't know how I could have forgotten. Hang on a minute, while I...'

Seeing the grimace of determination as Kat manoeuvred herself out of bed, Eleanor sprang back across the room to help, only to be met with a warning hand to keep away. She took a step back, aware of the deep, buried reflex of looking after her little sister stirring again.

'I'm fine, honestly,' Kat assured her tetchily. 'It's good to move. The doctors said. No one is supposed to lie around after an operation these days. They get you up and about as soon as possible.' She stood, pausing to let the crumples in her long white nightshirt fall free, and then moved steadily to a dark green and orange silk kimono hanging on the back of the bedroom door. She slid herself into it with a quick graceful shake of her shoulders, deftly knotting the cord into a big floppy butterfly-bow off her hip. 'We're going to my study. Prepare to be surprised.' She tapped her nose and grinned, looking so restored and pleased with herself that Eleanor did not have the heart to do anything but follow her downstairs.

Kat's study was a cosy end-of-corridor room containing a desktop computer, a voluminous orange beanbag, an oak chest spilling with sewing equipment and a tailor's dummy swathed in a sari of lilac silk. Kat went straight to the desk and plucked a sheet of A4 out of the tray of her printer. 'My surprise is this.' She shoved the paper under Eleanor's nose, beaming. 'It arrived this morning. Talk about a blast from the past. I want to hear your *views*.' She pronounced the word as if it was a great joke, sliding past Eleanor and settling herself on the beanbag, from where she began to adjust some lower folds in the lilac silk, her small, nail-bitten fingers working nimbly. 'I printed it off so it was easier to read. Take your time,' she mumbled, managing, in spite of having several pins between her lips, to communicate impatience.

The paper was an email. Noting who it was from, Eleanor leant back against the desk in a subtle bid to steady herself, marvelling both at the timing of its arrival and the reminder of her little sister's relentless and unfailing ability to wrong-foot her.

From: N.Wharton@QueenElizabeth.org.sa
Subject: Greetings
Dear Kat,
This is just a friendly enquiry to ask how the hell you are. Something perhaps to do with the big Four Ohhh being on the imminent horizon, wanting to take stock, etc. Where did twenty years go? That's what I keep asking myself. I hope you are well and happy. Are you well and happy?
As for me, doctoring took me to dermatology and for the past ten years I have been working as a consultant at the Queen Elizabeth Hospital here in Cape Town. (Hence the above email address!) I have a South African wife, Donna, and two beautiful daughters (they take after their mother!), Natalie and Sasha, aged fifteen and thirteen. We are lucky enough to live in Constantia, a beautiful area outside Cape Town (in case you didn't know!), in a house with a big garden, pool, etc., and views across the valley towards the city and the famous Table Mountain.
Donna is very happy being near her family (we moved here ten years ago from London, where I worked at King's after my elective). Her father is a successful property developer and they have a superb estate in Rondebosch where she and the girls are able to keep their horses and go riding. (Yours truly prefers tennis!) Living relatively far out of town, Donna is kept very busy running around after the girls – they go to school in the city and have hectic social lives!
Well, Kat, I was just wanting to touch base. A friendly line after twenty years. It would be good to hear some news back from you if you had the time.

By the way, how's Eleanor these days? Say hi from me if you see her.
Best wishes,
Nick (Wharton)

Eleanor read slowly, trying to hear the Nick she remembered between the sentences. There were a lot of brackets and exclamation marks, she observed wryly, her expert eye scanning the text. Far too many. Only nerves could account for it, she decided, feeling a flutter of the old bitterness that, after so many years and all that had happened, Nick Wharton should still betray such signs of jitters when placing himself across the path of her little sister.

'Well? What do you think?' Kat urged. She had finished with her repinning and was back in the beanbag, sitting cross-legged now, her knees neat bulges under her silk gown, her big blue eyes electric and staring. 'Nice that "friendly line" bit, don't you think?'

'Yup. Very nice.' Eleanor was trying to picture Nick in Cape Town in a white coat, being a proper doctor.

'Well? Do you think I should reply?'

'It's up to you.' Eleanor smiled. It was one thing to be wrong-footed, quite another to show it.

'But what do you think?'

Eleanor shrugged. She found it hard to believe that Kat really wanted her opinion.

'If you help me,' Kat added impishly, 'it will take no more than a few minutes.'

'Me? Help you? Why on earth would you want me to do that?' Eleanor set down the letter and moved away from the desk. Kat was putting her through some sort of sick test, she decided, prodding her emotions to see what came out. She had forgotten the power of her sister. Kat did what she wanted and everyone else dealt with the consequences. She either didn't care, or didn't notice.

'It would take me hours, but you'll be able to do it in two

minutes,' Kat pleaded. 'I'm crap with words, all dyslexic and rubbish, not like you, always so brilliant.'

'Don't be silly,' Eleanor murmured, something inside her softening nonetheless. Nick Wharton was such water under the bridge. Ancient water. Ancient bridge.

'I'll tell you what I want to say and you make it better,' Kat instructed, leaving her perch to turn on the computer and then pressing Eleanor into the desk chair. 'We'll do a cheerful potted history like he did, preferably *not* mentioning the jolly business of having had some of my gut removed—'

'You've got follow-up checks and things, have you?'

'Oh, heaps. Now let's get on with it.' Kat settled herself back into the dent she had left in the beanbag, lying on her side this time, one arm protectively cradling her lower stomach. 'Start with "Hi Nick".'

Eleanor obediently began to type. Kat, for whatever reason, had decided she should help with the letter. Test or whim, it was what she wanted. 'And you're sure Howard won't mind...'

She glanced up in surprise as her sister hissed an expletive and slapped the bean bag.

'What?'

Kat was sitting bolt upright, glaring at her. Eleanor stared back in disbelief. It occurred to her that if she had needed reminders of why they didn't see more of each other, Kat could not have been doing a better job. A long time ago, her sister had simply stopped liking her, Eleanor reflected bleakly. It was the only explanation. The sole wonder was her own difficulty in accepting the fact.

'Judging me,' Kat snapped. 'Bossing me. Like you think you have some sort of right. Because of... well, just because you're older.'

'I never think like that.'

'For your information – not that it is any of your business – Howard and I respect each other's privacy. We give each other space. That's one of the reasons I married him. He lets me *be,* unlike most other people I've come across... like Nick Wharton, for example. Oh my god, the man was such a limpet – it's all coming back to me.' Suddenly she was snorting with laughter. 'Mr Clingy... aagh... no wonder I was horrible to him.' She rolled her face into the beanbag, pretending to chew the fabric.

'Why don't you leave him alone then?' Eleanor asked quietly.

Kat stopped her rolling and sat up. 'Because not replying might just seem rude. And where's the harm?'

For a moment Eleanor imagined picking up the computer keyboard and hurling it across the room. She pictured the dummy falling, its robes of lilac flapping like a giant bird, pins pinging in showers of silver rain. But it would upset Kat again and that would be bad. The kimono had fallen slightly open, affording a clearer view of the outline of the bandaging thickening her sister's slim waist. 'You are right,' she conceded softly, quickly looking away, 'so let's get on with it. Where were we?'

'Hi Nick, I think.' Kat plucked at a thread on her gown. 'You're just so serious sometimes, Ellie. It can drag people down. And you're not to be too clever for this, okay? I'll suggest stuff and you phrase it nicely. But the letter's from me, remember, the muggins who scraped five GCSEs, not the bright star who went to Oxford.'

Ten minutes later, Eleanor read out the completed version, a wholly collaborative effort apart from the exclamation marks, which she had scattered liberally, telling herself that writers with sick, spoilt, bafflingly manipulative little sisters had to get their kicks where they could.

Hi Nick,
What a surprise to hear from you after so much time! It was great to get all your news of what sounds like the most wonderful life. I have never been to Cape Town but know of the famous Table Mountain, of course. How incredible to wake up to that every morning!
You asked for news of me and mine, so here goes. I have also been lucky with how things turned out. I stayed as a fashion dogsbody for

a few more years but gave up work after I got married in 1998. Hard to believe that was fifteen years ago! My husband Howard is a Fund Manager with Bouvray-Smith. We live near a place called Fairfield in East Sussex, not a million miles from Broughton, which perhaps you remember?! We've got three kids, Luke, who's 13 and brainy like his dad, Sophie, who's 11 going on 25(!), and Evie who's 7 and probably most like me! We are also lucky enough to have a lovely house and garden – lots of space for the kids to run around in. We even have a pool, though the English weather probably means we don't use it quite as much as you do yours! Howard has to commute, which is a pain, but apart from that life is pretty good. I do a bit of dress-making but otherwise spend my time being a mum - like your wife Donna, by the sounds of things – running around after the little darlings!

Well, Nick, thanks for your email. I can't imagine you forty years old, I must say. Though of course it will be my turn in a few more years! Eleanor is visiting at the moment and says hi back.

Take care and all the best for the next forty!

Kat (Gallagher these days, but I still use Keating sometimes. Was that how you tracked me down?)

'By the way, you know if you end with a question he's more likely to write back.'

'Is he?'

'It's human nature.'

'Is it?'

'Do you want him to write back?'

'Dunno.' Kat frowned. 'Oh, I guess not. Take it out then.'

'Out it goes.' Eleanor deleted the second sentence in the bracket.

'Oh, and add a kiss please. Just one. Lower case. Everybody kisses everybody these days after all, don't they? A kiss means literally *nothing*.'

'Does it?' Eleanor murmured, adding one small cross next to Kat's name and resisting the urge to point out that Nick's signing off had been much more formal. Kat could still have any man she wanted, she reflected, with a twist of weary pride. Age, motherhood, illness made no difference. One snap of her little sister's fingers and men fell like nine-pins. They always had. They always would.

An hour and a half later, after tea and some delicious ginger biscuits reputedly made by Hannah the babysitter, they were on the doorstep, conducting farewells in the glare of Eleanor's taxi headlights. Kat had by then showered and changed into a grey glitter-flecked mohair jumper, loose black trousers and bright red Converse trainers. The jumper shone in the light, catching the sparkle in her eyes. She looked radiant, transformed.

'Would you come again,' she said suddenly, 'if I asked?'

'Of course. Whenever. If you ask.' Eleanor bounced the phrase back casually, knowing Kat was laying down her terms. She had in fact reached a state of longing to be gone, to be on her own. Ill or not, her sister was such hard work, so ready to fight, so good at making her feel there was something she needed to apologise for, if only she could figure out what it was.

'Okay. Cool.'

'Or you could come and see me in London,' Eleanor offered, 'take a break from Howard and the kids. We could have lunch or something.'

'Oh yes, we must,' Kat cried, as if she might even mean it, when they both knew she didn't.

* * *

Ten minutes into Eleanor's train journey, a text came through from Megan.

You okay? Long time no hear. xx

Eleanor gripped her phone, seeing again her friend's husband's big, square, dismayed face peering at her over the mangled sheets of her bed linen three weeks before. The morning mortification had been mutual. Billy had loped off like a whipped dog and she had stumbled to the toilet to throw up with a violence that she knew was as much about self-abhorrence as her hangover. The Trevor Downs commission had come through on the very same day; a flimsy lifeline, it had felt like, the pretext she needed to clean her act up and start again.

Eleanor stared at the message. She was pretty sure Billy wouldn't say anything, but that didn't make it any better or easier. Slowly she typed back:

Fine. Mad busy. In touch soon. xx

Megan would also have noticed her recent lack of communication on social media, she knew. Shutting the world out was a lot easier, she was discovering. Fewer mistakes got made. Less money got spent. Aloneness was the key.

Eleanor rested her forehead against the cold grimy train window, her mind drifting back to Kat's bullishness over Nick's email. Yet it had been easy in the end. Words pinging into an inbox on another continent. Sunny sentences. The past was the past after all, a foreign country, as someone a lot wiser than her had once pointed out.

She closed her eyes with a sigh. Human lives were so messy, that was the trouble. It all began simply enough: one got born, but then stuff started to happen, blocking pathways, burying love and truth till only a fraction of anything made sense.

2

Nick Wharton logged into his work email. There was always lots to attend to. Through the window in front of him he could see his two daughters splashing in the pool, trying to push each other off the big inflatable dolphin, a toy owned and played with for so long it was a wonder it stayed afloat. The house was solidly built, double-glazed against the winds that could pick up suddenly across the Cape. It reduced his daughters' joyful shrieks to muffles, contributing to a sense of cocooned solitariness that Nick found he couldn't quite enjoy in spite of having sought it out. Donna was under the parasol at the table, busy on her iPad, a bottle of one of her expensive mineral waters parked in an ice bucket beside a tall lead crystal glass. She had made the most of the hot January weather by swimming and was wearing a white muslin kaftan recently bought from one of her favourite designer outlets in the Waterfront mall. It looked fantastic against her olive skin and with the black lines of her bikini peeking through the mesh.

Bored by the correspondence most in need of attention, Nick scrolled back to the emails he had been firing off to old acquaintances in the weeks since his milestone birthday and the various replies. It had been enjoyable as well as reassuring to find how easy it was to track people down and to hear news of their busy lives. It had also made him realise, a little wistfully, how far he had moved away from his early doctoring days in England. Coming across what Kat Keating had written back the weekend before, he paused, skimming again through the sentences. The tone was typical Kat, he decided – exuberant but faintly dismissive, skating over the surface of things, not wanting to get stuck in. She had seemed such an alluring locked box of a girl, but when you got close it was like there was nothing to come out, or at least nothing she was prepared to give. And, of course, someone like that had landed squarely on her feet, back in the Home Counties, a rich husband in tow. He would have expected no less. A golden couple with a swanky country house. No wonder the email was so light, so watertight, so insouciant.

Through the window, Donna caught his eye and held up her arm to tap the silver bracelet-watch on her wrist. The pool was now empty, the dolphin abandoned, bobbing in a far corner on a jet from the filter. It was time for him to take Natalie to her dance class. His wife had her sunglasses on, but Nick didn't need to see her expression to know she was irritated. He held up his hand, spreading the fingers to indicate five minutes, and moved on through the correspondence to another reply, a very funny one this time, from a man with whom he had spent many happy youthful hours – good old Peter Whycliffe, erstwhile eccentric student, now a professor of cardiology, making life-and-death decisions in an Oxford hospital. It seemed ridiculous they had ever lost touch.

Nick began to type a funny letter back until a tapping made him look up again.

Donna had taken her sunglasses off and was using them to rap on the window. 'Now,' she mouthed at him, stretching her beautiful curved Cupid's bow lips into an angry O, her blue eyes flashing.

Nick nodded, leaving his desk and putting his head out into the hall to call upstairs. 'Nat? Are you ready?'

'Nearly,' she yelled. There was the squeak of bare feet scampering along the wooden landing floor, followed by the slam of a door. 'Sash has taken my shoes.'

'Have not!' yelped her younger sister.

'Sort it, you two,' Nick warned, adding, 'Five minutes, tops.'

He turned back to his laptop, reluctantly closing down the tabs. When he glanced up, his eldest daughter was lolling in the doorway, her ballet kitbag slung over one shoulder. Noting his air of preoccupation, she shot him a look of wary puzzlement.

'What? We're not that late, are we?'

Nick closed the lid of his computer. 'No, we are not. And you're a good girl.' He kissed her head and picked up the ballet bag, whistling and tossing his keys as they made their way out to the car.

3

OCTOBER 1992

The mushroom was the size of a dinner plate. Behind it, blackening its profile, stretched the steely dawn sky, the sun a brushstroke of pink across its middle. Eleanor blinked in wonderment, her sleepy brain conjuring images of an Alice in Wonderland-style dinner party, attendants seated round the mushroom's flat, sleek ebony top. Beside her, Kat started humming softly. She was barefoot, up to her ankles in the dew-damp grass, her party dress testifying to another all-nighter. Gold strappy shoes dangled carelessly from the middle finger of her left hand.

'Still pissed off I got you out of bed?'

'I was awake anyway.'

'Yeah, right.'

They both stared at the mushroom. It was Kat's idea of a gift, Eleanor guessed, an effort to be nice on her last morning at home.

'It could be breakfast, I thought.' Kat swung the shoes.

'Eat it, you mean?'

'Yes, Dumbo.' She bulged her tongue into her lower lip. She looked exhausted, wild-eyed, wild-haired, glorious. The dress she was wearing was one of the ones she had lately started

running up herself, using their mother's old sewing box and
Singer machine – a tight red bodice sprouting a concoction of
silk and lace panels in electric colours. From somewhere in the
tangle of hair behind her left ear, she extracted a flattened roll-
up, slipping it between her lips but making no move to light it.

'For all we know it could be poisonous.'

'It's not.'

'And how would you know?'

'Because I do.'

'You shouldn't smoke.'

'Fuck off.'

Eleanor turned to face her younger sister, arms folded, her
gaze steady. The hostility was old hat now, she had got used to it.
'And where were you last night?'

'What's it to you?' Kat smiled slyly, displaying the small gap
between her front teeth that, for some reason Eleanor could
never fathom, made her look cute.

'I hope you are careful?'

Kat rolled her eyes, feigning shock. 'Oh yes, we must be
careful, mustn't we. Like you would know so much about that,
wouldn't you, Miss Big-Brain? You're not Mum, so don't try to
be,' she added nastily. 'And if you want to tell Dad then go right
ahead.'

'You know I wouldn't tell Dad,' Eleanor murmured. In just a
few hours, she was going away to start university, starting her life
it felt like. Kat could be Kat – wild and bad – without her having
to worry about it. The mighty mushroom was auspicious for *her*,
Eleanor decided. Her stomach cramped with sudden joy and
terror at the prospect of heaving the old suitcase her father had
dug out of the cellar into the trunk of her English teacher's mini
and journeying to the sandy-stoned college that had, miraculously, offered her the chance to spend three years doing
nothing but reading and writing about English literature. There
would be some Anglo-Saxon to study too, Miss Zaphron had
told her – stories about someone called Bear-Wolf and a green

knight – a dreamy-eyed look had come into her English teacher's eyes as she described them.

Eleanor stole a glance at Kat, who was smoking the cigarette at last, screwing up her eyebrows and doing her best to hold it like a man, between her thumb and index finger, the hot tip tucked into her palm. Pity rushed at her.

'You can come and visit me, you know.'

Kat looked away. 'Like that's going to happen.'

'You'll be sixteen soon, he'll let you then.'

'I wouldn't want to anyway. All those dull Oxford weirdos.' She crossed her eyes.

'Thanks.'

'You're welcome.' She flicked the roll-up into a patch of soft mud, where it sat smoking.

'Dad would be better if you left him alone more. If you didn't always... get at him.'

'Don't fucking tell me how to deal with Dad.' She dropped to a crouching position and circled the mushroom with her arms. Her bony knees stuck out from under the bunched-up panels of the dress. 'We simply must eat this,' she crooned. 'Fried. On toast. Loads of butter.'

Her lips looked raw round the edges, making Eleanor wonder again about the night, whom Kat had been with, what they had done. Anxiety heaved, but so, dimly, did envy. In her own case, boys seemed to steer a wide berth, apart from Charlie Watson, the son of their farmer neighbour. Charlie had a straggly sun-bleached fringe and a crooked smile that masked a jumble of teeth. Whenever Eleanor saw him bouncing along in a farm vehicle, or striding across a field with his father, he waved and grinned. But whenever they got close he seemed to shrink into himself, stuttering inanities, unless they were actually kissing. She knew her height didn't help. Standing up, his eyes were level with her collarbone. It made her want to run away sometimes, just to put the poor boy out of his misery.

From somewhere among the voluminous panels of her

dress, Kat had whipped out a tiny penknife and was hacking at the stem of the mushroom.

Eleanor released an involuntary gasp. 'Don't. I told you, we don't even know if we can eat it.'

'And I told you, we can,' Kat sneered. 'It's *okay*. The same kind are in the shops, just smaller. Christ, you're such a scaredy-cat.'

'I just don't want to die,' Eleanor muttered, adding to herself, 'at least not today.' She looked away, unable to watch.

'Got ya,' Kat cried, plucking the mushroom free and holding it over her head like a ghoulish trophy, heedless of the shower of earth raining into her silver bush of hair. 'Wow, Ellie, look at that. Just huge. We should get a camera. Take a picture.'

'Mark the day you poisoned me, you mean.' They caught each other's eye and laughed properly and joyfully, and suddenly Eleanor was so sad to be leaving, she could have wept.

They walked back in silence across the field, that year an empty square of weeds and compacted earth, Kat carelessly swinging the mushroom by its stalk.

'Just don't let Dad get you down, okay?' she ventured as they neared the garden gate, 'he can't help how he is.'

'Can't he?'

'You know he can't.'

'He should be taking you today.'

'What?'

'Today. He should be driving you. It's not right.'

'But Miss Zaphron wants to. It is only because of her that—'

'Oh shit, I'm going to have to leg it.' Kat jerked her head in the direction of a light that had flicked on at the largest of the vicarage's top-floor windows. 'If he catches me like this...' She thrust the mushroom at Eleanor and set off at a run, taking the long way round the garden, under the lee of the hedge that fringed the silver birch wood.

Eleanor sighed and walked on, picturing how Kat would race up the drive and down the side of the house where the four stone steps plunged to the unlocked cellar door. From there she would scamper up the back staircase to her bedroom, silent as dear old Titch, the vicarage cat, prowling round their stop-start comings and goings on his neat tiger paws.

Entering the kitchen ten minutes later, Vincent's eyes widened at the sight of the mushroom, which Eleanor had wiped clean and placed on a chopping board next to the frying pan. 'What wonders the earth holds in store.' He bent down to study it more closely, putting on his half-moon spectacles and taking them off again.

'Kat says it's okay to eat.'

'Does she now.' He tugged at the thinning grey fringe of his beard.

'She does,' Kat announced, appearing in the doorway behind them, miraculously spruce in her school uniform, her hair fastened into a ponytail that corralled the whorls of her hair into an explosion at the nape of her neck. 'And you trust me, Daddy-oh, don't you?'

'Indeed I do,' Vincent replied mildly, not looking at her. He turned to Eleanor instead, asking her if she was packed and ready. When she said she was, he said he had a gift for her. He disappeared to his study, returning a few minutes later with a small dog-eared dictionary. 'To help you with all those essays you are going to have to write.'

'Thanks Dad.' Eleanor found it hard to speak. He was so rarely attentive, it caught her off guard.

'Yeah, why use one short word where four long ones will do?' snorted Kat, pushing between them to take charge of the cooking.

'Not a morning for silliness, is it,' said Vincent tightly, pulling out a chair to sit down. Eleanor could see the vein in his left temple twitching.

Kat had tied the frayed stained kitchen apron over her uniform and was slicing the mushroom into chunks, tossing them into a pool of melted butter in the frying pan. She stirred with a wooden spoon till the pieces hissed and shrivelled.

She was so needy and Vincent wouldn't see it, Eleanor reflected sadly. Kat longed for attention and approval, but he blocked her at every turn. And maybe that wouldn't have mattered if he hadn't once done the opposite. It didn't matter for her, she was used to being on the outside, negotiating the dark tunnels of her father's moods. But Kat had never tried to negotiate anything. She just bulldozed on, making trouble. 'Kat was the one who found the mushroom,' she gabbled. 'So clever of her. Inspired.'

'She must have been up and out early for that.'

'I was.' Kat threw him a look from under her long mascara-blackened eyelashes. She lifted the frying pan off the hob, shaking and tossing the mushroom chunks as if they were a pancake. 'Very early. I couldn't sleep. I went for a walk.'

'I'll do toast,' Eleanor muttered, rummaging for a knife and sawing with a desperation that went beyond the hardness of the bread. She shook the loose crumbs into the toaster, which hadn't worked for years, and slid three fat slices of bread under the grill.

Seated in front of their food a few minutes later, the slabs of toast serving as hefty plates for the heaps of fried mushroom, Vincent pressed his palms together and closed his eyes, as he always did. Kat scowled at Eleanor, as she always did. *I can't wait to go*, Eleanor thought wildly as her emotions seesawed again. The routines between the three of them were so wearing, an invisible vortex, sucking her down. To be free of it would be like coming up for air.

The mushroom wedges, sodden with butter, were as soft and succulent as steak. Eleanor was too sick with nerves to eat much, but Kat wolfed her portion and Vincent had seconds, wiping the last of the grease off his plate with a ragged crust of toast. Afterwards, he patted his stomach, these days a notable bulk beneath his cassock, and stifled a string of husky burps.

'The Lord provides *bountifully*, doesn't he, Daddy,' quipped Kat, giving Eleanor a look of disgust, 'if you know where to seek.'

Vincent swivelled his gloomy eyes to his youngest daughter, the pupils narrowed to pencil dots. Kat merely smiled back at him, one of her big, bold, toothy smiles that dimpled her cheeks and lifted up the corners of her mouth.

And suddenly Vincent was smiling back at her, an ice-berg melting. 'The Lord certainly does. Exactly.' He pulled out a grubby handkerchief and dabbed cheerfully at the grease-specks in his beard.

'You're missing bits,' Kat cried, leaping round the table to pat his face with a dishcloth, pushing too far as she always did, so that Vincent was soon glowering again, flapping his hands at her to be left alone.

Eleanor took refuge in the washing up, spinning round with an involuntary cry of relief when a car horn sounded in the drive. Kat hugged her from behind, briefly, and then bolted into the hall to watch proceedings from the window seat, belting her arms round her shins and pressing her teeth into her knees.

When Eleanor appeared from upstairs, laden with bags, Vincent trundling ahead of her with the old suitcase, Kat swiftly averted her gaze, keeping it fixed on the window.

'Bye Kat,' Eleanor called softly.

'Bye.' She snapped the word like a whip.

Out in the drive, Vincent had stowed her case in the boot and was engaging the English teacher in the usual animated exchanges he managed for outsiders. Eleanor pawed at the gravel with the toe of her shoe. The lump in her throat ebbed and swelled; maddening, given how keen she was to be gone.

'Well, goodbye, child,' Vincent growled, turning to her at last and placing his heavy spade-hands on her shoulders. 'You are all clear on money, aren't you?' He looked at her – for the first time in years it felt like – with the big dark eyes that were such a mirror of her own.

Eleanor nodded. The money was a princely eighty-pound

monthly allowance, on top of a full government grant. It was another thing that made her feel guilty, but also thrilled.

'Study hard.'

She nodded again, aware of her English teacher on the far side of the car tactfully staring in the opposite direction, towards the sloping tail-end ribs of the Downs.

'And remember,' Vincent went on mournfully, still pressing her shoulders, 'the Lord gives each of us talents, just as he gives each of us burdens. We must accept both with good grace.' He released his hands at last, such a heaviness lifting that Eleanor had a strong sensation of floating rather than walking the couple of feet to the car. The feeling stayed with her for several minutes after she had settled into her seat, contributing to the sense of flying as she and Miss Zaphron took off down the lane, the wheels of the little car rocking and thwacking between the potholes and ridges.

Eleanor waited until the bend to look back. The drive was empty, but Kat was still there, her face a white smudge behind the hall window.

4

'So, are you coming?'

'In a minute... I just need to...' Eleanor gestured helplessly at the books piled around her corner of the library table, an ill-constructed semicircular wall, sprouting pencils and torn scraps of paper, where she was trying to keep track of relevant paragraphs. The books weren't the ones she had been recommended; those had already been whipped out of the library by the smarter, faster members of her year group. Instead she was trawling through turgid tomes that were in no demand whatsoever, desperate to unearth any snippet of information that might assist in the otherwise impossible task of tackling an essay entitled 'Beowulf: Poet or Warrior?'

It was on being presented with these four words the previous Wednesday, her third week of term, that Eleanor had started facing up to the realisation that she was stupid. Worse still, she was a fraud. Since arriving, she had so far cobbled together just one composition, on whether Thomas Hardy was more of a social reformer than a novelist, managing an answer of sorts by drawing heavily on *Tess of the d'Urbervilles*, which she had been fortunate enough to study in the sixth form with Miss Zaphron. It had garnered a few dry words of encouragement from her college tutor, a softly-spoken Irishman with kind grey eyes, who had then offered a respite of sorts in the form of a two-week spell looking at Dickens, with whom she was also lucky enough to have had some previous acquaintance.

But Anglo-Saxon was another matter. For that, she and her peers had been directed to attend the overheated, chaotic rooms of a man called Dr Pugh, who resided in another college and who preferred to rain down his words of wisdom, and much spittle, from the top of a set of library steps parked against one of his many book-stacks. With his domed hairless head, beady black eyes, glittering behind thick lens spectacles, Eleanor found herself unable to look at him without thinking of a bald-headed eagle, about to swoop onto his prey. When he announced the Beowulf essay, flinging down each word from his favoured perch, along with fluttering copies of a recommended reading list, the rest of her group had jumped to catch the pieces of paper like gleeful children chasing leaves, but Eleanor had stayed in her chair, frozen by the certainty that there was no way she would be able to answer such a question satisfactorily in seven years, let alone seven days.

'So, are you coming or not?'

Eleanor could hear the mounting impatience in her companion's voice. She was a girl called Camilla, also a Fresher, but studying History not English. Her own few books had been cleared away and buckled into the smart leather bag she wore across her chest. She occupied the room next to Eleanor's in the modern honeycomb of a block where the college housed most of its first-year students. Bumping into each other within hours of their arrival, they had braved the first meal in hall together and stuck to each other's sides ever since.

'You go on,' Eleanor urged. 'I'll catch you up.'

'But we might not eat lunch there. Billy said there was a chance of hooking up with some others—'

'That's fine.'

Camilla fiddled with the strap on her shoulder bag. 'The

point being, that if you don't come now you might not find us.'
She spoke in a whisper, even though it was past one o'clock and
they were the only two people left in the library.

'I know. That's okay, honestly.'

Still, Camilla hesitated at the corner of the library table. She
was well brought up. She had heavy straight blonde hair, cut in
ramrod lines, so that her face looked as if it was perpetually
staring out of a small window. She had come from an estab-
lished girls' boarding school and acted with all the confidence
Eleanor both feared and expected to find in the produce of such
places: a strong voice, strong opinions, coupled with a brusque
self-confidence. She played hockey and tennis and had signed
up for college rowing. She had big green eyes, set at a feline
slant, and wide nostrils that flared when she was amused, which
was quite often.

'Are you spoken for?' she had asked Eleanor, having invited
her in for a coffee just minutes after they met. Her own identical
box of a room had already been transformed into a homely,
softly lit collage of lamps, beads, spreads, posters and knick-
knacks, causing Eleanor to reflect with shame on the lacklustre
efforts of her own unpacking: a few books on the desk, her
toothbrush and paste on the edge of the basin, the big old suitcase still spilling with the heavy winter clothes that had proved
too bulky to cram into the room's meagre wardrobe.

'No,' Eleanor had admitted shyly, thinking of and dismissing
the unsatisfactory and intermittent fumblings with poor Charlie
Watson.

'Clever you. Good. I dumped mine before coming up. We
might have some fun then, might we not?'

Eleanor had nodded, grateful – and faintly alarmed – to have
found such an amicable and adventurous friend so early on. But
three and a half weeks into term and Camilla was tiring of her,
she could tell. With the proximity of their rooms, she suspected
she had merely provided a convenient starting point for Camilla's social ambitions; the first rung on what would be a tall

ladder. She had not yet stopped Eleanor from sharing her company, but an air of endurance had crept into the arrangement. Several other people were now being made much more obviously welcome; people like the charismatic Billy Stokes who was behind that day's nebulous lunch plan.

A fellow historian with a cherubic smile and the big square body of a seasoned rugby player, Billy was one of those who seemed to know everyone he passed in the street, sharing not only Camilla's armadillo confidence but also her apparent determination to put having fun above the priorities of academic work. Eleanor marvelled at and envied their insouciance. She did not dare to slack off her own studies for a moment. Stupid people had to work harder, she knew that. More to the point, she literally could not afford to enjoy herself in the cavalier manner that they did. Lunch with Billy and his friends would mean drinks, food, then more drinks, necessitating the recurring shame of having to remind them all that she was on a tight budget.

It had taken Eleanor a couple of weeks to realise this herself. What had once felt like riches was evaporating at terrifying speed: books, stationery, tea, coffee, milk, bread, sugar, the couple of subs for societies to which she had boldly and misguidedly committed herself during the course of Freshers' Fair had already proved such a drain on her finances that she was starting to wonder how she would last the term, let alone the year. Her new friends claimed to share such anxieties, but then joked easily about increasing overdraft limits and wheedling more money out of their parents. Eleanor laughed with them, inwardly picturing Vincent's granite face, knowing there was nothing more to come out of him, financial or otherwise.

Camilla at last conceded defeat and took off. Eleanor twirled her pencil in a show of careless farewell, but the moment the library door swung shut, she stabbed the pencil's lead point into her palm, repeating the attack until she had created a circle of deep pink indentations in her skin.

The silence of the old room was suffocating. No one else needed to work through their lunch hour, she reflected bitterly. No one else was so *stupid*. 'The Pride of Broughton' the Head, Mrs Mayfield, had called her in Leavers' Assembly. Looking back on it now, recalling the self-conscious prickle of pleasure on her scalp as all heads in the small school hall had turned to stare, Eleanor could have laughed out loud.

When the door creaked open a few minutes later, she hurriedly pretended to concentrate on her notes, watching out of the corner of her eye as a tall young man with dusty brown hair strode down the central aisle, peering between the bookshelves, clearly in search of a person rather than a book. He was wearing a shapeless cabled grey jumper that looked home-knitted, and loose black jeans, from the bottom of which protruded the pointed toes of scuffed desert boots. He clicked his fingers as he walked, as if keeping beat to some rhythm inside his head.

Eleanor adopted a studious frown and started to copy out a sentence from one of the dense texts in front of her. *Beowulf is composed of 3182 alliterative lines...*

'Excuse me?'

She glanced up. He had wide blue eyes and a clean-shaven face. A year or two older than her, she guessed. His hair was remarkably thick, the sort of hair that swelled outwards as much as it grew downwards. He had a pencil tucked behind one ear and several pens sticking out of his front jeans pocket, snagging on the hem of the jumper.

'Have you seen Miss Coolham?'

'Er... I don't think so. Who is she?'

'The college librarian,' he said, clearly surprised. 'Very tall, quite old. Hair like a Luftwaffe pilot. Scary lady.' He pulled a face. 'She normally sits over there, under Samuel.' He gestured at the large desk set at the foot of a plinth sporting a marble bust of a man with a bulbous nose and long hair.

'Samuel?' Eleanor echoed faintly, inwardly still cowering at the ignorance of having forgotten the name of the person in charge of her own college library.

'Johnson. The dictionary man.'

'Yes, of course, the dictionary man.'

Later, Nick would tell her that she had looked terrified, and that this had both amused him and made him faintly curious. At the time, he had merely shaken his head, disappeared between the bookshelves and then re-emerged with a heavy leather tome, which he settled down to read at the other end of her table.

Eleanor laboured on, making more notes, doing her best to look engaged and scholarly.

'That sounds painful,' he said at length.

'I beg your pardon?'

He pushed his book away and tipped his chair onto its back two legs, crossing his arms and hooking his knees under the table for balance. 'Your stomach.' He grinned. 'Unless there is a gremlin living under your section of carpet.'

Eleanor felt the blood rush to her face. Only too aware of the rumbles emanating from her empty stomach, she had been working with one arm pinned across her lap in a bid to stifle the worst.

'Call me Sherlock, but my guess is you haven't had lunch.'

Eleanor shook her head, still dry-mouthed with embarrassment.

'Me neither,' he confessed cheerfully. 'We could grab something together if you like. Miss Coolham can wait. And, frankly, with all the noise your innards are making, I'm not taking in much of this anyway—'

'God, sorry—'

'I was joking,' he pointed out, looking bemused. 'I'm Nick, by the way. Nick Wharton.' He leant across the table, all mock formality now, to shake her hand.

'Eleanor. Keating.'

'So, do you fancy a bite of lunch, Eleanor Keating?'

'Yes. Okay. Thanks.' She set about trying to tidy away the circle of books, which tumbled, messing up her precious markers.

'You could just leave that lot,' he ventured after a few moments. 'I mean, it's hardly likely to get nicked, is it?'

'No. Yes. Of course. Good idea.' Eleanor fumbled the books into yet more chaos, aware of him watching and of what felt like the liquid state of her brain.

He held the door open for her to go down the entrance steps first, announcing as they set off that he knew a good place in the Covered Market.

Outside, the November wind tore at their clothes, rendering it impossible to talk even in the relatively high-walled protection of the college's main quad. Once in the high street, Eleanor double-wrapped her scarf round the lower half of her face and concentrated on keeping up with her escort's long stride, sneaking sideways glances to marvel both at the apparent warmth of the heavy cabled jumper and the simple pleasure of walking beside someone who was taller than her by several inches. He had to be six foot three at least. He moved loosely, hands in his pockets, cocking his head at the handsome spired buildings and the grey sky as if it was a balmy summer day.

Eleanor had passed through the Covered Market several times but only to enjoy its jumble of artisan stalls and peer through the windows of its boutique shops. Nick led the way to a tiny café she had never noticed, a handful of tables in chequered cloths next to a counter in front of an open cooking range. He instructed her to commandeer the only free table while he queued for two plates of sausages, baked beans and scrambled egg, having assured her that it was the only thing on the menu worth eating and offering to pay.

He ate ravenously, talking between mouthfuls about the travails of being a third-year medic and how if it hadn't been for the pressure from his father, a consultant neurologist, he would have applied to read English.

'I'd even like a crack at Anglo Saxon,' he admitted ruefully, after Eleanor, sufficiently restored by some food and the openness of his manner, had confessed to the creeping sense of despair over tackling the Beowulf essay. 'It's a bit like German, isn't it?'

'I don't know what it's like. I've never done German, only Latin and French, but that's a fat lot of good.'

'But what about the rest of your year – how are they getting on?'

'They sort of keep to themselves. There are only six of us and they're so brainy compared to me... the boys especially. There's one other girl, Megan, but someone told me she's really into the Christian Union...'

'Oh blimey, you'll want to steer well clear of her in that case.' He paused briefly in his eating to skewer a finger to his temple. 'But I bet those others aren't brainier than you,' he went on amiably. 'Boys are really good at pretending to appear as if they know what they are talking about. Trust me, I know.' He closed his mouth around his last forkful of beans, his dark blue eyes flashing.

Eleanor smiled back shyly, her mind fast-tracking through the unpromising males with whom she had hitherto been acquainted, all of them classmates, some of them glib talkers, some not, like Charlie Watson, with his big kind face and thickset body, who had carried his own silence and shyness like a heavy load. It had been one of the main reasons she had felt drawn to him.

'It's mostly bluff,' Nick concluded, watching her carefully, 'remember that. So where did you go to school, anyway?'

'A tiny place in East Sussex, Broughton – you wouldn't have heard of it.' Eleanor hesitated. It didn't seem a good moment to mention that she was the daughter of a vicar. A motherless daughter of a vicar. Even without the Christian Union thing, all of it felt embarrassing, like something that needed confessing to, rather than fodder for general conversation. 'I am the first person in the entire history of the school to have done Oxbridge,' she said brightly instead. 'I only managed it because I had masses of extra lessons. There was this teacher there who liked me... she...' Eleanor stopped. She had been about to say that Miss Zaphron had *believed in her,* but it sounded too grandiose.

'Wow. Congratulations in that case. Loads of people feel daunted here at first,' he added kindly. 'It soon wears off. Don't be afraid to use your own brain would be my advice.' He beamed at her encouragingly.

Eleanor felt her insides dissolve, not with hunger, but something else that she would have found impossible to describe; close to embarrassment but more pleasant, and without the side-effect of the red face. It somehow made it difficult to continue eating. 'So, you would have liked to study English?' she prompted, grabbing at the question purely as a way of diverting attention from the sensation.

'Oh yes. Sort of. In my dreams, at least.' He sat back, smiling and pushing his empty plate away.

'And who are your favourite writers... if you don't mind my asking?'

It was like she had pulled a trigger. He seemed to explode forwards onto his elbows, landing with such vigour that the table tipped sideways. 'Amis. Obviously.' He held the table down, as if it might leap again of its own accord.

'Obviously.' Eleanor slowly carved a tiny piece of sausage. She assumed he meant Martin rather than Kingsley. But she hadn't read either.

'Mainly for *The Rachel Papers*, but *Money* is right up there too. Then there's Fowles, because of *The Collector*. And D. H. Lawrence, not so much for *Sons and Lovers,* or even *Women In love,* or *Lady Chatterley* – not that one can discount any of them, but in my view *The Rainbow* is his true masterpiece. And then there's Forster of course, not so cutting-edge but still a genius; though when it comes to geniuses, Nabokov has to take the biscuit, for *Lolita*, obviously, but then there's *Laughter in the Dark* and...'

Eleanor gawped as he plunged on, scooping up Conrad, T. S. Eliot and Shakespeare in his wake. It was like watching a small typhoon. A typhoon which made her heart race.

'He was a lepidopterist, did you know?'

It took a moment to realise he was expecting a response. 'A... what? Who?'

'A butterfly lover. Nabokov. And as soon as I found that out, I just thought it was significant... I mean...' A new group of students were hovering, pointedly eyeing their empty plates, clutching discarded coats and hats, their faces pink and steaming from the outside cold. Nick did not seem to notice. He was still talking in a rush. 'Take *Lolita* – it's almost like he has ensnared this beautiful specimen of youth, of nascent sexuality, and he wants to keep it – to keep her – pinned under a glass so he can scrutinise and feed off it and...'

'Isn't *The Collector* also a bit like that,' Eleanor ventured, seizing one of the rare moments when he paused for breath, 'at least, doesn't a girl get taken prisoner...' She lost courage, having only indirectly heard about the Fowles book from Camilla, who had pronounced it the creepiest thing she had ever read; but Nick was already slamming the tabletop in delight.

'Brilliant. That's a great thought. A great connection...' The people clutching their coats exchanged glances and shuffled to another vacated table. 'Fowles and Nabokov as literary lepidopterists... hey, that works really well.' He sat back, subdued but visibly pleased. 'I like the way things connect if one looks at them hard enough.'

'"Only connect" is Forster's mantra, isn't it?' Eleanor burst out, still shy, but starting to enjoy herself. 'In *Howards End*? It's the only one of his I've read, but I really enjoyed it. "Only connect the prose and the passion and both will be exalted..." or something.'

'Wilcoxes and Schlegels.'

'The Wilcoxes being the Prose, the Schlegels the Passion.'

'Joining forces.'

They looked at each other happily. Nick had a wide, generous mouth, Eleanor noticed, crammed with astonishingly even teeth, and there was a fleck of egg on his cheek, which she dearly wished she could brush off.

'Wouldn't they let you swap subjects?' she asked eventually. There were a million other things she wanted to ask or say. She was aware of them queuing up inside her, full of excited hope, bumping into one another. But there would be other conversations, she told herself. Other opportunities. He was in her college after all and only in his third year. Medical degrees took ages – she couldn't think straight enough to remember how long. And she was only in her first term. This was just the beginning. Her skin tingled.

Nick was shaking his head glumly in response to her question. 'They'd say no. Subject-changing is really frowned upon. More to the point, my father would kill me. Literally. A knife through the heart. While I slept. Whoosh.' He demonstrated with his fork, flashing a ghoulish smile. 'Though medicine isn't too bad,' he rushed on. 'In fact, I sometimes think I might make quite a good doctor.'

'Oh, I bet you will,' Eleanor cried before she could stop herself. She never wanted the lunch to end. Ever. It was too perfect. There was something coming off him, a sort of confidence – she felt it in waves across the table, not crushing her like all the other male confidence she had encountered, so bullying, so point-scoring, but something generous, holding her up, it felt like.

A man with a dishcloth over his shoulder rapped the table to get their attention. 'Are you two going to get anything else or not? There's other folk waiting to sit down.'

Eleanor leapt to her feet, apologising, but Nick took his time, because the guy deserved it for sheer rudeness, he explained, once they had left and were standing under the row of beef haunches and plucked turkeys outside the butchers next door.

'Back to the library then.' Eleanor dared to inject a note of regret into her tone.

Nick pulled back one of the heavy sleeves of his jumper to check his watch. She glimpsed fine gold hairs on his wrist and lower arm.

'I've got to be somewhere else. I'll catch Miss Coolham another time.'

Disappointment pumped inside her chest, making her miss a breath. 'Bye then. Thanks for lunch.'

'Bye.'

Eleanor ducked into the throng of shoppers streaming through the market, letting it carry her towards the High Street. Not looking back felt important. She did not want him to detect the extent of her reluctance to be walking away. But suddenly he was in front of her again, striding backwards, laughing as he bumped into people.

'Hey, you don't fancy coming to the PPP on Saturday night, do you? They're showing *Rosemary's Baby*. A classic. Mia Farrow... Oh, but you've seen it,' he cried, misreading the shadow of doubt that crossed her face, which was about the acronym rather than the invitation. PPP, she had learned recently, referred to an academic course. Philosophy, Psychology and something she couldn't remember. Now it was a cinema.

'I haven't seen it.' She laughed. 'Mia Farrow gives birth to the devil's child, doesn't she? Who could refuse an invitation to see that?'

'My thoughts exactly.' He laughed too, turning and falling into step beside her.

'My dad's a vicar,' she said in a rush as they emerged onto the High Street. 'At home, thinking about devils having babies, let alone going to see them, is banned.'

'Another reason to go.'

'Absolutely.'

'Porter's lodge at seven? If I don't see you before.'

'If I don't see you before,' she echoed.' Her face ached from grinning.

In one of Camilla's many women's magazines she had read an article about the importance of 'playing hard to get' if a man took your fancy. But, really, such tactics were impossible, and unnecessary, Eleanor reflected happily, giving Nick a wave as he took off up the High Street, pausing to admire the grace and agility with which he wove through the crowds. Why would two people play hard to get if they liked each other?

She strolled back towards college with her arms swinging and her scarf free and flying, the cut of the cold November air now only making her feel more alive.

5

Outside, the muggy March afternoon had turned thunderous. Silver slugs of drizzle were trailing down the big square hospital windows. Nick could never suppress a mild outrage when the Cape weather was poor, in spite of rain always being sorely needed. They were out to dinner that night and he didn't have a coat, let alone an umbrella.

Pat Driscoll, his secretary, put her head round the door. 'Your wife just left a message. She's running late and will meet you at the restaurant. She said she tried your mobile but it was off.'

Nick rummaged for his phone, lost under the pile of papers on his desk. As usual he had put it on silent for a consultation and then forgotten. 'Thanks Pat.'

His secretary hesitated, hanging off the door. 'Is it still okay for me to go early?'

'Oh goodness, your daughter's birthday, how could I have forgotten? Yes, go now. This minute,' he commanded with mock ferocity when still she hovered. 'And I'm on an admin stint, you'll be pleased to hear.' He rattled his in-tray, a pagoda of papers and patient files. 'No stone unturned.'

Pat laughed. 'Thanks, Doctor Wharton, see you tomorrow.' She paused to adjust the Monet print that hung beside the door.

A few minutes later he heard the soft thwack of her footsteps receding down the corridor.

Nick turned his phone's volume back on, wryly noting the number of missed calls from his wife. The dinner was with old family friends of hers, a couple she liked and he barely knew, so the chances were she would let it pass. With Donna, one never knew.

Nick sighed, embarking on a desultory shuffle through his in-tray and then shifting his attention to the greater administrative task of filing emails. He worked quickly and ruthlessly, going back over the weeks to weed out whatever correspondence he could, and saving more important letters under their various relevant subject tabs. It was thirty minutes before he reached January and the flurry of exchanges with old friends. Seeing Kat Keating's name, Nick experienced a sudden visceral memory of the turmoil she had once caused him; a reminder of what he had eventually been so relieved to walk away from twenty years before.

And yet it would be decent to round things off, he reasoned, give them a proper end.

Pressing the reply button, he wrote:

Dear Kat,
Just a quick, very late thank-you for your reply. Trust me when I tell you that I am happy – and not remotely surprised – to hear how well life has turned out for you.
As you say, good luck with the next forty.
Cheers,
Nick

As he pressed send, his mobile rang, displaying Donna's number. Nick picked it up at once, saying warmly, 'Hello, hon, Pat gave me your message. That's fine. I'll meet you there. I just hope it's something nice that's caused your change of plan?'

There was an audible intake of breath, warning him that the

warmth hadn't been enough. 'I know your patients matter more to you than I do, Nick. I *know* that. But if you could just do a better job of hiding the fact from time to time then I would be most grateful. And don't call me *hon*. I have a name, and, funnily enough, I am quite attached to it...'

'I did not mean to upset you,' Nick interjected hurriedly.

'No, you never do,' she said bitterly.

'I'm looking forward to dinner,' Nick tried again, determined not to rise to the bait but marvelling, as always, at his wife's readiness to be angered. 'A great idea of yours to go there. Pat said she saw a review saying it's the new best place for seafood, better even than Riley's.'

'Yes, well...'

Detecting a softening, he took heart. 'It's lucky one of us has her finger on the pulse.'

'It's not cheap,' Donna admitted, 'but then top-quality things seldom are...'

Nick noted, with some astonishment, that a reply from Kat had dropped into his inbox. He reached for the mouse and clicked it open:

By the way, I'm glad you grew to like being a doctor .

Donna was still talking, appeased in exactly the way he had hoped, moving from the merits of the restaurant to the promise to drop in on her father, which had warranted the last-minute change of her evening schedule. 'It will mean two cars between us tonight which is crazy, but—'

'Take a taxi. Then you can enjoy a drink.'

She laughed. 'Okay. If you're sure.'

'Of course,' Nick assured her happily, relief at the truce flooding him as it always did. 'It's a weeknight, so I'm only going to have a glass anyway. Give the girls a kiss for me.'

'Okay. See you later.'

Nick put the phone down and, after thinking for a moment, wrote back to Kat:

Did I say I like doctoring??!! But yes, I suppose I do. Mostly. Got to go now. Might drop a line another time. Nick.

When yet another reply popped into his inbox a couple of minutes later, he shook his head in bemusement.

Write if you want,

She wrote this time.

but no raking up of the past, okay? And nothing 'personal', thank you very much. At least not if you expect a reply.

He typed back, chuckling

I'll bear that in mind.

For the next hour Nick continued with the administrative duties he had set himself, while other, broader memories of the Keating sisters drifted into his mind. It was impossible to discount Eleanor, he reflected fondly, if only because she had led to Kat. The two were indivisible. Not that he had known that at the time. But then one knew so little of anything at the time.

6

It had stopped raining at last, though the sky was still a low canopy of metallic grey. Under Eleanor's knees, the dark, grainy wood of the hall window seat seemed to have hardened to rock. She and Kat had been wedged side by side on it for what felt like hours, passing the time by breathing mist onto the glass and tracing pictures in it with their fingers. Kat had drawn the number eight, because it was her birthday, then the sun, then the cat, Titch, who had come with the vicarage and was curled up asleep behind them in the sagging weave seat of the hall chair. Sensing Kat's mounting boredom with the game and not wanting her own anxiety to show, Eleanor switched from pictures to letters.

'This is what you drew, Kat. S-U-N. See? Spell it out for me, Kat. Say the letters...'

But Kat stuck her tongue out and licked the word off the glass instead. It provided a new diversion, Eleanor puffing clouds onto the pane and writing in a race against Kat's quick, wet tongue, until suddenly, just as they had forgotten to listen out for it, there was the crunch of car wheels in the drive and the old black Vauxhall appeared, exactly as Eleanor had longed for it to, fresh mud from the lane splattered thickly up its sides.

They pressed their noses to the smeary windows as their mother, upright behind the wheel, her face rigid with concentration, and pale but for the usual gash of red lipstick, steered between the gateposts. Catching sight of their faces, Connie tooted and waved. Behind them, Titch opened one eye and closed it. Keeping expectations low being a game they were all learning to play.

As Kat scrambled off the window seat, Eleanor hesitated, experiencing the usual jumble of emotions: joy, because her mother had returned at last, with her cloud of hair and her lemon-coloured coat and her slim legs steeply angled into one of the towering, shiny pairs of shoes that Mrs Owens liked to plough at with the hoover, as if they were monsters that needed driving back against the skirting boards; and fearful doubt, just in case it was going to be one of those new strange days when the energetic mood with which her mother left the vicarage was not the same one that accompanied her home. Since the main object of the journey that afternoon had been the secret purchase of a birthday cake for Kat, the doubt was worse than usual. A birthday tea and no cake – Eleanor couldn't imagine how her little sister would be comforted. They were supposed to have baked one for her – just the two of them, her mother had promised, whispering in her ear as she tucked her up the night before. Kat could watch her beloved cartoons, she said, and they would be girls together, just the two of them, creating heaven in the kitchen.

Quite how and why this promise hadn't materialised, Eleanor still wasn't sure. They had been woken extra early so that Kat could be given her birthday bicycle before their father went off on his Saturday church duties. Shaken out of a deep sleep, chilly in her nightie, Eleanor had sat hugging her knees on the end of her parents' bed while Kat bounced and squealed at the unveiling of her gift but then refused to sit on it, not even when Eleanor patiently pointed out and explained about the stabilisers. Kat had nestled against the bike instead, stoppering her thumb into her mouth as she stroked the chubby white wheels. Eleanor had retreated to her own bed, only to find Kat crawling in next to her and asking for Jeremy Fisher, but then falling asleep before they got to the exciting bit with the fish.

The rest of the morning had dragged by, the rain crawling down the windows and Kat forcing her to play baby games. Eleanor, remembering the promise of heaven, had put her head hopefully round the kitchen door on several occasions, only to find her mother with her head in one of her clothes magazines, a tall glass of her special water at her side. 'Later, Ellie,' she muttered less volubly each time, barely looking up, 'you're so impatient.'

But later came and went. They ate lunch – cold chicken and bread – and were then allowed to watch television. Kat chose the old *Snow White* video – her favourite – and made a nest in the sofa cushions. Eleanor slipped out of the room with more high hopes, only to find her mother in her yellow coat by the front door, her hair smooth and full of air, her lipstick sticky-fresh.

'No time for cooking now, Ellie darling. I'm going to whizz out and buy one instead. Not a word to your little sister, okay?'

Eleanor nodded even though it wasn't okay. Lots of things weren't okay that could not be mentioned. She blamed the move from London. Everything had been different in London. Different and better. In London, there had been Maria from next door who sat and played with them all the times her mother was busy. In London, they had been in a street with other houses and shops, near a library and a playground. In London, she had been ten and now she was eleven. Only four months and yet sometimes it felt as if she had left her whole life behind.

With the weight of these morning disappointments still upon her, Eleanor took the precaution of crossing her fingers as she slid off the window seat to greet her mother, skidding down the hall to catch up with Kat. The finger-crossing was a tactic she reserved for emergencies and which hadn't often let her down; unlike praying, which, in spite of her father's regular solemn recommendations, had let her down so badly that she had lately given up on it altogether.

'Oh girls, my good girls,' Connie cried, as they charged outside.

'But where did you go?' Kat howled, barrelling into her mother's thin bare legs.

Eleanor hung back.

Connie swayed from the force of Kat's hurtling embrace, rocking onto the big square heels of her blue shoes and then forward again onto their round tips. Her lipstick had faded to a dry rusty line and she looked wide-eyed, like she was thinking about lots of things beyond birthday teas and Kat's wretchedness. She patted Kat's head and then bent down to kiss it. 'Well, I'm back now, aren't I, silly lamb? And Ellie looked after you, didn't you, Ellie?' Connie straightened and smiled at Eleanor, absently trailing her fingers through Kat's knotty white frizz as her sister continued her sobbing.

Eleanor stood a little taller, meeting her mother's gaze. She had done as she was told and that felt good.

'I missed you,' Kat croaked, doing fake-crying now, Eleanor could tell, milking the moment because she liked having her head tickled.

Connie kissed Kat's hair again and then shifted her to one side so she could reach into her coat pocket for her cigarettes. 'There now, sweetie. Mummy needs a moment.'

Kat, who could never be interested in anything for long, not even being miserable, skipped off, sniffing, her candy-floss head bobbing, and was soon lost to an inspection of the large patch of green slime that had been growing for weeks under the broken drainpipe by the kitchen door.

Eleanor shuffled nearer the back of the car, unhooking her crossed fingers at the sight of two shopping bags, one of which had spilled its contents sufficiently to reveal the corner of a promising-looking bright pink square box.

Catching her mother's eye, she pointed at the cake box,

licking her lips and rubbing her stomach. Connie offered a half-smile back through the grey frills of her cigarette smoke, pressing a finger to her mouth to indicate the need for secrecy. She meant about the cake, Eleanor knew, though it made her think of other things too, like the cigarette, which she wasn't supposed to have, and leaving them alone, which she wasn't supposed to do. When it got to tea, she would ask to light the cake candles, Eleanor decided suddenly, in a blaze of happy certainty at how the day might yet work out.

'And did you two stay inside like you know I need you to?' Connie asked sternly. 'No wandering off into these woods or down by that railway line?' She threw a backward glance at the silver birch wood skirting the vicarage drive, and then the other way, towards the green sea of fields and hedges that lapped round the islands of the distant hill-tips everyone called the Downs. 'You remember how Daddy had to tell you off last time?'

Eleanor nodded earnestly. She remembered the telling-off only too well; the biting whack of the hairbrush on her bare backside, Kat whimpering as she waited her turn. 'I tried to make Kat ride her bike,' she confessed, 'but only in the hall. She still wouldn't. Then we drew pictures.'

Connie dropped her cigarette, twisting it into the broken gravel under the ball of her foot. 'And no answering the phone?'

Eleanor squirmed, shaking her head. There had been a phone call that afternoon, but it was only Mrs Owens, whom her mother didn't like, asking if she had left her gloves from Friday.

'And no one at the door for Daddy?'

'No one,' Eleanor assured her eagerly. In London, there had often been visitors for her father, but it didn't happen in Broughton.

'Darling girl. You are *such* a good girl. Come here.'

Connie crouched down opening both arms. Eleanor ran into them, happy that Kat was too busy with the green patch to do her usual thing of trying to join in. She buried her face in her mother's shoulder, smelling her flowery smoky smell, remembering dimly the time when it had just been the two of them, before Kat and going to school and all the other emerging horribleness of growing up. Through the tangle of Connie's hair, she blinked at the silver birches. In the late afternoon light, they had become tall, floating ghosts. Eleanor squeezed her eye-lids shut. The realisation of how things could change if you stared at them hard enough was new. It made her afraid to look properly sometimes.

'Swimming,' Connie cried, standing up so suddenly that she knocked Eleanor off balance. 'Kat, you'd like that wouldn't you?' she called. 'Swimming? A birthday treat? For my big grown-up eight-year-old girl.' Connie laughed at Kat, already stomping through the island of slime in celebration, squawking and flapping her elbows like a chicken.

Eleanor did her best to summon some excitement about the swimming. 'You mean go swimming *now*, Mummy?' she ventured.

'Of course *now*, you doodlebug,' her mother retorted, the edge in her voice as good as a smack. 'Daddy's always saying we should get to *know* the area. Well, when I was out I saw a sign to a leisure centre.' She carved a large loopy square in the air to demonstrate. 'And Kat wants to and it's Kat's special day, isn't it my chickadee?' she called, waving at Kat, who waved back. 'Fetch the swimmies for us, Ellie, there's a love.'

'I don't know where they are.' Eleanor spoke in her smallest voice. One of the panicky surges was coming at her, a longing to be back in their old house in a normal street, where everything, not just swimming things, had been in its right place.

'Oh, never mind,' Connie muttered, managing to suggest that Eleanor should mind quite a lot. 'You watch your sister.'

She strode towards the house, wavering a little on her tall blue shoes, and then reappearing what felt like an age later with three towels rolled into fat sausages poking out of a thin plastic bag that was splitting down the sides.

'What about the cake?' Eleanor tried to speak quietly.

'The what?'

'The cake...' She glanced at Kat, who had taken off one of her wellies and was using it to scoop water out of the puddle. 'Should we put—'

'We'll have it with Daddy, later, little Miss Fusspot. Okay? Now, help me persuade madam here to get in the car and *not* kick up a stink about being strapped in. I can't have her clambering around the car today, I just can't.'

They were halfway down the drive, within sight of the main road, when the Vauxhall performed a lurch and sank sideways into a soft bank of mud, its wheels spinning. Connie, who had just started her warbling version of Snow White's 'Whistle While You Work' to entertain Kat, clamped her mouth shut and pumped at the car pedals with her right foot. The engine roared and raced, a rocket trying to take off.

'Bloody car. Bloody place.' She tugged at the steering wheel as if it was a plant she was trying to pull out by the roots. 'Bloody hell.' She dropped her forehead onto its top edge with a thump that made Eleanor need to look away. Behind them, Kat started to cry.

'Should we get out?' Eleanor stole a glance at her mother, to whom this obvious possibility did not seem to have occurred. Instead, she had wound down her window and was staring into the army of silver trees that surrounded them, as if they alone contained the answer to their predicament. Which sort of turned out to be true, since an instant later the towering figure of their father appeared through the ghostly mesh, the panels of his long black cloak flapping round the skirts of his cassock, the ridges of his thick-soled walking boots swinging up into view with every stride.

Eleanor waved madly, too strangled with relief even to speak. Beside her, Connie put her hands to her face with a soft groan.

'Daddy, Daddy, Daddy,' Kat shrieked, kicking her feet madly into the back of Eleanor's seat and yanking at the belt across her belly.

'Trouble, ladies?' Vincent bellowed with a grin that split his dark, grizzled beard. 'Stay where you are.'

They watched in silence as he waded towards them through the sludgy mud, swinging his arms from side to side like a speed-skater.

'Oh, Vince.' Connie extended a hand through the open window, fluttering her fingers as if they were the only part of her still able to move.

He seized her hand, shooting her a glittering look as he pressed it to his lips.

'Daddy.' Kat was in torment on the back seat.

'Okay, Kitty-Kat, you first.' Vincent opened the door and swung her out onto his hip, jigging her like she was still a baby until she fell silent. 'Where were you going, my love?' he murmured, throwing Connie another look.

'Swimming,' Kat answered for her, trumpeting the word into his ear and then inspecting the wooden crucifix that hung round his neck as if she had never seen it before. 'For my birthday.' She gave the cross an elaborate kiss, holding it to her mouth with both hands.

'Yes, swimming,' Connie echoed. She looked very tired suddenly. Even her hair looked tired, all falling round her face.

'Okay.' Vincent shifted Kat higher onto his waist and tweaked her nose. 'Well, I'd say it looks like we need a change of plan, doesn't it?' He seemed the opposite of tired, Eleanor noticed, as if there was nothing that could have made him happier than finding his family submerged in a mud bank as the sun dropped behind the trees on a dank Saturday evening. 'I'll ask Mr Watson to come by with his tractor and pull the old girl free—'

'It's not a girl, Daddy,' Kat interjected crossly, 'it's a *car*.'

'Quite right,' he laughed. 'But you are a girl, aren't you? A big good girl, who is now eight years old.' He set her down carefully in the middle of the lane and then came round to Eleanor's side, just as she had been hoping he would, if she waited long enough and didn't fuss. 'I'm going to put you on dry land too and then look after Mum. All right?'

'There's *cake*, Dad,' Eleanor whispered, locking her sturdy legs round his broad waist as he swung her out of the seat, 'for Kat's birthday.' She pointed towards the boot. 'Mummy bought it, but I think she might have forgot.'

'Cake. Brilliant. Well done, Mum.' Vincent set her down next to her sister and squelched back through the mud to retrieve first the shopping, slinging both bags over one arm, and then Connie, squatting down in the open car door so that she could climb onto his back.

'Mummy's having a piggyback,' Kat yelped, clapping her hands. 'I want one. I want one.'

'But you are the leader,' Vincent declared solemnly. 'We are all going to follow you.'

Kat paused, as the gravity of the appointment sank in. She then set off at a gallop, steering a stomping course through the gullies and pools of water, stretching down the lane ahead of them like a chain of stepping stones. The vicarage was just visible in the distance beyond the bend, the cloudy light glinting off its tall windows.

Vincent carried Connie and the shopping all the way, making a show of copying some of Kat's dancing steps if ever she glanced round. Eleanor went last, watching her mother's long blue heels bounce against her father's black robe. Kat had got a head-start and her father walked so fast it was hard to keep up. He was like a tree, Eleanor decided, a huge old tree with a gnarled face and thick branches for arms and legs. Her mother looked like a doll in comparison, clinging onto his back like her life depended on it. It occurred to Eleanor in the same instant that, just as there had been a time before Kat, there had been one before her too, when it had just been her mother and father. The thought made her feel funny, as if it was one she wasn't supposed to have.

Her father took charge that night, as he usually did since the move, putting them in the bath and making scrambled eggs, which he said had to be eaten before the cake could be cut. There were no candles, so he used upturned matches, which he insisted – when Eleanor asked – that only he could light and which fizzed like sparklers and left black specks in the icing from Kat's efforts to blow them out. Kat said a breathy inaudible wish with her eyes closed and then Vincent helped her cut four hefty slices, making the jam and cream spill out of its creases. Like blood and guts, Eleanor pointed out before she could stop herself, earning a telling-off.

'It's only words, Vincent,' murmured her mother, taking a slice, but then moving the cake round her plate instead of putting it in her mouth.

'Do you think your sister enjoyed her day?' Vincent asked Eleanor later, coming upstairs to settle them after Connie, stretched out on the sitting room sofa, had summoned them to her side for goodnight kisses. Kat was already asleep, her hair a yellow fan across the pillow. Eleanor wriggled deeper under her covers, feeling with her feet for Mottie, her old bear, who lived at the bottom of the bed.

Vincent turned off her bedside light and sat on the mattress, the weight of him rolling her towards his knees.

Eleanor thought of the beautiful bike, which Kat had seemed to love but then refused to ride. And then of being left alone for the afternoon. And then of the abortive attempt to go swimming. But Kat had been happy enough, most of the time, as she always was. 'Yes. I think so.'

'That's good. And what about her big sister, did she enjoy it too?'

'Yes,' Eleanor lied, because the day had ended so well and because of the recently acquired, hardening instinct that confessing to unhappiness was somehow disloyal. To him. To all of them.

'Did Mummy leave you on your own today?'

'No.' The word flew out of her mouth, but it sounded wrong. 'Just for a little bit.'

'For a little bit. Okay.'

'She had to or the cake wouldn't have been a surprise. I looked after Kat fine.'

'Yes. I know.' He had placed his hand on her chest but was looking round the room like he had forgotten he had left it there. Eleanor could feel her heart thumping under his palm. 'You can have your own room soon,' he went on in a dreamy voice, 'just as soon as I get around to redecorating this old place – you'll like that, won't you?'

'Maybe, but Kat won't.' Eleanor spoke in a rush. 'Kat likes being with me.'

He shook his head, lifting the hand at last. 'Yes, but we all have to grow up sometime. Even your little sister.' He traced a finger down her cheek, looking sad. 'You are ready for a room of your own. More than ready. All that reading you do.' He kissed her forehead and then made the sign of a cross where his lips had been. 'But none of that bookworming tonight, okay? It's too late and you'll ruin your eyes with that torch of yours. Don't forget to say your prayers.'

'I don't know what to pray for.'

'Pray for everybody, including yourself.' He stood up.

'I prayed not to leave London,' Eleanor confessed in a tight voice. 'And it didn't work.'

'God has his reasons.'

'Did you pray not to leave London too then?'

He pulled on the wispy ends of his beard, like he always did when he was thinking. 'I leave big decisions to God. I trust him. He knows best.'

Eleanor thought of her new school in Broughton, wondering why God thought it best that she should hate it and have no friends. She had done one term, enduring the ignominy of being the only new pupil to arrive halfway into the year. A classmate called Clarissa Mayfield had hung around her, but she was the universally disliked, spoilt, crybaby daughter of the Head, and so it didn't count. The person who counted was a girl called Isabel Kirby, a girl whom Eleanor had quickly learned to do her best to avoid.

'I hate school.' She knew it was a terrible thing to say. The landing light blazed like a sun behind her father's head, a halo, casting him in shadow. In his sermons he sometimes said that God was light, shining in the darkness of the world.

'But it's the holidays.' He sounded genuinely surprised.

'I never want to go back.'

'You're too bright, Ellie, that's your trouble. It makes the other kids feel left behind. You ask too many questions. Know too many answers. But the teachers like you, which is what matters. Life isn't a bed of roses, my child, it can be a struggle. It's *supposed* to be a struggle. For all of us.' He spoke emphatically, clasping his hands so tightly that for a moment Eleanor thought he might be about to drop to his knees to pray. She had walked in on him doing so the previous weekend, hunched on his study floor between all the messy piles of paper, head bent like someone expecting execution.

'But why? Why is it a struggle?'

'Because if it was easy it wouldn't mean anything.' His voice was harsh, but then he ruffled her hair. 'Now. Goodnight, Chatterbox. God bless.'

Eleanor rolled onto her side, cradling Mottie gently between the arches of her feet. The bear was eleven like her and had bald patches; but they were soft and good for rubbing. She moved each foot in turn, getting the soothing rhythm that helped her feel sleepy. The things her father had said drifted in and out of her mind. She didn't understand them, but if she was clever, like he said, then she would one day, surely. And for the moment this seemed a great comfort – that answers existed, even if they were beyond her grasp.

As she closed her eyes, she saw again their evening procession down the muddy lane: Kat up ahead, thinking she was in charge, skipping and splatting, Connie pinned like a yellow butterfly to their father's back. She and Kat were the children, but it was their mother who had needed carrying; Eleanor tried to hold onto this thought, sensing that it might take her to the brink of understanding something, something momentous. But the image slithered free and blankness came instead, pulling her into the world she liked best, the one where nothing had to be understood because you didn't even know you were alive.

7

Vincent held the phone a little way from his ear as Mrs Owens talked. She didn't want to interfere, it wasn't in her nature. She had been in agonies about it all week. Agonies.

The telephone flex had lost its neat regular curls and become a stiff tangle, destroyed by hours of fiddling. Vincent let his gaze drift out of the kitchen window, where the sun was still gathering power, a low-wattage light bulb labouring in a dark room. The window faced south, framing the edge of the wood that skirted the drive and offering a shadowy view towards the broken horizon beyond the vicarage's wide sprawling garden. It was the point where the South Downs fizzled out, tailing off into a few last low ridges; giant, distant waves breaking on a flat shore.

Vincent allowed the cleaner's voice to come back into focus. She didn't think it was right that his girls had been left on their own while Mrs Keating was seen in town. She didn't blame the vicar, he had been laying poor Tony Mossop to rest, God bless his soul, but the thought of those little girls...

'Thank you, Mrs Owens. I value your concern. Really, I do. It was just one of those complicated days – the girls were left briefly, it is true – Connie was organising a surprise for Katherine's birthday. Nothing that is likely to arise again. I had no idea you had telephoned. I hope Eleanor was helpful. She's very grown-up for her age. Pardon? No, I don't think your gloves have turned up. But I'll double-check with Connie, of course. Hopefully, we won't be needing gloves much from now on, not with the weather getting so much warmer... Oh, they were rubber? Extra-large pink? I've got it now. Yes, have a nice holiday. And thank you again, for your concern.'

Vincent glanced back out of the window. The tops of the silver birches were on fire suddenly, just for a few seconds; a miraculous combination of light and angles. He could feel his soul swelling. It always helped to see the sun.

Vincent knew people talked. They had in South London and they would in Sussex. That Broughton was not only a much more scattered but infinitely less hectic community than his Wandsworth parish made no difference. It was still a goldfish bowl. Parishioners watched and judged, with expectations that were not only high but also unashamedly proprietorial. How a priest comported himself was their business. Connie was a Belisha beacon, even when she kept her head down; even when she didn't do stupid things that she had promised never to do again.

In the early days, scrutiny had been an aspect of his calling that Vincent welcomed. After all the years of false starts, the twists and turns of dead-end jobs, the failed relationships, it had been a joy to emerge from the purging of the seminary at the grand age of forty-one and embark on a life that was contrastingly singular and transparent – both to God and to those whose spiritual health he had vowed to serve.

Then, God bowled him a googly. He sent Connie. Of course, God *sent* Connie, because, Vincent reasoned, even as he edged into the maelstrom of the feelings that she stirred in him, being human could still be a highly complicated business and God had every right to remind him of the fact.

As with so many momentous things, it had happened

quietly, unexpectedly, on a Wednesday afternoon. It was the first Wednesday of the month, which in those days had come to mean a visit to the flagship property of the Home for Hope project, a scheme Vincent was pioneering to wrest some of the large dilapidated houses in his parish back from squatters and convert them into volunteer-run refuges for the homeless. It was an ambitious project, launched on good faith rather than good economics. Local government had promised support and then withdrawn it. Five months in and the energies of the volunteer team, not to mention the wherewithal to keep even this first home open, were flailing badly.

Mulling over the problem, Vincent had taken his time covering the half-mile between the paint-peeling front door of his own run-down accommodation and the newly restored gleaming black entrance gates of the refuge. He walked with his head down and his arms clasped behind his back, preoccupied for the first time in a while by chipped paving stones and the ugly smears of spat chewing gum rather than the glories of the world. He had envisaged opening several more homes across South London, each a pearl of succour and hope for those most in need; a working testimony to the force of God's love on earth. He had seen it so clearly that just to contemplate the possibility of failure made his skin crawl with shame.

Since his last visit, a thick, splintering crack had appeared across one of the panels of coloured glass set over the refuge's main entrance. The result of a thrown bottle or stone, Vincent guessed sadly. Almost worse were the empty crisp packets and beer cans blowing around the splitting folds of two bulging black plastic rubbish sacks which had been propped carelessly against the overflowing dustbins. The rubbish men must have driven past without stopping. Again. Such details mattered. It would have to go on the agenda that afternoon. Again.

He braced his shoulders, punched in the new-fangled security code that had sucked up too much of the Hope Project funds and pushed open the door. And there was Connie, swabbing the tatty lino of the front hall. She was barefoot, wearing a red T-shirt and faded blue flared jeans with straggling hems. Her feet looked muscled, as if they were used to being shoeless. Her long, astonishing curly, white-blonde hair was swept back into a plain ponytail with a brown elastic band, the sort one might put on a parcel. Strains of some music were coming out of a room down the corridor and she was very subtly moving the mop and her body in time to it. *'I'm so tired of being alone, I'm so tired...'* Vincent would only register the tune later. At the time, he wasn't able to take in much beyond the fact that he had forgotten what a woman could look like; the sheer power of female physical beauty. It was like being blown off his feet.

'Hello there.' He offered his hand, glad of the priestly mask of his clothes, careful to behave exactly as he would towards any of the residents or volunteer employees. 'You must be new. I'm Father Keating, in charge of this place and the whole Home for Hope project.'

'Oh, reverend... but I am Connie.' There was a soft trace of upper-class refinement in her accent. Home Counties, public school, ponies, twin sets and pearls – unappealing, clichéd associations skidded across Vincent's brain. But it was her use of the word 'but', sounding so like an apology for existence, that snagged on his already shredding heart. How did such a creature get to be so uncertain? She had fresh skin and the most piercing translucent blue eyes he had ever seen. They sought his and then dropped quickly, back to the sopping strands of the mop-head and the task at hand. After the squalor of the bins, Vincent could have loved her for that alone. He wondered how old she was. Thirty? For a few moments he felt like some creature in a fairy tale, literally rooted to the spot. All he wanted was to make her look at him again.

'Not reverend,' he corrected her, finding his voice at last and speaking much more gruffly than he intended, '...Father Keating is fine,' he added hurriedly, seeing the trace of panic scud across her face and recognising it as no moment to start explaining the business of ecclesiastical adjectives and nouns. 'You're doing a great job on that floor. Thank you.'

The meeting flew by. For every agenda point, Vincent had an answer – an inspired answer, inspirationally delivered. The world not only glowed again, it was full of solutions. His ears strained for sounds in the hallway – the swish of the mop, a light footstep.

And who was the new helper, he asked at last, once issues of bin-collection and social service involvement and fresh fundraising had been dispatched. He let the question out slowly, steadily, like a lungful of held-in air.

'Oh, that's Connie,' he was told. 'A real treasure. Turned up last week, needing a place to tide her over till she gets a new job. Problems in the past with alcohol. Estranged from her family, from what we can make out. Came with good references though, from St George's, where she's been working for the last year as a part-time receptionist. She's so willing to help out, she puts everyone else to shame.'

It wasn't until much later, in the deep quiet of his own bed, fighting unseemly thoughts, that Vincent referred the matter to God. He waited, expecting scolding, warnings, suggestions for hair-shirts, but none came. Instead, the voice in his heart, the one Vincent had learnt to trust and listen out for, told him to be patient and follow his instincts and see what mysteries lay in store.

Connie started appearing in his church soon afterwards, always sitting quietly at the back, her vivid hair peeping out of the edges of a headscarf. Vincent would feel her eyes on him as he performed his duties and when he stepped into the pulpit to deliver his sermon. It made him pull his shoulders back and stand taller. It made him speak with greater fluency, finding ever better ways to set the hearts and minds of his small, growing congregation jangling with awe and understanding.

Soon, Connie was giving more and more of her time to helping run the home. Schemes for raising money proved an

impressive forte – bring-and-buy sales, renting the church out
for concerts and keep-fit groups, bombarding the council with
begging letters – she was tireless in her efforts to support not
just the parish, but Vincent himself. He needed looking after,
she would scold, arriving on the doorstep of his small, shabby
church house with a basket of food, her long ponytail swinging
as she dodged past him and his remonstrations in order to turn
the contents of the basket into a meal. Vincent would follow,
helplessly, a stunned rabbit in the glare of her radiance, all the
more hapless for doing his best not to appear so. After she had
gone, he would remember each detail of her clothes, every pleat
and crease, every hemline. For, as Connie's confidence grew, so
her wardrobe had smartened, to tight-fitting skirts, dresses and
tall shoes; outfits which presented the added complication for
Vincent of making her lithe, ballet-dancer body even harder to
ignore.

He stopped sleeping. Connie might have been a heaven-sent
inspiration, but Vincent wanted to have sex with her. More
exactly, he wanted to tear her clothes off with his teeth and
crush his mouth against hers until the thick red lipstick she had
taken to wearing was gashed into smears across her cheeks and
chin. He wanted to bury his face in every crevice of her body; to
smell her, taste her, drink her, *consume* her. He prayed feverishly
for guidance. The Anglican priesthood required no vow of
celibacy, but Vincent had made one with himself anyway. He did
not want to want Connie. He did not want to want to serve
anyone but the Lord.

Vincent took three days off and went on a retreat. By the last
morning, he was longing to leave; longing to see Connie again.
He drove back to London in a trance. The traffic, the world,
streaked past. He did not see it, he saw Connie. The words he
wanted to say to her tumbled round his brain. God *had* sent
Connie. Not as a test but as a gift. Even more importantly, there
was something in Connie that needed saving. She could not say
it – no one who needed saving ever could. It was difficult enough

to get her to speak about what she had been through; all he had gleaned were a few heartbreaking details – the family banishment, the blackouts, the mortification, the endless men who had let her down, the final brief terrifying period on the streets that had led to the rock bottom of a police cell and the decision to get proper help. The subsequent slow grind of sobriety and temporary jobs. She had endured so much and shown such strength, but the fear in her eyes was plain to see; the need to be properly cherished, kept safe.

* * *

Twelve years on, Vincent could still summon, at will, the mounting, joyous certainty of that day; the peace that at long last re-entered his heart, the sense that God was watching, as, of course, he always had been, not laughingly, but tender and glad. The sight of Connie on his doorstep in her rumpled black overcoat, her face grey with fatigue, and the strain of having missed him, as she immediately, shyly confessed, almost came as no surprise. Of course Connie had been there, waiting for him. Of course. This was his path in life, requiring only that he acknowledge and commit to it. Four months later they were married.

'Vincent?' Connie's eyes blinked slowly.

'Hello, my darling. I let you lie in.'

Vincent approached the bed, Mrs Owen's clumsy words of interference still ringing in his ears. He marvelled at the calmness of his wife's face in repose, at how little change over a decade and two children had wrought. Her looks astonished him still, the dusting of freckles across the high bridge of her cheekbones, the violent blue of her irises, the neat indents of her knees and ankle bones. But she had got thin. That in itself was a bad sign. Quite apart from the other signs, the ones that had propelled him to get them out of London.

'Did you?' She struggled upright, digging her knuckles into her eyes. 'Oh no. What's the time? Where are the girls?'

'The girls are fine. I have given them a job in the garden. The veg patch. I found an old trowel and fork in one of the sheds. They are digging, clearing the weeds. Eleanor is in charge, as she likes to be.' He smiled, sitting on the bed and crossing his legs. It felt good to be free of the cassock for once, in jeans and an old grey sweater. It was one Connie had patched at the elbows during the early days, using squares of leather and tight neat stitching, which she said she had learnt in Domestic Science at school. 'I'm keeping today simple,' he said. 'A visit to Tony Mossop's widow this afternoon – otherwise I'm taking it off. I thought I might get some paint.'

'Paint?'

'For Eleanor's new bedroom.'

'Oh that. Yes.' She flopped back against the pillows. 'Are you sure she wants it?'

'Of course she wants it. Look, I made you some tea.' He nodded at the mug he had left on the bedside table, watching with satisfaction as she grabbed it with both hands and drank deeply. The lilac smudges under her eyes were growing darker, Vincent observed. She had never been an easy sleeper, not even during the good years, fighting the bedclothes, taking trips to the bathroom. It was one of the things he had hoped the countryside might improve, fill her up with good health, good air. 'We need to talk, Con.'

'Oh really? What about?' She swigged more tea, half hiding her face.

Vincent's heart twisted at the sight of her absorbing his challenge. Though motherhood had initially provided an anchor, it had gradually lost its purchase, so gradually that it had taken him a very long time to notice. Too long, and for that he blamed himself bitterly. She was so adept at concealment, that was the trouble, hiding not just the bottles, but the wherewithal to buy them. Even now, safely away from all her old haunts and under his greater control, she somehow managed. She was canny, calculating, strong-willed, her own closest ally, as well as her worst enemy. Vincent wished Connie could understand how such contradictions only made him love her more. He was her rock, Vincent reminded himself. Without him she would be adrift.

'You can't leave the girls on their own.'

'On their own?'

'Con, I've just had Mrs Owens on the phone. Last Saturday she rang the house and got Eleanor. I was doing Tony Mossop and you were seen in town. I knew anyway because Eleanor told me, but hadn't wanted to make a fuss.'

She slammed the mug down on the bedside table, slopping tea onto her pack of contraceptive pills. 'I needed... some space.' She bunched up her knees, hugging herself.

'Connie.'

'Fuck off, Vincent.'

'Connie, look at me.'

'I said fuck off. You're getting people to spy on me now, are you? Nosy neighbours? The girls? And all you are really worried about anyway is whether I am *screwing* anybody else. Isn't that right? I could drink myself into oblivion and you wouldn't mind. It's my *body* you care about, isn't it? Not my *health*.' She tore back the sheets and threw herself out of bed, fighting off Vincent's efforts to put his arms round her. 'I need to fucking pee.'

'Okay, my love, okay.' Vincent stayed where he was, studying the backs of his hands. The veins bulged. He waited for the clank of the loo flush, a long chain, ancient like all the vicarage fittings. 'Better?' he said when she returned, but she didn't smile.

'I need to get dressed.'

'Con.'

'And I don't require an audience, thank you.'

'Con, talk to me.'

'I'm not some poor sod in a confessional box, Vincent, needing to spill their miserable innards for *absolution*... Hey – stop it. Stop it. Let me go.'

Vincent had taken hold of her shoulders. 'No, I am not your

confessor, Connie,' he whispered urgently, 'nor anyone else's for
that matter.' He squeezed her slender frame more tightly, aware
of his own strange excitement, building as it always did. 'I am
your husband. Your *husband*. And if the worst stuff is starting
again, then I need to know the extent of it, so that I can help—'

She swung at him, elbows and fists. It took all his strength to
keep her in the vice of his arms. For her safety, he told himself,
for her safety. Somehow, in spite of the squirming, he swivelled
her round to face him. She was so small. He always thought that
when he held her tightly. The fight went out of her suddenly
and she stared up at him. The specks of black in her eyes had
spread, darkening the blue. Like a cat's, Vincent thought, when
steadying itself to pounce.

'Help me?' she said quietly. '*Help* me? Like the way you *helped*
me by bringing me to this godforsaken place.'

'It was time for me to try a new parish—'

'Like hell it was. It was time to get me out of London, more
like. Wasn't it? Lock me up and throw away the key.'

'Don't be ridiculous—'

'To make me your prisoner.'

'You are not my prisoner. There is a good life for you here, if
only you would see it. Connie, I've been... I am... so worried
about you.'

'Worried that I might have a good time? Too good a time?
Because that's what you mean by the "worst stuff", isn't it? The
danger that I might remember how to *enjoy* myself. Maybe even
talk to other *men*?' Her black-blue eyes glittered.

'I don't call drinking yourself stupid having a good time.'
Vincent spoke slowly and heavily, doing his best to imbue the
words with the weight of his sorrow rather than admonition. At
the back of his mind meanwhile hovered images her accusations
had conjured, the ones that cut as deeply as she intended: her
nakedness in the embrace of another man. Such imaginings
came at him all the time, searing his brain. There had been
evidence of such goings-on in London, the bruised look to her

lips, the times in the night when he woke to find her gone, just to the spare room she said, and he had never caught her out. But he wasn't sure. He wasn't sure of anything.

'Oh, well thanks for the hot tip,' she sneered. 'I'll bear it in mind, oh *Wise* One, oh Servant of the Lord who has all the answers.'

'Connie, don't talk to me like that. Stop this, please.'

She had started twisting again and he had to hold on harder, more roughly. He tried to call on God, to ask the voice for help. When no answer came, he wondered suddenly if Connie's taunts were justified; whether all he had was the desire for faith rather than faith itself. Connie certainly had lost faith in him. He was a sham, she liked to claim now, a control freak masquerading as a priest. Her own show of early religious zeal had shrunk to the occasional charade, for the sake of the girls, she said, rather than the outside world. During one of the recent late-night arguments, triggered by his plea that she attend church, she had snarled that the outside world could go fuck itself and then taken the eiderdown and her pillows into the bathroom for the night, sliding the bolt across when he tried to come in.

'You are not yourself,' Vincent said hoarsely as one of his elbows caught her chin, knocking her head back. If only she didn't fight so hard. 'I know you are not yourself.'

'Oh yes I am. This is me, Vincent. *Me.*' She spat the word, flinging specks of spittle onto his cheeks and eyelids. His elbow had left a small red mark on her jaw. 'The woman you married.'

Vincent flinched but clung on. They became one creature, locked and wrestling. He used his greater strength to steer her towards the bed. When it was behind her, he pushed with all his might, falling heavily on top of her as she hit the mattress. 'Connie.'

She thrashed her head from side to side. He had to wait for the right moment to kiss her, biding his time, like a boxer watching when to throw a punch. When his mouth found hers, she fought more fiercely, pushing upwards with her hips, but then relented suddenly as he had known she would. He put his knee between her thighs, forcing her legs apart. She fell silent and he knew he had won, that she was his again, for that morning at least.

8

Eleanor reversed slowly away from her parents' half-open bedroom door and ran downstairs, not stopping until she was back by the shed where her father had taken her and Kat to choose gardening tools that morning.

All she had been able to see was her mother's arms and legs, sticking out from under the bulk of her father as he lay on top of her. The arms and legs had looked small and oddly floppy, as if she might almost have been asleep. But her father had been moving – rocking – saying her mother's name and holding her as if he never meant to let go. He had all his clothes on, but his trousers were loose, halfway down his pants, the belt undone.

Her mother was sick, Eleanor reminded herself, slowing to a walk when she reached the path from the shed to the patch where she and Kat had been digging. She was sick and needed special looking after, as their father had lately grown so fond of telling them. It was why he had recently made Connie throw all the cigarettes he had found onto the fire and why she wasn't to drive the car again, he explained, not until she had got her strength back.

The ants' nest which had scared Kat and made her run for help was still spewing its angry red inhabitants. Like a miniature volcano, Eleanor decided, crouching down to poke at the mound with her trowel, watching, mesmerised, as the larva of insects glowed brighter.

The thickness of the silence crept up on her slowly. Where was Kat?

She straightened, looking about her properly. 'Kat?' she called crossly, thinking how typical that her sister should create a stir and then be fine. 'Are you hiding? Come out if you are.' It was only then that she noticed the gate into Mr Watson's field hanging half open on its big rusty hinge.

Eleanor ran through into the impenetrable jungle of thick green stalks that had recently burst into being. Too high to see over, they shimmied and swayed in the morning sun, as if riffled by giant invisible fingers. She stumbled through them, calling Kat's name, fighting her way to the stile that led into the next field, the one she and Kat had been forbidden from exploring because of its proximity to the railway line.

Her wellingtons made it hard work; clods of mud glued themselves to the soles, weighing her down and making her feet slide off balance. Within minutes, her socks had rucked into uncomfortable tight rolls round her toes, leaving the thin bare skin on her heels at the mercy of the boots' rough lining. At every moment, she hoped to see Kat, squatting over some object of fascination, or maybe even lying on her back as she did in the garden sometimes, claiming to be watching for when the door to heaven opened, granting her a peek – she said – of an angel. But Kat liked running even more than lying on her back, Eleanor reflected unhappily. She had been famously speedy since toddlerhood – nippy and up to mischief – as their parents had often observed fondly; not a clodhopper like her big sister.

At the stile, Eleanor clambered onto the top plank, looking out rather than down, which she knew would make her dizzy. Using her hand as a visor, she peered back the way she had come, half fearing, half hoping that one or both parents would come into view. But the only sign of movement was a flash of ginger as Titch scooted out of the tall green shoots and into the hedge, on one of his urgent private missions.

The wood of the stile was damp and Eleanor slipped getting down it, grazing her arm. She lumbered on, heading towards the section of fence that overlooked the railway line, the panic swelling inside her. As she ran, she pictured what she would find: Kat at the bottom of the embankment in a bloodied mess, limbs twisted, a ghost of recrimination in her open, glassy, lifeless blue eyes. She had a vivid imagination, that was her trouble. It had already been remarked on by Miss Zaphron, her new English teacher. 'Your mind takes off,' she had declared in front of the whole class, before going on to demonstrate the fact by reading out one of Eleanor's compositions, publicly awarding Eleanor a top mark for it and putting the seal on her already manifest lack of popularity.

Reaching the railway fence at last, it was with a sort of curiosity that she wriggled underneath. What would Kat look like dead and mashed to pieces?

Eleanor peered over the edge of the siding. Her little sister came into view at once, not bloodied or dead, but crouched awkwardly on the slant, her skirt bunched up, having a pee. 'Kat, what are you doing?' she yelled. 'People will see.'

'Only if there's a train,' Kat shouted back, tugging unevenly and inexpertly at her pants, which had got hooked over her wellingtons. 'And there isn't.'

'Get back up here,' Eleanor shrieked, the bubble of worry bursting into anger.

'No, Bossyboots.' Kat stuck her tongue out, but then started to climb back up the bank anyway.

'You should never just run off,' Eleanor scolded, grabbing Kat's arm and giving it a shake. 'We're not allowed here, Dummy. Remember what happened last time? Which means we have got to *run* back home, fast as we can.' She burrowed back under the fence and Kat followed, but then stayed lying on her belly.

'I'm tired.' She plucked disconsolately at the sparse grass.

Eleanor stared down at her sister in disbelief. The sting of the hairbrush was still vivid, a memory of humiliation as much as pain; being commanded by her father to roll onto her stomach and pull her pyjamas down, baring her bottom. Her innards went liquid just thinking about it. 'We'll get told off again,' she reminded Kat with queasy urgency. 'Punished. You don't want that, do you? We've got to hurry.'

'It didn't hurt.'

'Of course it hurt.'

'Did not. It didn't touch.'

'What? Get up, come on.' Eleanor yanked Kat onto her feet and then set off back towards the stile at as brisk a pace as she could manage, dragging her along behind. 'What do mean didn't touch anyway?'

'The brush.'

'The brush didn't touch you?' She stopped, dropping Kat's hand.

Kat shook her head importantly. 'Daddy did pretend hitting.' She darted on ahead suddenly, reaching the stile first and riding it piggyback until Eleanor caught up with her. 'I'll say you looked after me, Ellie,' she offered, perhaps reading some new heaviness in her sister's step. 'If we get told off. Okay?'

'Okay.'

'Don't be cross, Ellie. I don't like it.'

'If Dad asks, just say we walked as far as the stile, okay? Here.' Eleanor thumped the top plank. 'To the stile. Nothing more.' Her voice was a croak. She felt hollowed out.

'Nothing. More. Nothing. More.' Kat cawed the words, flapping her arms as she leapt off the stile into the lake of shimmering green, ploughing through it like a small, rogue wave.

By the time they reached the garden, Vincent was back, digging at the overgrown beds with his hefty fork, whistling. Eleanor braced herself. Kat was too young to be trusted with a lie, too young to know about consequences. But when her father looked up, he was grinning.

'Bad girls, playing in Mr Watson's fields.' He winked, resting on the fork to wag a chastising finger. His eyes looked shinier than usual, Eleanor noticed, and the bit of his face above the edges of his beard was bright pink, like when he was sunburnt.

'Is Mummy still in bed?' Eleanor plucked at a tall grass stem, pretending to study it closely. The glimpse through her parents' open bedroom door slid back into her mind. She thought of how crushed her mother had looked under her father, how tightly he had been hugging her and wondered how that could really help with getting her strength back.

'Yes. She's especially poorly today, as I've already told you. So you have to be extra good and grown-up.'

'Gardening, you mean?' Eleanor ventured more brightly, retrieving her trowel, the relief at not being told off starting to take hold. Days with her father at the helm were always smoother; no sofa-lying or false-start expeditions to swimming pools; no false promises.

'Gardening, yes, and shopping. We shall go to the super-market and stock up the fridge, so poor Mum doesn't need to leave the house this week. And we'll buy the paint for your new room, get cracking on that.'

Eleanor glanced at Kat, busy now trying to entice Titch down from the gate post. Her own room. It felt odd to want something and not want it all at the same time. 'Could it be blue?'

'Blue? Of course it can be blue. It can be anything you want. You can choose. But first to our labours here, eh?' He swung the fork at the ground, ramming it up to its hilt under a cluster of tall thistles, making their purple bell heads shake in protest. '*We plough the fields and scatter,*' he sang in his shouty voice, '*...but it is fed and watered by God's almighty hand.*'

Eleanor crouched down to dig more gingerly at a patch of nettles. She was sorry her mother was still so sick, but it did feel much better having her father back, working alongside them.

9

APRIL 2013 – CAPE TOWN

Nick's serve landed exactly where he had planned, springing wide over the tramlines, but not with as much pace as he had intended. His opponent, a seasoned club member in his early forties, was on top of it in seconds, firing a low cross-court drive and racing up to the net in preparation to administer the obvious volley winner. Nick arrived late to the ball but managed a last-minute flick of the wrist as he struck it so that instead of shooting back on the obvious trajectory, it sailed high over his adversary's head, landing an inch inside the baseline and securing him the crucial five–three lead he had been hoping for. It was the final set. He had only to break serve again, or hold his own, and victory would be his.

Nick glanced at the stands where his daughters and Donna had based themselves, only slightly disappointed, and not remotely surprised, to see that they were empty. The three of them had been popping in and out regularly during the course of the final, for snacks and toilet breaks, and to watch Mike Scammell, their neighbour, who happened to be playing as a doubles guest on the next-door court. Nick was deeply touched that his family had bothered to come at all, even if two lame horses had been the reason. The tennis club ran so many tournaments and he often did well in them, so it was hardly a momentous occasion. In addition to which, the April weather was blowy, not ideal for sitting out in.

As they changed ends, Nick paused to swig from his water bottle. Through the fencing behind the stands, he glimpsed Donna's red jacket and a smudge of blue that was probably Nat's denim one. Sasha was in her old grey hoody, but he couldn't see her. Doubles was always more fun to watch, but as a player Nick preferred singles, the focus it required, the absolute responsibility it demanded. To concentrate completely on something – anything – was a form of relaxation, as he had found himself trying to explain to Kat when he eventually got around to writing a proper email back to her, latching onto the subject both because it interested him and because it seemed to fulfil her somewhat curious stipulations. *No raking up of the past. Nothing personal.* Whatever did that even mean anyway? How could one write to an old acquaintance without being 'personal'? And Kat had, for a couple of years anyway, been integral to his past, so that didn't make much sense either. Brooding on such questions after what had proved a very pleasant evening with Donna's relatives, Nick had resolved not to bother with a proper reply.

During the ensuing days, however, the matter kept pestering him, like a loose tooth. Soon, Kat's stipulations began to feel like a challenge from which he had shied away. Possible subjects began to present themselves, including the art of tennis. His response, when he got to it, became something of an essay, a relaxing act of concentration in itself. He crafted and reworked several versions before eventually sending it on its way. When there was no immediate response, Nick wondered if Kat had suffered similar doubts and changed her mind.

But then, after a week, a witty email arrived, describing the tribe of humanity – of which Kat claimed to be an affiliate – mysteriously incapable of making contact with any moving sporting objects. Nick had replied in the same light-hearted vein, asking if she had ever considered tiddlywinks or poker as alternative pastimes. A series of amusing and enjoyable exchanges had ensued, covering the degree of hand-eye coordination required for firing plastic counters and whether gambling could ever be regarded as a sport.

Next it had been clouds – had Nick heard of the Cloud Appreciation Society? (he hadn't); then theories as to why pet owners grew to resemble their pets; then some joint musings as to the reasons jazz music sent some people into ecstasy and others crawling up the wall. And so it had gone on, sporadic, harmless, left-of-centre exchanges which invariably made Nick chuckle, or stop and think, and then be eager for more. There was such clarity and colour in her language, and yet an alluring down-to-earth-ness too. If ever – rarely – he caught her out on some detail, she was only too happy to retreat and apologise, usually with a joke at her own expense.

Kat, can I say how much I am enjoying our communications, he had ventured in a recent missive, *it makes me wonder what we talked about when we were together. What the hell DID we ever talk about??*

I've no idea, and it doesn't matter, she had shot back, *and you are breaking the cardinal rule. The olden days and private stuff are out of bounds, remember?*

It took a while for Nick to realise that the tennis match was slipping from his grasp. Not only had his opponent managed to hold his service game but had done so with such ease that he was now attacking Nick's with new and dangerous self-belief. The man's first two returns had been clear winners and he was now springing round on the balls of his feet, eager to slam the third. Nick took a deep breath. At a certain level, sport was always a battle of minds. He had let his concentration drift, that was the trouble, done exactly the opposite of what he had told Kat he was good at. He had allowed himself to believe that the work of winning was done when it was still all to do. He might write to Kat about that too, one day.

Nick took his time assembling himself to serve again. The girls were back in their seats, although there was no sign of Donna. Natalie was on her phone, but her younger sister was watching him intently, looking faintly troubled. An ace, Nick told himself, straight down the middle, shaving the outer edge of the line. He shot Sasha a wink and began to bounce the ball. He bounced it seven times, slowly, rhythmically, shutting out not just his daughter but the whole world, making his opponent wait, making the moment his.

10

Vincent ran his finger round the inside of his dog collar. He could never remember an April being so hot. It was almost May, but still. Even in the cool stone interior of St Winifred's, he was sweating.

He checked over his shoulder again, across the empty pews, for any signs of arrivals for his new Bible Reading class. He had been mentioning it at the end of services all month and pinned a reminder in capital letters on the church board. And yet already the hands on his wristwatch had edged round to ten minutes past the appointed hour.

People led such busy lives, he reminded himself. Only a foolish priest would feel personal rejection.

His Bible lay open on his lap, a pleasant balanced weight across his knees. An anchor. Vincent dropped his gaze, experiencing a rush of joy at the familiar words. St John, chapter 3. Nicodemus quizzing Jesus. But then the page blurred and his head was full of Connie, the need to make her see sense, to guard her from the treachery of the outside world.

Vincent forced the page back into focus, tracing the tip of his index finger down its tissue-smoothness. The poetry of the language alone made him want to weep. Jesus spoke so beautifully and yet Nicodemus had been so literal-minded. Every time Jesus described a truth, the hapless man had pressed for more: *The wind bloweth where it listeth and thou hearest the sound thereof, but canst not tell whence it cometh, and whither it goeth: so is every one that is born of the spirit.*

And yet still Nicodemus hadn't been satisfied. Good old Nicodemus. Like him, needing to have things spelt out, prosaically, in order to fend off the rages of doubt. Rages of doubt were normal. That was the consolation.

Vincent sighed as he read on.

For God sent not his Son into the world to condemn the world; but that the world through him might be saved... light is come into the world, and men loved darkness rather than light, because their deeds were evil.

Light and dark. Dark and light. Polar opposites and yet sometimes it was hard to know the difference.

A creak ricocheted into the silence like a gunshot. Vincent spun round to see that St Winifred's stout oak door had swung ajar. A cloud of light hovered in the gap, illuminating silver flecks in the grey stone slabs of the floor and walls.

'Hello?' Vincent carefully closed the Bible and stood up, peering towards the hazy beams. 'Con?'

Please God, he prayed, *let it be Connie.*

That morning he had tried to persuade her to come to the class. Not deploying 'religious' reasons – he knew far better than to raise those – but saying she might find it interesting. She had muttered darkly and turned her back on him, her body a hard S under the bedcovers.

Wanting the S to soften, Vincent had tried to kiss her, meeting only the sharp ledge of her cheekbone through her hair. She was still cross with him about Kat, he knew; with Eleanor in her new room, their youngest had tried the night before, and on several previous occasions, to crawl into their bed and he had had to be firm.

'I love you, Con,' he had murmured that morning, nuzzling

his nose deeper to drink in her scent but also wanting the reassurance that there was nothing untoward laced within it. There
couldn't be, of course, not any more. Not now they had the new
routine. He dropped the girls off in the morning, leaving the
exact bus money for Connie to make the return journey to fetch
and accompany them home. Vincent would have preferred she
didn't go out at all, but with busybodies like Mrs Owens around,
it was important to keep up appearances, to stifle fuel for gossip.
Apart from that, Connie had no funds and was no longer
allowed to go anywhere unaccompanied. The car had been out
of bounds for weeks. He kept both sets of keys on him to be sure.

But recently Vincent feared he had detected the hint of
something alien on her skin in spite of these precautions – not
just alcohol, but possibly aftershave. His thoughts had lurched
to their neighbour, whose ramshackle farmhouse was set in a
dip of land barely half a mile behind the vicarage. Broughton's
main street might be a three-mile hike away, but the Watson
man was close. Still only in his thirties, the farmer was swarthy
and lonely, having lost his wife to cancer several years before. All
he had now was the boy Charlie, who was at school all day. To
have such thoughts sickened Vincent, but it was Connie's fault.
She had history and she was determined; that was the problem.
Anything was possible with Connie.

And yet outwardly his wife seemed to have embraced the
new curfew. She was surly, but he was used to that. Behind the
surliness, he had been sensing a new docility to her. Doing the
supermarket shop that week, now a strictly joint venture at his
insistence, she had thrown several bags of lemons into the
trolley and then, the moment they got home, diligently set about
converting them into curds, sorbets and tarts. The girls had been
briefly interested but drifted away when it became clear their
assistance was surplus to their mother's requirements.

And just that morning, in spite of the sulking, she had swept
into the kitchen just as he and the girls were finishing breakfast,
pulled on her tatty, stained apron over her nightie and declared

that the day's project was to be lemon cordial, the old fashioned-kind. She had asked him to reach down her favourite green jug from the top shelf and started lining up the chopping board and various pudding basins, chattering to the girls about how delicious it would be. She had paused in her preparations to help them find their satchels and kiss them goodbye, and then rushed out to the drive to kiss them again.

Before the lemons, there had been sewing, days and days of it. She had ransacked cupboards and drawers, unearthing clothes that needed attention. The sitting room sofa had been her station for the task, the garments growing around her like a carapace as she stitched and patched, replacing buttons, letting seams out and hems down, driving the girls mad with her demands for their cooperation.

Sitting in the hot church, Vincent experienced a rush of tenderness as he pondered these labours. The daily cleaning chores were being neglected as usual, but they had the old sourpuss Mrs Owens to pick up the slack there. Connie was trying hard, that was what mattered. It reminded him of the bursts of energy during the early days – the fundraising ventures and all the sweet second-guesses of his own meagre bachelor wants – days when Connie had welcomed her need of him instead of resisting it. Days when no force had been necessary. But he would win her round again, Vincent vowed. Get her to see the rightness of submission, rejoice in it.

The church door swung shut with a groan, taking the cloud of light with it and bringing Vincent fully to his senses. It was obviously time to give up on the class. If he was quick, he could grab a bite of lunch at home. He had a busy afternoon ahead of him – a long-promised visit to The Bressingham nursing home, followed by the monthly Monday meeting with his churchwardens. They would be gathering as usual at Hilda de Mowbray's imposing manor house on the far side of Broughton, under pressure to do so from Hilda herself, a formidably wealthy widow and churchwarden whose generosity to the church funds made her bidding difficult to refuse.

Vincent was dreading it, both for the tedium of the largely administrative agenda and Hilda's palpably oppressive sense of self-worth. He would sip Earl Grey, which he didn't like, from the hand-painted heirloom bone-china cups, doing his best to steer the meeting rather than give up on it, wondering all the while how far Mrs Owen's concerns about his private life had spread beyond Mrs Owen. The cleaner had been cooperative and dead-pan since her Easter holiday in the West Country, but that told him nothing.

Village talk was like the leak in the vestry, Vincent mused gloomily, quickening his pace as he hurried under the shadowy canopy of the birch wood, finding new outlets even after you thought you had got it fixed.

* * *

During lunch break that day Eleanor took her book to the patch of shade in the corner of the playground. It meant she could keep an eye on Kat through the meshed fence dividing the Broughton Grammar's senior and junior school playgrounds while at the same time tracking Jane Eyre's doomed attempts to escape the clutches of the hateful Reed family.

Eleanor didn't like the heat much and would have preferred a quiet nook in the library, but that wasn't allowed. Breaks were for 'fresh air', her form teacher said, even when, like that day, it didn't feel particularly fresh. Rainy air was fresh, in Eleanor's view, but when it rained, they were made to stay inside. She had made this very point in class that morning, only to be told off for being 'precocious'. Looking the word up in the school library dictionary, she had been confused. How could someone be told off for *having faculties that develop early*?

Though the junior portion of the playground was much smaller, they had a lot more fun by the look of things. At least,

Kat always appeared happy. That day, she was part of a hopscotch group, waiting her turn to throw a stone into the chalked squares and then launching off on one of her spindly legs to retrieve it. When she saw Eleanor watching, she was halfway through a go. She waved and overbalanced, making a meal of the fall. Eleanor anxiously got to her feet but sank back down when it became clear the writhing was thanks to giggles. Kat's little companions were soon clustered about her, hands on hips, joining in with the laughter.

A book could be used as a shield, Eleanor had discovered. A book said *I am busy, go away.* If held at the right angle, she didn't even have to see the gaggle of girls she most dreaded, the troupe who trailed round the sharp-eyed, sharp-tongued Isabel Kirby like weedy bodyguards, hanging on her every word. That lunch break they were on the gym steps as usual, sniggering and pretending to smoke pencils, their grey school skirts hitched halfway up their thighs. They had bagged the back row of the classroom on the first day of the summer term, from where they exerted their dark, invisible pressure on the class, making rude gestures and faces when teachers' backs were turned and flicking pellets at the necks of those refusing to share the joke. Eleanor, sitting in the front row, had become so frequent a target that she had taken to wearing her thick dark brush of hair loose, for protection. The pellets were made of paper and spittle and if fired hard enough could sting as well as cause annoyance.

'What's that you're reading then?'

Eleanor's eyes stopped mid-sentence, but she did not look up. She had found *Jane Eyre* on a returns pile in the library the week before, read it in one gulp and decided to start it again. She was still in the opening pages, sharing Jane's ordeal of being locked in the 'red room', where the ghost of the uncle prowled the shadows. Even in the heat, on a second reading, it was giving her goosebumps.

'I asked you a question.'

Eleanor allowed her face to appear over the top of the pages, aware as she did so of the faint scent of lemon on her clothes. It made her think of her mother, the new version who was always ill, or asleep, or busy with other things, like sewing and cooking. She looked as she always did, and said the same sorts of things she always had, and yet it felt increasingly to Eleanor that she didn't *mean* them. Like she was there, but also not there. Occasionally, like someone bursting out of a dream, she would seem to try and make up for this absence by lunging at her and Kat with hugs so hard they hurt and whispering soft things they couldn't understand. Like that morning, running out of the house to grab them in the drive, her rings and nails snagging in their hair.

Isobel Kirby sniggered. 'Cat's got her tongue.'

In spite of the discomfort of the moment, Eleanor felt a surge of frustration at having a mother so patently unsatisfactory compared to the ones other children enjoyed. Children like the girl before her, with her cocky plaits and tight skirts, who was deposited and collected at the school gates by a handsome ruddy-cheeked woman driving a dirty green Land Rover crowded with dogs. Not even looking back on London helped Eleanor any more. The past had sunk beyond reach, overlaid by the incomprehensible disappointments of the present. Like her mother still not driving, not even to take or fetch them from school. Like the horrible blue walls of her new bedroom; a blue she had chosen, but which, under the slap-slap of her father's paintbrush, had somehow transformed itself from the milky beauty in the tin into a dingy murk. It felt like failure to have got the colour so wrong, too stupid a failure to admit to. She had to console herself by whispering her sorrows to Mottie instead, having promoted the bear from the bottom of the bed and into her arms to make up for the emptiness of the space that had once contained her little sister.

'It's called *Jane Eyre* and was written by Charlotte Bronte,' she replied at last, when the sniggering became unbearable.

'Ooooh, *Jane-Eyre*-by-Charlotte-Brontty,' mimicked Isobel

Kirby, glancing at her friends for approval and then making a sudden swipe for the book. But Eleanor held fast, crossing her arms and pressing the novel to her chest. 'It looks swotty. Don't you think?' Isobel threw another look at her smirking companions. 'And who does she think she is anyway? I only wanted to take a look at the fucking book, didn't I?'

Inwardly, Eleanor quailed. At home, the Lord's name wasn't allowed in vain, let alone any swear words. Even Isobel's followers exchanged awestruck glances.

'Maybe it's poetry,' sneered Isobel next, taking a step closer. 'Well, here's some poetry for you: Swot and Spot. How about that? Spotty Swotty.'

Eleanor hugged *Jane Eyre* tighter, hooking her chin over the top of it. Out of the corner of her eye, she was aware of Kat still hopping on the other side of the fence, her fizz of white hair bouncing half a beat behind. Eleanor kept her gaze on the dusty tarmac under her legs, not speaking, not moving. Jane Eyre had tried to be nice and it had got her nowhere, and when she had finally retaliated – fighting back at the bullying John Reed – the consequences had been even worse. The thought had no sooner formed in her mind than Isobel's leg swung out from the folds of her rucked-up school skirt and delivered a sharp, penetrating kick to Eleanor's shin. The troupe pressed in a closer circle, sensing blood.

In spite of her recent resolution, Eleanor decided to pray for the bell. It was the only thing she could think of that might break the spell, release her.

But, instead, the narrow peaky face of her English teacher appeared over the heads of the girls. 'Ah, Eleanor, there you are. I need you a moment.' The gang parted, meek and defused. 'There's an essay competition I think you should go in for and Mrs Mayfield agrees. Come along now, I haven't got all day. And you lot, find *something* to do other than loafing, can't you? If you like *Jane Eyre* you could write about that,' Miss Zaphron added briskly as they walked away. She cast Eleanor one of her arch smiles, peering down her beaky nose at the book, still clutched in Eleanor's white-knuckled hands, keeping her afloat, it felt like, in the stormy seas of another difficult day.

* * *

A wasp hung over the dirty mixing bowl, dropping every now and then to dunk itself in the ridges of lemon and sugar. The back door had been propped open with an upturned bucket. A loaf of bread sat half out of its bag, greyish and rock hard.

Vincent ran himself a glass of water from the kitchen tap, fighting irritation as he surveyed the scene. After the walk from the church, he was hotter than ever. He could feel pools of moisture trickling from his armpits and down his sides. He opened the fridge, reaching with some difficulty past the green jug, full to the brim now with bright yellow liquid, and the several foil-covered dishes stacked round it, to pick at the bony carcass of last night's chicken.

'Con,' he shouted, aiming his voice at the hall, 'have you had lunch? I've only got five minutes.'

The ground floor of the vicarage echoed back at him. Tearing off the one drumstick still with a few threads of meat left on it, Vincent stepped outside the back door to check that he hadn't dreamt seeing the car in the drive. He hadn't. It was still there. As of course it had to be because he had the keys. He scanned the garden, tossing the chicken bone into a bush and licking the grease off his fingers.

'A husband is for life but never for lunch, is that it?' Vincent called, chuckling at his own joke as he stepped back into the kitchen and hastily cobbled together a meal out of cheese, a slice of the stale bread and an apple.

He ate doggedly and quickly, for fuel rather than pleasure. The wasp had been joined by several relatives. It was ridiculous – wasps so early in the summer, and not good for Kat, who was allergic. Vincent batted at them with one of Connie's magazines, managing to kill a couple. If the sticky lemon dishes weren't washed up, soon more would come in.

Vincent booted the back door shut and tried calling up the stairs. 'I've got to go.'

The clank of bathroom plumbing echoed back at him. From their bathroom by the sound of it. She often took a late bath these days.

Vincent started up the stairs but checked himself. He didn't want to crowd her. Nor did he have time for an argument. 'Okay. I'm off then. When you've washed yourself, the kitchen could do with some similar treatment. Wasps all over the place. Not good for Kat, remember?'

He hurried out to the car only to realise he had forgotten the bulging manila folder in which he kept everything relating to matters of church management. Striding back inside, along the hall to his study, the thump of pipes upstairs assailed him again. Vincent fought down a wave of deep frustration. Nothing in the vicarage worked as it should. The entire place needed rewiring, replumbing, reroofing. As a bachelor such things hadn't mattered, but with a family, they mattered greatly. His London accommodation had eventually deteriorated into a condition of such dire need that he had fought to be moved into a small terraced house instead, a supposedly temporary solution that had lasted until they left.

The mess on and around his desk dampened his spirits further. He was a preacher not an administrator. Why did one have to be both?

Having located the folder, Vincent paused, arrested by his desk photograph of Connie on their wedding day. She was holding her bouquet and had her head thrown back, her mouth open, laughing. Confetti floated across her face like snowflakes.

Vincent picked an old envelope out of the mayhem on his desk and scrawled: *Darling Connie, came home for a 10-minute lunch. I love you. Vx.*

He propped the message on the bottom stair and raced out of the house.

* * *

'It's a pity, vicar, that's all I'm saying. A great shame. One expects... well, you know, there is a certain expectation, is there not?' Hilda de Mowbray paused, teapot poised over her cup. She had offered Vincent a refill and he had refused. The other members of the meeting had gone. Vincent too, had tried to leave but had been pressed back into his chair with an urgent request for a private consultation. It was a conspiracy, he realised now. They had all got to Hilda's before him to agree tactics: letting the meeting proceed, covering the usual nuts and bolts and then withdrawing to leave Hilda to corner him about this other matter, the one he had feared, but coming at him from not quite the angle he had feared it. Having prepared himself for atmosphere, maybe some exchanged looks, he had been entirely caught out by what was apparently a mandate to speak for all of them.

She was loving every moment, Vincent realised with some wretchedness, noting the twitch of Hilda's thin pastel pink lips as she continued to seek the right words to tell him that his wife was not a sufficiently bright beacon of godliness.

'You mean she doesn't go to church enough.'

Hilda hesitated. 'Yes, that. Partly.' She patted the thin mousy helmet of her hair. 'Not that how people live their lives is anyone's business.'

No, it is not. Vincent let the retort reverberate inside his head where it could do no harm. He needed this woman's allegiance. He needed Broughton. '*Indeed*,' he said instead, giving the word great emphasis. 'Freedom to worship as we each choose is important.' He spoke with the sort of put-on pious tone he had once despised, but which he had learnt could be lapped up by certain types of parishioners. 'I entrust that freedom to my wife, as I do to anyone else.'

'Quite.' Hilda replied. 'Are sure you don't want me to freshen the pot?'

'Quite sure, thank you. I have a busy afternoon. I really can't stay long...' Vincent faltered, suppressing an eagerness – a bomb inside him it felt like – not just to be gone, but to charge, hollering profanities, out of Hilda's pristine museum of a home, with its fussy tie-back curtain tassels and exactly positioned lace doilies, ideally making sure he barged the two stone cherubs on her doorstep as he went and, for good measure, trampling her preciously mani- cured front flower beds until every stem was snapped and their flowers mashed to a pulp. He let his big dark eyes meet hers, filling them with all the calm power he possessed. 'I would also ask you to take into account that my wife has been struggling somewhat with the transition from London. She is still finding her feet. She supports me as much as she can. She has, in addition, been poorly lately, a nervous condition, barely able to leave the house. In such circumstances, I would never command her to attend church. What sort of priest, or husband, would I be then?'

'I am sorry that your wife has been unwell, naturally. I am only trying to help and... to do what is right.' Hilda fiddled with the delicate handle of the teacup, shifting sideways in her chair.

She had thick ankles, Vincent noticed viciously.

'The fact is,' she continued crisply, 'one might feel obliged, at a certain point, to say something to the Archdeacon.'

Vincent stood up, involuntarily, as if the bomb inside him was starting to go off. 'I really do not think that would be either necessary or... or... charitable.'

Her sharp grey eyes darted up at him, steely, but with a trace of indignation. 'I can assure you I am the most charitable of women. I give freely of my time, and money, both to the church and several other deserving organisations. I also care dearly for this parish and the members within it. I speak only with their welfare in mind. And, as you may know, Reverend Cope set the highest standards.'

Vincent clenched his toes inside his shoes. He would have liked to clench his fists but knew that would not do. He tried to open the door inside his chest, the one to the guiding voice he needed. *Help me God, with this abominable woman,* he prayed. *Help me love her and understand her and not cross her.*

'Your commitment to this parish is wonderful, Hilda, no one could disagree on that. But I can assure you, so is mine. I will, of course, speak to Connie, express some of your concerns. But can I ask in return that you give her a little more time to... settle... that you are not too quick to judge?' He managed a smile, and then somehow got himself out of the sitting room and into the broad hall, past the pedestal sporting a vase of lilies and the vast oil painting of a schooner on a stormy sea.

Hilda trotted behind him, her stout heels smacking on the polished herring-boned floor. On the doorstep she fiddled with the large pearls studding her small, pale earlobes. 'Rest assured, I shall take no further action at present. I just felt something had to be said. I hope no offence has been caused.'

Of course it hadn't, Vincent assured her. He quite understood. He would look forward to seeing her on Sunday as usual. It was simply splendid that she had volunteered, again, to read the Lesson.

Getting out of the drive required a three-point turn. He was aware of Hilda, framed between her cherubs, watching the entire manoeuvre, the solid orb of her permed hair shining in the sun. There was a wasp in the car, beating its head against the passenger window. After a few minutes, Vincent pulled into a layby to lean across to release it, thinking of Connie as it bounced off into the hot blue air.

* * *

Connie walked fast, the train timetable leaflet flapping in her hand. She had taken all the big decisions in her life quickly. This was something to be proud of, she told herself, something to hold on to amid all the mess. Leaving home, the first abortion, then the second, accepting banishment by her family, finding her own way in London, tripping over and getting up, only to fall again, each time further, each time harder. Attaching herself to men who let her down, or dragged her down, or both. She made mistakes, but always moved on, with speed. That was something she had learned how to do at least.

Picking out Vincent had been a quick decision too, one of those light-bulb moments. Near the end of yet another tether (there had been so many), Connie had seen the hunger in his dark earnest eyes and resolved, instantly, dripping mop in hand, to target him, see where it led. Such an impressive bear of a man, with his blazing faith, he had seemed a sure bet, the surest of her life. The way he loved her, displaying a flatteringly feverish intensity she had never previously encountered, had been disarming too. It had been easy to place her trust in such powerful emotions, easy to imagine that they would more than make up for the flakiness of feelings on her own part, deriving as they did from an instinct for self-preservation rather than love. Marrying Vincent, Connie had believed she was boarding a ship; a big strong ship, that would keep her steady.

It shocked her still, the myriad ways in which such a belief had proved misguided: the corrosive, daily struggle to live well, the rebel in her fighting at every step, wanting to succumb to the pull of her own demons. Most shocking of all, however, had been Vincent himself, not a ship as she had supposed, but a man overboard, floundering in his own ocean, grabbing at whatever he could – God, her – to keep his head above the waves.

The girls had helped for a time. And then not helped. Made things worse. Even as babies, Vincent had been jealous of them, their needs, the time they took.

Connie slowed. Sweat was pouring into her eyes, making it hard to see. She mustn't think about the girls, except that she had failed them. The sun was pounding her head, making her dizzy. The horizon of fields skirting the scrag-end of the Downs zigzagged in the distance, a series of unreadable lines. She had drunk the bottle too fast, that was the trouble. Digging it out of the earth like a dog, she had been too relieved at the sight of its smeared glass and half-torn red label to hold back. It was just a half-bottle, the last of her treasured stash, painstakingly acquired during the recent, gradual constriction of her world, funded first from savings eked out of her meagre housekeeping allowance and then, as Vincent tightened his vice, from coins rootled out of every dusty corner of the vicarage – under furniture, between floorboards, behind cushions, in jars and the occasional gift of a note in the gritty bottom of a trouser pocket. Wretch that she was, the girls' piggy banks were lighter too. She had been scouring the house for weeks. There was nothing left to draw on.

Connie forced herself to walk on, wrenching her ankles as her flip-flops slid between the lumpy blocks of compacted earth. Money mattered. She had always known that but had taken a while to realise quite how much. It was freedom. And she had none. Back in the day, walking away from her family, she had imagined that her looks would see her through, open doors. Which they had, only the wrong ones. It was a measure of how parlous her situation had become that she had alighted upon Vincent as the opportunity for financial as much as emotional security. A Church of England salary was meagre, but at least it was steady and came with a free house. Vincent had a big heart too, or at least he had seemed to when they met, always eager to give her extra money when he could, for treats like nice clothes, nice shoes. Because she was blessed and beautiful, he would say, tacitly exacting payment in the form of the dominating sexual embraces he preferred and which she had been more than willing, in those early days, to give.

But then the girls came, bewitching and bewildering, draining. There was neither time nor money for treats like new clothes. Vincent's generosity soured into possessiveness. Responding to his endless physical demands, keeping him happy, was something Connie had learned to wring out of herself, from a knot of sheer willpower. Sex was proof she still loved him, he would say, applying a force that contained extra relish if ever he detected a hint of reluctance. After the girls, he began to tighten his hold on other aspects of her life too. He started watching, interrogating, distrusting. It had begun to feel as if she was living under a microscope, pegged out for scrutiny.

The day she decided to drink again was joyful; like stumbling across a lost soulmate. She would keep it under control, she vowed, save it for when her energies were at their lowest. And for a time she had managed. For a time there had been balance. Until Vincent realised and the portcullis came slamming down in the form of the secret applications to get them to Broughton, away from dear Maria and the couple of other friends she relied on to see her through. Contact with London had been forbidden from the start. It was the only way to break the cycle, Vincent said. From the first glimpse of the vicarage, its grey roof-tiles poking over the bone-white trees as they rounded the bend in the long-overgrown drive, Connie had felt he might as well be burying her alive.

Connie reached the stile and leant on it to catch her breath. An image of Kat came to mind, curled up in the middle of their bed the night before, her head tucked under her arms like a puppy, seeking refuge – again – from the new emptiness of her bedroom. Connie's heart had fluttered with the old joy – the feel of a new-born in her arms, drifting in and out of sleep as she suckled, Vincent powerless and curious beside them. But Vincent had scooped the child off the bed without a word, carrying her back along the corridor and then locking their bedroom door on his return. There were things he needed, he said, his eyes glittering at her in the way that they did; things only a wife could provide. It was about love, he growled, coming round to her side of the bed; about her proving it was still there.

Connie had turned over before he asked, thinking of the roll-up she would sneak out for afterwards, and the precious half-bottle still buried by the back gate, a reward for being good.

As Connie climbed the stile and set off across the second field, she was aware of beads of sweat tracking down her ribcage and the backs of her knees. Her cotton skirt clung to her thighs. Her hair was like glue on the back of her neck. She bunched it up angrily, wishing she had brought one of her hair ties or a rubber band. Breathing hard, she paused to examine the timetable again. Twelve minutes, give or take. She was going to have to get a move on. Inside her a wave was breaking; the urge to look back, to see how far she had come and perhaps catch a last glimpse of what she was leaving behind, but she checked herself. Always look forwards, that was the key. Make a decision and move on. Vincent was the longest she had stuck with anyone. And the girls.

But she mustn't think about the girls.

Her brain circled back at her, an enemy regrouping. Connie swung her arms, stiffening her neck, propelling herself forwards. She had grown useless with her daughters. It ate away at her, the uselessness, fed off itself, got worse. Vincent, for all his faults, was good at being a father; purposeful, strong, consistent. All the things she wasn't.

The way out had arrived in Connie's mind that morning, drifting in on the lemony steam of the kitchen like inspiration, its approach unseen, crystallising instantly into the blindingly obvious. It was the only option. She had no money. She was powerless. Regrets were for sissies. And Connie had been many things in her thirty-eight years on the planet, but she was never that.

11

Mrs Owens sat in the square of shade offered by the breakwater, her ample backside bulging below the frame of the deckchair. Her basket was next to her, containing the empty crisp packets and foil wrappings of their picnic, and the bag of knitting which she had started and then abandoned, as her chin dropped further onto her chest. Her short stout arms were neatly placed across her stomach, the palms hanging slightly open.

Kat reached across and tickled one of her veiny ankles with a straggly seagull feather she had found.

'Don't, Kat, you'll wake her up,' hissed Eleanor

'Won't. Look.' Kat waggled the feather more energetically. 'Her tights make her not feel it. And she should wake up anyway, shouldn't she? In case we drown?'

The question, with its impossible connotations, made both girls look at the sea, a retreating, mesmerising choppy mass some ten yards in front of them, breaking noisily on the shingle. In the vicarage garden that morning the air had been balmy, but here it blew noisily off the water with a force strong enough to lean on, as Kat had gleefully demonstrated while they were eating their picnic, spraying bits of cheese out of her sandwich as she arched her whippet frame into it, stretching her arms wide as if in preparation to skydive off a cliff. Mrs Owens had shaken her head and clicked her teeth, saying what a wee slip of a thing she was, but then adding in the same breath, so that the two thoughts were inextricably, crushingly, connected, 'And your big sister badly needs a new cozzie.'

Eleanor had shovelled the last crusty portion of her sandwich into her mouth, her cheeks burning. She dug her fingers into the pebbles around their towels, feeling for the cool wet mud with her fingertips. Putting her bathing costume on that afternoon – under her shorts and T-shirt ready for swimming, as Mrs Owens had instructed – she had been distressed to find how the straps cut into her shoulders and the way the sides rode up over her hips, forcing the flimsy material to gather uncomfortably in the crevice of her bottom. She had stood on a chair to try and get the measure of these difficulties, using the small mirror above her chest of drawers, fighting the dispiriting notion, as she tugged and twisted, that this newly burgeoning body was in some way betraying her. Arriving at the beach, she had attempted to keep the betrayal secret by tying her jumper round her waist even after she had stripped off her shorts and T-shirt. Sprawling on the towels beside Kat, bare and flat-chested in her frilly pink bikini pants, she had felt like a lump of dough next to a rose petal.

'I'll speak to Dad about it, Eleanor love,' Mrs Owens had continued, either not knowing Eleanor wished her dead or not caring. 'You're growing out of all your clothes. And we'll see about getting you a brassiere while we're at it. Don't you worry, we'll soon get you fixed.'

Eleanor had unknotted her jumper and run at the sea to get away, flopping down on the sharp stones in the shallows just to hide herself. She had kept her back to Mrs Owens, willing the woman and her hateful words to evaporate. There was no end to anything bad now; not since the hot April afternoon three months before when her mother hadn't come on the bus to get her and Kat from school and Isobel Kirby had kicked her leg.

Eleanor glanced down at the still lumpy brownish scab on her shin. At the time she hadn't noticed it was bleeding until Miss Zaphron had handed her a tissue. In subsequent weeks it had become a ritual to let it heal and then pick it open again. It was like a reminder of what had happened. A boundary line between the Before and the After.

'Look, Ellie.'

Eleanor turned round to see that Kat had abandoned the feather and was busy instead tying messy knots between the laces of Mrs Owens stout walking shoes.

'Kat, you shouldn't.' Eleanor giggled, wriggling across the towels to help.

When the job was done, they picked their way down to the water's edge and stood as close as they dared to the crashing waves, letting the icy water pool round their ankles.

'Okay?' Eleanor had to shout over the roar.

When Kat didn't answer, she reached for her hand and held it hard. Then they both just stood there, narrowing their eyes in the onrush of wind, their hair blasting from its roots, facing not just the sea on their own, it felt like, but the whole world.

'Girls!'

It was with a reflex of hope that Eleanor swung round. It wasn't their mother, of course. It couldn't be, ever again. There had been other such moments, each one its own rollercoaster. Like the previous week, glimpsing a lady with big blonde hair striding in high heels down Broughton High Street; Eleanor had found herself starting forwards, an involuntary jerk against the iron grasp of Hilda de Mowbray's hand. But, in the same instant, the woman had turned, confirming a profile that bore no relation to her mother; an ugly square chin, full cheeks. The hair was wrong too, straight and dry and stiff, like straw.

'Eleanor, Kat – you can't be here alone, surely.' The voice belonged to her English teacher, barely recognisable in a wide-brimmed floppy straw hat and a long halter-neck sundress the colour of tangerines. She was out of breath, and had the flat of one hand pinned on top of the hat while the other held the sides of the dress out of reach of the lapping sea.

'No, we've got *her*.' Kat stuck a thumb in the direction of Mrs Owens, who was stirring. 'We don't like her much. She cleans our house.'

There was a time, Eleanor realised, when she might have felt awkward, or even duty-bound to apologise, for her little sister's bluntness. But now it made her love her more dearly. Kat speaking out had come to feel like an important part of what they were both going through; they both felt the same things, but only Kat could actually say them. It helped ease the knots in her own heart, Eleanor had found, especially when it came to tackling the new silent fortress of their father. Eleanor couldn't look at him, but Kat was fearless. 'I am going to sleep with Daddy,' she had declared stoutly on the first airless night, when Connie was merely missing as opposed to dead beside the rail-tracks. 'He will need me, won't you, Daddy.'

'Yes,' Vincent had croaked, swivelling dazed eyes to look at her. They had all slept together in the end, heaped in the middle of the wide bed like mangled wreckage.

'But this is so lucky,' Miss Zaphron exclaimed, releasing her dress hem to the perils of the beach so that she could squeeze Eleanor's shoulder. The silky orange panels billowed round her thin legs like flames. 'Because I was going to call you today anyway... my dear child, you've only gone and won the competition.' Her big brown eyes shone, making her nose look small.

Beside them, Kat had stopped listening and was doubled over in a private, miming imitation of Mrs Owens, now testily sorting out her criss-crossed shoelaces.

'The writing competition?' Miss Zaphron prompted, when Eleanor did not speak. 'The *national* writing competition? They have chosen your essay about *Jane Eyre*. It is going to be published in a magazine. You are a clever, clever girl and should be jolly proud.'

'Yes, I suppose I am.' Eleanor smiled. A dim, unreachable

part of her was pleased. Far more vivid was the sting of the salty water finding out the freshly picked crevices of the scab on her shin. The pain was taking her back to the deserted forecourt of the school, waiting with Kat under the big tree, leaning against their satchels as if they were cushions. Kat had scratched a hole in the dry ground with a twig. She was herding ants into it and then raining down blobs of spittle on top of them. To see if they could swim, she declared solemnly, catching Eleanor's look of disapproval.

Eleanor had whiled away the time looking over what she had written during her talk with Miss Zaphron. The competition title was, 'Why Does Reading Matter?' Entrants were invited to use a favourite book to answer the question, Miss Zaphron had explained, reading from a leaflet and suggesting Eleanor jot down any first thoughts there and then. Eleanor, thinking at once of *Jane Eyre*, had written, *a story is real life, but also an escape.* When she showed the sentence to Miss Zaphron, the teacher had beamed, saying she thought it would make an excellent starting point.

While they sat under the tree, various teachers had drifted past, each pausing to ask if they were okay. She and Kat had kept saying yes, not looking at each other, mutually eager to hide the ignominy of having been forgotten.

'Mummy's toooo busy at the *moment*,' Kat cooed, when the first expression of serious concern arrived, via Mr Posner who taught Eleanor Maths and who had a deeply pockmarked face, as if it had withstood a hail of tiny bullets. By then it was some forty minutes after the official end of the school day. 'But she will come soon, and then we go on the bus together,' Kat had chattered, displaying the assurance that made Eleanor want to hug her. The Maths teacher had patted Kat's head and offered them both a fruit Polo, saying he would pop back to check on them again soon.

It was fifteen minutes before anyone reappeared. And then it wasn't the Maths teacher, but Mrs Mayfield, approaching at speed, the vulture-wings of her scholar cloak flapping. There had been a misunderstanding, she said. Their father, not their mother, would now be coming to fetch them from school.

'Well, you *should* be pleased,' Miss Zaphron declared in a scolding tone that ripped through the images in Eleanor's head.

Eleanor was grateful. She didn't want to remember. When the two policemen came to the vicarage front door the following morning, helmets off, heads bowed, Vincent had dropped to his knees with a howl. She and Kat had huddled in the doorway of the kitchen behind him, waiting to be noticed.

'You have such talent,' the English teacher went on, the wind whipping at her sentences. 'We must look after it. I've been speaking to Mrs Mayfield. We are going to move you up a class, keep a special eye on you.'

Mrs Owens, her laces back in small tight bows, her wide flat face visibly disgruntled, slid gingerly over the pebbles to join them. Out of the lee of the breakwater, the wind blew her short grey hair up into stalks, flinging her paisley dress tightly round her stocky body.

Miss Zaphron introduced herself, quickly relaying Eleanor's good news.

Kat took it on board this time, shouting, to no one in particular, 'Ellie is a brainbox.'

'Oh, but your father will be pleased, won't he, love?' Mrs Owens put an arm round Eleanor's shoulders, which she endured, inwardly cowering. It was true though, it might make Vincent happy, and that was a welcome idea. Because her father didn't seem to like doing anything much these days, except his praying, stopping suddenly in the middle of something quite normal – like walking or washing-up or reading – to close his eyes and move his lips fast over whispered words. Eleanor hated it. But she couldn't say so. She couldn't *say* anything.

'Oh my goodness, yes, I'm sure he will,' exclaimed Miss Zaphron. 'I am going to call him this afternoon. Tell him I'm going to call him, Eleanor, will you, dear?' She was losing the fight with the hat. The brim was bouncing like a flying saucer wanting to take off. 'I want to propose some extra tuition with me. Reading books and talking about them. You'd like that, wouldn't you? I'm thinking of university one day... maybe Oxford. What do you say, Eleanor? The city of dreaming spires.' She laughed, as if she had told a good joke, and gathered up her dress to continue her walk along the shoreline. In the distance a man in green shorts and a yellow T-shirt waved. She waved back and broke into a bounding run towards him, a flapping orange bird charging along the fringes of the surf.

* * *

Vincent peered through the blind, widening the flimsy plastic slats with his fingers to create a gap. He had thought he heard a car, but what he could see of the drive was empty. The sun had been drowned by cloud, great thick banks of it rolling in over the distant horizon of hills like fog. He was in the small lavatory on the top landing, studying a calendar that Connie had hung on the wall, deploying a thick, rusted nail left by one of his predecessors. The calendar was one he had given her for Christmas, of Renaissance masterpieces. For weeks it had been stuck on April, but since his last visit to the top floor someone had moved it on to July. Mrs Owens most likely. Or maybe Eleanor. Eleanor had a stealth about her these days, a quietness. Kat was wilder, needier, easier. Vincent gave them what he could. He gave everyone what he could. Including God. The trouble was, it wasn't enough. He knew, because God no longer answered back. No matter how he begged, there was nothing but silence. It had left him empty. What he managed for the outside world was a shell. Inside he was rotting, echoing, stained, without a soul.

Vincent fell against the wall, breathing hard. The calendar picture for July was Botticelli's *Birth of Venus*. It was a painting he had been made to study once, during some class on something or other, a hundred years before. His entire life felt like a hundred years before, the sad history of someone he didn't know, someone who thought he had found salvation only to fail at that too. The woman in the shell looked like an image of perfection, but she was flawed, Vincent remembered. The artist had cheated to create the effect. Her left arm was far too long, serving to accentuate sinuous female curves rather than biological reality. She wasn't standing in the shell so much as floating at an awkward angle on the front edge of it, one foot virtually in mid-air. Perspective, that was what the Renaissance artists had struggled with and finally mastered. Perspective. But all it amounted to was trickery with their brushes. A con. Vincent's eyes darted around the grimy avocado walls of the small toilet. They were closing in, sliding on invisible rollers. Soon he would be crushed flat, a fly slammed between two hands.

He stumbled into the passageway, stalling at the sight of Kat on the top stair. She was lost in one of her private games, clinging to the landing as if it was a cliff edge, her head bobbing up over the edge.

'Daddeeee,' she squealed when she saw him. She scrambled to her feet and charged at his legs, chattering about the beach and something to do with Mrs Owens' shoes.

Vincent clasped her against his knees. He had to fight to stop himself gripping too hard. It wouldn't do. But he wanted to. He needed to.

'Kit-Kat.' He lifted her up, sniffing her soft nest of hair. It was cold as silk against his cheeks and smelt of the sea. *I could drown in this*, he thought. Then God and the world would cease to matter.

'Mrs Owens said we couldn't have ice creams.'

'Did she now.'

'Tell her off, Daddy.'

She tightened the clench of her legs round his waist for the journey downstairs, tugging on his crucifix and yelping giddy-up. *I am a beast*, Vincent thought.

Mrs Owens was seated at the kitchen table with a cup of tea

and a biscuit, browsing through the *Radio Times*. When they appeared in the doorway, she started slightly, as if she sensed his deep wish not to have her there. He needed her, that was the trouble. Just as he needed all of them, all of the people who had been so quick to gossip and find fault. Since the horror of April they had been giving their services for free. Food arrived on the doorstep in Tupperware boxes and foil containers, while offers of help looking after the girls were posted through the letterbox on a Sunday night – schedules of dates and times and phone numbers written in Hilda de Mowbray's neat sloping hand. It had started straight after Connie's funeral, and continued into the summer holidays. Christian charity in action. The only problem being that Vincent didn't feel Christian. He didn't feel anything, except abandoned. By Connie, but mostly by God. What sort of deity would bestow such a gift on a man only to rip it so cruelly away?

It made it worse that the Charge of the Righteous was being led by Hilda de Mowbray. Hideous Hilda. On the outside a paragon of organised compassion. But behind her sorry smile, Vincent detected the sulphurous whiff of something toxic and triumphant. He was sure she had wanted to see him brought low, and her desire had been granted. Why this should be so was one of the many questions he had flung heavenwards, only to receive a mockery of silence in return. As the days crawled by, it was this not-being-spoken-to that he was finding hardest to bear. It made him feel as if he didn't exist.

'We met one of their teachers at the seaside,' said Mrs Owens.

'Ellie won,' shrieked Kat into his ear, yanking his beard so sharply that Vincent had to set her down to stop himself throwing her across the room. 'She's going to be in a *book,* Miss Zaphron said,' Kat chirruped. She leant her back against Vincent's legs as if he was a doorpost, inspecting and sucking a few salty strands of her hair.

'Eleanor's composition is to be published in a magazine,'

Mrs Owens explained, pondering, as she closed the TV magazine, how exactly the vicar resembled his brainy eldest daughter,
with his hefty frame and big sad brown eyes. 'Nice to have a bit
of good news.' She brushed the biscuit crumbs off her chest and
went to rinse her mug under the tap.

'Yes. Absolutely. Goodness.' A pain was sliding in and out of
Vincent's left temple, a needle puncturing and pushing, up to its
hilt and then withdrawing. He rubbed the spot, aware of how
the vein throbbed, as if there was too much blood in his head.
'Splendid news indeed. And where, may I ask, is the victor of
this great prize?'

Kat twirled out of the room, shouting to Eleanor.

Mrs Owens hung the mug back on its hook and folded the
drying-up cloth into a padded rectangle. 'Will you be wanting
any more help today? There's some cold meats for supper. A
spot of salad.' Grief, even in more straightforward circumstances
took time, she reminded herself, even for men of God; even
those men of God misguided enough to have burdened themselves with such pitifully unsuitable wives. The woman's death
was a shocker, of course. It was no way for anyone to die. The
final verdict had been accidental death, but for weeks gossip and
local papers had swirled with speculation, because of the
alcohol content in her blood and the lack of a handbag or train
ticket.

The cleaner stole another glance at the vicar's big chiselled
face, admiring the stoical strength that seemed to radiate from it,
but wondering if, on some undetectable level, it masked a sense
of release. Such a tragedy – especially for the two dear girls – but
there was no denying (God forgive her) that the man was better
off alone. All of Broughton thought so, it wasn't just her.

'They wanted lollies, but I'm afraid I said it would ruin their
appetites.'

'Quite right, Mrs Owens. Thank you. Cold meats. Splendid.'

'So I'll be off then. Till Friday.'

'Till Friday. Exactly. Thank you... *thank* you.' Vincent hurried into the hall to see her out, sensing, as ever, that his responses were inadequate, but lacking the wherewithal to improve on them.

He found Eleanor on the sofa with Kat, watching television. They were propped together like two rag dolls, pink-faced from the beach, their hair tangled and full of air. Kat had stoppered her mouth with her thumb as usual and was sucking rhythmically, her eyes half closed.

'I gather congratulations are in order. Well done, Eleanor, well done indeed.'

'Thanks Dad.' Eleanor spoke softly, sheepishly, not looking at him.

'You're a clever girl.' Vincent perched on the arm of the sofa and delivered a pat to the dark springy roof of her head. 'And... and... Mum...' The effort in the word was audible to all of them, an unwieldy mouthful, close to choking him. 'Mum would be pleased too. Pleased and proud. Okay, Eleanor? Okay?' His voice rose, as if he was asking himself the question as much as her.

'Yup.' Eleanor nodded, keeping her gaze on the telly. A man in a gorilla costume was trying to eat a banana but kept missing his mouth. 'Miss Zaphron said she's going to call you. She wants me to have extra lessons.'

'Oh yes? And do you want extra lessons?'

Eleanor shrugged. It was impossible to relish the idea of more schoolwork, but the opportunity to escape her class definitely held some appeal. After her mother's death, the taunts and paper pellets had stopped, but for the rest of term it was as if a bell jar had been lowered over her. She had been set apart, stared at, pitied, examined. 'Miss Zaphron said maybe I'll go to Oxford one day.'

'Did she now?' Vincent was watching the milky evening light fill the window. He found it impossible to envisage the end of the day, let alone the tunnel of six years that might or might not allow his parlous finances to stretch to the accommodation of his eldest daughter attending university. 'Well, no harm in aiming high, I suppose.'

Eleanor, detecting the drift in his voice, the trace of what sounded like disapproval, returned her attention to the television. The volume was almost too low to hear, more of a drone. The gorilla was using his banana to point at the hands of a big clock.

Beside her, Kat suddenly plucked her thumb out of her mouth and sat up. 'I want Mum,' she wailed. 'I want her. She shouldn't have gone to the railway. She told us not to. So why did she?'

'Mum is in heaven,' said Eleanor grimly, not looking at their father. Unlike Kat, she had been able to pick up on some of the speculation. It had made it hard to think straight sometimes, even after Miss Zaphron had gently taken her to one side to explain that it meant nothing, that journalists, like people, made up stories just to seem interesting.

Vincent reached across Eleanor and picked Kat up, cradling her as she continued to sob, her arms and legs splaying out awkwardly, like a rangy pet. 'God has reasons for everything and we must accept them.' He sounded like he did when giving one of his grand sermons, as if he was speaking to the air rather than a person. They both had to attend church every Sunday now, always sitting with Mrs de Mowbray in the front row. 'A bath before supper tonight,' he added, in the same loud flat voice, 'wash all that salt off. We'll leave the water in for you, Eleanor.'

Kat had gone limp in his arms, not asleep, but like she had given up a fight. He carried her out of the room. As they went through the doorway, her head bobbed up over his shoulder, the tears dry smears on her cheeks, her eyes already fresh and sparkling. She locked her gaze onto Eleanor and shot her a secretive smile, like she knew she was being spoilt and was sorry about it.

12

JULY 2013 – CAPE TOWN

Nick carefully peeled off his gloves, oily from the service he had given the lawnmower, and went into the kitchen. The grass hadn't needed a cut, but he had given it one anyway, wanting the excuse of fresh air. Their gardener, Joseph, would be put out, but there were plenty of other things for the man to get on with.

He poured a tumbler of water and ice from their big American fridge-freezer and watched the wind lift the edges of the pool cover as he drank. It was a grey Saturday afternoon in early July and Donna and the girls were shopping before their usual weekend ride at their grandparents, so he had the luxury of at least two more hours to himself.

He drank a second glass of water and then stowed the gloves at the back of the cloakroom shelf, sufficiently buried, he hoped, to prevent complaint. Donna did not like dirt in the house of any kind. She probably wouldn't be too pleased that he had mowed the grass either, since Joseph's surliness would fall on her.

Under the shower, Nick slapped on the bodywash with such carelessness that a glob of the stuff got in his eye and he had to soak it with a cold flannel. He leant against the tiled wall with both hands as the stinging subsided, letting the shower water bounce off his back.

Once dry and dressed, he fetched a beer from the fridge and took it back upstairs, settling himself on the floor beside the ever-growing stack of medical journals that lived under his bedside table. Nick worked through the journals quickly and intently, folding the occasional page that contained anything of significance and deftly hurling the rest into the bedroom's large metal wastepaper basket. When his bottle was empty, he threw that in too, landing it squarely in the middle of the papers. Unplugging his laptop, charging next to the bed, he then set to making notes on the pages he had turned down. A reward would be another beer, he told himself, but quickly growing so absorbed that he forgot.

When his backside grew numb, he shifted onto the bed to finish up, and then spent a few minutes googling fast-track teacher-training courses in the UK, pursuing a germ of an idea that had lately taken hold.

Only after that did he succumb to the temptation to scroll to the most recent cluster of emails from Kat. Three months in and they had covered so many subjects that Nick would have struggled to list even half of them. Somehow, through it all, they had stuck to her rules about what was out of bounds, in spite of Nick finding it a matter of growing frustration. A person and their views about life were one. To insist on keeping the two so separate had begun to feel not only weird, but increasingly impossible.

But then, that week, there had been an abrupt change of tack from Kat herself and Nick was still trying to get his head round it. The trigger had been a passing reference he had made to the loneliness of his mother since the sudden death of his father three years before. Half-expecting to be told off – it was a personal piece of information, after all – he had instead found himself reading the first missive that had clearly come straight from Kat's heart, blasting all her blessed boundaries to smithereens.

Dearest Nick,

I am so sorry for the loss of your father. Grief can be such a monster.
If there is one thing in the world I understand, it's that. Though I wish
it were otherwise. People we love are taken away from us, and each
time is worse than the last. They say time 'heals', but it doesn't really.
All that happens is that one learns to live with the sadness. I do not
remember my mother at all well – I think a part of me has tried not to
– but she is there nonetheless; or rather, her absence is there.

I am sorry your mother is now struggling on her own. I was never
particularly close to my father, but it still pains me to think back to the
state of lockdown he went into after Mum died, basically shutting out
everybody and everything but God. He has Alzheimer's now – which I
fear is simply another way to lose someone, even worse in many
respects. I do visit him, of course, but I can't say I like it. In fact I
bloody loathe it. Which no doubt makes me a terrible person.

Here's a UK weather report by way of a cheery change of subject:
Rain today and more forecast for tomorrow. I bet you don't miss
English summers. X

Nick had written back.

You are not a terrible person and of course I had not forgotten about
your mother.

For you and Eleanor to lose her when you were so young, let alone in
such circumstances, must have been unspeakable. It is one of several
things that, looking back, I wonder we didn't talk about more. But
then – MENTIONING THE PAST ALERT – our relationship was a total
fuck-up from the start, wasn't it? We were never right for each other. I
could tell I irritated the hell out of you! When we split I knew it was the
right thing.

Trust me, I'm not trying to get 'heavy' here or anything. For the record,
I am happily married, as I am sure you are too. It is purely this new
friendship of ours that I am enjoying. Friendship. Dare I say that
maybe that was what was lacking between us before!

Very enjoyable weather report, by the way. Perhaps you could

manage a few updates on the Test Match next time? Assessment of
form, views on the Ozzie batting order, some stats and predictions,
that sort of thing... nothing too taxing.
Nick x

Several days had passed before she replied, with an email
that once again surprised him, but this time for being so
incoherent.

Can't do cricket. Hate cricket.
As to 'friendship', dunno. dunno anything, except that in 'real' life
conversations are hard. god it's depressing. life is so fucking short.
regrets about crossed wires AFTER death are just POINTLESS... I
KNOW that. yet it doesn't make being open and honest with those we
love while they are alive any easier...
Shit. BAD day.
Expectations of happiness are the problem I think. as in, We all
believe we have the right to be happy. Ha ha.
Sorry. difficult stuff going on here. not at my best. forgive me

What 'difficult stuff'? Nick had asked at once, intrigued but
also now faintly concerned. Maybe I can help?
Her reply was the most recent he had received.

There are some things no one can help with. I shouldn't have said
anything. Breaking my own rules is despicable. Pathetic. I am
pathetic. Trust me, sharing confidences would lead nowhere good, for
either of us.

I do trust you, Nick had replied, curiosity and desperation
mounting, but then what are friends for other than sharing
problems?
There had been nothing since.
Nick tipped his head back among the bed's many scatter
cushions and closed his eyes, deflated at having reached the end.

He had been reading their exchanges almost like a page-turning book, he realised, as if he did not know what might happen next. Which he sort of didn't. Because who knew what was round the corner? That something in her life was clearly going very wrong only made the suspense worse.

Downstairs, a window shutter started banging in the evening breeze, the sitting room one, Nick guessed, which had a loose hook. He checked his watch. There was still time to write again, come up with something reassuring. And yet how impossible to offer reassurance to someone without having a clue what the matter was. Being funny was the safest bet, he decided, starting to type. She must not feel harried or anxious. He must make sure he nailed that above all things.

Subject: Status Report
From: N.Wharton@QueenElizabeth.org.sa
Date: 5/7/13
To: KitKat123@hotmail.co.uk
Dear Kat,
You will no doubt be thrilled and fascinated to hear that I have now reached the sort of age where pushing a lawnmower makes me happy. Indeed, that is how I have spent a large portion of my afternoon. It wipes me out too, unfortunately – aching muscles, etc. In fact, instead of writing this email, I should probably be taking a nap. By the way, I also like tinkering with machines these days, especially lawnmowers. I'll be polishing my hubcaps next...

He continued in a similar fashion for a while before signing off with the jokey request for a passport photograph. *So I can see the toll the years have taken on you in their worst light. Why is it that passport photographs make us all look like criminals???*

He sent the email on its way and set off to attend to the flapping shutter, only to get halfway downstairs and race back up again when his ears caught the faint ping of a new message.

Thank you for the gardening/health report. So very detailed. By some miracle, I even managed to stay awake while reading it. I assume you soak your false teeth in bleach?

No to the photograph.

Nick started to write back at once, delighted to have caught her in front of a screen. And she had cheered up, a little. He had cheered her up.

To: KitKat123@hotmail.co.uk

Great to hear back so quickly. You are very strict with your strictures, did you know that?

What about sending me three words to describe yourself instead then. As you are now. A measly THREE words. Surely that's not too much to ask?

To: N.Wharton@QueenElizabeth.org.sa

No. Not three words and not ten. No one ever sees themselves as they are. It is an impossible, as well as unreasonable, request.

To: KitKat123@hotmail.co.uk

Such a response can only come from someone who has learnt to see themselves very clearly.

But perhaps I could give you a kick-start. Based on my (albeit limited) observations over the last three months, I would humbly suggest that you are:

1.OBSTINATE.

2.STRICT.

3.???

That only leaves you needing to find one more word.

As for me, you can be assured of total and thoroughly scientific objectivity when I offer the following (current problems of sleepiness and muscle ache notwithstanding)

1. Not too fat (yet).

2. Not too grey (yet).

3. Very accommodating to strict people.

There. A fully rounded, current picture of Yours Truly. (And yes, I am

aware I have used phrases rather than single words in my self-
portrait, but it is my game and so I can do as I choose.)
Your turn.
One more word.
And I am going to have to hurry you, a) because I am on tenterhooks,
b) my family will soon be returning from my in-laws.

A good ten minutes passed. Nick was starting to despair
when his inbox lit up.

To: N.Wharton@QueenElizabeth.org.sa
Deceitful. That is my third word.
This needs to stop.
Sorry. But it does.
To: KitKat123@hotmail.co.uk
What??? You are completely overreacting. We have done nothing
except exchange a few thoughts across the airwaves. Where's the
harm in that?
To: N.Wharton@QueenElizabeth.org.sa
No, Nick. This is over.
I am sorry. I had no idea I would do this today. Though, if I am honest,
I have known from the beginning that it would have to be done.
It's my fault, not yours. I should never have written back.
I am sorry. Take care. Forgive me. I have very much enjoyed our
emails.

The slam of the front door made Nick start. He had forgotten
to keep an eye on the time, forgotten everything. As he closed
the laptop, he heard Donna calling out about the flapping shutter. He reached the landing in time to catch Natalie wrestling
her way through the door with a shopping bag over one
shoulder and carrying the saddle with the girth that was always
snapping. On seeing him, she pulled a face that told him the
afternoon had not been without its dramas.

'There you are,' said Donna in an exasperated voice,

appearing at her side, 'the house was so dark and quiet, I thought you'd been kidnapped. And what's wrong with that bloody window?'

'I was on my way to fix it. It just needs a screwdriver.'

Nick hurried to relieve his daughter of the saddle and headed towards the utility room. He was aware of having to work hard to be himself, of acting as they would all expect him to act. And yet what he had written to Kat was true, he reminded himself. They had nothing to feel guilty about. They had exchanged words on a screen; random ideas about the world – about life, nature, current affairs, music, sport, the weather, tennis. It had been nothing. And now she had ended it anyway.

Later that night, leaving Donna under her eye-mask and with her earplugs in, he broke one of his own cardinal rules and checked his laptop. Finding no further word from Kat, he held down the delete button until their entire correspondence was eradicated. Out of sight, out of mind. It was a shame, but done with. He tiptoed back to bed, breathing deeply till his pounding heart had settled.

13

'I want it to stop. All the help, I mean. I couldn't be more grateful, I really couldn't. But it is time it stopped. I can manage now.' Vincent couldn't see Hilda's face properly. It was dappled with the sunlight falling through the beech trees guarding the entrance to St Winifred's. 'Everyone has been so... charitable. All summer. But now we must manage. Alone.' Vincent was aware he was talking in strange bursts. He found it easier to be fluent standing before his congregation, with the structure of a service to follow.

Hilda's small grey eyes were widening with dismay. It was the last Sunday of August and she had hovered on the path after the service, pinning the girls into conversation while he shook the hands of parishioners. Attendance to all his services had surged since Connie's death. Vincent liked to think it was more than pitying curiosity but knew in his heart that it wasn't.

His daughters, released from Hilda's attention, were playing tag around the gravestones, leaping dots of colour in his peripheral vision. Kat skipping and squealing. Eleanor in more lumbering pursuit at her heels. His eldest was growing fat, Vincent had recently observed, turning, in spite of her height, into an ungainly lump of a girl. It pained him to see, though the reasons were obvious: too much sitting around with her head in a book. Too many snacks and summer ice creams. He couldn't wait for the autumn term to start.

'It has been the least I – all of us – could do.' Hilda fiddled with the big round buckle on her handbag. She was wearing a blue dress with padded shoulders and a wide belt that accentuated the vertical lines of her thin torso. In recent weeks her hair had undergone a transformation, the lifeless brown helmet converted into layers of dusty blonde. Feathery tresses flicked neatly off her face in two symmetrical wings.

'School is about to start,' Vincent pressed on, 'and Eleanor is old enough to be in charge of Katherine on the bus. She is very grown-up for her age, as you know, and loves the chance to take charge. And Kat, as I am sure you have also noticed, adores her.'

As if in validation of the claim, Kat, caught at last in the tag game, shrieked her sister's name in gleeful acknowledgement of surrender. The two of them slumped down against one of the big lichen-speckled sarcophagi, giggling and catching their breath.

'They are dear girls,' Hilda murmured, unable to resist adding, not for the first time, 'and Kat more and more the splitting image of her mother... that alone must be so very hard for you. But also, I hope, a consolation.' She reached out and squeezed Vincent's forearm.

Vincent dropped his eyes, regarding the gesture numbly. Hilda's fingers were thin, the nails long and filed into neat white crescents. In widowhood, she kept the fourth finger on the left hand laden: a wide gold band next to a large sapphire circled by diamonds. His own fingers looked fat and shapeless in comparison. It occurred to Vincent that he loved nothing properly any more, least of all himself.

Below the line of his and Hilda's arms, he could see the black skirt of his robe falling to the path. The hem was scuffed and grey. He had another that was even shabbier. He was never out of his priestly clothes these days; not for the provision of solace or loyalty they inspired, but simply for camouflage. Looking the part had become paramount; the least – and the most – he could manage.

Hilda released her grip. His silence filled her with confusion, making her ramble on, dropping more grains of salt into the open wound. 'Such an uncanny resemblance, the extraordinary hair colour, and those eyes...'

Vincent shifted his gaze to Hilda's throat, which moved as she talked. He imagined his hands closing around it. He had done that to Connie sometimes, taken her to the edge by keeping his thumbs on her windpipe. She loved to be on the edge, to live dangerously. He had understood that about her, in spite of her denials. A fresh, violent sense of loss coursed through him, pinpricking his body with sweat and flooding his mouth with some strange juice, acrid and salty.

'Yes, indeed. There is a remarkable likeness.' It was hard to speak. He swallowed. 'And now, if you'll excuse me, I should lock up the vestry. And the girls need—'

He was rescued by the girls themselves, running up to them, Kat in the lead, Eleanor chasing in her cumbersome way behind.

He put an arm round each, pulling them a little roughly against his body. 'And now we will be visiting the graveside, of course.'

'Of course,' Hilda echoed faintly. She looked fragile suddenly, her new thin hair lifting off the tops of her small, pale ears.

'Thank you again for all your help during the past difficult few months,' Vincent went on, recovering himself, 'but, as I have said, the three of us can manage alone now. If you could pass the word on.'

'I see, yes. I am just so fond of you all,' Hilda blurted. '*All* of you. So never be afraid to come to me if you need anything. All right?'

Vincent nodded, keeping his grip on his daughters as she walked away.

He had buried Connie in the lower reaches of St Winifred's graveyard, a strip of land bordering a field which had recently been bought by a developer finalising plans for a housing estate. Several wooden notices advertised the fact, pitched at wonky angles along the dividing fence.

Kat flopped down next to the still fresh-looking mound, sitting cross-legged and cupping her face in her hands with a dramatic sigh. 'Do you think Mummy still likes our flowers?' She gestured with her chin in the direction of the small pewter tub of sweet williams which they had brought along a few weeks before. The flowers had grown ragged, but their orange and yellow still glowed against the square granite headstone. *Connie Keating*, it said, *1947–1985 Loved and Missed.*

'Of course she likes the flowers,' Eleanor said sharply, looking at their father, who had lowered himself onto the grass and was sitting with his arms round his knees, staring into space. Eleanor held out a hand to Kat, who took hold of it, shifting closer. They looked at each other, waiting, since Vincent normally said a prayer.

Vincent was staring at his legs. His cassock had ridden up a little, revealing his weathered leather sandals, grey ankle socks and meaty calf muscles. Outlined on the inside of his right sock was the folded envelope on which he had scrawled his message on that fateful day. *Darling Connie, came home for a 10-minute lunch. I love you. Vx.*

It was both a comfort and a torment to Vincent that he had written it. A thousand times in his mind he had replayed propping the envelope on the bottom stair. Whether it had been missed, or seen, he would never know. She could already have set off on her fateful walk. The clanking pipes he had heard could have been just that, trapped air, not a running bath. The coroner's verdict had offered no solace. She may well have meant to die. Or she may not.

The sickly metallic taste was back in Vincent's mouth. She had gone for a walk, that was all, he told himself. She had got hold of a drink, from God knows where, gone for a walk, decided to cross the line and the train had come. It had caught her by surprise. She had stepped back but, with her senses dulled, not quite in time. That was why she had been thrown as she had into the undergrowth. Why the train had sped on unknowing. Why it had taken their neighbour, Farmer Watson, chasing after one of his ill-disciplined dogs the next morning, to find her. Before that it was weeks since he had so much as caught a glimpse of her, the man had assured Vincent when he asked.

'Daddy? There's a bee on the flowers.'

Eleanor's face came in and out of focus.

'Yes. Bees are good. We like bees. They help flowers to spread their seeds.'

'But Kat...' Eleanor bit her lip. Her little sister's allergy to wasps and bee stings was ancient family lore, drummed into her thanks to an incident she had been too young to remember. Kat, stung in her pram at three months, had swollen up like a football and been rushed to the hospital down the road from their house in London. But her father's thoughts were far from that now. He was getting himself into position to pray at last, levering with visible effort onto all fours and then sitting back on his heels.

'Dear Lord...'

Eleanor and Kat scrambled quickly into position, pressing their palms together and crinkling their eyes shut.

'Dear Lord,' Vincent intoned, 'please look after Connie – Mummy – whom you called from this earth before we were ready to lose her. Help us to accept her loss and to live our lives in ways that would make her proud. We know she is looking down on us...'

Eleanor peeped through the slits of her eyes. Her tummy was rumbling for lunch. The bee was gone. She tried to think about her mother, but also not to think about her. The memories hurt, so it was easier just to push them away. It felt, increasingly, as if she was missing something she had never really had. Eleanor stole a glance across the grave.

Vincent was still pressing his palms together, his eyelids trembling. It was a long prayer this time. In fact, he was starting to repeat things over and over, as if he couldn't find a way out of his own sentences.

Eleanor shifted her weight, her knees tingling. Inside, she was aware of a rising, terrible urge to get up and run away, not to the vicarage, but in the opposite direction, across the lumpy fields towards the line where the land met the sky. But there was Kat, she realised, flicking her eyes to her little sister. Kat would have to run too. She couldn't leave Kat behind.

Vincent sensed his daughters' restlessness, but he didn't care. *My words fly up but my thoughts remain below.* Who had said that? He couldn't think straight. He couldn't think about anything except that he was alone and lost, all the more acutely for having once believed himself found.

PART II

14

2013

Subject: Question
From: N.Wharton@QueenElizabeth.org.sa
Date: 3/8/13
To: KitKat123@hotmail.co.uk
Dear Kat,

I wish I properly understood why you suddenly decided you had to
stop writing to me, however many weeks ago it was. (Five I think.) It
was like something made you afraid. Please don't be afraid, Kat. I
also keep thinking about the 'difficult stuff' you mentioned and hoping
it has now been resolved.

You hurled the word 'deceit' at me when I was only mucking around.
No, I had not, as it happens, mentioned our correspondence to
Donna, or anyone else for that matter, but that's hardly a big deal.
Whether you had told your husband or not doesn't bother me either.
We were enjoying a private (if not 'personal'!!) exchange of emails.
End of.

Can I reiterate that I have been happily married for sixteen years and
have every intention of continuing that way? Donna and I are fine.
Like rocks! We have different interests, having been together long
enough to recognise the importance of being separate as well as a

'couple'. I saw my correspondence/friendship with you as falling into that separateness – something harmless to her and pleasing for me. The reason I am dropping you another line now is because it looks like we might be in England for a week in September and I was wondering if you would let me take you and Eleanor out for a cup of tea/coffee. It would be fun to catch up and talk about old times. We go back a long way the three of us, and life is short.

All the best,

Nick

Subject: Reply

From: KitKat123@hotmail.com

Date: 4/8/13

To: N.Wharton@QueenElizabeth.org.sa

No I do not think meeting up would be a good idea. Not now. Not ever.

Please try to forget that we were ever in touch.

Subject: PS

From: N.Wharton@QueenElizabeth.org.sa

Date: 5/8/13

To: KitKat123@hotmail.com

I meant to say, I would tell Donna about it of course. Coffee with two old friends, i.e. You have nothing to fear!

Nick

Subject: Request

From: N.Wharton@QueenElizabeth.org.sa

Date: 14/8/13

To: KitKat@hotmail.co.uk

Dear Kat,

Your silence speaks volumes.

So may I – by way of a last favour – ask your opinion on something I have been brooding over for a while? (And no, I haven't run it past Donna yet because I know already what she will say... one of the hazards of having been close to someone for nearly two decades!) Lately I have been toying with the idea of a major change of track. So much about my life out here is good but, as I was once only too eager to tell people (and as you remembered!), I used to harbour serious reservations about pursuing medicine. Recently those reservations have been creeping back over me. In fact, I can't seem to shake off the idea of retraining as a teacher (English? Science? Some cricket/tennis coaching thrown in?!) and leading a rather different, slower-paced sort of life in the run up to my dotage. Possibly in England. I miss England, I really do.

Try not to laugh at me. I would value your thoughts.

Nick

Subject: Reply

From: KitKat123@hotmail.com

Date: 15/8/13

To: N.Wharton@QueenElizabeth.org.sa

If you value my thoughts, then hear this:

To retrain as a teacher would be the act of a lunatic. You think you miss England, but you are probably hankering after an idyll – nostalgic for something that never actually existed and never will.

Dreams are best left in our heads, where they can do no harm.

Hold fast to what you have. You never know when it might be taken away.

Goodbye Nick and good luck.

15

1992

'So, is he good at kissing?' Megan blew one of her smoke rings, big and blue, which stretched and thinned as it floated free of her mouth.

Like a jellyfish, Eleanor decided, sleepily tracking its tremulous progress towards the ceiling. It was three o'clock in the morning on the last Monday of their first term. She and Megan were propped on cushions on the floor of Megan's room, among the soggy remains of the two Spud-U-Like baked potatoes that had constituted their supper, four flattened cider cans and an almost empty bottle of wine. The room's oak-panelled walls glowed and shifted in the shadowy light cast by the candles Megan kept on her shelves and windowsills, sputtering now out of the tops of older, long since emptied bottles of alcohol.

Megan was one of the few freshers to have been quartered in the original body of the college, at the very top of the staircase that ran between the chapel and the dining room. It was a space that filled Eleanor with envy every time she entered it, in spite of the notable proximity of the college clock, which induced Megan to work, and often to sleep, in a pair of large purple earmuffs. Eleanor, who had fallen asleep on the sofa countless times during the course of their late conversations, never minded the bells. The way the city chimed was one of the many things she had grown to love about it, a counterpoint to the bustle, unchanged and unchanging, like birdsong, so integral to life that one forgot to listen.

'So, he's bad at kissing,' Megan prompted, with the bluntness that Eleanor liked and which sometimes reminded her of Kat; Kat, whom she missed occasionally, but felt bad about for not missing more. They had spoken just once, early on, when Eleanor phoned from a call box to wish her sister a happy fifteenth birthday. Kat had sounded her usual self – bolshie, resentful, disinterested. Everything was fine, she declared coldly; home, school, her birthday, their father, all were all *fine*. Even when Eleanor explained that she had posted a birthday gift, several yards of soft pink and green tweed which she had not been able to afford, Kat said only that it hadn't arrived yet, managing to communicate indifference as to whether it ever did.

Letting the heavy phone box door fall shut after the call, closing out the stale stench of urine and cigarettes, Eleanor was aware of her home life shrinking back to the dot to which she had consigned it, and being glad. She had her new life now, made up of things like *Beowulf*, with whom she still tussled, but happily, and nineteenth-century novelists, with whom she struggled not at all; and drinking, and new friendships like Megan, and surviving on a shoestring; and Nick Wharton, who was a friend but also something so much more. Every moment of every day was hectic, all-consuming. She didn't want the term to end.

Eleanor blinked slowly at Megan's questioning face, aware of the effort of sliding her lids over her eyeballs. They had drunk too much, as usual, but more than anything, she was exhausted. She wondered idly if she looked as terrible as Megan, whose face was the colour of putty, with dark circles under her pale green eyes and a fringe so overgrown and unkempt she looked like she was peering through the bars of a cage. Megan in fact was very pretty, though she never thought so herself, injecting any discussion about looks and clothes with disconsolate slaps to her solid backside and strong stocky legs. Her figure was certainly on the square side, but Eleanor, burdened with her own heavy rangy limbs, admired its compactness, the impression of contained energy. Even the way Megan walked had a spring to it, bouncing on the balls of her feet as if in a permanent state of readiness to break into a run. The Christian Union affiliation had turned out to be a rumour. Megan liked hymns she said, but only because she was keen on the tunes and enjoyed singing; otherwise she regarded herself as mostly Buddhist, thanks to an inspirational couple of months spent travelling in India and Nepal in her run-up to university.

'Nick Wharton is not a bad kisser,' Eleanor conceded at last. 'In fact he's the opposite of bad.'

'As in good?' Megan giggled.

Eleanor sighed. 'Very good.'

She rolled onto her back, shoving one of the cushions under her head. The need to talk about Nick was surging inside her. Megan had had her usual outpouring about Billy Stokes, whom she despised for his public-school arrogance, but with whom she claimed to be in love nonetheless. But there had been a development with Nick just that afternoon – unexpected, game-changing – and Eleanor was still reeling from it, not quite ready to offer it up for one of her new friend's well-intentioned but clumsy interpretations.

She was good on some things, Megan, like work and college gossip and sadness. When Eleanor had confided the fact of her mother's death, she had simply crawled across the sofa and put her arms round her, not saying a word. Not even Nick had managed such a perfect response, reacting to the same news with an expression of pained compassion, but then gently changing the subject, like he was steering her away from harm. On other matters, however, such as relationships, Megan had proved less reliable. The yearning for Billy Stokes, for instance, hadn't prevented her from having several one-night stands with fellow students, only to howl with self-recrimination afterwards. Yet when Eleanor had ventured a few confidences about Kat's surly attitude and wildness with boys, Megan had offered the view, albeit in a tone of speculative apology, that Eleanor's little sister sounded like a bit of a jealous slut.

'I should go,' Eleanor murmured, closing her eyes, enjoying the solidity of the floor under her spine too much to move. All her dates with Nick were floating through her head, a procession of details and pleasures. There had only been four kisses, five if she counted their first brief lip contact under a street lamp on the night of the film date to the Penultimate Picture Palace five weeks before. A mere brushing. Nick had pulled back so suddenly that Eleanor feared something last-minute might have put him off. Like bad breath, or the sight of her face close up, which, she knew, had manifold imperfections. Back in her room afterwards, she had scrutinised her reflection brutally in the small mirror above her washbasin, tugging at her skin, trying to see what Nick might have seen.

But then there had been the second kiss, ten days later. A proper one this time, as they strolled back to college after having a pizza. His tongue had found hers, gentle and exploratory, solicitous if such a thing were possible, Eleanor had wondered, reliving the experience again and again in her mind, comparing it cruelly to Charlie's clumsy foraging. Nick had tasted faintly of cheese and mushroom and red wine and Eleanor had loved this too. She had fallen against him afterwards, dizzy and exhilarated, feeling like a film actress.

'You have the nicest eyes,' he had said gruffly. They had been in a side street near the college, half leaning against some railings. It was the most intimate thing he had ever said to her, but even as Eleanor luxuriated in it, his mood seemed to change, grow awkward. There was no more kissing, just the walk back to college, Nick keeping a pace ahead, doing his finger-clicking while casting out staccato comments about how much work he had and how he needed to get some sleep. When they reached the tangle of bikes in front of the porters' lodge, he had said a breezy goodnight and cantered off up the steps, his long legs taking three at a time. Eleanor had trailed after him, bewildered. Catching a last glimpse as he ducked under the arched entrance to his staircase, he seemed to pause to wipe the back of his hand across his mouth. Like he was wiping away their kiss, Eleanor had thought wildly. She had slept fitfully, the pizza cheese heavy in her stomach, her heart veering between elation and the old fear of some part of her having been found repellent.

But a few days later he asked her out again. The third kiss had followed. A week later, the fourth. Each lasting longer. Each getting better. Kissing was something that could be learnt, Eleanor had realised. It made her feel sorry for girls like Kat and Megan with their promiscuity, always in a rush, questing after the next sexual experience the moment one was done. She and Nick were the opposite of being in a rush, Eleanor decided ecstatically. The slow, unhurried intimacy of the way his tongue touched hers still took her breath away. It stirred a new, animal part of her, something that felt like recognition as much as physical need, as if her body had been waiting just for him to come alive.

But then that morning had happened. She had been in the library in her usual place, pulling together her findings for her final essay, when Nick appeared in the doorway, miming an invitation to lunch. They had gone to what had become their usual café, where he had eaten at even greater speed than usual, casting pinched looks across the table, as if there were things he might say if his mouth wasn't otherwise engaged. Eleanor had sensed something building – some declaration – and been foolish enough to feel excited. She even wondered if he was going to invite her back to his rooms there and then. Sex in the afternoon. She would need to pee first, she realised frantically, her bladder being full and the café not extending to the luxury of a loo. She had felt shy of that more than anything –

confessing the need to stop in the icy toilet on his landing, the sound of her pee, the sound of the flush.

Her instincts had proved correct, but also misguided. Nick had indeed been steeling himself towards a declaration, just not the one she had expected.

'Over?'

He had waited until they were back in the street. Eleanor was aware of her jaw hanging gormlessly open and the need to snap it shut. It had seemed important, facing this new crisis in her life, not to look gormless. She shifted her legs to a wider stance, needing physically to steady herself.

'I am... committed elsewhere.'

Shoppers and tourists steered round them, giving them a pocket of space, as if they sensed the magnitude of the conversation.

'Where?' Eleanor found herself scanning the busy street, as if the person to whom he was referring might leap out and present herself. But it turned out the person wasn't even in Oxford. She was called Tilly and was back home in Wiltshire, training to be a nursery nurse. Eleanor had managed not to gasp at this. Indeed, it gave her hope. Nick could not stay forever with someone called Tilly who was training to be a nursery nurse. It was ridiculous. Quite impossible, even if they had, as Nick explained, blurting and wretched, known each other since primary school and been going out since they were fifteen. For six years in other words. Six years. They were each other's first and only love. While apart they wrote regularly and rang each other at prearranged times several nights a week. She kept a curl of his hair in a locket round her neck and he had a treasured picture of her face in his wallet. They were as good as engaged. He missed her like mad. She missed him so much, she often wept herself to sleep. He waggled the wallet picture at Eleanor as if it was the final proof she needed in order to accept his words.

'Over?' she repeated stupidly, her brain snagging on the

thought that something could not be over when it had barely started. There was so much still to do. So much that she had wanted and imagined. Her future. Their future. He couldn't just wave a photo and take it away. 'Maybe...' She stopped, astonished to see tears in his eyes. She had never seen a man cry. Even when her mother died, her father hadn't cried. He had gone silent instead, ossified, as if to protect some deep unassailable part of himself.

'I'm betraying her by seeing you,' Nick growled, swiping at his face and rubbing his nose on the sleeve of that day's baggy jumper. He had several: the grey cable, two blues and a bright green Fair Isle one that Eleanor had teased would be appropriate in a golf club. 'I like you, Eleanor. I *really* like you. But this is wrong. Tilly and I... we have sworn... we are... we have always said...'

Watching his struggle, Eleanor experienced a sudden flooding calm. This man, whom she also liked, so very much, was trying to walk away from her and she had to find a way to stop him. And seeing him unhappy was unbearable too. It cleared her head, made her thoughts sharp.

'But, Nick, we can be friends, surely?' She put her hand on his arm. 'You haven't betrayed anybody. All you've done is kiss me. Four times. Five if you count when we left the PPP.' She held his gaze, blazing a coolness she did not feel. She even smiled. 'You've been amazing. The model of restraint. And I like you too. A lot. So let's settle on being friends. Okay?'

'Okay. Just friends. Great. Thanks, Eleanor.' Relief gusted across his face, relaxing its handsome features. He pulled her to him and they hugged fiercely.

So this is love, Eleanor thought. *This is love and it hurts.*

16

2013

Subject: January
From: N.Wharton@QueenElizabeth.org.sa
Date: 23/9/13
To: KitKat123@hotmail.co.uk
Dear Kat,
We are now coming to England in the middle of January instead. I am
telling you in the hope that you might change your mind about that
cup of tea with Eleanor?
It would be fun, surely, to lay some old ghosts to rest. Who was it who
said life was lived forwards but understood backwards...? Nietzsche,
I think?
Look, just don't rule it out, okay?
Nick x
Subject: Reply
From: KitKat123@hotmail.co.uk
Date: 24/9/13
To: N.Wharton@QueenElizabeth.org.sa
I do rule it out.
It was Kierkegaarde.
Understood or not, the past is best left where it lies. I knew that once,
but temporarily forgot it.

Now please forgive me for that by leaving me alone.

17

1992

Eleanor was the only one at the bus stop, a leaning pole on the main Broughton road, half a mile on from the vicarage turn-off. The New Year was four days old and had produced nothing but rain, churning the countryside to sludge. Eleanor stayed on the tarmac to protect her footwear – a pair of brown suede ankle boots purchased with Vincent's Christmas cheque – hunching her shoulders inside her thin coat against the cold. The skies were leaden but sealed and smooth in a way that she hoped would last all day. Her hair, freshly washed, had looked nice enough in the mirror but could still turn into a black frizzy blanket at the first hint of drizzle. It was Pre-Raphaelite hair, Nick had remarked once, not in any overtly romantic way, just firing the comment across the table during one of their many shared meals the previous term, as a statement of fact.

A brief letter had arrived from him two days after Christmas, suggesting a date for a pub lunch and offering to pick her up from the vicarage if she gave instructions. Eleanor had written back at once to say she would take the bus and meet him at the railway station instead, because it was easier to find. Nick's plans centred round an early January visit to a godfather who lived in Lewes. He was to spend one night there, he explained, and would have time to make a detour to visit her on the way back home to Salisbury the following day. He had added that he would be driving a black Volkswagen, a loved ancient family car with an engine so raucous she was likely to hear it long before she saw it. At the bottom of the letter there had been a small cross next to his name, the sight of which had caused a stab of hope and longing to shoot up through Eleanor's groin and into her heart.

She had taken the letter upstairs to devour again, many times, in the privacy of her bedroom, picking the nuances out of it like meat scraps off a bone. The kiss meant there was still genuine hope, she decided, quite apart from the wonderful fact that he wanted to see her. Saying their farewells at the end of term, Nick had muttered something about getting together in the vac, but Eleanor hadn't dared believe him. Even the gentle humour about the car had delighted her; of course Nick Wharton would drive a croaky old car. He was that sort of man – loyal to cars as he was to people – not flash. Not superficial. Which was why, for the time being, he was staying true to the girl called Tilly. A lesser person would never have shown such restraint, such integrity. In her reply, Eleanor had carefully signed off with a cross beside her own name, a bit bigger than Nick's, but not too outrageously so. Before sealing the letter, she kissed it for real. A dozen times. Invisible kisses. Who was to say they didn't have equal power?

With the lunch date to look forward to, the post-Christmas drear of the vicarage had dissolved round her like mist in sunshine. She stopped caring that her father's terse enquiries about university life rarely incorporated the time to hear her answers, or that Kat, having initially greeted her like a dog starved of affection – yelping, kissing, jumping round her in the drive – had then, with almost comical speed, retreated back into her state of studied distracted indifference, as if her big sister was some dimly recalled, irksome acquaintance from a previous existence.

The prospect of seeing Nick burned inside her like a secret light. The days towards the date dragged, but in a way, Eleanor relished the anticipation. Nothing got her down during the course of them: not the murky blue walls of her bedroom, now sporting black cobwebs of mildew across the ceiling corners; not the creak of the floorboards in the small hours as Vincent did his customary pacing, muttering his lonely prayers; not even the rain-leaks landing in the new cluster of metal buckets outside her and Kat's bathroom, loud enough to wake her every time the rain started. Love was armour against the world, that was the discovery.

Eleanor swung from the bus-stop pole to celebrate the fact, tipping her face to the stony sky. No wonder people died for it. No wonder doughty, plain little Jane Eyre had stumbled back across the wild, unforgiving moors for another chance at it with her beloved, blinded Rochester. Love was the gravity pull of one human being to another, as irrefutable as physics.

But it was one thing to read of a great truth and even more thrilling to experience it. Eleanor pirouetted out into the road. She was meeting Nick Wharton for lunch. *She was meeting Nick Wharton for lunch.* He could talk gibberish and she wouldn't mind. Indeed, it would unman her, just as she had been unmanned when he had confessed, near weeping, to the existence of Tilly. She skipped another circle round the road, beating her arms to keep warm, chuckling at her own silliness and excitement.

A horn blasted and Eleanor hopped onto the safety of the boggy verge, her heart pumping. A sports car tore past, spattering her thin coat and adding to the mud now gluing itself to the edges of her precious suede boots. Eleanor stared down at the mess and then laughed loudly, scaring off a magpie which had landed to peck at a crushed snail in the middle of the road.

Her confidence didn't falter until she actually saw the little black Beetle, parked neatly in the grid of white lines outside the station entrance. Having virtually run all the way from the bus stop, Eleanor came to a halt, the joints of her knees suddenly feeling too loose to rely on. But then the driver's door swung open and Nick emerged, in stone-washed jeans and a dark blue duffel coat, his hair longer and thicker, his face pale but smiling. He came to greet her, kissing her lightly – easily – on the cheek, smelling of the stuff he liked to use that she didn't know the name of.

'How was the godfather?'

'Great. Plied me with whisky. Told me funny stories.' Nick held the passenger door open for her before settling himself back behind the wheel. 'He's got this brilliant dog, too – Dougal, an Irish wolfhound – we took it on a couple of long walks along the coast, one yesterday and another this morning... bloody early. He's ex-army, unbelievably hearty. I've been up for hours. I'm starving. Have you thought where to go? I'm afraid I don't know these parts at all. Got lost several times getting here. Hope you had a good Christmas, by the way.'

He was nervous, Eleanor realised, liking him all the more on account of it. 'If you turn left out of the station, there's a pub called The Green Man a couple of miles away which does decent food.' She tried to sound casual, as if the option had occurred to her on the spot rather than being agonised over for days. She had even consulted Kat on the subject, braving the jeering glint in her sister's eye both at the revelation of the lunch and so overt an acknowledgement of her superior local knowledge. 'Wow. I see what you mean about the noise,' Eleanor remarked as they set off, having to raise her voice over the throaty racket of the Volkswagen.

'Careful. No insults.' Nick patted the dashboard protectively. 'She's called Harriet and she's very temperamental. Responds only to compliments. She once belonged to my Mum but is now for me and my sister to use when we're home.'

'In Salisbury.'

'Yes, sunny Salisbury.'

'And what's your sister do?' She wasn't sure he had mentioned a sister before.

'Medicine – what else?' He pulled a face. 'She's six years older than me and much more committed. Went to Cambridge, then Tommy's. Wants to get to the top, and I can tell you she will do just that. Neurology is her thing, which pleases the old man, of course.'

'Shouldn't that have taken the pressure off you then?' ventured Eleanor. 'About being a medic, I mean?'

Nick laughed with the trace of bitterness that always seemed to edge into any discussion about his chosen career, no matter whom it was with. 'You do not know my dad. And anyway, I am going to be a good doctor, remember – we agreed.'

'Yes, we agreed,' Eleanor murmured, happy not only at his easy recall of their conversation the previous term but at the word 'we' tripping so effortlessly off his tongue. 'Anyway,' she rushed on breathlessly, wanting to say something she had been saving up. 'Who says you have to be *one* thing? I mean, Keats was also a doctor, wasn't he?' This was a fact gleaned from her recent holiday reading, preparation for the following term's studies. 'He wrote in one of his letters that a poet was a physician for the soul... or something like that...' She let the sentence hang, having forgotten to whom the letter had been written and why.

Nick was looking doubtful. 'I don't really know any Keats. Or much poetry for that matter. Apart from T. S. Eliot, I don't mind him.'

'Right... no, of course... I only meant... that is, I only mentioned it as an example of someone being medical and liter-ary. Like you.' Eleanor glared at the brown fields sliding past the window, cursing her ineptitude, but Nick was smiling and nodding.

'Oh, I see. Well, thanks very much in that case. I shall bear it in mind. And, by the way, for what my opinion's worth, you are a seriously bright girl and should never let any of those pompous idiots at Oxford allow you to think otherwise.'

Eleanor kept her eyes on the window so he couldn't see the flush of happiness his words caused.

* * *

The Green Man was jammed, both round the bar and in the main dining area, where a shooting party, decked in plus-fours and cartridge belts, was in rowdy form, occupying several tables, laden with plates of food and open wine bottles.

Nick fought his way through the throng to buy two gin and tonics while Eleanor made a beeline for a tiny bench-table next to the fireplace, where several sturdy logs blazed. They bundled their coats at their feet and ordered off the chalkboard of specials, Nick opting for roast beef and Eleanor following suit, though her stomach was too knotted to care.

The bench seat soon grew hot. 'Can't exactly 'turn down' an open fire, can you?' Nick joked after a few minutes, peeling off his jumper, a close-fitting bright blue one that Eleanor guessed had been a Christmas present, and managing in the process to give her a glimpse of a dark neat arrow of hair down the centre of his stomach. She looked quickly away. Her own black woollen dress, so apt a choice in the morning chill of her draughty bedroom and an excellent match with the suede boots, had become a slow-cooker. Every inch of her felt as if it was being steadily roasted. 'Hey, this is good, isn't it?' Nick rubbed his hands gleefully.

'Have you told Tilly?' she blurted. 'About today?' She prayed he would say no. No would mean he harboured feelings that warranted stealth. No would nurture her few tender tendrils of hope.

'No,' he confessed, but then quickly ruined the moment by adding, 'she finds it hard enough, with me being away at university, making new friends.' He shot Eleanor a pained, rueful look from under the light brown mop of his hair.

'Yes, yes of course.' Eleanor chewed her cheeks. 'I hope you didn't mind my asking—'

'No, it's fine. It's good to talk... to be open.'

Although awkward, the exchange seemed to clear the air and they chatted more easily when their lunch arrived, Nick doing his usual job of concentrated demolishment of the entire contents of his plate, while Eleanor picked at the slabs of meat and vegetable mounds with a fork, still too tense and hot to muster a genuine appetite. He offered up more tales of the hearty godfather and his dog, while she managed to make him laugh with a couple of anecdotes about her spell at home, including Vincent's dire, endless Christmas-morning sermon, delivered against a mounting cacophony of mutinous children, and the terrible meal served by Kat to which they had returned afterwards. Left in charge of cooking at her own request, her sister had jettisoned their small supermarket turkey in favour of two packets of fish fingers, mashed potato and mountains of frozen peas and sweetcorn. Vincent, surveying the table, had ignored the flashing defiance in his youngest daughter's eyes and merely fetched the ketchup, before tucking his napkin deep into the rim of his dog collar and pronouncing the longest grace either of them had ever heard, in Latin.

'God, my family is so conventional,' moaned Nick when he had finished laughing. 'Brussel sprouts, stilton and toasts to the Queen. Yours sounds much more fun.'

'Believe me, it isn't,' Eleanor said stiffly.

'Not that I'm saying...' He broke off, looking stricken. 'I mean, from what you told me... not having your mum around and so on... that must make it hard.'

'It did. It does. Sometimes. Not always. The thing is...' Eleanor fought with her paper napkin, tearing it into shreds. She always wanted him to concentrate on her but then found the glare of his attention overwhelming. 'At home we never talk about anything,' she admitted dully, 'not a single thing.'

He laughed. 'Mine neither. All we ever discuss is bloody doctoring.'

Eleanor smiled, knowing he was trying to be kind. The thing she really wanted to say was jumping inside her head. She needed Nick to know it so that he understood her – more of her than the rest of the world did. 'But the trouble is,' she pressed on slowly, 'with us, there has been some stuff... big stuff that really needed saying. And now it's too late.'

'What sort of stuff?'

'About my mother.'

'Ah, yes—'

'She drank, you see.'

Nick had been nodding sympathetically, but he stopped, staring at her in surprise.

Eleanor hesitated, still hating what she had to say, but a part of her also now managing to savour the intensity of the moment, the trust that had brought it into being. 'She had what is commonly known as a "drinking problem". Kat and I were too young to realise. It was only after the accident, picking up on the gossip, stuff about the alcohol levels in her blood, whether she had meant to walk in front of the train or not – jolly things like that.'

She tried to smile, but her jaw seemed to have locked. She felt Nick's hand close round her fingers, sealing them, keeping them safe, it felt like.

'The point is,' she pressed on, 'at the time I would have liked to know more... to understand... more. I waited, but Dad never said a word, not to me or Kat, or anyone. Not one word. He just buried himself in God instead. He still does.' The heat of Nick's hand was different from the hotness of the room, dry and warm, like balm. Eleanor could feel it filling her up, making her strong. 'But don't think I miss her that much or anything, because I don't. I mean, I don't even try to. It was a long time ago and remembering gets you nowhere.' She shrugged. 'All I know is that getting away to university has been the best thing that ever happened to me. And Kat will get away too,' she added with some urgency, 'if she can just pass a few exams, the idiot.'

Eleanor found herself laughing suddenly, dizzy with relief and incredulity at her own candour. She had never told anyone about the drinking thing, not even Megan. Kat knew, of course, but then Kat was as bad as her father when it came to discussing things.

'Sorry. None of this was on my list of entertaining conversation for the day.'

'Don't apologise.' He had released her hand and was sitting back in his chair, regarding her solemnly. 'Friends should be able to tell each other anything. Entertainment doesn't come into it.'

Eleanor wished she could stretch the moment out, but already the rest of the room was bursting back into focus. Someone in the shooting group had started thumping the table in time to the downing of a drink. It was with a twist of dismay that she caught Nick sneaking a look at his watch.

'We could have coffee at home,' she suggested desperately. 'It would be quieter. Both Dad and Kat are out.'

Nick flexed his eyebrows in a show of mischievous anticipation that made Eleanor's hopes bounce. But then uncertainty gusted in, taking the lovely look of mischief with it. 'Tempting, but I'd better not. I'll drop you wherever you would like first though, of course.'

'The bus stop would be fine, thanks,' she said quickly, her courage shrinking.

Once in the car, he fell into a silence that Eleanor found hard to read. He was fighting with himself, she decided, casting glances at the rigidity of his high cheekbones and the fix of his dark blue eyes on the windscreen. He wanted to spend more time with her but felt guilty, and that was understandable. In profile, the length of his eyelashes was astonishing; it made her want to reach out and run the tips of her fingers along them.

But then a hitchhiker came into view, a strikingly attired

hitchhiker, clad in high-heeled thigh-high gold boots and the stiff edges of what looked like a pink tutu poking out between the folds of a bright purple cape. She was hopping for warmth, hugging herself with one arm, thumbing madly with the other.

'Blimey, look at that.' Nick slowed right down, gawping.

'*That,*' said Eleanor, in a tone of affectionate exasperation, 'is my little sister.'

Nick shot her a look of disbelief and burst out laughing. 'Well, had we better pick her up in that case?'

'Yes, I suppose we had.'

'And I can drop you both home if you like.'

In spite of being consigned to the back seat, Kat wedged herself as far forwards as she could between them, draping her gold-coated lower legs round the gearbox as she chattered, lighting and relighting her damp roll-ups off the Volkswagen's temperamental cigarette lighter, and at one stage grabbing each of their hands to study their lifelines – palmistry being a skill she had learnt that very day, she claimed gleefully.

Exultant at the slight extension to Nick's visit, Eleanor gladly went along with the show, feeling a little proud of Kat's strangeness – seeing afresh what a cute oddball mix her younger sister was, all sweetness and faux sophistication, a funky kid playing at being a grown-up.

When they got home, Kat continued with the charade, insisting Nick come in for a cup of tea and shooing them both into the sitting room like some fussing middle-aged hostess. She puffed up the old brown sofa cushions and commanded them to do nothing but relax, before tottering off to clatter round the kitchen.

Nick and Eleanor exchanged bemused looks, talking quietly, until she made a re-entrance carrying a big old tray they never used, laden with every possible accoutrement for a formal tea that the vicarage's jumbled crockery cupboards could provide – including not just a teapot, cups, saucers, teaspoons and the old green jug for milk, but a proper sugar bowl with tongs and a silver dish Eleanor had never seen before, piled high with triangles of toast visibly oozing butter and jam.

Eleanor absorbed the sight in amazement, unable to suppress the hope that instead of being some new, perverse tributary of Kat's contrariness, a bigger conciliatory avenue in her little sister's attitude towards her might be opening up. She tried to catch Kat's eye, wanting her to confirm it, but Kat was too busy concentrating on 'playing mother', as she merrily put it, asking for exact instructions from Nick about milk and sugar as she poured and stirred.

'So, was it a fancy-dress party you'd been to?' Nick enquired politely, once tea and toast had been distributed.

It occurred to Eleanor in the same instant that, as well as being kind, there was an endearing innocence to him, an uncertainty; demonstrating that, for all the good looks and ability, Nick Wharton was a man still very much feeling his way along the course of his life rather than taking command of it. The thought made her long to take hold of his hand as he had hers in the pub, let him know that her support of whatever he chose to do with his life would be unconditional. She let her gaze settle fondly on her sister instead, curious as to how she would respond to the enquiry. Kat's clothes, she knew, had nothing whatsoever to do with fancy dress. Her sister made and wore peculiar things that somehow looked tremendous. It was what she did.

Kat was lying on the floor on the hearth rug, her mouth full of toast. 'What, because of this lot, you mean?' She tweaked the gauzy skirts of the tutu and lifted one gold-booted leg onto the table next to the tray, showing off badly laddered white tights that managed to highlight the slim sinewy curves of her thighs. 'It was a sort of party, I suppose. If you can count four people as a party. Then they all got on my wick and I needed to get home. And I didn't have any money. And luckily you found me.'

'Do you know when Dad's getting back? He told me last

night that he would be out for most of the day.' Eleanor threw a glance at Nick who was looking disconcerted.

Kat rolled her eyes at the ceiling. 'He's not out, he's *asleep.*' She pulled a face.

'Dad is a bit of an insomniac,' Eleanor explained, 'so he gets very tired.' Inwardly she fought down dismay that Vincent should have changed his plans, jeopardising the pleasures of the afternoon by threatening the necessity of awkward introductions.

Kat posted a last wedge of toast into her mouth, licking each of her fingers before wiping them in exaggerated swipes on her tights. 'Oh, and if he comes down, would you mind not mentioning my smoking, Nick? Not that you would. But please don't. He's got a bit of a thing about it. *So* boring.' She rolled her eyes in such a blatant further attempt to appear grown up that it was all Eleanor could do not to laugh out loud.

'No, of course I won't,' Nick assured her kindly, 'I wouldn't dream of it. Your secret is safe with me.'

'Who has secrets?' boomed Vincent, appearing in the doorway behind them, making them all jump. 'Ah, we have guest, I see.' He strode into the room, his craggy face flexed into the expression of winning interest that he always could manage for people he did not know.

Nick and Eleanor both stood up. 'Dad – this is Nick.' Eleanor did her best to sound unflustered. 'Nick Wharton. A friend from—'

'Ellie's friend from university,' Kat chipped in, pronouncing it *yooooniversity* as if it was something hilarious.

Nick shook hands with Vincent across the back of the sofa. 'You are most welcome, young man.' He clasped both his hands round Nick's. 'Most welcome. Do you study with Eleanor?'

'At the same college, yes, but not the same subject. I'm reading medicine—'

'Splendid, splendid,' Vincent interjected, breaking off to glower at Kat, who was still lying flat on her back, one gold-booted foot propped on the table. 'Sit up properly, child, can't you?'

'Sorry, Daddy.' She swung into a kneeling position with exaggerated speed, prim as a nun. 'Tea, Daddy?' She puckered her lips and set about pouring him a cup, holding the spout of the pot at such a great height that tea spattered everywhere. The saucer she handed to him contained a moat of brown liquid.

Vincent took it calmly, tipping the moat into the cup and reaching to the tray for a lump of sugar, using his fingers rather than the tongs. 'Hardly attire for visitors, my dear,' he said tersely, turning his back on her.

'I don't like the way you dress either,' she retorted.

'Kat – don't.'

Kat turned on her sister. 'Don't what? Speak?' She flashed a smile at Nick. 'Sorry, Nick, we are good at pretending to be nice, but we aren't really. Don't be fooled by any of us.' She snatched another triangle of toast and stalked out of the room.

Five minutes later, she reappeared as if nothing had happened, her expression serene and wearing a pair of dark blue jeans that gripped the straight lines of her narrow hips before flaring to wide skirts round the base of another pair of very high-heeled shoes, red ones this time, with toes as sharp as pencil-points. She had brushed her hair as flat as it ever went, compressing it into two fat silky plaits that bounced on her shoulders. In her arms she was clutching an old Cluedo box, dusty from the cellar by the look of it. 'I thought we could play a board game. Daddy would you like to play a *bawd* game?'

Vincent had been talking to Nick about the ordeal of medical training, with such fluency, such charm that, while glad, Eleanor had experienced a rising anger. Her father was nice. He was *normal*. And yet she was never on the receiving end of such treats. Kat riled him, but she did the opposite. She *tried* to be cooperative and nice. Why was that still not enough? To be noticed. Shown some affection. Was that really so much to ask?

'Not me, I fear, I have work to attend to,' Vincent replied

hastily. He cast an apologetic grimace at the Cluedo box, though it was perfectly clear he was going through the motions.

'And I too must be on my way.' Nick stood up.

But Kat stepped forwards in the same instant, tapping him on the chest with a corner of the box so that he promptly sat back down again. 'We are going to play a game,' she commanded. 'Then you must stay for supper. We are going to eat sausages. We have heaps of them. And mash. Daddy would like it, wouldn't you?' she called after Vincent's retreating back. 'Another *man* at the supper table. And Nick can stay the night, if he wants, can't he? In the yellow room. Ellie and I will do the sheets.'

There was a grunt of acquiescence from the corridor and then the sound of retreating footsteps.

Eleanor looked at Nick, her heart racing. It would have been impossible for her to ask him to stay, but coming from Kat it seemed all right... impudent, but all right. For a moment she wondered if she had ever loved her sister more.

Nick was shaking his head, laughing helplessly. 'Thanks, but no, I couldn't possibly stay. I'll play one game and then I really must be on my way.'

But he hadn't played one game, he had played at least ten: A Cluedo marathon, undertaken in a pedestrian manner until dinner and then rather more riotously afterwards, once Vincent had retreated upstairs and Kat had mixed a syrupy concoction of the limited contents of the drinks cupboard to serve as forfeits for every wrong guess, of which there were many. Nick's caving in to the invitation to stay overnight had occurred suddenly and easily, aided by another bout of pleading from Kat and perhaps by the smell of frying sausages which she said she would see to while he made up his mind. He asked for permission to use the hall phone and made a couple of calls, first to what sounded like a parent and then to someone who had to be Tilly, Eleanor decided, hovering in the open door of the kitchen to hear what she could of the conversations: *...bad news... Harriet has thrown a*

wobbly... yes, conked out on me... university friend... port in a storm...
see what the garage says tomorrow... a real pain... let you know
tomorrow... yes, me too.

So a man of integrity could lie. But did that matter if the
lying was for you?

* * *

Shivering under the bedclothes in the blue-black murk of her
bedroom some eight hours later, her head still spinning from
Kat's fiendish cocktails, the question leapt out at Eleanor again.
The good and bad of it felt knotted together. Wrong turns in life
had to be taken, she reasoned, before the right ones could be
found. All that mattered was that Nick Wharton lay, warm and
breathing, at the end of the passageway, sheathed between the
sheets that she and Kat, giggling and unsteady, had tugged
round the thin divan bed mattress in the small yellow room
where Mrs Owens had once liked to do her ironing. Nick had
watched them, arms akimbo, from the doorway, feigning impatience between fighting yawns and then chivvied them out,
saying they were useless domestic slaves and he would finish the
task alone. Eleanor had dared to cast a look back as they scur-
ried along the corridor, but seen only the closing door.

The divan bed would barely encase his long body, she
reflected now, and the room itself was an apology of a space,
more of a cupboard than a bedroom. Mrs Owens had long since
decamped to retirement in the West country and the ironing
pile, such as it was, lived in a plastic basket behind the door in
the downstairs cloak room. Vincent managed the occasional
shirt and Kat didn't bother. The sheets on Nick's bed, like all
washed linen in the house, were dry and dimpled, having been
bundled upstairs in the brutalised state in which they had
emerged from the tumble dryer.

Eleanor's brain hummed. The jug mix had been fierce: gin,
whisky, sherry. Her father, perhaps not surprisingly, wasn't a big

drinker, usually sticking – as he had that night – to beer. She had sipped her own forfeits for fear of choking, glad that her term at university meant she didn't feel a complete fool. Kat, on the other hand, had swigged hers without much apparent effect. Her head was hard, she had boasted to both her and Nick, and her stomach like iron. At one stage, she had rolled onto her back to demonstrate the point, slapping the bare white flatness where her stomach met the waistband of her jeans.

Eleanor pushed off the bedclothes and sat up. Nick was a few yards away, that was the overwhelming thing. She could feel her nipples harden in the cold, pushing against her T-shirt nightie. Thirty seconds, that was all it would take to get to the yellow room door. Possibly twenty. If she walked fast. Some things in life were about courage. About... Eleanor snapped her brain shut and spun herself upright, grabbing her dressing gown off her chair.

Once in the corridor, she froze nonetheless, hugging herself, listening. Vincent's three beers meant there was a better chance of him sleeping instead of pacing. Sometimes he snored. Eleanor strained her ears, hearing nothing above the usual creaks of the vicarage. She set off along the corridor, finding it sufficiently hard to walk straight for her to realise that she was still quite drunk.

The brass handle of the yellow room door was cold under her fingers. She turned it slowly, making no sound. Inside, the first thing she noticed was the moon, a mother-of-pearl button in the middle of the windowpane. He hadn't bothered to draw the curtains, which were flimsy anyway, scraps of yellow that Mrs Owens had strung up one afternoon, not worth bothering with. A silvery light illuminated the shape of Nick beneath the bedclothes. He was lying on his side, one arm up under the pillow, the other round what Eleanor at first took to be a bunch of bedding. It was only as she took a step closer that she saw it was her sister, tucked so closely against him that it was hard to tell them apart. Bare necks, bare shoulders, bare arms, threaded tight as twine.

Eleanor backed away, groping behind her for the open door. There was no sensation within her other than the desire to leave. She had nearly made it into the passageway when Kat's eyes sprang open. Her sister turned her head slowly, peering out at Eleanor from the nest of bedding. Then she smiled.

PART III

18

2013 - SUSSEX

Subject: Last Word
From: N.Wharton@QueenElizabeth.org.sa
Date: 2/12/13
To: KitKat123@hotmail.co.uk
Dear Kat,

Your silence, as ever, speaks volumes. You are sticking to your guns. You do not wish to correspond and have no desire to meet up, with or without Eleanor. (I wonder if you have even told her. I suspect you haven't.)

I sense such resolve in you now and cannot resist comparing it to what I remember about you from before. Not that you weren't determined! Landing a job in the fashion world in London at barely sixteen takes some mettle! (You lied about your age, as I recall.) But, don't be offended when I say you weren't exactly the most focused person I had ever met. You were out to enjoy life, it seems to me, throwing yourself at whatever came along that looked like fun (me, briefly!). You come across as being so much stronger now, not to mention more contemplative. Dare I say that I prefer it? (Yes, I dare. You are not going to reply anyway. Hah!)

Which brings me to the point of this email. I accept, at last, that you do not wish to see me. Not this year. Not in the New Year. Not ever.

Not for old times' sake or anything else. And I respect that, I really do. But I have also decided that this means I can finally abandon every last shred of trying to stick to your precious 'rules' and tell you something deeply personal and – I make no apologies for this – somewhat indulgent. It is something which you may take as proof, should you require it, that I really had laid our messy past to rest a long time ago. What I want to say concerns the first night we spent together. I mean the VERY first.

Do you remember that night? It was a long time ago after all...almost twenty years! I had come to take Eleanor out for lunch and we spotted you hitch-hiking, in a ballet dress! So we gave you a lift home and the pair of you persuaded me to stay for supper and games (with drink penalties!) and somehow I ended up agreeing to stay over. I was drunk, but I also remember being bewitched – literally – by you. You were still so young but seemed such a free spirit, and a beautiful one at that. Smitten would be the word! Sorry to be blunt, but that was the truth of it, as you know, since I was pretty soon telling you as much, ditching my girlfriend of six years and begging you to go out with me, which you eventually did, in a manner of speaking, albeit while somehow getting yourself to London, working all hours and generally squeezing me in between the hordes of other men queuing up to take you out!

But to get back to that first encounter. You cast your spell over me, Kat, and I remember, even before anything happened between us, feeling bad for Eleanor because she and I had got close, and because she was so straightforward and trusting and didn't have a clue. That night, not surprisingly given how much we drank, I pretty much passed out in that box of a spare room, only to wake and find you next to me. Your feet were icy. And your hands. You were shivering. I've never forgotten how you shook, as if you were afraid just as much as cold. I couldn't believe my luck! All you wanted was to sleep with me, you said. Just to SLEEP. And that is what we did. By the time I woke properly in the morning, you were gone.

And though rather more did happen between us, eventually, I was always aware that it was really only because I was so keen. (Bombarding you with phone-calls being my primary tactic, if memory serves. You caved in and I was too pleased to care how or why.) The point being, we never really were a 'proper' couple, Kat, because you never WANTED to be. I chased and sometimes you let me catch you. End of.

So I have decided that, looking back – (Kierkegaard!!!) – that night of sleep was in many ways our best time together. You went on to break my heart, Kat – never being straight, keeping me dangling – I can't tell you how desolate I used to feel getting that night bus from London to Oxford, the lurking conviction that you were glad to see the back of me – but that first night, for a few hours, something good happened. You were just a girl who needed to be held and I was there to do it. I have often thought how much better it would have been if I had left it there.

Your husband Howard, from what little you have mentioned, is clearly the rock you were looking for. And from your emails, I can state with some authority that he is a lucky man. I hope Eleanor has found happiness with someone too. I always felt bad at the way she steered clear once you and I started going out. We had already settled on being just good friends, but I still knew she felt shut out and hurt. When you and I finally went our separate ways for good, I remember thinking it a shame that I had somehow lost you both.

I wish you well, Kat. You were right about the dreams business, leaving them where they are. And about Kierkegaard! You have been right about so many things. It's been a pleasure and a privilege to get to know you a little better. But I promise, since you so clearly wish it, not to get in touch again.

When you next see Eleanor, please give her my love.

With great fondness,

Nick x

Eleanor printed off the email and then stood very still, forcing herself to read it again. Its contents felt like comeuppance. It had been stupid even to print it out. It needed deleting, obviously. As she had all the others, covering her tracks. All the months and months of it. Letting Nick think she was Kat. Shame coursed through her, a burning rush that dried her mouth and made her skin damp. *I'm glad you grew to like being a doctor*. One line was all it had taken. One line and Nick had been hooked. And a part of Eleanor had been elated by that alone – the quickness of his response, his cleverness in finding a way round her silly obstacles, how hard he had then fought to keep the conversation going.

Eleanor gripped the paper very tightly, but still it trembled. It was only an email, she reminded herself bitterly.

Eleanor let her gaze roam round Kat's study, messy with evidence of her faltering progress on the Trevor Downs manuscript: notes, half-started chapters. She had been chiselling away at the ghost-writing project all year, bringing it on her visits to her sister's house, using it, like the emails with Nick, as a distraction from what was going on. The old actor's ramblings remained in a state of mortifying chaos. Much like her life, Eleanor reflected darkly, as the hopes from January flashed across her mind: belief in the book commission, Kat's recovery. It had all been a lie.

Eleanor dropped her eyes to the printout in her hands, contemplating the sudden bleak notion that a long time ago she had placed her trust in the written word and all it had ever done was let her down.

The shredder made its usual terrible sound, like a machine that was broken instead of one doing its job. Nick's final, lucid, cruelly poignant missive went through very quickly. A loud whirring, it was over in seconds. Water back under its bloody bridge.

'Okay?'

'Howard. You startled me.' Eleanor pressed an involuntary hand to her heart as she spun round. Her brother-in-law looked drawn, his thin face etched with deepening lines, his short mousy hair scuffed in the way that showed the new spreading baldness at the crown. *His youth is being sucked out of him*, Eleanor thought; *Kat is going to take it with her to her grave.*

'Manage to get anything done?' He glanced at the shredder, where a few small curls of Nick's letter were still sticking out of the top.

'Not really. Difficult to concentrate.' She spoke quickly, brusquely, wanting only to divert Howard's attention from the jaws of the machine and its last pitiful

trailing evidence of her unforgivable duplicity. Her thoughts swung back to the May day on which it had all started seven months before. She had arrived at the house in a state of shock, summoned by Howard's report of a sudden relapse in Kat's condition. Expecting to be there an afternoon, she had stayed for a week.

It turned out that her sister's post-operative sprightliness had been an elaborate charade. The cancer was terminal and always had been. Kat had sworn him to secrecy, Howard had confessed miserably, coming to meet Eleanor in the drive, both about the diagnosis and the immediate, unwavering decision to undergo no further treatment beyond an initial operation.

She had wanted to enjoy what she had left, Kat had snapped when Eleanor's wretched gawping face betrayed her knowledge of this decision not to poison her already faltering system with pointless chemicals.

'Could you be useful instead of cross,' she had suggested archly, once Howard had beaten a tactful retreat. It was half-term and the children were out with Hannah at a theme park. Kat had been lying on the chaise longue in the conservatory, bundled between pillows and a duvet, thin as a twelve-year-old, the glorious silver-honey of her hair an assault against her pale skin. 'Howard is floundering. He is going to need help, especially with family admin. He's crap at that sort of stuff. The kids' comings and goings, parents' evenings and sports' days and concerts and outings – with three schools, there is so much going on – forms to fill in, subs to pay... I've already got rather behind. Everything takes such energy...' She had let the sentence hang, introducing a silence in which there was so much that Eleanor had wanted to say that she found she couldn't speak at all. 'In fact, perhaps you could go to my computer and take a look now,' Kat had snapped, cutting off the moment like a slamming door, 'print off anything that needs signing, ask me stuff you are not sure of.'

Eleanor had stumbled along the hallway to Kat's study to set about the task at once, grateful for any avenue to be helpful. The computer was open at her sister's email account and Eleanor had ploughed through the relevant correspondence, quickly syphoning out what needed action: a couple of dates for a concert and a sports day, and two forms requiring parental signatures – one for ballet lessons for Evie and another about a trip to a castle for Luke. As she worked, she was aware of the shadow of the tailor's dummy in the corner, still decked in the lilac it had been wearing in January. It took her back to the curious coercion by her sister that afternoon to help compose a reply to Nick Wharton. At the time, she had thought it was game-playing – Kat at her usual tricks. But sitting at the desk that cold May Friday, the new horrible knowledge of Kat's real prognosis churning inside, it occurred to Eleanor that her sister could have been playing a more generous game: wresting her focus to Nick Wharton, making jibes about visiting their father – maybe Kat had simply been throwing up diversions from being asked too many awkward questions about the excision of the tumour that was already a ticking bomb.

Eleanor had been roused from such musings by the arrival of a fresh email in Kat's inbox. And there it was. Nick's reply-to-a-reply, four months tardy and thoroughly dismissive, wishing Kat well for the rest of her life. The irony had been stark. But so had Eleanor's reflex of delight at the coincidence; the realisation that, out of all the million minutes in which Nick could have chosen to write back, he should have done so when she was logged in and looking on Kat's behalf. And it was because of that that Eleanor had fired back the comment about being glad Nick had grown to like being a doctor. She *was* glad. *Let him assume it's from Kat*, she had thought, not pausing to imagine any harm as she sent the message on its way. It had felt nothing more than a one-off chance to flash a detail of once treasured knowledge; something she would tell Kat about just as soon as the right moment presented itself.

Except, of course, she hadn't told Kat, and it had proved anything but one-off, because Nick had replied at once and so had she. And on it had gone, twelve weeks of the most enjoyable correspondence Eleanor had known since Igor, except with far more playfulness and empathy than her Russian lover had ever managed, and resulting in a growing desire to open up in precisely the way she kept insisting to Nick was out of bounds. Indeed, as the days ground on and Kat grew sicker, their correspondence had begun to feel almost like consolation. Something – the only thing – to look forward to between the stop-start efforts at writing Trevor's life story and ever longer spells at her sister's bedside. Guilt grew, a black flower in her heart, but Eleanor had ignored it for as long as she could, telling herself that emails were only emails and that the opinions she expressed to Nick were always her own. Never once had she even signed Kat's name.

Eleanor turned her back on the shredder and leant against the desk, facing her brother-in-law. She had done the right thing in the end, she reminded herself. Even if it had taken until July. Nick's playful request to describe herself had been the clincher. She had been alone in her flat that day, feeling so low, so powerless. She knew he meant to cheer her up, but all she could think of was *deceitful lying cow*. It had been like waking up from a wonderful dream, waking up to shame.

Nick hadn't made it easy, of course, finding reasons to write again, including the suggestion – of all things – that he meet with both her and Kat for a drink. Eleanor had had to laugh at that. A sharper reminder of why their communications had had to end would have been hard to conceive.

Eleanor folded her arms. Howard was still standing in the doorway, lost in one of his trances of sadness.

He nodded again in the direction of the scattered leaves of the Trevor manuscript. 'I like it that you work in here when you stay.'

Eleanor grimaced. 'It is not exactly *working*, to be honest. But I suppose an old actor's memoirs is never going to be Tolstoy, is it?' She endeavoured to smile, fighting down the unhappy reflection that the commission might perhaps have become some sort of literary masterpiece in the hands of a different, better writer; the kind of writer who would never have posed as a sister in emails to old flames, let alone a seriously ill sister, now locked in a losing battle with metastasising tumours. 'All Trevor has to offer is theatre gossip,' she said feebly, 'has-been theatre gossip from a has-been.'

Howard nodded, as if he sympathised with Eleanor's literary endeavours, when they both knew his mind was still in the big spare room upstairs where he had spent the two hours since his return from London. He had wanted to take time off work, but Kat had insisted against it. He needed his working life, she liked to point out crisply, both to keep him sane now and for later on. Being moved into the spare room had been another commandment. So Howard could sleep uninterrupted, she said. Though, from what Eleanor could make out, he spent most nights alongside her anyway. She often glimpsed him through the crack in the door in the early morning, sprawling in the armchair beside Kat's bed, his eyes closed, glasses hanging off his fingers, phone, iPad and charger wires strewn round his feet.

'She seems better today, don't you think?' Howard's voice was stern, as if daring Eleanor to disagree. 'Sort of calmer. And her face is a good colour. We had quite a chat. And she didn't do so much of that... you know... that twitching she does... when she's fighting the pain instead of taking more relief... Christ, why does she have to do that? I mean what the fuck is the point of *that*? All she's got to do is squeeze the fucking button.' He turned swiftly and dropped his forehead with a brutal thud against the door jamb, ramming his hands into his trouser pockets. He was still in his suit, his spotty city tie loosened and askew, his top two shirt buttons undone. 'Sorry. Long day.' He straightened and faced her slowly, breathing in and out, rolling his shoulders. 'Hannah's got the kids settled, thank god. Thank god for Hannah.'

There was a moment's silence while they both considered the virtues of the twenty-three-year-old who, during the course of the year, had developed from an ad-hoc babysitter into a full-time nanny. Through the worsening personal difficulties of her employers, she had continued to chivvy the three children through home and school routines with the cheery deftness of a sheepdog, somehow managing to do most of the household chores as she went. Watching the achievement had reinforced Eleanor's sense of helplessness and ineptitude. A round trip to the super-sized supermarket the day before had taken her three hours, and even then she had managed to return without milk.

What she found hardest of all was watching her nephew and nieces, continuing to function as their world unravelled. It was like observing innocents playing on a beach with their backs to an approaching tsunami. Didn't they see what was coming? It made a dim, deep part of her want to scoop them up and run for the hills.

And maybe the children saw the terror in their aunt's eyes because, in spite of her persistent efforts, they showed no let-up in a united determination to keep her at arm's length. Luke always had a screen at the ready – iPhone, tablet, laptop – an escape portal to dive into at the slightest pretext; while Sophie hung off the long-suffering Hannah like a vine, throwing tantrums at anyone who tried to intervene, especially if it was her little sister. Evie, meanwhile, was the one Eleanor found hardest to reach of all. Silent and impassive, even in the face of her big sister's histrionics, the seven-year-old's small earnest green eyes peeped out through her thatch of wild yellow-blonde hair like an animal monitoring the world from a lair. There was an intensity to the child, a fierce determination to stay separate, that tore at Eleanor's heart.

'There's a pie for supper,' Howard said dully. 'Ham and chicken. Hannah made it.' He had taken off the spotty tie and was winding it round his knuckles like a tourniquet. 'She's eaten early and gone to her room. Are you hungry?'

'Yes,' Eleanor lied, because going through the motions had to be managed, the very least any of them could do.

'Thanks for being here, Eleanor,' Howard blurted miserably. 'All your support over these last months... I know she's not the easiest patient, particularly as you and she... well, you've never been exactly close. But, in spite of that, I hope you realise that she does... she does...' He wiped his mouth.

'I know she does.' Eleanor busily set about gathering up her Trevor notes, patting the sides to bring stray sheets into line. Did her sister in fact love her? It was difficult to believe. Howard was wrong, of course. She and Kat *had* once been close, that was what made it so hard. The whorls of Nick's last email were still poking out of the shredder. *Bewitched*, he had described himself. Whereas she was *trusting and straightforward*. Christ. Talk about curiosity blowing up the bloody cat.

'You all right, Eleanor? You look tired.' Howard was still hovering, still needing something she couldn't give.

'I'm fine. As fine as we all are.' The email might have been pulped, but Nick's words were still reverberating inside her head, the simple truth of them. He had fallen in love with her sister. There was no one to blame, least of all Kat. Eleanor marvelled that it should have taken her two decades to see this properly. No one stole anybody. Love happened.

'So you'll go up to her before we eat?' Their eyes met for an instant, enough for Eleanor to see the gleam of her brother-in-law's fear, to know that it was a plea for help rather than a question.

'Of course. In a minute. I'll just finish clearing up here first.' She fiddled at the desk, aligning pencils and papers, aware of Howard drifting deeper into the room. He paused at the tailor's dummy, patting its lilac shoulder as if it were an old friend.

'And whenever you need to go back to London, for your work... or whatever... just say, because...' His voice tightened as he talked. 'Because, after all, we don't know how long she...'

Eleanor looked up to see that he had fallen against the mannequin, burying his face in its stiff pleats. 'Howard...' She hurried to his side and put her arms round him, aware as she did so of her own greater height. Her brother-in-law was lithe and compact, but several inches shy of six foot. He turned, sobbing quietly, into her shoulder. 'I am not going anywhere just yet,' she soothed, stroking his back.

'Thank you.'

'It will be okay,' Eleanor added, but only because he needed to hear it.

'Yup.' He pulled free, appearing smaller still. 'Somehow it will.' He tried to conjure a smile, tearing at his lower lip with his teeth. 'This just wasn't the plan, you know? This wasn't how it was supposed to go for Kat and me.'

Eleanor managed a rueful grin in return. 'But then life never is quite the plan, is it?' Nick gusted into her mind again, the Nick she had glimpsed in the correspondence that year, the one who loved seeking answers and ideas; the one who was funny and bold. 'I'll go up to her now. Then we'll eat.'

'Peas okay?'

'Peas?'

'Peas with the pie?'

'Oh yes. Whatever.'

Luke slipped out of the spare room as Eleanor rounded the bend in the corridor. It was a rule that the children could go into their mother whenever they wanted, unless specifically instructed otherwise. Seeing his aunt, he took off in the opposite direction, moving in that skulking way that Eleanor noticed in so many teenagers, as if they were trying to glide unnoticed through life, disassociate themselves from their own bodies.

The spare room had developed its own distinct smell, medicinal, floral. Howard brought fresh flowers every few days from the station, vast bunches, invariably involving lilies because they were Kat's favourite. Eleanor had once idly calculated what he must have spent since January, arriving at a figure that would have paid several months' rent on her Clapham flat.

Kat was on her back, her head raised by two pillows, her petite frame pitifully narrow beneath the covers, her cheeks flushed. Even so, suffering and illness had hardened the beauty of her face, drawing out the bones, accentuating the icy edge of her impossibly large blue eyes. She started talking the moment Eleanor entered, in staccato bursts, licking her lips between sentences. 'Do you know that Debra Winger film? *Ordinary People.* Do you remember? The kids all troop in to say goodbye. She tells the boy it is okay to hate her, but that later he will regret the hating. Howard and I watched it all cosy together one night years ago. Wept buckets, both of us. But it's not like that. It's not like you imagine. Luke doesn't hate me. He wants me well, which is much, much worse.' She plucked feebly at the bedsheet. Her fingers were so small and white as bone.

Eleanor stroked them, her mouth dry with pity. As usual, all the things she wanted to say had deserted her the moment she entered the room. There was talk of a hospice, but not yet, Howard insisted. Not till Kat said she was ready. All the business with Nick couldn't have seemed more pointless. Who cared what he, Kat or any of them had thought or done two decades before? It was the now that mattered. Kat still being alive. 'I remember that film,' she said eagerly. 'A real tear-jerker. In fact it annoyed me. I felt manipulated.'

Kat half closed her eyes, murmuring something.

Eleanor leant closer. 'Say again. I didn't hear…'

'I said that's typical of you…' She spat the words, causing Eleanor to jerk upright, and then blinked furiously as if it was an unwelcome struggle even to get her sister into proper focus, '... applying *critical* faculties, not wanting to be manipulated... not letting anything go... wanting control. And you're losing weight,' she went on accusingly, adding in a gleeful croak, 'the *big* sister shrinks at last.'

'Yes... I...' Eleanor glanced self-consciously down at her jeans, hanging ever more loosely off her hips as the weeks passed. Inwardly, she was still reeling. If anything, Kat's hostility had grown worse over the months of her illness; a hostility that stung all the more for being reserved just for her. But then, when had Kat ever made anything between them easy. She did her best to shoot her little sister a smile that was regretful instead of bruised. 'All my clothes are falling off me, it's true. Maybe I could borrow a belt?'

'Be my guest.' Kat raised a tremulous finger in the direction of the wall of wardrobes on the far side of the room.

'Thanks, I'll take a look in a minute. How are you feeling?'

'Fucking awful, thank you.'

'Is there anything...' Eleanor broke off as Kat convulsed suddenly, bending her knees to her stomach and screwing up her eyes. Eleanor gripped her hand, wretched and helpless, as a tremor moved up and over the wasted body, as visible as a breaking wave. 'Kat... darling Kat.' Eleanor tried to stroke her cheek, but Kat rolled her head from side to side. A moment later she fell still, releasing short sharp breaths through her nose. Eleanor laid the back of her hand against her forehead. The skin was hot and sticky. 'Is the morphine not enough?'

Kat's eyes flew open to deliver a withering look. 'I don't mind pain. I've always been good with pain. It's something... real...' She grimaced. 'Something to push against. Easier than other things.' She seemed to hold her breath and then relax. Her gaze grew more distant, then slowly her eyes closed and peace flooded her features, smoothing them.

Instants later she appeared to have fallen asleep, her lips slightly apart, each breath floating from between them with the soft evenness of a baby. Eleanor stayed by the bed, holding out against the urge to flee to the kitchen and eat peas and pie with Howard. They would drink wine. She would get drunk. With Howard. That was all she wanted to do.

'Go and eat,' Kat growled.

Eleanor stayed where she was. Tears had started tracking down her cheeks and she felt powerless to do anything about them. They flowed steadily, as if a tap inside her had turned and stuck fast. The rest of her was curiously calm, the sort of calmness that comes with giving up. 'You don't like me, Kat. I wish you liked me. I don't understand.'

'Don't be stupid.'

'That time I came, after your operation, back in January, did you make me help write back to Nick because you wanted to hurt me?'

Kat swivelled her head, alert in an instant, the incredulity in her translucent blue eyes unmistakeable. 'Nick the limpet? Oh Jesus, this is all I need. Why,' she added suddenly, her gaze sharpening, 'has he written again?'

'No.' Eleanor flung the lie out. The tears were still streaming out of her, emptying her. She had run out of patience, of compassion, of everything. 'I love you so much. Why don't you like me?'

'Oh just go and eat,' Kat croaked. 'Howard will be waiting.'

Eleanor didn't move. 'On the beach that day, with Mrs Owens. You knotted her laces, do you remember? And then we paddled. We held hands. And Mum,' Eleanor was sobbing now, 'you've never talked about her, you never—'

'She was a useless mother, that's why,' Kat interjected in a cold brittle voice Eleanor had never heard before. 'She was a drunk who killed herself. She left us when she didn't need to. You and me. She left her *children*, whereas I... I... me... with this fucking... *thing*... I would stay for mine if I could. Luke, Sophie, Evie... I would stay. I would give anything, Ellie... anything. But I can't.'

'Oh Kat,' Eleanor whispered.

'I've told Howard – I've told him...' Kat was speaking through a clenched jaw now, forcing the words out. 'When this is over – I don't want to be anywhere near her. I want to be burnt and scattered. In the garden. By the tree with the swing. Howard knows. Howard understands.'

Eleanor was stroking her arm and Kat didn't resist, though she turned her face to the wall. Eleanor made shushing sounds. Her tears had vanished. She wished she could retract everything, her own stupidity most of all. Already it seemed ridiculous ever to have minded for one second how Kat treated her, how difficult she was, how distant or aggressive. All of it was nothing compared to what her sister was going through. A part of her ached to offer flimsy consolations – that their mother's death could have been an accident – but she feared Kat would scoff and get vexed, and only suffer more. Instead, she said shush again and tenderly placed a kiss on her arm.

'And Dad only ever really loved her anyway,' Kat murmured, rolling her head to look at Eleanor properly at last, her big eyes cloudy. 'She was the one he always wanted most. Not us. Not you. Not me...'

Eleanor tutted softly, while in a corner of her mind a memory fluttered. The slither of a view into her parents' bedroom. Her father's trousers loose. Her mother pinned under him. 'Now that's just nonsense,' she murmured to Kat, 'you were always Dad's favourite. For all the aggro, he loved you best.'

Hearing a shuffling noise behind her, she turned to see Evie at the door. Her niece was half in and half out, hanging off the handle.

'Mummy.' She spoke in a whisper, but Kat replied at once in a firm voice.

'Come here, darling. Come here and give me a kiss and a hug. A huge one please.'

Evie flew across the room on the balls of her feet, brushing past Eleanor as she clambered nimbly onto the bed, choosing that side as they all did because it was the one without the morphine drip.

'Dear doodle,' Kat murmured, stretching out the arm for Evie to nestle under. 'Not for long because Mummy is tired tonight. Boring Mummy, always tired.'

Eleanor stood tensely, not knowing whether to stay or go, feeling like the intruder she was. After a few moments, remembering the offer of the belt, she backed away and opened the nearest door in the wall of wardrobes. The clothes, bunched on their hangers, stirred like people shifting their weight in a queue. Eleanor ran her fingers over the materials, most of them Kat's creations, silks and satins in electric colours, trimmed or trailing snippets of lace and gauze and velvet.

A faint scent floated out from between their folds, chalky sweet, the smell of the past. On the inside of the wardrobe door several silk scarves hung over a loop of gold braid, along with a couple of belts, one thin and white, the other much wider, of soft tanned leather. Eleanor pulled out the leather one and threaded it through the waistband of her jeans. It had a brass buckle that snapped shut with a click.

'Mummy said I could,' she explained quickly, noticing her niece's arrival at her side, her flinty green eyes that were so like Howard's narrowed in disapproval.

'She's gone to sleep,' Evie retorted, throwing a scowl in the direction of the bed.

'Would you like a story?' Eleanor put the question tentatively, such suggestions invariably meeting with rejection. 'You could lie in your bed and I would read it to you. Anything you like.'

Evie sighed. 'Just one then.' She turned and traipsed out of the room, clearly resigned to the knowledge that her aunt would follow.

A few minutes later they were settled on Evie's pink wooden bed reading a tale about a rag doll joining a circus. The book was slim, dog-eared, clearly an old favourite. Eleanor sat up with her back against the headboard and Evie lay alongside her, but awkwardly, the stiffness in her small body shouting reluctance. The story was repetitive, not that well-written. Eleanor read carefully, making each line as interesting as she could. As the minutes passed, she became aware of the mild soapy scent of her niece filling her nose, and the thickening of the child's breathing as she nestled closer, growing sleepy. It brought memories drifting into the fringes of her mind, of Jeremy Fisher and the big fish, of Kat's cold feet digging for warmth under her calves...

'Oi, you're holding me too hard...' Evie squirmed upright, all elbows and knees.

'Sorry... sorry... I was just...'

Her niece shuffled into a cross-legged position on the end of the bed, maintaining a safe distance, eyeing Eleanor gravely. 'It's okay. Daddy does it sometimes. He doesn't know his own strength, Mummy says.'

'Doesn't he? Right.' It was a relief to glance across the room and see Howard in the doorway, miming despair about a near-ruined meal.

He took over to tuck Evie up, patiently following a series of comically precise commands about saying goodnight to various soft toys propped on shelves around the room and how many inches wide to leave the door open. Eleanor waited in the passageway, the smell of her niece still on her skin, mulling over how childhood was childhood, no matter how one filled in the colours.

When Howard emerged, she rolled her eyes, smiling kindly, wanting him to know that she thought he was the most tremendous dad. When his expression imploded, she wondered for a moment if he was ill. Instead, seizing her elbow, he propelled her along to the landing, explaining in low hurried sentences that he had found Kat collapsed on the bedroom floor and both their doctor and an ambulance were on the way.

19

Nick waved a fly off the plate of uncooked steak and rummaged at the burning coals with the barbecue fork. Their undersides were ash-white, almost ready for cooking. Away from the barbecue, it was almost chilly, one of the evening winds having picked up. He thought with a start of guilt about the loose window shutter, but then remembered he had fixed it months before. On the day Kat said their emails had to stop. A grey July day he would never forget. And now it was December. A sudden gust whipped at the fire. Nick blinked as a scattering of hot ash-dust blew upwards. Wind or no wind, Donna would want to stick with her plan of eating outside and he knew better than to suggest otherwise.

A few yards away, in the alcove facing the pool, she had laid out the usual extravagant array of salads on their big outdoor table: green leaves and yellow peppers in a blue dish; farfalle pasta, tomatoes and basil in a yellow dish; a creamy potato salad in a red dish. Nick sighed. These three would already have been far too much. Both the girls were at party sleepovers. The only people coming were Donna's parents and their nearest neighbours, Mike and Lindy Scammell. What's more, the steaks were rib-eyes the size of books, and Donna ate sparsely, with great attention to her calorific intake. Yet Nick knew there were two further vast side dishes being prepared, one containing cucumber, sweetcorn and tuna, and the other a dense concoction of pulses that he could tell at a glance he wouldn't like.

Donna's parents had just arrived and were still in the kitchen. He could see the heads of the three of them bobbing in the window across the pool, talking intently. About him, Nick guessed grimly, his thoughts skittering to the days when he had imagined his in-laws to be friends.

Catching Jim Cruick's eye, he raised the barbecue fork in a salute, getting a head-nod in return. He guessed the Scammells would be late. They usually were, in spite of living only a couple of miles away on a similar gated plot with garden and pool. They had a daughter called Meryl who was in the same class as Natalie, which meant the convenience of sharing the thirty-minute drive to the girls' school. They were not kindred spirits by any means, but decent enough people. He hadn't seen Mike for weeks, but he would be back-thumping and cheerfully noisy, Nick knew, charged already with a couple of beers. Lindy, meanwhile, would be overdressed, in something a little too short, the heels a little too high. She would come and stand next to Nick at the barbecue and light her first cigarette of the evening, saying in her low smoker's voice that he was her favourite doctor because he never lectured her about her bad habits.

For all their families' interactions, Donna maintained she didn't like Lindy very much. Because the woman was in love with Nick, she claimed, blatantly chasing after him at every opportunity. That Nick wasn't interested in the advances of their neighbour, or any other female for that matter, was never of any relevance either to his wife's train of thought or the viciousness with which such accusations were flung out. Donna's bullying certainty about Nick's desire to be unfaithful had formed early on in their marriage, quickly establishing itself as an ugly and unrelenting thread in the tapestry of their arguments. The implausibility of the candidates and Nick's dogged efforts to convince her otherwise never did any good. Lately, he had stopped trying. Which was ironic, Nick mused, and possibly even connected to the fact that, for the first time in sixteen years of matrimony, Donna might actually have had some dim grounds for complaint. If exchanging a few emails counted as grounds.

Nick stirred the coals, bringing the outer ones into the middle and then spreading the whole lot flat. But it was over, he reminded himself. Whatever 'it' had been. He jabbed at the coals again, ruining the smoothness. He had half hoped his most recent missive – sent from his office the week before – might prompt a reply, in spite of its protestations to the contrary. He was still glad he had written it, Nick decided stubbornly, glad that Kat at least could now be in no doubt that he wasn't, and had never been, clinging to some rose-tinted version of the past. Deep inside himself, however, he knew her silence was right. It was that knowledge that had helped him delete every word of their stop-start correspondence, up to and including his most recent message. What was less understandable was the hole this appeared to have left in his life. In fact, most hours of most days, Nick was starting to feel as if someone had bulldozed the ground from beneath his feet.

As regards Lindy, it was clear to Nick that their neighbour's attentions remained innocuous. He had always found it hard to see the crime in one human being wanting to establish a teasing connection with another, even if it had faint sexual undertones. It was the choices one made about such undertones that mattered; whether they led to action or not. Nick had grown fond of Lindy's at times off-kilter flirty remarks, but only because they made a welcome change from the usual conversational paths to dominate his and Donna's otherwise predictable and privileged social circle, tending as they did to range between irritatingly competitive chat about the achievements of offspring, gripes over inept house-staff, and horror at rising crime stats. The pattern of it all could get him down.

It was also baffling and irksome, Nick decided, stabbing yet more chaos into the hot smooth bed of charcoal, that Donna should claim such dislike of Lindy and yet do so thorough a job of keeping the woman embroiled in their lives. Sharing the school run was an obvious tie, but beyond that there were innumerable invitations to lunch and dinner parties, with Donna rather than Lindy invariably leading the charge.

'Why are you using that?'

'Pardon?' Nick had been too lost in his cogitations to notice his wife arrive at the barbecue. She was in silver-strapped heels he hadn't seen before and a long purple silk dress that billowed on the evening breeze round her tanned ankles.

She pointed with distaste at the barbecue fork in his hand. 'That is for actual cooking. You *know* it is for cooking.'

'Yes, but—'

'So why the fuck are you shovelling at the fire with it? Christ, Nick, as if it isn't bad enough that you hide out here—'

'Hide?'

'How do you think that makes Daddy feel, or Mummy? Their own son-in-law, not even bothering to come and say hello?'

'But I assumed you would be bringing them straight out here...' Nick glanced hopelessly in the direction of the kitchen, noting that the heads of his in-laws had been joined by those of the Scammells.

'I have to do everything, do you realise that? Every-fucking-thing.'

'I'll come in now, of course. I just thought you...'

But she was already striding away, flicking her hand dismissively over her head in the I-give-up gesture that had the sharp, double power to make him feel both furious and ineffectual. He had often thought that to be treated as purely irrelevant would have been preferable. But Donna wasn't like that; she liked to poke him with a stick and then storm away, blocking the possibility of explanations or reconciliation. That came later, on her terms, and usually – maddeningly – without any willingness to discuss what had caused the outburst. Indeed, her most common default reaction was to behave as if the outburst hadn't even happened, precluding the possibility of solving its root cause. Her mood simply changed and she expected Nick to change with it.

Nick stared after his wife. Her lithe body swayed as she moved, making the shape of its curves tantalisingly visible through the expensive cloth of the dress. It still astounded him that such unpleasantness could erupt out of such beauty. Early on, he had felt not only attracted to, but somehow safe with Donna's looks; seeing them with mad subconscious logic as insurance against the possibility of ever leading an ugly life. It had taken years for the naivety of this assumption to sink in. Indeed, it was only really with the imminence of his fortieth birthday that he had started to face up to it, driven by unhappiness to the sort of introspection that he had spent a life-time avoiding.

The introspection had wrought a certain despair. Tilly had been strikingly pretty, a petite brunette who turned heads; Kat's wild elfin beauty had been in an order all its own; on his elective in Sri Lanka there had been a sultry Spanish nurse, in possession of a healthy sexual appetite and a boyfriend in Manchester. And then there had been Donna, jigging to keep warm at an inter-hospital rugby match soon after his return, chattering about how she had just started working as a PA in London. It had been a steely day at the end of February, seeping drizzle, and she had seemed to throw light at it. Two years later they were married. Six years after that, with his father-in-law oiling the wheels on all fronts, they had made the move to Cape Town.

Did female beauty make him stupid? Was he just a walking cliché?

Nick looked round for something to cover the meat. It had occurred to him that he needed to get into the kitchen fast, if there was to be any hope of re-establishing matrimonial peace.

But the fly had returned to the plate with a cohort of followers. The steaks were sweating and succulent, so red they were almost blue. He would just have to take them with him. Nick picked up the plate and hurried round the pool. As he reached the garden room doors, Donna stepped through them, followed by their guests. Jim, her father, came first, right on her shoulder, bearing an ice bucket containing – Nick could see at a glance – a different bottle from the one he himself had placed inside it an hour or so before.

'Nick. How you doing?' It seemed to Nick that the ice bucket was a pretext for not shaking hands. 'I brought something special – a Chardonnay – barrel fermented – from a Durbanville vineyard now being run by a friend of mine. Dean Cobalt. Good man. And the wine isn't bad either. It will win awards, mark my words.' Jim rattled the bucket. 'There's another keeping cool in the fridge. I brought a couple of his reds too, Cabernet Sauvignons. I've opened them to breathe.'

'Thanks, that's really generous.' Nick forced out the gratitude and accompanying smile, marvelling that gifts could feel so like coercion. There had been countless others in the past, ranging from horses to holidays. Even work. It was largely due to pressure from his father-in-law that he now did the highly paid day of cosmetic surgery at a private clinic downtown. It would see off the girls' university fees, Jim had pointed out sharply, when Nick had dared to express doubts about accepting the networking that had produced the possibility of the post. In the end, predictably, Donna had joined the fray and Nick had succumbed, accepting that the extra income made sense, since keeping up with his wife's idea of living well at the same time as privately educating their daughters was already blowing large, regular holes in his domestic budgeting.

But inwardly Nick had resented the strong-arm tactics. It had made him see more clearly than ever that his father-in-law was a man forged out of granite, with his own agenda. Physically, Jim Cruick exuded a powerful force too, his Dutch ancestry having dealt him the same piercing blue eyes he had passed onto his daughter and thick sandy-gold hair, which still showed no trace of grey and which he kept cropped in vertical spikes, like bristles on a boot-scraper. He had been a rugby player in his youth, tried out for the Springboks, and still had the wide neck and a tank of a chest to prove it. Well into his sixties, he now boasted about maintaining his fitness in the gym or through horseback riding round the formidable Stellenbosch property he had acquired and extended through his success in real estate. It was where Donna and the girls kept the horses he had given them, ensuring that riding with Grandad was always a favourite weekend treat.

'We are sorry the girls aren't here,' cried Lauren, his mother-in-law, her bangles jangling as she grasped one of Nick's arms with both hands. 'Aren't we sorry, Jim?' She threw the words carelessly in the direction of her husband, making the big gold loops lancing her ears swing like wind chimes. Her hair was white and expensively styled in high waves. She was wearing one of her tent-dresses, a medley of electric greens and blues designed to accentuate the lingering prettiness of her strong grey eyes and mask the swell of her sizeable midriff. Compared to Jim, she looked an old woman. The difference was almost comical.

Nick kissed her on both cheeks, feeling a burst of sympathetic affection. Living with his father-in-law could not be easy. Moving on to greet the Scammells, he was aware of the stiffening of his smile and the grit of tiredness under his eyelids. He had hit a particularly bad patch of sleeping, making trips to the bathroom just to relieve the tedium of lying in bed. Lingering in front of the basin mirror in the small hours that morning, he had found himself wondering how the years had treated the Keating sisters. Lately, he had been struggling to picture either of them clearly, even as young girls. Whenever he tried, all that came to mind, vividly, was the voice in the emails, intelligent, playful, fresh. Honest.

* * *

Rapidly and unexpectedly, the dinner party grew enjoyable. It helped that the wind, like a fan turned off at the mains, suddenly dropped, leaving a balmy warmth that caressed their bare skin. The pool, with its underwater lights, became a huge emerald mirror. On the table, the candles glinted in their vases like jewels in glass cases. The steaks were buttery-soft and Nick highly praised for his outdoor cooking skills. Jim's wines slid smoothly over the tongue and throat, making any resentment about being forced to consume them seem churlish. When Mike got out his iPad to start making notes of the grapes and labels, Jim insisted that he would organise a visit to Dean Cobalt's vineyard. A multi-course lunch of tastings for all six of them – it would be his treat and a great day out, he boomed, in the tone he favoured, the one that defied contradiction.

Donna floated off to the kitchen with the dirty plates and floated back again, bearing a tray of mountainous fruit salad, home-made chocolate brownies and a tub of organic vanilla ice cream. As it was the weekend they had sent their kitchen help home. After setting the food on the table, she took a detour to her own chair via Nick's, pausing to trail her fingers up the back of his neck and under the cuff of his hair. He was being forgiven. An involuntary shiver of pleasure rippled over his skull. Maybe the forgiveness would stretch to sex. That didn't happen often. Nick rubbed his arms, aware of the shiver of pleasure disappearing as quickly as it had come. He caught his father-in-law watching him, steel flashing in the dark blue eyes, as sharp as any sword.

After their guests had gone, and they were clearing up, the atmosphere of truce prevailed; an atmosphere that Nick, as ever, felt little inclination to jeopardise with defensive questions or recriminations about what had gone before. With Donna, saying the wrong thing was akin to pressing a detonator. Shouting, hitting. Sometimes things got thrown.

She had her back to him and was busy transferring the left-over salads to smaller containers for stowing in the fridge. The pulses had barely been touched. 'Daddy says he is going to put one of the flats in the new Waterfront condo in trust for Sash and Nat. Like a nest egg for them. Isn't that insanely generous?'

'Goodness, yes. Insane.'

She spun round, her cat-eyes wide with the readiness to take affront. 'Are you taking the piss?'

'No. I am agreeing.' Nick found a laugh escaping. Her quickness to take offence was absurd and yet somehow always caught him off guard.

She spun back to the fridge, restacking shelves to make room for the Tupperware. 'With your recent midlife career *crisis* it makes me feel more secure, anyway. For the girls' future, if not my own.'

'I haven't had a career crisis.' Nick braced himself. He had hoped the truce might be more resilient, one of those that lasted for several days.

'No, right. A top consultant wanting to become a teacher.' Her tone was sneering, but she still had the pretence of a grin fixed in place when she turned round. 'Not to mention all these sudden urges about visiting the UK.' She wagged a finger at him. 'Pretending you want to rush off and see your mother, whom you hate anyway, when it's perfectly clear you're really after a sneaky closer look at this school teacher idea, talk to some old *chums.*' She gave the word a faux posh English accent, the one that once upon a time had made him smile. 'And as for how you could even consider trading in what we have here for a life like that...' She shook her head in disgusted wonderment.

'I don't hate my mother,' Nick said levelly. 'She's hard work, I admit. Since losing Dad, she's not been the same, but that doesn't stop my sense of duty—'

'Which is why we are going in January. I have *agreed* we are going to bloody England in bloody January, have I not?' Donna's once professed fondness for his homeland had sunk over the years beyond her own recollection, let alone retrieval. She hated the weather, the food, the traffic, quite apart from her mother-in-law.

'Yes, you have. And thank you for that.' Nick spoke firmly and as warmly as he could manage, resisting the urge to remind her that the January plan was the poor compromise, reached thanks to her pulling out of the original agreement to visit England in September. A suggestion that he go on his own had proved one of those unforeseeable detonator moments. She didn't trust him, she had shrieked, throwing a mug that time; she didn't trust him with life choices, with women, with *anything*. The mug had somersaulted through the air, giving him plenty of time to duck. And since Kat had been half on his mind at the time, he had climbed down with guilt for once, rather than suppressed outrage, sweeping up the broken fragments, soothing her with the idea of postponing to a visit in the New Year instead.

'Though why your mother can't come and see *us...*' Donna started fiercely, but then let the sentence hang. This was slightly less safe ground. The last thing she wanted was a visit from Carol Wharton, as they both knew. What they also both knew was that since her mother-in-law barely ventured out of the small Cheltenham flat to which she had retreated in widow-hood, there was little chance of her bluff being called.

Nick hesitated. It was always a question of picking which battles to fight. 'Yes, well, you know how she is.'

'Yes, I bloody do.'

'So January it is.'

'Yes. But only if you promise to drop all this fucking crazy teacher talk once and for all,' Donna countered bitterly. 'You don't mean it, do you? You can't mean it.' She slammed the fridge door and turned to face him, hands on hips.

'It was just an idea,' Nick said quietly, regretting for the umpteenth time that he had ever been foolhardy enough to broach the subject out loud. 'Surely,' Nick went on carefully, 'one should be able to have a few off-the-wall ideas and share them with one's partner. As you know, teaching literature was something I used to want to do. And now that I'm getting past the age where...' He paused.

Donna was fiddling with the fridge magnets which had slipped out of their usual places thanks to her slam of the door. A Barbie logo, a figure of the Little Mermaid, a plastic hamburger, a smiley face; relics of a lost time, it seemed to Nick suddenly, of lost hope, lost innocence.

'I was just airing an idea,' he tried again, speaking very calmly and gently to her back. 'I love our lifestyle here, as you well know, and there is so much about being a doctor that I like too. I know I am good at it. And, as things stand, I couldn't afford to switch careers anyway.'

'Oh, you'd find a way.' It was an accusation not a compliment. She turned round, the nostrils of her small neat nose flaring slightly. 'You would go on a teaching course in England or something. You would make it happen. I *know* you hate it here. I know how you resent Dad – are jealous of him—'

'I do not hate it here. And I am neither resentful nor envious of your father.'

'The trouble with you, Nick Wharton,' she snapped, ignoring these reassurances, 'is you don't love me properly. You never have.'

'Yes, I—'

'You don't. Because if you did you wouldn't even talk about going to England.'

The obvious counter-challenge, that evidence of her affection for him had grown pretty scant in recent years, would get him nowhere, Nick knew. It would produce ructions. He could already feel her anger brewing. He had run out of ways of dealing with it other than stonewalling; and that night he didn't feel he had the strength even for that. He felt battered already, exhausted.

'To have doubts about a career choice and own up to them

has got nothing to do with not loving you,' he said instead, speaking wearily now, while inside a deeper tiredness heaved, for the whole sorry business of what they had become. With hindsight, it was pitifully obvious that they had married barely knowing each other; fallen for notions of what each might be, rather than with any firm grasp of one another's needs and personalities. Lately, Nick had found himself dreaming of Donna leaving him. But then, each time, he would hit the road-block of the girls. It took no crystal ball to imagine how hard Donna would make it for him to see them, or how rigorously her parents would take her part. The notion of being deprived of contact with his daughters, not seeing them for weeks on end, not being around to catch their breathy everyday stories about this and that, all the myriad, daily disarming moments when they forgot about trying to be anything other than themselves, Nick found impossible to contemplate. The pain of anything was still preferable to that.

Somewhere deep inside his pocket, his phone rang.

'Aren't you going to answer it?' Donna's sapphire eyes glittered. She was still teetering on the precipice, assessing her own levels of frustration and how to let them play out. She was gripping her upper arms so tightly the skin had gone white around her fingertips. 'Or perhaps I should?'

For one mad moment, Nick feared it might indeed be Lindy – which, he decided was what Donna herself was thinking. Both their neighbours had drunk a lot and there had been no disguising the way Lindy's soft sad mouth had landed a little too close to his as they said their goodbyes.

But the number flashing was Sasha's, their youngest.

'Hey, Dad, sorry to call.'

'No problem. Is everything okay?'

'I didn't want to try Mum in case she was asleep.'

'Quite right. Good girl.' Famously within the family, Donna was a delicate sleeper – easily woken and finding it hard to drop back off once disturbed. Nick's doctor's training meant he was the opposite, or so Donna had always told the girls once they were old enough to process and pay heed to such information. That this was not the case, that Nick too was, and always had been, a light sleeper, was one of the countless small deceits and disconnections that had threaded its way between them over the years, harmless in itself, but not so harmless in conjunction with everything else. Working the long hours he did, Nick had in fact been happy to let the myth ride, taking whatever opportunities he got to be a father, even if that meant being the first to soothe night terrors, strip bedding or hunt for a thermometer.

'It's Sasha,' he mouthed, in response to Donna's questioning look. She was at his side in an instant, clutching Nick's arm and trying to get her head near enough to hear the conversation. He eased Donna's hand off his arm and switched his phone to speaker mode so she could hear without straining. She was a good mother, he reminded himself. It was just him she had difficulty with. She needed to be able to let go, she had confessed once, a rare moment of candour piercing the calm that had followed a particularly bad explosion. She had thrown a butter dish that time. It had caught his cheekbone, leaving a red lump. It was because she trusted and loved him, she said, which meant being able to show her worst. And what if he were to show his 'worst', Nick had growled on that occasion, cupping his throbbing face, the shock at her behaviour numbing him as it always did, while inside the optimist in him wondered if so rare a disclosure might mean they had reached a turning point at last. For, in those days, he had still believed that every situation had its rock bottom from which good might yet emerge.

But Donna had expertly flipped the dynamic, as she so often managed, visibly shrinking from him and asking in a terrified whisper, 'And what exactly do you mean by that... your *worst*?' She had fumbled for her mobile, keeping big scared eyes pinned on his as she pressed the numbers – whether to call an emergency service or her father, Nick had no idea – the threat in itself being enough to make him backtrack.

Sasha's words were muffled, delivered with her hand over her phone, by the sound of it. She was feeling sick, she said. In spite of it being gone midnight, Nick could hear the dull thumps of the sleepover, which had been for her best friend, Adrienne's, thirteenth birthday, still going on in the background. She didn't want to make a fuss, she said, but could she be picked up and taken home. Nick said, of course, that he would be there as quickly as he could. Adrienne lived in Muizenberg, a good forty-minute drive away.

'I'll phone Mia, say you're on your way,' said Donna, patting a yawn away as she bent down to retrieve her silver shoes.

Nick had drunk too much to drive, but neither of them referred to it. It was a relief for both just to have the spotlight shifted from their own dysfunction, to step back into the safe world of parenthood.

'Drive carefully,' Donna called from the doorstep, waving Nick off as he nosed their hefty four-wheeler through the gates; as if they were any ordinary couple, who trusted and loved each other.

* * *

'You just say if you need me to pull over, okay?' Nick glanced sideways at his youngest. She had her head out of the car window, like a dog on a hot day. Her long hair, a sandier brown than his, streamed off her ears and neck. The mountain was a hulking shadow behind them, Cape Town a pincushion of lights, twinkling through the red alders flanking the road. 'What was it, too much chocolate cake?'

Sasha flashed him a scowl that quickly became a sheepish grin. 'No it was not.' She pulled her head into the car and then threw herself back into her seat with a sigh.

'Mind if I close it?'

'Sure.' She turned on her side to face him as the window

whirred up, folding her legs onto the seat and making a pillow of her hands under the headrest.

'Just tired?'

'Dad, I'm not going to throw up in the car, okay?'

'Good.' Nick smiled. 'Because that is *all* I am worried about, as you well know.' He reached out and touched her forehead with his palm, relieved to feel the coolness of her skin, but saying teasingly, 'Whatever it is, I think you'll live, Ms Drama Queen.'

'Am not. Just felt rubbish. I really did.'

'It's fine, I know you did. I'm glad you're a bit better now.' Nick drove faster as the road levelled out, enjoying the emptiness, keeping one eye on his mirrors for cops and one eye on her.

'Dad, can we get a dog, like as a Christmas present to the whole family?'

'An Alsatian, by any chance, like Adrienne's?'

'Bruno is the greatest dog. Ever. But no, it could be any kind of dog. Mum always says we can get one, but then it doesn't happen.'

'That's because Mum knows all the work of looking after it would fall to her.'

'It wouldn't. Nat and I would do it.' She yawned.

'And what about those other four-legged pets you lot keep at your Grandparents – Geeno and Lester and Impi? How would you have time to keep them exercised too?'

'A dog could come for riding at Grandad's – it would be perfect.'

'Except your grandfather doesn't believe in dogs as pets, does he? He just has his for guarding. And I'm not sure how those horses of yours would react either. You know how Impi likes to have you all to himself, doesn't he?'

Sasha smiled, as he had meant her to, temporarily defeated. The subject would be raised again in due course, Nick knew. It was because Donna hadn't said an outright no but kept them dangling with promises. It maddened him.

'Hey, Dad, it's not because of maybe going to England, is it? Because Mum says you want to make us all leave here and that you want to be a teacher instead of a doctor. Is that true?'

Nick reeled. This was low, even for Donna. 'No. Those were just thoughts that crossed my mind one day. Mummy was wrong to tell you about them.'

'Don't you like being a skin doctor?'

'I do like it.' Nick patted her leg, smiling. 'But we've each only got one life and sometimes I think about trying out other things too, things that being a doctor doesn't give me time for.'

'But you play tennis a lot.'

Nick laughed. 'Yes, I do, and I enjoy it very much, especially when you lot are off riding.'

'So what else do you like doing?'

'Books... reading. You know I like that.'

She snorted. 'Yeah, you're always reading.'

Nick couldn't help laughing again at the derision in her voice. 'Yes, mostly boring medical stuff.'

'So what would you *teach*?' For a moment she sounded as scathing as her mother.

Nick knew it was time to stop the direction of the conversation, make her feel safe. 'Nothing. It was just something I mentioned to Mummy one day. She shouldn't have bothered you with it. And when we go to England it will just be to visit Granny.' As Nick spoke, a vivid, unsettling image of the young Kat chose the moment to burst back into his mind; the mad frame of alabaster curls; the scores of faint freckles, invariably concealed under a layer of powder that had tasted like some strange dusty soap; the eyes, blue bottomless pools, drawing him in but then never seeming to take him anywhere, no matter how desperately he had wanted them to. He shuddered, relief coursing through him. The sudden certainty of a bullet dodged.

For a moment the big car seemed to drift out of his control. Nick wound his own window open to clear his head. Sasha had fallen asleep. He glanced at her, finding solace in the fatherly love that flooded his body like warmth. She had shifted into an endearingly gormless pose, her cheek squashed against her pillowed hands, her mouth wide open, showing the very slightly gappy teeth of which he was so fond but which the orthodontist – and Donna – insisted would soon be clamped into brace-tracks.

Nick sped on, keeping a close eye in all his mirrors. He must get home safely. Make sure Sash really was all right. Sleep. Get up. Go to work. Christmas was barely three weeks away. There was a lot to do. There always was. And the secret to a smooth life, as he had been in danger of forgetting, was taking one step at a time, resisting gawping over one's shoulder at what might have been, or straining to see too far ahead. That was when the trip-ups came. It was like playing good tennis, Nick warned himself: the key was to stay balanced, to keep one's eye on the ball instead of the place where one wanted to hit it.

20

Trevor,

I know we had a session booked for next week, but I am afraid I have to cancel it because my sister...

Eleanor slumped back, hurting her spine against the hard, unforgiving angles of the kitchen chair. Overhead, the bunches of dried herbs which Kat, with her usual arty flair, had strung up along the kitchen's handsome beams, stirred in the warm air rising off the Aga. The email to Trevor came in and out of focus on her laptop. Eleanor narrowed her eyes, but still the words wavered. How could one begin to describe the weight of someone's absence anyway? It was an oxymoron. As she had tried to explain to Nick once. A million years ago. Back in the days when he thought he was writing to Kat. Back when Kat was sick, as opposed to dead.

The doctor had put it best. 'She's gone,' he had announced gently, arriving minutes after Howard's summons two nights before, shaking his round grey head as he pressed Kat's thin wrist between his fingers in a bid to find a pulse. Eleanor had watched from the end of the bed, unable even to blink, aware only of being very still. She could still smell Evie's skin on her from their bedtime reading.

The spare-room door had been closed against the possibility of prying children. They would need to be told, obviously, when Howard was ready. The need to be supportive to her brother-in-law had coursed through Eleanor, a hot energy. Kat had once requested that of her and she would do her best to manage it. This unhappy ending was what had been expected, what they were all supposed to have been ready for.

In fact Kat had died moments before the doctor got there. Eleanor had realised but said nothing because Howard, having laid her back on the bed, had been stroking her sister's arms and fingers, crooning endearments and reassurances, hanging on to his hope like a man on a cliff-face. Eleanor had already been at her stance at the end of the bed, gently cradling Kat's feet through the covers. The dying had been almost invisible – no discernible last breath to speak of, no dramatic finale. Kat's face had simply seemed to tighten as a shadow passed across it, infusing a tinge of grey into its delicate pallor. Instants later, the doctor was ushered through the door by a puffy-eyed Hannah, who, with her usual tact, then quickly withdrew.

To Howard, the doctor's words were terrible. As the man lowered Kat's eyelids and stepped back, dropping his head in respect, closing his leather bag, Howard threw himself onto the body with a force that made Eleanor flinch. Alive, her sister would have squirmed with pain to be held so hard. Unbreathing, her wasted frame looked even smaller, frailer. Only the extraordinary hair, which she had been so anxious to preserve, looked cruelly alive; big bright curls burning across the pillow. Howard rolled his face in them, sobbing.

Eleanor remained where she was, keeping her distance like the doctor, biding her time, giving Howard his moment. Inside, it began to feel as if something was exploding, slowly. The bedroom floorboards were shifting under the carpet, dissolving it felt like, until she was standing on nothing.

The steady noise of the kitchen clock snagged on Eleanor's brain. She shivered as the half-written email to Trevor came back into focus. The ticking of time was good, she told herself. It was a reminder that bad moments would pass, just like the good ones. Under her jumper, she was aware of the buckle of Kat's belt pressing into her stomach. It was on the tightest notch now, her new slimness heightened by two days of consuming nothing but sweet tea. Hannah's pie had never been eaten. Its blackened remains were in the kitchen bin, chiselled off by her at some unspeakable dawn hour, while Howard, at his own request, had been left alone upstairs with the children. Over the noise of her scraping knife, she had heard the occasional wail or sob, but mostly it had been very quiet.

My sister, who as you are aware, has been ill for many months... Eleanor typed from her slumped position in the kitchen chair, ... *passed away the day before yesterday. I know you will therefore forgive me for not being able to make our meeting on Monday. I will, however, definitely be able to manage a session before Christmas. In fact, let us say in two weeks' time, 18 December at eleven. I'll come to yours as usual. Life, as they say, goes on.*

Eleanor signed off and sent the email on its way. She had plucked a date at random. She didn't care when she saw Trevor. She didn't care about anything. The emptiness of the spare bedroom was still within her, a coldness. She had ventured in that morning to strip the bed, catching her breath at the smell that had come to mean Kat: a mix of the faint odours emanating from the cluster of medicines still on the bedside cabinet and the richer aroma of Howard's most recent flowers. She had grabbed at the bedding, the sheets and countless pillows that had done so little in the end to provide comfort, wrenching off their covers in what felt like a war, with herself, with Kat, with life's refusal to be easy.

There had been no grand deathbed reconciliations, but there had at least been some new understanding; a sense of forgiveness, if not the thing itself. And for that she should be grateful, Eleanor had told herself, stumbling through the twisted bed linen to fall against the window. The wintry browns of the garden, tipped still with morning frost, blurred under her eyes. The completeness of her sense of loss was so vast, so overbearing, that for several moments she could not breathe. It bore no relation to what she or Kat might or might not have meant to each other. Her little sister was gone, taking what felt like the past, the present and the future with her. Forever.

'I suppose he needs to be told. It's only right.' It was Howard, speaking from the kitchen doorway.

He looked like a man who had been hollowed out, fragile to the point of translucency. For all Eleanor's efforts at support, she found that she hardly dared speak to him sometimes, for fear that even her voice might have the power, literally, to shatter him to dust.

Hannah had taken the children back into school that morning. Sticking to their routines would help, someone had said. Eleanor couldn't quite remember who. Possibly the doctor, possibly a family friend, possibly Hannah herself. The house had steadily filled and emptied each day of helpful people – local friends, other parents, the priest, undertakers.

'You mean Dad.' Eleanor slipped her hand under her jumper and clasped the buckle of the belt. The metal felt comfortingly warm from the heat of her body.

'Vincent, yes. Not that it will mean anything to him.'

'No, but of course you are right. I feel bad not to have done it already. I'll go today.'

'Kat got him into that place.'

'I know.'

'She thought it was where he would most like to be.'

'Yes, she did well.'

'She hated seeing him, you know, but she went once a week.'

'Yes, Kat was good like that. Much better than me. She said Dad didn't care about her, but he did.' Eleanor stood up, her chair legs shrieking against the limestone floor. 'I'll go now.' She unhooked the keys to Kat's car that hung on a board next to the fridge. She had been using it for months, for convenience on her visits.

'It won't mean anything to him, of course,' Howard repeated heavily. His task that morning was to go to the undertakers with clothes. He had asked Eleanor to help him choose them and then begged her to leave. Even now, she didn't know what he had selected. An image of gold knee-high boots fluttered across her mind.

'I read once somewhere that grief is like fear,' she gabbled, twirling the car key, 'like being afraid. I think it was C. S. Lewis. I am pretty sure that is what I am feeling. Afraid. Are you?'

Howard's eyes met hers with an expression of puzzlement and hurt. 'I've no idea. All I know is Kat shouldn't have died. She was thirty-five. It's not right, not for me, not for the children, not for her.'

'No.' Eleanor glanced away, trying to think of something more helpful to say, but by the time she looked back he had gone.

* * *

Eleanor took the longer route to The Bressingham, through Broughton, which meant driving for the first time in many years past the turning to the vicarage and the dead-end lane that led to St Winifred's, a quarter of a mile beyond. She slowed, marvelling at the smart brass-tipped wrought-iron gates marking the entrance to a residence now described, in big brass letters on a marble plaque, as 'The Paddock'. Behind it, the winding muddy drive that had defeated family cars and left a crusty brown fringe on Vincent's priestly robes had been transformed into a crisply gravelled lane, bordered by a formidably thick feathery hedge that served to keep the silver lake of birches from view, as well as much of the sky.

It wasn't possible to see the vicarage itself from the road and

Eleanor was glad. She didn't need to see the place to know how it would look: extended, repointed, rewired, snugly fitted with pipes that didn't clank and neatly overlapping roof tiles that gleamed when the sun shone. No gaps in the guttering like a gaping mouth of bad teeth. No knotted old vegetable patches. No rusting hinges. No patches of green slime.

Eleanor accelerated and then, having almost changed her mind, swung a little sharply into the church lane. These days, the sturdy wooden doors of St Winifred's were permanently closed, the parish Vincent once served having been streamlined to offer larger, more accessible buildings for worship. It was a development that Vincent himself had taken personally, never settling into the new role of roving priest to which he had been assigned. The dementia had set in on the back of these changes, with lightning rapidity. Self-absorbed with her own life at the time, in the thick of things with Igor, Eleanor had been shamelessly happy to let Kat take charge of the situation. As Howard had grimly reminded her that morning, Kat had risen to the challenge with her customary brilliance, getting Vincent into a place he had not only served and loved but which was also a mere thirty minutes from her own doorstep.

Eleanor pulled up onto the grassy verge and turned the engine off. The church's stocky square tower and grey mottled walls looked squat and stoical beneath the two, now giant, beech trees guarding its main door. Their upper branches, entangled over the years, resembled arm-clasping old friends. Eleanor rubbed a porthole in the steam on her window, trying to picture her father as he had once been, shaking parishioners' hands, his beard bushy, his sandals and thick socks poking out from under his skirts. Instead, marching into her mind like a parade of ghosts, came other presences from her childhood: the sharp twitchy face of Hilda de Mowbray, tracking her and Kat like a greedy hawk; old Mrs Owens, wheezing reprimands and warnings with the gruffness of one resigned to being ignored; and the Watsons, the old man's face sun-wrinkled and half hidden under his tatty tweed cap, and dear Charlie half a step behind, in mud-caked wellies and terrible mustard cords. Eleanor blinked tears as she peered up at the sky, all the sadness about Kat merging with the weirdness of the past, how it could feel at once so unreachable and so close.

It took immense resolve to get out of the car. She wasn't even sure why she had come. Death was death, Eleanor had no illusions on that score. She had never believed Connie to be more in a churchyard than she was anywhere else. And Kat was right, when it came down to it, she had been a crap mother.

After the fug of the car heating, the early December cold was like a slap in the face. Eleanor tunnelled her hands into her coat pockets and trudged up the path, past the church and across the lumpy grass, down to the lower strip of ground that housed Connie's grave.

Nearly three decades on and the small headstone had weathered to bare legibility. Eleanor stared at it, making an effort to summon fresh thoughts for once – fresh sadness – but all that came to mind was the usual tired, shrunken stock of memories: a smile framed by red lipstick, a yellow coat, a pale-face, alert and erect behind a car wheel, or tired and stretched out under a blanket on a sofa. Everything else – everything that mattered, Eleanor realised suddenly – such as how Connie had sounded, or spoken, or felt to hold – was lost.

She would not let memories of her sister fade in the same way, Eleanor vowed bleakly. She patted at the soft brown earth of a molehill with the undersole of her shoe, thinking fondly of the hours she and Kat had endured as little girls on their knees in that very spot, peeking out of closed eyes to pull faces at each other as Vincent intoned prayer after prayer, keeping them there on purpose, it felt like, testing them.

Eleanor let her gaze drift to the field. There had once been talk of a housing development, but it had clearly never happened. Today the sole occupant was a brown horse, a rough blanket on its back, nosing disconsolately at the thin, half-frozen grass.

Spotting Eleanor, it pricked its ears up and trotted to the boundary fence, snorting frills of steam from its nostrils.

'Hello horse.' Eleanor approached warily. Horses put her on edge. They were so huge, so beautiful and with eyes that suggested a knowledge of suffering.

It tossed its head.

Eleanor forced her cold hands out of her pockets and bent down to pluck a few tufts of grass to feed it. As she did so, her attention was caught by something metallic, half buried in the earth. She dug it out with the tip of her shoe, aware of the horse waiting and watching. It was a small pewter tub. A gleam of black and yellow blazed in her mind: sweet williams on a hot summer day. Now it was packed with twigs and mud. Eleanor let it lie and offered a good pile of grass across the top of the fence for the horse. She kept her palm flat as the animal chomped, enjoying the tickle of its big, velvety mouth and the way its moist breath warmed her hand. She blew softly at it through her lips, causing it to stop chewing for a moment, looking surprised.

'My Mum is buried here,' she told it. 'And now Kat has died. And I've got to break the news to my dad, who never liked me much and won't understand anyway. But still.'

But the horse had lost interest. As she spoke, it ambled back into the field.

The sun chose the moment to burn through the shield of cloud. The pewter pot caught in the light, a blinding flash. Eleanor picked it up and shook it with sudden desperation, a futile hope that a clue might fall at her feet. She wanted things to add up, that was the trouble. She wanted the world to make sense. Instead, for as long as she could remember, her existence had felt as if she was lurching round in the dark, groping for doors that weren't there, backing into corners she couldn't see. All that fell from the pot was earth and stones. Eleanor flung it away and strode back to the car. As she was about to start the engine, her phone rang.

'Where are you?'

'Howard? I stopped... Never mind. I'm on my way to see Dad, remember? Are you okay?' He didn't sound okay.

'Yes... no. Evie needs picking up. I've had a call from her school. There's been some sort of incident. I can't get hold of Hannah.'

'I'll go.'

'I knew we shouldn't have sent them in. I knew it was too early. Fuck it. Fuck.'

'Don't worry. I can be there in ten. Twenty at the most.' Eleanor pictured him at the undertakers, gripping the bag containing her sister's burial clothes. She hoped suddenly that he had remembered shoes. Not the gold boots, but perhaps a pair of the soft leather flats or, better still, the red Converse trainers. Kat had always loved those.

* * *

Her youngest niece had locked herself in the end cubicle of a row of toilets housed in the oldest part of her school, a once private stately home set among several acres of garden. Crouching down to peer under the door, Eleanor could just make out the scuffed pink ballet pumps – chosen in spite of Hannah's gentle admonitions that morning – dangling well above the chessboard tiled floor.

'Evie, it's Eleanor, can you unlock the door? I've come to take you home. Daddy and Hannah couldn't come right this minute, but they'll be home soon too. And Luke and Sophie.'

'She said she wouldn't come out and now she won't talk,' the headmistress had explained, wringing her hands. 'The Year Threes only come into this block for Friday Assembly. She must have slipped in during morning break. When her class teacher reported her missing, it took a while to find her. Such a relief, mind you.' The head threw a pained glance at Eleanor. She wore a plain black polo-neck jumper that heightened the severe pallor of her skin and the plain strong features of her face. It was a face that looked proud of its hard work, Eleanor had decided, where kindness seemed to fight with determination. 'Removing the door is the only other obvious answer,' the Head went on, 'because the gaps top and bottom are so small. As I say, this block is not supposed to be for our young ones. It's long overdue for refurbishment,' she had added bitterly. 'Our handyman took some while to contact but is on his way. Perhaps now you are here he won't be necessary.'

'Evie, did you hear me?' Eleanor tried again, her first effort having met with no reply. When the silence continued, she lay flat on her stomach so as to be able to press her mouth right up against the narrow gap under the door. 'Evie, dearest, please undo the lock if you can. If you can't, don't worry. Just tell us, so we can take the door off instead. The main thing is that we all want the best for you. I bet you just want to go home, don't you? I certainly do.'

The ballet shoes swung slightly. Eleanor could feel her heart leaping against the cold floor.

'Or we needn't go home, not straightaway. Not if you didn't want to. We could go somewhere in the car instead. Are you hungry? We could buy something extra nice to eat... like choco-late biscuits, or ice cream, or sweets... any sweets.'

Behind her Eleanor was aware of someone arriving along-side the head, the clanking of a ladders and tools.

'Just tell me what you want, Evie...'

'Mummy,' came the sudden screech, echoing round the stone floor and walls. 'I want MUMMY.'

Eleanor remained very still, half her face squeezed tight into the crack between the door and floor. 'I know,' she said softly. 'I want her too.'

There was a long pause. Then Evie's voice echoed out again, much more quietly, 'Is she in heaven?'

'Yes, she is.'

'And so when I go to heaven I will see her again?'

'Yes, you will.' Eleanor was acutely aware of her own childhood loss flickering in her mind: Kat seeking comfort and reassurances that their father, for all his godliness, had never been able to give. 'But Mummy wants you to do a million things with your life first,' she pressed on hoarsely, pushing the images away. 'She is watching you right now and if she sees you are unhappy that will make her unhappy too. All she wants is for you to unlock the door so I can take you home.'

Eleanor watched, holding her breath as the scuffed suede soles of the small shoes were slowly lowered to the ground, just a couple of feet from her face. A moment later, when she was still clambering to her knees, there was the grinding of a metal lock and the toilet door flew open, giving her niece little option but to step into her arms in a way that felt almost natural. Eleanor had never embraced the child so thoroughly before. She felt sinewy and fragile, like a sapling. 'That was very brave indeed,' she whispered. 'To come out when you didn't want to.'

'Oh yes, well done,' trilled the head, dancing round them, dots of colour in her pale face, gesturing at the man and his ladder to be gone. 'Clever girl. And lovely Aunty Eleanor for coming to get you.'

Eleanor got them away as quickly as she could. In the car park, she tried to take Evie's hand but was shaken off. Instead, her niece maintained a distance of several feet as they crossed the forecourt. When they reached the car, Evie set about delivering several kicks to each wheel with her soft pink shoes, saying in a small angry voice, 'This is Mummy's car, not yours.'

'Yes it is,' Eleanor admitted sadly, holding the passenger door open till she had finished, glad of the chance to wipe away her own tears.

'I'm not saying go crazy, I'm saying maybe buy a few bottles. Je-sus.' Donna rolled her eyes round the table in a manner suggesting an amusement that belied the hostility of her tone. 'I love my husband's *English* thriftiness, but really... there are times.' Having elicited sympathetic grins from both Lindy and Mike Scammell, as well as her mother (her father had taken himself off to the wine shop), she shook her head at Nick in mock despair. 'We are here partly to support a family friend, remember? A friend who has given us the most incredible lunch, not to mention—'

'You are right, darling.' Nick stood up abruptly, cutting her off. 'I shall follow your father to the wine shop forthwith.' He waved his wallet, smiling and nodding in a bid to mask the deep irritation that had prompted the climbdown. Most over-whelming had been the appeal of a pretext for leaving the lunch table. Shelling out a few more thousand rand for twenty minutes' peace – yes, that seemed cheap at the price.

Family friend? It had been all he could manage not to snort out loud. Dean Cobalt, the vineyard owner, was simply an acquaintance of Donna's father, mentioned for the first time at their barbecue the weekend before. They had met the man –

and then only briefly – on arrival. As far as Nick could see, the entire lunch wine-tasting project, pushed through by Jim Cruick in his usual bulldozer fashion, was simply an excuse for two rich old men to show off to each other.

After a hectic week that had included packed clinics and Sasha's party sickness evolving into a diagnosis of mild glandular fever, Nick had found it impossible not to wake that morning without resentment in his heart at having to give up virtually an entire Saturday to so unworthy a cause.

The vineyard's wines, a selection of which had been served with the three-course lunch, were indisputably good, but in Nick's view far too pricey for everyday drinking. His father-in-law's decision to set off to the shop to purchase several cases had been announced with typical fanfare, only making Nick even less keen to succumb to the pressure to follow suit. At the time, he had still been reeling from the exorbitant cost of the meal itself – all the more painful for the apparent misapprehension that they were there as Jim's guests. That had been Nick's firm understanding, and yet when the bill arrived, his father-in-law had cast a quick look at the total and suggested they cut it down the middle, treating the Scammells between them. Rich men were so often mean-spirited, Nick mused, striding away from the table and then slowing in a bid to savour his few minutes of freedom.

From a distance, the dining area – a stone terrace set under a billowing awning of white silk – looked ready for a wedding party. Each of its four corner-posts teemed with purple and scarlet bougainvillea. Spread around them was a spectacular panorama of the wine valley, basking that day in sunshine that made the rows of vines planted along its undulations look as soft as goose down.

Nick sighed as he moved on, aware of observing the extraordinary beauty of the location without the wherewithal to be moved by it. The sense of detachment made his heart heavy. Once upon a time, the stunning topography of southern Africa had touched his soul. Once upon a time, he had believed Donna's claim that trading London for Cape Town would solve all their problems. Once upon a time, he had lived with hope in his heart.

From deep in his memory, a quotation surfaced, from the redoubtable Dr Johnson, one of those engraved by an English teacher he had revered before science had come to dominate his studies: '*He who has so little knowledge of human nature as to seek happiness by changing anything but his own dispositions, will waste his life in fruitless efforts and multiply the griefs which he purposes to remove...*'

Nick grimaced, nostalgia as well as self-recrimination flooding his heart. Moving to South Africa had achieved nothing except to intensify the spotlight on his and Donna's dysfunction. He was dumber now than he had been as a teenager. It was a dispiriting notion.

Dr Johnson. The marble bust of the famous lexicographer that had sat at the entrance to his college library floated into his mind, bringing with it a sudden vivid memory of Eleanor Keating on the day he had first come across her – such a towering, shy, powerhouse of a girl.

Nick chuckled to himself, remembering how endearingly flummoxed she had been at his suggestion of lunch. A moment later, however, despair flooded in, not over Eleanor Keating, but for all that he had once been and all that he had since become. A wind-blown tree arched across the path and he leant against it, pretending to drink in the view. Unhappiness was in danger of warping him. He had to stay on his guard. Live in the real world instead of inside his head.

* * *

In the roomy warehouse of the vineyard shop, Jim was leaning on the counter by the till, informing the young girl manning it that a palate for wine was something that could be learned, like all things.

'Take Nicholas here, he said,' swinging out an arm as Nick approached. 'This man is a skilled doctor – a dermatologist who understands human skin like no other – and yet he refuses to learn how to ride a horse. I have tried to persuade him, but he won't budge. He says it's too late to learn, but it's not.' Jim smacked the counter with his palm, barking his sharp confident laugh. 'We shall see who wins, shan't we?' The azure eyes glinted, telling Nick, as they always did, that far more was being discussed than the subject in hand. 'I'll leave you in the capable hands of this young lady then, Nick. I am going to take a natural break, then find Dean for a word.' He winked at the girl and wandered off in the direction of the Gents.

Nick chose four bottles from the selection served with their meal and paid with his credit card. The girl at the till had very bad skin, he noticed, which she had smothered inexpertly in make-up that would only exacerbate the condition. Nick smiled kindly at her. A better diet, a course of antibiotics would work wonders. It occurred to him suddenly that Jim had made reference to his dermatological specialty without any thought for the possibility of causing embarrassment to the girl. But then his father-in-law never factored in other people's feelings. He was a bully. Like his daughter.

The truth of this hit Nick as if for the first time. He was married to a woman who used physical assault as part of a formidable arsenal which she liked nonetheless to describe, when challenged, as a protest connected to love and trust. What sort of love and trust could ever allow for violence?

'Sir, your card?'

He had left it in the machine. Nick hurried back to retrieve it. 'Thanks. I'll pick the wine up when we leave, if that's okay. Won't do it any good to sit in a hot car.'

Outside, the mid-afternoon sun was already dropping, taking

some of its intensity with it. A skittish breeze bowled up the path, stirring flurries of dust and flower petals. Nick walked briskly back towards the restaurant terrace, but then, spotting Lindy and his mother-in-law sitting alone at the table, veered off past a sign that said 'Deliveries only'. He found himself following a path that ran behind the kitchens, past bins and a skip of masonry, and ending at a loosely slatted wooden door set into a high stoned wall. Nick peered through the slats, making out what was clearly some kind of kitchen garden. Closest to him was a large ground box of what looked like herbs: lavender and sage were the only ones he recognised. He widened the slats to get a better look, more to delay going back to the lunch table than because he was genuinely curious. The view broadened to include a sprinkler trained on a bed of low green bushes. Rainbows flashed through its wet haze. Two people were walking behind it. Donna and Mike. His wife and Mike Scammell. Nick blinked. There was nothing untoward. They were side by side, a foot apart at least, pointing out plants as they went. Mike bent nearer to say something and Donna laughed her soft easy laugh.

Nick could feel the hairs on the back of his neck standing up. Donna and Mike were just walking and talking, yet there was an air of familiarity between them that he had either never noticed before or not been in a position to acknowledge. Intimacy. Yes, that was it. They were two people who *knew* each other. As he watched, Donna stopped suddenly and turned to Mike, offering her face up towards his. Nick braced himself. But it appeared his wife had something in her eye. Nick watched, transfixed, as their burly neighbour cupped Donna's left cheekbone with one hand and tugged gently at the offending eyelid with the other, peering and frowning and shaking his head. When he released his hold, it seemed to be with an air of reluctance. Nick squinted, wondering if he was imagining things.

It was time to go. Donna and Mike were clearly leaving too, having made their way to a crumbling section of wall that Nick hadn't at first noticed, right on the periphery of his frame of vision. He was on the point of turning away when they kissed. A snatched brushing of mouths. An instant later, they were both ducking to get through the hole. Donna went first. Mike followed, placing a light, proprietorial hand over the curve of her right buttock. Then there was just the piece of broken wall and the heavy afternoon air, and a flash of blue from a swooping dragonfly.

* * *

'Mike and I found where they grow the veg,' Donna reported, once they were all seated back round the lunch table, draining the dregs of lukewarm coffee and picking at a saucer of melting mint chocolates. 'It's like this secret garden. We felt like trespassers, kept expecting to be shouted at or have a guard dog set on us.'

'Oh, I wish you'd told us,' cried Lindy. There was a pile of menthol cigarette stubs in the small clay ashtray next to her saucer, their white cork tips smudged with pink lipstick. 'Lauren and I thought you were just going to the toilets.'

'We were, but then we took a wrong turn and decided to have a bit of an explore. Didn't we, Mike?'

There was a beat of a pause before Mike agreed that they had indeed taken a wrong turn, before quickly reassuring his wife that it hadn't been that big a deal. 'It's kind of run-down, to be honest, like seeing behind the scenes at a theatre.'

'Hey, good analogy, Mike,' Nick blurted, clumsy in his desire to appear normal. He felt numb more than anything. It would wear off. And he must be prepared for that, he told himself. It was like the shock of any injury – the first rush of natural anaesthesia before the pain kicked in. It was one thing not to love one's wife. It was quite another to realise one had been made a complete fool of. For years, Nick guessed. Years. Not only bullied but blind. Deflected always by Donna's jealousy. It was worthy of fiction. But this was far, far worse because it was real life. His life.

He stared across the table at Donna with something like

wonderment. She had her hand on Lindy's and was reeling off ingredients for a recipe, ignoring her mother as usual. Mint ice cream, using fresh herbs, she instructed, pronouncing it *erb* in that affected faux American accent she liked to use sometimes, a reminder to all that, courtesy of her father's deep pocket, she had once spent a year studying in New York. Or, rather, a term, because she hadn't liked the course. She had landed in London soon after, another chapter in her life sponsored by Jim and his connections. The silver bangles on her slim, tanned arms tinkled. One of them, the biggest, was engraved with the words: *Darling Donna, with all my love, Nick.* It had a circle of tiny diamonds set round its middle. He had given it to her a couple of Christmases before, telling himself the cost was worth the look of pleasure on her face, the affectionate gratitude it would ensure came his way, for a week or so at least.

Nick stole a glance at Lindy's face, thinking how bound they in fact were and how little she knew it. Lindy was looking flushed and tired and his heart went out to her; but then it had been a long meal and they were all running out of steam.

22

2013- SUSSEX

As the funeral started, it began to snow. The shadowy flurries dancing behind the stained-glass windows lent an impression of movement to the bright gowned figures they depicted, as if they were frames on a reel of film. The Bible was just stories after all, Eleanor reflected bleakly.

The pews of Fairfield's airy church were packed with people whom she did not know. Processing in behind Howard and the children, Vincent being wheeled beside her by a burly assistant from the care home, she had avoided eye contact with anything except the rich black of Howard's spruce, tailored city coat, trying to erase from her mind the argument they had had that morning. The subject, ridiculously, had been her father, whom she had suggested they collect from The Bressingham themselves, rather than having him fetched and delivered like a parcel.

'I think I've got enough on my plate today as it is.'

'I know, but if I am happy to do it...'

'Stop interfering. The arrangements are all in place.'

It was very early in the morning. The children were still asleep and the pair of them were in the cellar, rooting out the wines Howard wanted to serve at the wake. He was picking out bottles from the various wine racks lined up along the wall and handing them to Eleanor to put into boxes for carrying upstairs.

'How can I be interfering,' Eleanor ventured in a small, tight voice, 'when we are discussing Kat and my father?'

Howard examined a label and rammed a bottle back into its slot. 'Never mind.'

'I do mind.'

'To be honest, I don't even see why he needs to be there. You went over and did the business of telling him. For which you know I was grateful.'

'You cannot mean what you are saying,' Eleanor interjected fiercely. Seeing through the task of visiting her father, the depressing certainty that her terrible news fell on deaf ears, had added another dimension to the already extreme distress of the week. 'You just can't.'

'I do. It will be a hassle for us and be of no significance to him.' Howard plucked out two more bottles and dropped them noisily into a fresh box.

'A hassle?' Eleanor laughed incredulously. 'A hassle? Well, *hassle* or not, it is only right that Dad should be there. Kat would have thought so too,' she added, close to tears, partly because of the turn the conversation had taken and partly because in her new sister-less state, eruptions of sadness were only ever a pinprick away from the surface. 'And surely that's all that matters.'

In one swift movement, Howard had swung round from the wine racks and raised a warning finger at her, his eyes bright with emotion and hostility. 'Do not,' he hissed, '*ever* presume to tell me what my wife would or would not have wanted. Is that clear?'

Eleanor had turned and fled up the cellar steps, too distraught, too fragile herself to manage any further defence. He had found her in the kitchen a few minutes later and apologised, mumbling about being stressed out, saying he would prefer to keep the Vincent arrangements as they were, if she didn't mind, and Eleanor had agreed.

Eleanor glanced down at her father now. The carer had parked the wheelchair at an angle beside her in the aisle before tactfully withdrawing to the back of the church. Her father's poor big head with its pitiful gauze of snowy hair flopped onto his chest, directing his blank-eyed gaze permanently somewhere in the region of his knees. Eleanor reached out and laid a comforting hand on the back of his neck, wondering if pity could turn to love, hoping with all her heart that it could. For all the distance between them, he was all she had left.

At the other end of the pew, Howard was staring resolutely at Kat's coffin, parked on trestles in front of the altar. On top was a single heart-shaped wreath of scarlet roses and a large framed photo of the entire family, Kat radiant at its centre.

Between her and Howard, the children were seated like Russian dolls, in ascending order of height, Evie at her side and Luke next to his father, Sophie in the middle. Since the rescue from the school toilets, there had been a faint sense of a bond between Eleanor and her youngest niece, an invisible guy-rope. Nothing had been said, but Eleanor had been aware of the child hovering nearby from time to time, as if she wished at least to be noticed if not addressed. Since sliding into the pew next to Eleanor for the service, Evie had been swinging her short legs rhythmically, looking straight ahead. When the vicar embarked on his introductions, about the gathering being an act of celebration rather than mourning, she rolled the service booklet into a cylinder and began alternately sucking one end of it and raising the other to her eyes like a telescope. While the rest of the congregation struggled through the first hymn, she continued to look through it, training her gaze round the church, making no attempt to sing herself.

After the hymn, it was time for the tributes. With Howard's encouragement each of the children had prepared a brief list of what they had most treasured about their mother. As they filed out and took their places in front of the coffin, he buckled visibly, crossing his arms and gripping his ribcage. From the congregation there arose a soft collective intake of breath followed by a tender, expectant silence, a cushion of support it felt like, as if to catch all three of them, should they fall. Luke's paper shook, his thin face twitching as he read out brief, gruff descriptions of Kat's sense of humour and inability to understand the rules of cricket. There was an eloquence to some of the phrases that suggested a painfully adult attempt to process the occasion. It made Eleanor want to put her fingers in her ears. Sophie was more natural, reading too fast about having all her party dresses made for her and the special French plait into which Kat had often tied her hair.

'Hannah does it now,' she muttered by way of a conclusion, self-consciously tweaking the thick braid, and nudging her little sister to take her turn.

Evie spoke in the clear ringing voice of a creature who hasn't begun processing anything. 'Mummy made nice cakes,' she said. 'And I liked it when Mummy hugged me.' There were stifled groans from her audience. Collective pain. Evie stared back at them, her green eyes wide and inscrutable. She lowered her piece of paper. 'She couldn't find my rabbit Choccy and we think it died.'

Both her siblings looked startled. Sophie nudged her again, this time to indicate a move back to the pew. Howard was pressing his face into his hands.

'And now Mummy might see Choccy again,' Evie continued, 'but I am not sure because after this we are going to burn Mummy's body and we didn't burn Choccy's. Mummy said she wanted to be burnt because it will turn her into a cloud. And clouds are part of heaven. But I think God is mean,' she concluded stoutly, 'to take Mummy when we still need her.'

The silence in the church had stretched tight and thin, as delicate as blown glass. Even Vincent seemed to tremble in his chair. Only Evie appeared oblivious. She led her siblings in the return to the front pew, stomping in her smart patent leather shoes and dodging Howard's outstretched arms. She did not look at Eleanor as she sat down but resumed her leg-swinging, more frantically. Eleanor edged closer, so her arm was pressed against her niece's, aiming to offer comfort but also needing to feel the heat of the small angry body against hers.

Outside afterwards, it was snowing lightly, the flakes too wet to settle. The Bressingham nurse was waiting with the back of his van open and the ramp down, ready for the journey to the crematorium. Eleanor kissed the top of Vincent's head as she handed him over. Twenty-four hours, she told herself. Twenty-four hours and she would be back in London and it would all be done with.

'I am going to get drunk,' Howard announced later that night, emerging from the cellar as Eleanor stepped from the kitchen into the hall. The food caterers were long gone, the house tidy as a shop. Kat's ashes had been scattered, all of them taking a turn, under the tree by the swing. The children had been mute by then, drained, like the rest of them. All three had fallen asleep in front of the telly in the den, and Howard had carried each to their beds in turn, even Luke, who was as long and unwieldy as a plank. Howard held up the bottle he was carrying to show Eleanor. It looked old and special, covered in dust, its label half torn. His hands and fingers were visibly dirty. His once crisp white funeral shirt was open and askew, hanging forlornly out of his smart black trousers. 'I am going to drink this. Then some whisky. A lot of whisky. And I would prefer to do it on my own. If you don't mind.'

Eleanor shrugged, nodding. Her head was throbbing. She couldn't wait to be on her own, to close her eyes, even though she knew she wouldn't sleep.

'But thank you, Eleanor.' He dipped his head in a brief

formal bow. 'All these months. All you have done. Thank you. Kat and I asked you to be here and you came. That was good of you. Setting aside your work. Dealing with her. Dealing with me. None of it can have been easy. I want you to know I am grateful.' His voice was clipped and polite. 'I have ordered you a taxi at nine-thirty on my account for your morning train. Hannah's coming at eight. I shall be up too of course. Say a proper farewell.' He hesitated, frowning. 'That was one thing with Kat, at least. We had time. To say our goodbyes. Not that it makes a fucking difference now.' He spun on his heel and trudged towards his study, cradling the bottle to his chest like a newborn.

Eleanor went upstairs and lay on her bed. The snow had resumed, blowing with soft thuds against the windowpane. Somehow she dozed, dreaming of trains, screeches and whistles, but then suddenly she was wide awake and desolate. She listened for Howard, but all downstairs was quiet. She hadn't drawn the curtains and could see that the snow had stopped again. The sky was black, blacker than she had ever seen it. And starless. She needed tea. Whisky. Something.

In the kitchen, the heat coming off the Aga was comforting, like sliding under a warm bath. Eleanor moved slowly, filling the kettle, setting it to hiss on a back ring, picking a mug off one of the hooks along the dresser. She was unscrewing the tea caddy when Howard appeared in the doorway, maintaining his balance with the visible effort of the seriously inebriated.

'Tea?'

'Nope.' He swayed and then steadied himself.

'I couldn't sleep.' Eleanor picked out a teabag and screwed the lid back on the caddy. She felt nothing but compassion for Howard. She would have drunk herself stupid too, if she had thought it would help.

'He touched her, you know.'

Eleanor paused, holding the caddy. 'Who touched who?'

'Your father. Touched your sister. Nothing too mind-bending. Just enough to fuck her up.'

'Howard, you are very drunk.' Eleanor spoke evenly, continuing with the business of putting the caddy back on its shelf but finding that it seemed imperative suddenly to set the tin in exact equidistance from its counterparts bearing the labels 'Coffee' and 'Sugar'.

'She made me swear never to tell you.'

'I think you should get yourself to bed.' Eleanor kept her back to him, the row of tins blurring before her eyes. Her heart had started fluttering oddly against her ribcage, like a trapped bird. 'It's been a long day—'

'She made me swear never to tell you and now I've told you.'

Eleanor hoped that if she didn't speak, the conversation might end; that if she waited long enough, she would turn around to find that Howard had gone; that maybe she had even imagined him ever being there. But when she turned round, Howard was still hunched in the doorway, watching her from under the hoods of his eyes.

'She would have told me such a thing.' Eleanor spoke stoutly. The kettle whistled and she took it off the heat, splashing water as she filled her mug. 'She wouldn't have told you and not me.'

Howard straightened himself, swaying. 'She was afraid what you would think. She was always afraid of what you would think.'

'I would have known.' Eleanor shook her head, denying his words, though it felt curiously like a denial of her own. Inside, a terrible logic was forming. An obviousness. Like something that had always existed but never been acknowledged.

Howard lurched for the back of a kitchen chair and held on to it, positioning his legs wide for extra balance. 'She said I had to know everything about her before we married,' he went on in a tremulous voice. 'She said, that's what love was, knowing someone and allowing yourself to be known in return.' The alcohol was still working on him, felling him. Gaps were starting to appear in the wrong places between his words, like he had forgotten how to speak.

'When?' Eleanor leant against the Aga, folding her arms.

'It was just a few times, she said, in her teens,' Howard mumbled wretchedly; 'from when she was fourteen, I think. After she told me I wasn't allowed to ask again. It was never full sex, she was clear about that. Just....' he groaned softly, '...touching. She said she thought it was because he was deeply lonely. She said she had forgiven him. That I made her happy.' He dropped his face into his hands. 'I swore not to tell and now I have.'

'And now you have.' Eleanor felt no compassion for him now. She was too lost in her own shock. Everything was making dreadful sense, but a hopeless, retrospective guilt was swamping her too. She had thought she was wiser, cleverer, and yet she had been blind. 'Tell me what you know,' she instructed in a brittle voice. 'Everything. Now.'

'But I have—'

'Now.' She banged the kitchen table, making Howard jump and stagger and cling hopelessly to his chair. Eleanor carried on clutching herself, waiting for him to go on, seeing only Kat's electric blue eyes glaring at their father, challenging him, taunting him, picking at him like a wound.

23

Nick could feel his skin tightening under the early-afternoon sun. Given the number of melanomas he saw, his own relative lack of caution was inexcusable. Donna thought so too and was keen on reminding him of the fact. She used a cabinet's worth of creams on her own skin, whether lying in the sun or not, different ones for different parts of her body, some promising rejuvenating benefits that Nick did his best not to remark on, since he knew the remarks would not be well received.

A week had passed since the wine-tasting lunch in Durbanville. It was the Saturday before Christmas and they were at a cove the Scammells had mentioned with affection several times, summoned there by a last-minute plea to help Mike celebrate his thirty-eighth birthday. The girls had been dispatched to the Waterfront Mall under the watchful eye of their neighbours' Dutch au pair, with money for Christmas shopping and pizzas afterwards. The cove was on the Atlantic side of the cape, formed by two vast arms of rock reaching out from a stretch of coast too wild and too far north of Table Bay to be frequented by tourists. They could not have picked a better day; the sea was choppy thanks to a brisk breeze but glassy blue under the beam of a cloudless sky. The lines of breakers rolling onto the beach were only waist-high, regular and foam-topped, perfect for bodysurfing. After the swim, they were heading back towards town for an early dinner at Mike's favourite restaurant, a seafood shack hidden among the docks beyond Milnerton.

Both the Scammells were already in the sea. Donna had settled herself in the lee of her windbreaker with her iPhone, her expression unreadable behind her big black winged sunglasses. She was wearing a new white sun hat with a long pink sash that streamed in the breeze like bunting.

Nick sat up and looked towards the water where their neighbours were signalling for them to join them. 'You coming in?'

Donna kept her gaze on her phone screen. 'You go. I'm barely warm enough as it is.'

Nick let his gaze remain on his wife for several moments. Somehow, the conversation wasn't about warmth or swimming. It struck him with sudden force that very few of their conversations were ever really about what they seemed; the real dialogue was always unspoken, a subtext. Donna not swimming was unusual. She was excellent and hardy in the water, the legacy of a childhood spent beside pools and beaches, and more than up to bodysurfing on a hot breezy afternoon. And it would give her the chance to be near Mike.

Nick turned his gaze to the water edge, where their neighbour was now clowning around, putting his solid square body through collapsing handstands and cartwheels while the hapless Lindy clapped like a seal.

'Okay.' Nick got off his towel and stretched until his back clicked. He waved at Mike, wondering if it was the show the man was laying on for his wife that was deterring Donna's entry into the water. Presumably the pair of them had swum together countless times, before and after making love, in their respective swimming pools, on snatched picnics by the sea. Nick let the images form, staring them out in his mind's eye. He had been doing a lot of this in recent days, discovering that the more head-on he came at them, the less potent such images grew. There had been a sense of sadness too for a while, but that was utterly gone now. It wasn't possible to mourn losing something already so well and truly lost.

'Hey, Nick?'

'Yeah?'

She had taken the hat off, placed the phone face-down on her stomach and was staring at him. There was something in her voice that sounded true for once. *Maybe she knows I know,* Nick thought suddenly. *Maybe she is going to say something.*

Instead, she said, 'Just to be clear. If I wanted any work doing on my face, you would do it, wouldn't you?'

Nick laughed. He couldn't help it. Not because it was a ridiculous idea – though it was – Donna's skin was drum-tight, over a face and body of such robust bone structure that it was clear she would remain a standout beauty of whichever decade she inhabited – but because of the crude indication that potentially she still regarded him as having certain uses. 'You don't need cosmetic surgery, Donna. But to answer your question, no I wouldn't do it.'

'Well, that's just fucking great,' she snapped, either not seeing or choosing to ignore the compliment veiled in his refusal. 'What's the good of being married to a guy who's only prepared to make other women look better?'

'It is not about that, as you well know. Of course I wouldn't stop you having work done if you really thought you needed it. It is just that I couldn't be the one to do it. It is about being a doctor versus being... a person. For me the two worlds are separate and need to stay that way. In addition to which, as you also know, it is not my favourite area of expertise. My day at the clinic is purely to pay bills.' Nick tightened the waist string on his Bermudas. He had been losing weight recently, without trying. He was simply burning more energy, he could feel it. Getting through every day, every conversation, took effort. 'And besides, you couldn't look more beautiful than you already do,' he added with some force. It was true after all. 'Beauty is not your problem.'

Donna, who had picked up her phone, slowly lowered it again. 'Oh yes? And what is my *problem*?'

There was the usual menace in her tone, but Nick could sense the new uncertainty in her too. Something had shifted between them and she couldn't put her finger on it. He wondered sometimes if this was the main reason he hadn't said anything yet about Mike. It wasn't how he had planned to tackle things, but somehow the days had been slipping by and still he had put a confrontation off. 'I'm not sure, Donna. To be honest, I'm still trying to figure it out.' He turned and strolled towards the sea, but then turned parallel to it, deciding to take a walk first. He kept his shoulders loose. He knew she was watching and he wanted her to think he was fine. In a way he was. Finer than he had been in years.

* * *

Eleanor raised herself onto her elbow and lifted up the thin curtain covering her bedroom window. Below her the muddy scrub separating her block of flats from the rail embankment bore testament to the dankness of the late December weather. The trains had kept her awake again, all night it felt like, shaking her back to consciousness every time she was on the verge of sleep. Like a form of torture.

It had to be late morning, but the day held no light to speak of. Eleanor tried to recall when she had last seen the sun. Two weeks ago? Three? She endeavoured to think forwards instead. Christmas was six days away. She pictured Howard and the children, the rituals they would all have to go through; the rituals they would expect her to go through. There had been a card that week, inviting her to join them; one line in Howard's miniature cobweb writing.

Do please come for Christmas. Kat would have wanted it. We want it.

Eleanor propped herself up on her elbows, shoving the curtain out of the way. A large piece of dirty plastic clung to the lower branches of a tree. It had been blowing round the garden for as long as she could remember, gusting into different positions, getting dirtier, tattier.

When the landline on her bedside table rang, she shuddered. She had thought getting back to London would make everything easier, but it hadn't. It had made things the opposite of easier. She stared at the phone for ten rings and then slowly lifted the receiver to her ear.

'Eleanor?'

Eleanor hesitated. 'Megan?'

'I just heard about Kat,' blurted her old friend, 'Billy heard – from a rugby mate who works with Howard in the city... Jesus, Eleanor, I am so sorry, I had no idea. Now I know why you've been silent for months and months – and I've been so busy – but I wish you had told me. You should have told me... but, oh God, how are you, darling girl? Are you coping?'

'I... I'm not sure.'

'Fucking cancer. Bowel, Billy said, is that right?'

'Yup.'

'But, of course, you probably don't want to go into it all now... on the phone...'

'No, I...'

'I need to see you. Talk properly. I can't get away this week but maybe could you come and visit us instead? Pack a bag this minute. Come for Christmas. Billy would love it too. Fresh Welsh air, dogs and cows, not to mention our three thugs who can be quite sweet when required, I promise you...'

Eleanor rubbed at a smear on the windowpane with her fingers, making it worse. She thought of Billy, his wide, wonky rugby player's nose and deep-set eyes, blinking sheepishly at hers as she opened her flat door to him. Bumping into each other at the nightclub. London heaving in the Christmas party season. Her on one of her mad nights. Him on a stag do. The shared taxi. So many rotten decisions. Was it genes or bad luck that made a supposedly clever person so repetitively stupid?

'Thanks, Megan, but there's still a lot to... sort out... you know.' She saw out of the corner of her eye that it was almost midday.

'Oh, yes. There must be... of course... Oh, Eleanor, I am just so very sorry for your loss,' Megan's voice was cracking. 'I never met Kat, but I know she...' There was a silence, the chance to speak. And Eleanor would have filled it, if only she could have thought of a single thing she could say. 'It will have to be in the New Year then,' Megan went on firmly. 'I'll come to London, kick off the wellies, take you out to lunch. In fact, what about the nineteenth of January, as I have to be in town that day to talk to someone about cows. The nineteenth, Eleanor. Four weeks from now. Will that work for you?' She spoke with great vehemence, as if she sensed the need to keep a grip on something more than the conversation.

'The nineteenth,' Eleanor echoed, already resolving to pull out. 'That would be nice. Thanks.'

'And you are doing okay, are you, apart from being sad?'

'Yes,' said Eleanor, a dim part of her thinking that losing her best friend, as well as her sister, was the least she deserved, given what she had done. She looked round her room, wondering what Megan, who these days ran a herd of prize-winning cattle as well as her family of three sons, would say if she could see her, still marooned on the grubby island of her bed in the middle of the day, surrounded by an ocean of dirty laundry, her phone and laptop cold, and nothing in the fridge but an out-of-date pot of humus. 'I mean, at least with cancer you have a chance to say goodbye,' she managed, snatching at the words Howard had used like a lifeline.

The moment Eleanor put the phone down it rang again. She picked it up automatically, thinking Megan had wanted to add something, but it was Trevor Downs.

'Sweetie, you're not answering your mobile, and you're not here. Are you okay?'

'Not there?'

'Yes... er... we had an arrangement that you would come today at eleven. I know it's a Saturday, but we have done that before...' Trevor hesitated, acutely aware of the tragic business of the sister. He nearly hadn't rung. 'You are writing the story of my life, remember?' he cajoled gently. 'We once had a deadline of Christmas and have got rather behind. I live in Chiswick, and in the normal run of things you get on a train to come and see me...'

'Oh God, Trevor, sorry. I... somehow... I forgot.'

'Darling, don't apologise. We can leave it.'

'No, I...'

'Though it would be splendid if you came,' Trevor pushed on, because they were badly in need of the session. 'I'll rustle up some lunch. Just get here as soon as you can.' Trevor put down his phone with a compassionate sigh. His ghostwriter had been hard to like at the beginning, such an Amazon of a girl, bullying with her tape recorder and her timelines. The illness of the younger sister had softened her. Progress on the book of his life had faltered accordingly, but it had seemed impossibly churlish to mind. With the loss of his own dear Larry still so raw two years on, his heart had gone out to her.

Trevor set about making a duck salad, propping his recipe book against the fruit bowl and flicking the radio to Classic FM. They were playing Mahler's second. It was near the end, when the mezzo soprano took off. Resurrection and redemption galloping in on white chargers. Trevor started on a bottle of Prosecco and sang along in the falsetto that he reserved for times of absolute privacy, breaking off as a title for his memoirs popped into his head. *For My Sins.* Sincere. Faintly saucy. Yes, it had distinct possibilities.

He sang on, happier. He would run it past Eleanor. Grief might have caused the poor girl to lose a bit of focus, but he still trusted her literary judgement. Indeed, given the calibre of her background – the first-class Oxford degree and the well-reviewed book written on behalf of some eminent Russian academic – the cheapness of her fee had seemed astonishing. It was because the book on Igor Strovsky hadn't sold, his agent Julian had explained at the time, adding the unnecessary but compelling detail that Eleanor and the Russian had also been lovers, until the man bolted back to his wife and his homeland.

She was on his doorstep within the hour, her face gaunt, her long frizzy hair as black and wild as a thunderstorm. 'Trevor. What can I say.' She plucked at the frayed strap of the bulging canvas satchel in which she kept her notes and laptop.

'Say you'll have a glass,' Trevor said briskly, ushering her inside. 'I've got a bottle on the go. Not proper fizz but it's cold and dry and packs just the punch one needs on such a dingy day. Roll on Christmas.' He flung his arms up in theatrical despair as he led her through into his recently completed glass-domed conservatory, inwardly bracing himself for a barrage of compliments, since Eleanor had borne witness to some of the disruption the work had caused. But Eleanor dropped wearily onto his new scarlet sofa without a word, dumping her workbag at her feet.

Trevor trotted back to the kitchen to fetch another glass of Prosecco and pressed it into her hands. He had been saving a funny story to tell her about a fan cornering him in the supermarket, but noticing how stiff and low she seemed, he sat down next to her instead. 'My dear, you look really carved up. I was a bully to make you come. Forget my silly book. Let's just have a nice lunch.'

Eleanor took a sip of her drink. The bubbles felt like needles, stabbing her throat, pleasantly sharp, something to push against as she swallowed. *Something to push against.* It was what Kat had said.

Trevor started to say something else but she cut across him, blurting, 'I can't go on, Trevor. With your book. With anything. I can't do it.'

'There now. Goodness me.' Trevor hid his dismay, patting her knee. 'My dear girl, you are in the eye of the storm. The grief will – it does – get better.' He withdrew his hand, guiltily aware that he was rather enjoying offering comfort.

Eleanor sank backwards, staring at the ceiling, her glass lodged precariously between her thighs. 'There have been terrible things... unforgiveable things...' She chewed at her beautiful mouth.

Trevor hesitated, curiosity vying with compassion. 'Unforgivable is a strong word, sweetie.'

'I impersonated my sister,' she snarled, flinging herself round to face him, her dark eyes glassy with self-disgust. 'My sick, now *dead* sister. Is that *unforgivable* enough for you?'

Trevor picked a speck of red sofa fluff off his trouser leg. 'I think unhappiness can make one do all sorts of things,' he said carefully, his mind filling with all the nights he had worn Larry's clothes, standing in front of the mirror, weeping. 'You can't rush these things, sweetness. And of course you are probably angry with her, for dying. A lot of grief is simply a sort of rage.'

Eleanor stood up stiffly, as if he had insulted her. 'I'm afraid what Kat and I went through doesn't fit into any kind of easy category.' She set her still full glass on the table and picked up her bag. 'I am sorry, Trevor, I shouldn't have come. I'm wasting your time. I'll speak to Julian about finding someone to take over.'

'Take over?' Trevor could feel his toes slide to the front of his brogues as he got to his feet. The shoes were too big, but Larry had bought them for him so it didn't matter. 'Come on now, you need to take a deep breath.' He spoke urgently, genuinely alarmed now by the wild look in her big brown eyes. 'I don't care whether you have impersonated your sister or the man in the moon. I need you, Eleanor,' he added grandly. 'Shall we do some work? Would that help? I have had all sorts of new ideas... stories coming back to me for that middle section which we are agreed is a little thin. The time in Hollywood – the box-office flop – there is so much I can add. Quirky stuff, sad stuff, happy stuff. It brought me Larry, after all.' He had hoped to soften her expression, to divert her a little from her own woes, but she didn't even blink.

Instead she was shaking her head again. 'I can't do it. Writing. Making sense. Of life. Your life. Anybody's life... I am an imposter, Trevor. I am not what I seem.'

'Oh, but we're all imposters,' Trevor cried, almost laughing because she was so much wiser than she knew, 'It's only the brave ones who admit it.'

But she had stopped listening and was striding away to the front door. 'You have been so patient,' she said in a hollow voice, when he caught up with her. 'Thank you for that and for being so nice. Really, truly, *nice*.' She opened the door, letting in jets of icy air that flicked round their ankles.

'Don't decide anything today, okay?' Trevor talked fast. She was poised on the front step, clutching her bag to her chest, steeling herself in a way that made him think of a parachutist crouched to jump. 'This impersonation of yours, sweetie,' he rushed on, 'I suppose it was for... money?' He tried to recall the sister whom she had showed him a picture of once on her phone, months before – a petite creature, a long loose tangle of silver-white hair, big baby-blue eyes. Impersonation in any real sense seemed improbable.

A moment of involuntary surprise lit up Eleanor's face. 'Oh no, nothing like that.'

'What then?' Trevor pressed. He had assumed it was something to do with penury and forged signatures. His ghostwriter was clearly poor. It oozed out of her – the ancient tiny phone, the big scratched laptop, the racehorse figure decked in charity shop clothes.

'I can't tell you.' Her face had gone blank again. 'I can't tell anyone.'

'But surely nothing is that bad,' Trevor began, but she had

already launched herself off the step and was grappling with the stiff handle on his gate.

* * *

It was three o clock by the time Nick returned from his stroll to their patch of beach. Mike and Lindy were back messing around at the water's edge, Mike hoisting her onto his shoulders, rising from the water like a dripping leviathan, and roaring with laughter as he tipped her off sideways. Lindy was shrieking with delight, playing the game. It made Nick feel sorry for her. It almost made him feel sorry for Donna, having to watch. Almost. If she loved Mike, it must be hard.

Nick plunged into the surf, relishing the shock of the Atlantic cold. After joshing round in the shallows for a bit, he sprint-crawled away from his neighbours and the handful of other swimmers and made for the middle of the bay. It felt good to be properly on his own. He trod water for a few minutes, admiring the big rocky arms of the cove, stretched out round him like an embrace, and then swam on until he was in the great blue canvas of the open sea. The water was chillier, choppier. He flipped over onto his back and floated, letting his limbs drift and ride the swell. The sea was a silky mattress beneath him, moulding itself to his body. Overhead, the sky was already its rich afternoon blue. It seemed to bear down; as if he was a specimen on a glass slide, Nick decided dreamily, closing his eyes.

Nick floated. Mike and Donna. The truth had been laid bare. And though it was a truth that brought burdens, it also had manifold blessings. Already there was the new dynamic at home. He felt empowered. More surprising perhaps was that he had been enjoying work much more too. Each day that week, swinging into his reserved slot in the Queen Elizabeth car park, he had felt more positive, more hopeful. No one could deny he had forged a fantastic career. He had done well. He could remain a doctor or give it up. He had options, on all fronts.

The current was pulling on him, little tugs. Nick began composing an imaginary email to Kat.

Happy Christmas!
Change your mind about January. Please. I want to meet the Keating girls!
What harm could one drink do? It could be any drink you like! Wine. Coffee. Tea. Water...

Nick opened his eyes. He had thought he heard something, but it was only the roar of the sea in his ears. The sky was the same. The sea felt even colder, though, and much more active. He righted himself, observing with some amazement that he had drifted well beyond the reach of the cove and was out in the open water. The figures on the beach had shrunk to the size of pin men. A couple were moving, most were lying still. One seemed to signal in his direction, but it was hard to be sure. Nick waved back anyway and started swimming. The cold had numbed him to a point, almost, of not noticing it. Sharks didn't like the cold though, he reminded himself, which was good. The bay wasn't that far away, perhaps a half mile, and he was a strong swimmer.

Within a few minutes, however, Nick found himself wishing he had made more of the brunch Donna had thrown together before they left the house. It had been a busy morning – a long work phone-call about a patient, chivvying the girls because they were dilly-dallying as usual and Donna, packing for the beach, was getting irritable. He had eaten a banana. A piece of toast, a mouthful of cheese, two tomatoes. Nick forced himself to calculate the details as he ploughed his way back through the water, trying to take his mind off the mounting physical effort and a sudden raging thirst. But it was hard work and the tide fought him back, stroke for stroke.

He fixed his eye on a jagged rock near the mouth of the cove and started counting. Ten. Thirty. Fifty. One hundred. The point seemed to get no closer. In fact it looked further away. Nick swam on against the current, keeping his head down now. He wasn't a quitter, he reminded himself. He wasn't even that tired yet but should probably try to pace himself. He stopped counting and switched to slower strokes, squinting in a fresh effort to make out what was going on at the beach, but it had shrunk to a slim band of white, stretched between two rocky sections of the coast.

The sea had begun churning into frothy peaks, flinging spray and salt into his eyes, making it hard to keep them open, let alone see. Drifting for a while would be fine, he told himself. If it came to that. The cove was isolated, but Donna and the Scammells had almost certainly summoned help. It wasn't like he was having a heart attack.

Nick paused to look behind him, treading water, catching his breath. There had been a speedboat earlier on, but now the horizon was empty.

* * *

On the train after leaving Trevor's, Eleanor found a new, numb calm overtaking her. She decided to text him, put on a show of the normality she did not feel.

Sorry for being an idiot.

She took her time, picking a word calculated to reassure. Choosing words was one thing she did at least know how to do, she reflected darkly.

Eleanor pressed send, but the screen on her phone went blank. She tapped it, shaking the phone urgently, panic gushing back in. The battery had died. When the train pulled into the next station, even though it was too soon, she got off. It didn't matter where she was. She needed to move, to breathe.

In the street, she saw a sign to Wandsworth Common and followed it, walking fast.

Nick was flooding her head suddenly. He seemed to do that, as if it was something he controlled rather than her. Always at her weakest moments, pouncing like a need that could not be satisfied. A thwarted first love, it was pitiful to have got so enthralled again. Eleanor summoned to mind the beautiful South African wife and two teenage daughters, the wretchedness of her deceit, allowing Nick to believe he was writing to Kat. Kat, who was dead. Kat, who had been touched – *touched* – by their father. Eleanor stopped in the middle of the path. A man hurrying behind her steering a bike, cursed as he dodged past.

Further questioning of Howard had got her nowhere, not even the next day when he was sober. It had been a few occasions during Kat's early to mid-teens, he had repeated miserably. Fumbling, touching, never full sex, usually – from what he could gather – when Vincent had had a few drinks. It had messed with her head, but Kat was adamant that she had got over it, even forgiven the bastard, in spite of the fact that Howard himself could not and would never forgive him. It was why he had been so reluctant even to have the man at the funeral, Howard had explained, before pleading with Eleanor to leave the matter alone. He had told her all he knew – he swore – all that Kat had ever told him. What seemed to distress him most was that he had broken his pledge of silence.

The shock waves of abhorrence and betrayal had followed Eleanor back to London and then settled, a darkness in her head that teemed with new understanding. Kat's souring as she hit adolescence, the hostility – even the promiscuity – she saw it all in a new light now. As to what her sister had actually been through, what Vincent might or might not have subjected her to, the dread Kat must have felt on his nightly prowls, Eleanor could not bring herself to imagine. Instead, worsening like a pain as each day passed, was the longing to speak to Kat herself: to ask her why she had not shared this most terrible of secrets with her own sister; to offer her what clumsy comfort she could; but, most of all, to say sorry, for having been too blind, too self-centred, to see what had been under her nose.

But Kat wasn't around for speaking to. And never would be again. Like their mother. Only the ones who deserved to be dead were still alive.

Eleanor started to run across the common, her feet catching in sludgy drifts of old wet leaves. She stumbled, veering left away from the main path and weaving through a sloping bank of thin trees. Ahead, some fencing came into view, high and rusted. Through its metal lattice she glimpsed an embankment snarled with brambles.

Straightforward and trusting, Nick had written. But she wasn't even that. Kat had known it. Kat hadn't trusted her. Kat had endured hell rather than trust her.

Above her a train crashed past, deafening. Faces flashed at the windows. Eleanor stared up at them through the cage of brown wire fencing, her eyes streaming; the outsider looking in. The people in the carriages had families and livelihoods to go to, jobs they were on top of, pasts that made sense. Their lives hadn't stalled. Or been built on lies.

A few yards to her left a gap in the fencing caught her eye. It was a tempting hole with spiked, bright curling edges, recently cut. From there it would be a two-minute scramble up to the top. The trains were so frequent. So fast. Maybe her life could make sense too. Circles could be completed. It took courage, that was all. Courage that her mother had had, and Kat too, in her way.

* * *

Nick returned to swimming with maximum effort, working through his repertoire of strokes to give his various muscle sets time to rest. Crawl. Breaststroke. Backstroke. Fifty of each. He thought about Natalie and Sasha. He wanted to be a part of their futures, whatever they held; he wanted to be involved in all of it.

As for Donna... But as he tried to look ahead, his mind looped backwards, to Oxford, the cradle of the supposedly 'gilded' youth into which he had never truly settled, and to Eleanor and Kat. Such a striking, intense pair, with their strange priestly father and tragic childhood loss. They had instantly stood out from the crowd, both of them. The thought catapulted Nick back into the café in the covered market, Eleanor talking at him across a red gingham table cloth, a plastic flower between the salt and pepper pots, flashes of doubt and intelligence scudding across her big honest brown eyes. Fowles and Nabokov. Lepidopterists. Prisoners. Later, on a few occasions, there had been kissing.

The threads of memory fluttered behind Nick's salt-sore eyes, easing the aching cold and the tiredness of his body. Life wasn't a line, he realised with sudden lucidity. It was simply a widening circle. Nothing got left behind. All of it was there, always.

The sluggishness of his limbs was worsening, like they were forgetting how to swim. His temples thumped and his throat was sticky. Nick flipped onto his back to rest again. The sun had sunk to a point almost in line with his vision, a thick beam straight into his face. He let his eyelids fall closed, relishing the soothing cool of the water lapping round his hot pounding head. Drifting. Let the current take him. Yes, that was okay, that would do. He was good at drifting. A master.

Nick made another monumental effort to think properly about Donna, about what he was going to *do*. But new rows of thicker higher waves were starting to arrive, flooding his mouth, his nose, his ears. He fought them off, windmilling his leaden arms, trying backstroke. His thoughts spun to being happy, how he missed it, how he deserved it, how hard it was to achieve. Kat had said something about that once in one of her emails, but he couldn't remember what. And loss, she had said things about that too. Wise, moving things. She had been through so much, known so much. Nick began to shout. In frustration. Despair.

For Kat. For help. But the waves kept coming, pummelling his head, punch after punch.

* * *

Trevor peered gingerly under the sheepskin trim of his left glove, checking his watch for the umpteenth time. It was still only four-thirty – not five hours since Eleanor had stumbled out of his house, and only twenty minutes since the start of his vigil on her doorstep. Overhead, the security light kept coming on and off. He had taken the precaution of wearing his fleece liner under his cashmere coat, as well as a scarf to plug the gap between his fedora and the top of his collar, but was cold to his bones nonetheless. He had poor circulation, that was the trouble. Thanks to low blood pressure, which was supposed to be good. Larry had been the opposite – high blood pressure, so dangerous that they had eventually lived like vegans – but in the end it had been a stroke that got him, not his heart. A massive one. Bed with a headache one minute, waxy-skinned and lifeless beside him the next. It still made Trevor tremble to think of it. Death was always such a violent shock, even an expected one, like slamming into a brick wall. Trevor wished he had thought to mention this to Eleanor.

Thirty more minutes, he decided, hugging himself and humming some of the Mahler from the radio. Hearing the click of approaching footsteps on the pavement – female footsteps, he sprang forwards hopefully. But it was a chunky girl, bare-legged in stilettoes and a mini-skirt. 'Hiya,' she trilled, giving a sassy wave as she tottered past.

Trevor shuffled back into the lee of the doorway and crouched down, cursing his creaking knees and wishing he hadn't come. Watching the taxi meter race, he had felt only foolish – rushing to the aid of a woman who almost certainly didn't want or require it, feigning drama for his own needy purposes. He was sure that was what Larry would have said.

The block of flats had given him something of a jolt. Clapham still had its seedy patches, he knew, but the peeling windows and pebble-dash front, set against a backdrop of bramble thickets and litter that included a broken chair, a washing machine and several items of clothes, had depressed him deeply. He had ducked into the small portico entrance like a soldier seeking cover, relieved and faintly moved to see proof of Eleanor's residence at the top of the panel of buzzers, written in solid thick italics: KEATING FLAT 3. But there were no lights on in the building and no one answered when he rang.

Twenty more minutes, tops, Trevor decided, leaning back into his corner. But no one came and after a while the discomfort turned to a sort of paralysis and he found himself closing his eyes.

* * *

It was six o clock by the time Eleanor turned into her street. Her limbs dragged with fatigue and a blister had formed on her left heel, but she did her best to walk fast. Home, a bed, refuge, was at last in sight. Soon she would be able to sleep, close her eyes, shut out the world. Somehow she had lost her bag, but her keys were in her pocket. She sought them out, gripping their sharp edges till her fingers hurt.

Already what had happened was starting to recede, the details dissolving with the rapidity of a dream. There had been the hole in the fence, she remembered that much, big enough to crawl through, though the spikes had torn at her clothes. Her concentration had been fixed on the task in hand. Accept defeat. It was possible for life to become too much. A deep new wave of understanding and forgiveness had moved through her, melting a long-buried knot of blame and incomprehension. Her mother had given up, that was all. And she was, after all, her mother's child.

Once through the fence, she had fallen onto all fours for the climb up through the tangle of the embankment. The earth had felt solid under her knees, the snagging brambles no worse than pesky insects. She had swiped and swatted. Her sole aim had been to reach the metal track above.

She was almost at the top when the ground started to come alive under her. A train was on its way. Her train. Eleanor had paused, straining to hear, desperately sure of the importance of getting the timing right. But as she did so, something other than the sound of a diesel engine burst inside her head. It was a voice. A shout, so loud that she jumped and then froze. She looked over her shoulder but there was nobody there. *No*, it had said. And in that instant it woke her up to the terror of what she was doing. And once the terror was there, it had been impossible to continue.

Eleanor had slithered back down the embankment and sat hugging her knees, trembling as the train, a long goods one, roared past.

On spotting the old man in a brown felt hat, curled up in the corner of the entrance to her flat, Eleanor's only thought was how to get past without waking him. But the automatic light flashed on, glaring and buzzing.

'Trevor?'

The old actor scrambled to his feet, disconcerted, tugging at the rim of his hat, wiping his mouth. 'I was worried,' he stuttered. 'When you left... the way you left... what you had said...' He looked at her properly. 'Good God, child. What has happened?'

Eleanor gripped the keys harder in her pocket. The concrete under her feet was starting to heave and the shout was back inside her head, repeating and repeating. It sounded like Kat. But it couldn't be, because Kat was dead. 'Worried? About *me*?' Her voice was small and disbelieving.

'Have you been mugged?'

'No, no... but I seem to have lost my bag. Luckily I had these in my pocket.' She plucked out the keys, holding them high so he could see.

Trevor rubbed his legs which had stiffened badly and were hurting. He was still foggy-headed, and incredulous that, a resigned insomniac for two years, he should have managed to fall so deeply asleep on an icy concrete floor in a dingy doorway. 'Oh Lordy,' he said, bringing Eleanor sufficiently into focus to note the smears of mud on her coat, the bits of twig and leaf in her hair. She had clearly been through something. But she was safe and now all Trevor wanted suddenly, very badly, was to return to the comfort of his own home. His conscience was clear. 'Here, let me.'

'I can manage, thanks.' She kept him at bay with her elbow, continuing to work with both hands at twisting the key. There was a streak of mud on one temple, and cuts on the backs of her hands. There were even some scratches on her neck, Trevor noted grimly, his thoughts returning to the possibility of assault.

When the door opened at last, she jumped round, keeping her back to it, like an animal defending a lair.

'I'd invite you in, but I'm afraid I meant what I said today and so there's no point. Also I have nothing to offer. Literally, nothing.' Her big dark eyes glittered. 'Not even milk. So thanks for coming by but... perhaps now you wouldn't mind... leaving me alone?' Her words had started coming out in rushed clusters, as if she was having trouble timing her breathing between sentences.

Trevor hesitated. She was giving him a way out and he wanted to take it. 'I'll see you upstairs first. And I'd like to use the bathroom, if I may.'

She gave a moan of what sounded like exasperation and led the way inside.

Trevor took the stairs slowly. There were a lot of them and they were uncarpeted and covered with stains that he tried not to examine too closely. At the top, she opened the door quickly and easily, but then stopped, dropping her forehead against the jamb.

'It's a tip okay?'

Trevor nodded, but then could not contain a gasp as the door widened. 'Oh my word...'

'The bathroom is that door there,' she said fiercely, pointing across a sea of domestic detritus that made his stomach churn. It was clearly the main living room of the flat. He could make out a couple of armchairs and a table, though, like the floor, they were submerged under clothes, papers, books, notepads, dirty crockery, empty bottles and cans, boxes of takeaway, shoes, coat hangers – there seemed to be a lot of coat hangers. In the middle sat an open suitcase, empty but for a hairdryer and a couple of socks, looking somehow as if it were responsible for spewing out the contents of the room.

'Does it contain a bath?'

She flinched visibly. 'What do you mean?'

'A bath. Does your bathroom have one?'

She nodded. 'You want a bath?'

Trevor smiled, a little sadly. 'No, my dear. Not for me. For you.' The desire to be kind was flooding him now. He smiled at her tenderly. 'I am going to run a bath for *you*. If there was a drop of bubble bath, I would like to add that too. If there isn't, I shall purchase some when I go out. Because while you soak yourself – a long soak – I am going to rustle us up something for supper. A curry, I think. Very light – snow peas, coconut milk, chicken, basmati – nothing to startle the stomach.'

He began picking his way across the room, not looking back in case she detected the fact that he was flying blind.

'It takes courage to admit one needs help,' he went on, emerging from the bathroom a couple of minutes later to find her still standing by her open front door, her face slack and frightened, as if she might take off down the stairs at any moment. 'You've clearly been through a lot.' He surveyed the room, bending down to tug a piece of something sticky off the side of his shoe. 'It's in danger of burying you. We are all in danger of getting buried. Sometimes we need other people to dig us out.'

Eleanor put a hand against the wall. Trevor and the room were spinning. 'Why should you—'

'Because I want to. Because you have helped me this year more than you know.' Tears had started spilling silently down her face, but it seemed kindest to ignore them. 'I am going to the shops now. I won't be long. I'll take those keys of yours, if I may.' Trevor spoke sternly, aware of the importance of appearing in charge. Inside he was still quailing. They may have worked in tandem for ten months, but the meetings had been sporadic and they barely knew each other. 'Are you sure we have nothing we need to report to the police?'

She slowly shook her head, looking stunned.

'Except the missing bag, of course,' he added quickly, 'but we'll get to that.'

He took the keys from her, suppressing a twist of panic at the idea of all her notes, his precious half-formed life story, falling into a stranger's hands, being scrutinised, mocked. His heart raced. But that would happen anyway, he realised. Readers were an audience like any other. Some would boo and some would cheer.

'I am so stupid,' Eleanor muttered, not looking at him. 'I've got everything wrong. I don't matter. I've never mattered.'

In the doorway Trevor paused. He felt a lump swell in his throat, a reflex of sheer, visceral pity. How did a creature of such capabilities, such beauty, get whittled into so pathetic a state? For a moment he was glad he was helping, simply because it might provide some answers.

'Everybody matters,' he said gruffly, going back to put an arm across her shoulders and steering her towards one of the chairs. She stood, her head hanging like a castigated child, while he removed the various items smothering it, and then pressed her gently into its sagging seat. Trevor picked up a pillow in a greying stained case off the floor and tucked it behind her head. 'Now, do not move, sweetness. That's an order. Okay?'

Eleanor nodded, the fight seeping out of her; a fight that felt as if it had been going on all her life, though quite what it had been about, she couldn't at that moment have said.

24

CHRISTMAS 2013

The puppy staggered to the edge of the box, wagging its little tail so hard that it lost its balance and fell sideways, exposing a smudge of white in the silky jet-black of its underbelly. Its fur was crinkled in places, adding to the impression of a creature zipped into an outfit still several sizes too large. Having got back to the edge of the box, it toppled out face first, righted itself, and then waddled across the sheets of newspaper to the large corner basket that housed its Labrador mother and siblings, already plugged in for an afternoon feed. The litter belonged to a neighbour of Hannah's family. It was Christmas Eve and the slower puppy had already been picked out as a favourite. Still only three weeks old, it would be early February before it was ready to go its new home.

A puppy for Christmas. It was sheer genius. Eleanor stole another glance at her sister's family, in line beside her, rapt and quiet, falling in love, healing. After a week in Trevor's tender care, she was starting to feel almost healed herself. The kindness of the man, so unexpected, had been like balm. Trevor had arrived at nine on the dot each morning, like Mary Poppins, ready to clean and organise and cook, fixing things as he went. Every inch of her pokey flat now shone, looking, as a result, a lot less pokey. Scores of bin bags had been filled and disposed of. Light poured through the clean windowpanes, falling in bright squares across the polished wood floors. Even her ancient and sorry array of defeated pot-plants, draped and wilting around various windowsills, were sitting up pruned and perky. Laundered linen bulged neatly on the shelves of her bathroom cupboard. Chiselled free of glaciers, her freezer door opened and closed properly for the first time in years. Below it, the racks in the fridge, scrubbed of mildew and stains, housed a dizzying spread of appealing food – fresh pasta, greaseproof paper parcels of deli cheeses and meats, yoghurts, a cooked chicken. The salad drawer contained salad and the egg holder bobbed with eggs. Even more extraordinary, Trevor had managed to track down her lost bag, returning from one of his shopping forages with it strapped across his portly chest like a handbag. Someone had found it hanging on a branch, he explained breezily, and had the good sense to hand it in to a police station.

'It's only two nights. You'll be fine,' he had told her in his kind, commanding way that morning, posting her into a taxi to catch her Christmas Eve train to Fairfield and sliding a twenty-pound note into her hand before he slammed the door. He was setting off himself later in the day to spend the entire Christmas and New Year break with a couple he referred to as his 'Dorset cousins', an elderly pair of women about whom he was amusingly disparaging but of whom he was clearly very fond. 'Just be gentle with yourself. Don't *try* too hard. And if you are not up to visiting that father of yours, then don't do that either.'

Eleanor had spent the train journey in a state of gathering nervous tension nonetheless, worried about her hastily cobbled gifts, tucked among a few spare clothes in her holdall, and dreading a three-day charade of festivities in a house still trembling with loss. Hovering on the edge of such worries, like a patch of thin ice where she still feared to tread, was her recent meltdown on the common. Near-madness in retrospect. Yet Trevor had helped immeasurably with that too, probing for details as to what had happened and why, but always as he scrubbed or cooked, so that Eleanor was faced with the easier task of directing her answers to the back of his head.

It was almost as if their roles had been reversed, Eleanor had mused wryly: she pouring out every sorry twist of her life story, while Trevor listened. Except that, unlike her, her new friend never seemed burdened by the need to make things add up, contenting himself instead with flinging out occasional and refreshingly pithy comments along the lines that life was a bugger and families a mess-up and unless Eleanor dropped the habit of blaming herself for every bad thing that had happened, she might as well leg it back to her railway line. Not even the Nick business fazed him. Love and grief were both forms of madness, he assured her, and could produce all sorts of strange behaviours. The only thing she mentioned that produced a vehement response was the voice that had brought her to her senses. That was her inner self, Trevor had pronounced solemnly, pausing in his labours to give Eleanor his full atten-tion; it was the core of her, yelling its desire to survive, and she should bloody well listen to it.

The moment Eleanor had seen Howard, striding towards her along the small country station platform, grinning warmly, his arms outstretched to relieve her of her bag, all the apprehension had dissolved.

'Thank God you came.' He had hugged her hard, keeping hold of her for several seconds. 'I so wanted you to. I've made the children wait in the car. I needed to say sorry to you first. I was too hung-over to manage it last time.' He stepped back, keeping a grip on her elbows, compelling her to look him squarely in the face. 'How I behaved at Kat's funeral was terrible. Getting so drunk afterwards, telling you what I did. Can we put it behind us? As Kat herself would have wanted?'

Eleanor had tried to speak, but he ploughed on, drowning her out. The platform had emptied round them.

'Every word I said was true,' he went on urgently. 'Kat did

always care, deeply, about how you might judge her, but I also know – what I was in too much of a state to articulate properly – is that part of her motive in not telling you was to protect you.'

'Protect *me*?' Eleanor had let out a laugh of disbelief.

'Yes.' Howard had eyed her gravely. 'What your father did was so... ugly.' He paused, his thin face trembling. 'She wanted to protect you from the burden of knowing about it, not let it cast a shadow over your life as it had hers. The trouble was,' he added quietly, 'that seeing you always reminded her of it, and she found that hard. At least, that's my theory.'

Eleanor had taken a deep breath before answering, still processing what he had said, wanting so badly to believe it that she didn't quite trust herself. 'Thank you,' she said finally. 'It's a good theory.'

Along the platform behind him, Evie had edged into view by the exit, wearing what looked like a brand new pink anorak and matching wellington boots.

'I think someone is losing patience,' Eleanor had murmured, waving at her niece over his shoulder.

'Hey, bad girl,' Howard called, scooping up Eleanor's bag and setting off at once to retrieve his daughter, any suggestion of real anger belied by the grin splitting his face. 'I thought I told you to stay in the car. Didn't we agree that getting a puppy for Christmas would only happen if you were *good*... I know it's mad,' he added, glancing back and laughing at the expression on Eleanor's face, 'but a near neighbour of Hannah's has a litter of black labs to find homes for and it felt like it was one of those things that was meant to be. We are going straight there now, there having being a general consensus round the breakfast table that it would be nice to have you to help us choose.'

It was a small thing perhaps, in the grand scheme of all that had happened, but sitting on a kitchen floor with puppies clambering across her knees, and afterwards back in the hubbub of the car, Howard chairing a fierce back-seat debate about names, the smell of the pups still on her skin, Eleanor was aware of a warmth inside her that went beyond the efficient heating of Howard's Range Rover. The children chattered and shouted and didn't listen to each other. Howard laughed and told them off with idle jokey threats. It was Kat's family, and she was part of it.

Shooting over the Roman Bridge, long since mended from the flooding at the start of the year, Eleanor found her mind travelling back to her arrival at Fairfield station almost twelve months before, the taxi driver so irritated by the queue for the bridge repairs, Kat still frail from her operation, awaiting her with that prickly cheerfulness for which Eleanor had learnt to brace herself. It was like looking back to different lives, different people, and yet all that had altered was her understanding. And Kat was gone.

Eleanor stared out at the tight white wintry sky, an awning over the flat brown fields, all of it blurring as Howard cruised along the country lanes. *At least I am staring life in the face again*, she consoled herself, *at least I am not looking the other way*.

As soon as they got to the house and Luke had made a touchingly adult to-do of carrying her bag upstairs for her, Eleanor pulled on a purple beanie of Kat's from off a coat peg and slipped out into the back garden. The swing hung forlornly from the tree branch. Under it the grass was much thinner than the rest of the lawn and pitted with patches of hardened mud. Eleanor watched her feet as she approached, reminding herself she was treading on bits of Kat. Howard had asked if she wanted to be with them for the ash scattering and she had said no. 'Sorry, darling,' she said to the air now. 'I was too sad. Too afraid. I let you down. Again.'

A gust of wind blew through the garden, stirring the swing. Eleanor took hold of it and sat down, pulling the beanie lower over her ears and dropping her head to lean on one of the ropey arms. She wanted to think of Kat, but it was a memory of Connie that surfaced; of their mother's fast lithe fingers folding squares of coloured paper into animals, flowers, boats. Around them, the floor was a sea of shapes and coloured papers. Kat, fluffy-headed and dimple-kneed, toddled through it, kicking and whooping. Connie had scooped her up and grabbed Eleanor's hand. 'Now to the sea, my chickadees,' she cried, dancing them to the bathroom, where she put Kat on a stool and filled the basin, setting three little paper boats on the water, one pink, one blue, one yellow. 'Go, little boats. Run for your lives. Escape while you can.' She blew gently, making the little flotilla bob between the taps, while Kat and Eleanor huffed and puffed, giggling at their new-found power.

Eleanor looked up and saw Evie watching through the kitchen window, palms and nose pressed flat against the glass. She smiled and waved, aware of the origami afternoon still floating inside her, a bubble of comfort, one of several that had been emerging since her recent meltdown.

Evie disappeared from the window and appeared skipping across the lawn a few minutes later, her new pink wellies flapping audibly against her shins.

'Can I push you?'

Eleanor laughed. 'I was going to push *you*.' But Evie already had two hands on her back, and was groaning dramatically at the physical effort of the task. Eleanor gave a gentle push-off to help and was soon swinging so freely her only worry was knocking her niece off her feet.

* * *

Howard's Christmas gift to her was a lilac pashmina, weightless and soft as gossamer, immaculately wrapped in layers of crisp white tissue and gold festive paper, tied with matching ribbon and a gold tag. There was a new bond of candour between them, and in spite of the indomitable Hannah's extensive culinary preparations on their behalf, Eleanor and Howard muddled through the Christmas meal together. They forgot several of the trimmings and poured so much brandy onto the pudding to get it lit that, had the children not opted instead for Hannah's mince pies, they might well have passed out. If ever Eleanor fell silent for too long, she would look up to find Howard throwing her a questioning glance of sympathy and she did her best to offer the same in return; although, happily, Howard, in demand on all sides, seemed little in need of it. Rather to her surprise, Hannah joined them soon after the Christmas lunch had been cleared away. There were difficulties at home, Howard explained quietly, sensing Eleanor's reaction.

As well as Howard's scarf, there were gifts from the children, which he had clearly overseen: a box of organic soaps from Sophie, chocolates from Luke and a home-made stapled booklet of a story about a butterfly from Evie, which she read to Eleanor several times, scattering crumbs of dried poster paint over the sofa and brazenly changing the events on every run-through. Because it is *my* story, she told her aunt solemnly, so I can make happen whatever I want.

Eleanor followed Trevor's advice and deliberately pushed her father to the back of her mind. The decision to visit The Bressingham arrived of its own accord, fully formed, a few hours before she was due on her Boxing Day train back to London. She asked to borrow Kat's car, but Howard said at once that he would take her and drop her at the station afterwards.

'I won't come in,' he said, pulling up outside the entrance, 'but I'll be out here if you need me.' He squeezed her arm. 'You don't have to do this.'

'I want to. I must.'

'Okay. Good luck then.'

Eleanor got out of the car and walked steadily across the drive, aware of the weight of her father's old Bible in her handbag. She had put it in at the last minute and spent the journey devising exact plans for how she would hand it over, what she would say. It didn't matter how little Vincent understood. She needed to speak out for her own sake. Her sister might have forgiven and moved on and generally been an all-round saint, but what had happened was part of her own life story too. And what Eleanor most needed to communicate to their father was that he disgusted her.

Once inside Vincent's room, however, Eleanor found the clarity dissolving. A rotund soft-faced woman with tired, kind grey eyes accompanied her there, offering her tea before disappearing. Her father was parked in his wheelchair by the window, granting a view of a cluster of holly bushes studied with cherry-red berries. Since the funeral, he seemed to have shrunk even further into his frame. His legs, their outline visible under his blanket, were thin pipes, his arms like sticks. His hands sat open on either side of his lap, the joints visibly bulging with arthritis. Even his beard had thinned, to the point where it was almost as wispy as the hair on his head. Eleanor dug for hatred but found only pitying repulsion.

'I *know*, Dad,' she began, in a wavering voice, standing before him, the weathered old book clutched in both hands. 'This is Eleanor, your daughter, speaking and I know what you did. To Kat. I know and I will never forgive you.'

Vincent's fingers twitched briefly. On the windowsill someone had put a poinsettia. The leaves were as blood-red as the holly berries through the glass behind them and threaded with lines like veins.

Eleanor held the Bible upside down and shook it to release the scribbled message that Kat had been so quick to dismiss back in January.

Darling Connie, came home for a 10-minute lunch. I love you. Vx

'This means nothing,' she cried, flapping the envelope near his face. 'Do you hear me? Nothing. Words are just words. Mum still left us and you have to know why.' For a moment Eleanor was in the thick of that last morning, with Connie flying out of the front door to pull her and Kat against her for a second farewell, the scent of lemons on her skin and clothes, burying wild kisses in their hair. Eleanor's heart thumped, just as it had then, when all the love for her mother had been swamped with a nameless fear. 'Why did she do it, Dad?' She was shouting now. 'Why?'

A moment later the door opened.

'All right in here, are we?' It was the grey-eyed woman, back with the cup of tea Eleanor had said she didn't want.

'Yes, fine, thank you.' Eleanor's hands were trembling. She slipped the note back between the pages and held the Bible behind her back. 'It gets upsetting, that's all, not to be understood.'

'Oh, I think he understands. Don't you, Vince, dear?' She set the cup of tea down and squeezed Vincent's shoulder. 'Lovely to have your daughter here, isn't it, Vincy?' She spoke slowly and loudly, as if addressing someone deaf as well as stupid. 'Well, I'll leave you to it,' she murmured, flicking Eleanor a hard look as she closed the door.

Eleanor knelt down in front of the wheelchair, this time placing the heavy old book on his lap. 'I hope you can hear me,' she said bitterly. 'Because Kat was... What you did was... Jesus, Dad...' Sobs began to overtake her. 'All that godliness of yours...' She rapped the Bible with her knuckles, making his big limp hands jump. 'Was it just for show?' she choked. 'Something to hide behind?'

Vincent's jaw hung slackly. His eyes seemed to have fixed on an area of wall behind her back. Wearily, Eleanor got to her feet. Her plan had been to rip up the message the Bible guarded before her father's eyes, shred it to pieces like the trust he had betrayed. But now doubts were resurfacing. Maybe the note did mean something after all. Maybe, for all Connie's problems, Vincent really had loved her; Kat had certainly thought so.

Eleanor stood very still, seeing again the view through the gap in her parents' bedroom door: her mother on the bed, her father moving on top of her. Submission rather than consensual sex. Or maybe that wasn't right either. Eleanor shivered as a terrible new possibility occurred to her. Kat had been such an uncanny replica of their mother. Could that have been what her sister was referring to? That Vincent's violations were simply a perverted quest to experience an echo of what he had lost. In which case it might have been purely Eleanor's resemblance to her father that had kept her safe.

Slowly, Eleanor took the Bible from Vincent's lap and placed it next to the poinsettia. There had been darkness in her childhood, a darkness she had sensed rather than seen. She had to accept that and learn to live with it. She would never have all the answers.

'Goodbye Dad,' she said bitterly, sliding out of the room, leaving the tea the carer had brought her untouched.

She had reached Reception when a disbelieving voice said, 'Eleanor?'

It took a moment for the broad-bellied man in a black anorak standing by the door to merge with the shy, short boy who had waved at her from tractors and pressed his mouth so keenly over hers whenever she let him. 'Charlie Watson, oh my goodness.'

Charlie shook his head incredulously. 'Eleanor Keating. Wow.' He reached to shake her hand and then clumsily kissed her cheek. 'I can't believe it. What brings you here?'

'My father. It's been a long time now... Alzheimer's...'

'Oh, I see. Oh dear.' His round face fell, genuinely crestfallen. 'That's too bad. He was nice, your dad... at least.' He smiled sheepishly, showing some of the jumble of his teeth. 'Well, he was weird and like something from the Old Testament and we were all terrified of him, but apart from that he was really nice.'

Eleanor laughed a little sharply but was glad Charlie was just as sweet and kind as she remembered. 'What about you? Do you have someone here too?'

'Not as such. My sister, Gill – half-sister – Dad remarried – works here, but her car was playing up so I dropped her off. But how the hell are you anyway?' he went on eagerly. 'Are you living round here now?'

'Oh no, I'm in London.' Eleanor looked pointedly at her watch. She had no desire to tell Charlie Watson how she was. It was nice but also unsettling to have bumped into him, proof, though she hardly needed it, that the past never quite left anyone alone. 'I'm good thanks, but I am afraid I can't chat.'

'No. Fine. Here, let me get that.' He leapt forward gallantly to open the heavy front door before she reached it. Then followed her out.

Outside, it was already dark and much colder. Eleanor tucked her hands into her coat. 'So, do you still farm?'

Charlie flipped up the hood of his anorak, shaking his head ruefully. 'We were only ever tenants and it just got impossible to make a decent living. My wife and I run a garden centre at Crowsborough now – the one on the roundabout – everything from tomatoes in a bag to cappuccinos. Hey, you wrote a book, didn't you?' he blurted, giving her an awkward nudge that reminded her of the shyness she had once liked so much.

'Oh, that was ages ago. Nowadays I mostly teach... idle kids doing retakes... you know the sort of thing.' She looked round with mounting desperation for Howard's car, but it wasn't where he had dropped her. 'Well, Charlie, nice to see you. I'm glad life's clearly treating you well.'

'Can't complain,' he agreed. 'Got the mortgage and the marriage and the two-point-two kids...'

Eleanor had spotted Howard at last, parked under a hedge and she gave him a wave.

'I am glad you've got someone,' Charlie murmured, following her gaze.

'Yes. Thanks. You too. Good luck with everything.'

'Someone you know?' enquired Howard when she was back in the car.

'Yes, from way back. Charlie Watson. A neighbour from

Broughton days. Nice guy. I didn't tell him about Kat, though, I couldn't face it.'

'No, I find that. You have to choose who you tell, don't you?'

'Yes, you do.'

'Because it takes so much to manage it.'

'Yes, it does.'

They both sat in silence for a moment.

'So. How did it go in there?'

'I don't want to see him again. Ever. All I want is to speak to Kat. I want to tell her sorry. I want to tell her that she was brave and a total idiot. I want to hear her say she loves me.'

Howard put out his arm and pulled her close enough to rest her head on his shoulder. Eleanor wept quietly for a few moments and then sat up, apologising for leaving smears on his coat.

At the station, Howard held her in a proper hug, similar to the one with which he had greeted her three days before. When they pulled apart, his green eyes were moist. 'It would be nice to see more of you. Can we see more of you?'

'Yes, I'd like that.'

'Soon?'

'Soon.'

The train thundered in. Howard waited on the platform until she was seated and then walked alongside, waving as it pulled away.

Subject: Meeting
From: EleanorKeating@googlemail.co.uk
Date: 19/1/14
To: N.Wharton@QueenElizabeth.org.sa
Dear Nick,
I hope you are well.
I have reason to believe you might be in the UK around now. In which case, I was wondering if you would have the time to meet with me for, say, an hour at the very most? I am afraid it concerns matters of great sensitivity and seriousness connected to my sister Kat. Which is why I must stress that I will only be able to talk freely if you are able to come alone.
Sorry to fire such a bolt from the blue after so long.
I hope to hear back from you soon. My mob is: 07836569911.
Best wishes,
Eleanor Keating

Eleanor sat back in the café's weather-beaten leather seat, chewing a rough bit of skin by her thumbnail. She had been writing and rewriting the email all morning and now only had a few minutes until Megan would be joining her for the January lunch that she had somehow never got around to cancelling. Her trepidations about getting together remained vivid, but so did a mounting desire to see her old friend.

It felt peculiar to be communicating with Nick as herself, and so formally too. Pangs had kept arriving, for how they had written before, when he thought she was Kat – the rush, every time, of hearing back from him, the clarity and directness of his thinking, the moreish glimpses of his playfulness.

Eleanor scowled at the screen. Truth mattered, she reminded herself; if there was one thing the last few weeks had taught her, it was that. No matter how old, or how horrific, the mere fact of facing up to reality brought its own comfort.

A stream of sunshine chose that moment to burst through the café window behind her, making the email hard to see. Eleanor stopped her re-reading and stabbed the send button, flopping back in her seat, her long dark curly hair splashing around her shoulders. The heat felt good on the back of her head, cradling the stiffness in her neck that had resulted from the new daily regime of hard work with which she had launched herself at the New Year. A string of private pupils was in place to help see her through to the summer. Better still, Trevor's manuscript was starting to take shape at last, growing out of the paper mayhem round her laptop. Its paragraphs were not only double-spaced, spell-checked, chaptered and readable, but they had exactly the blend of comedy and poignancy that she had striven for and failed to achieve in all the years of abandoned attempts at fiction.

Since the rollercoaster of Christmas, the sentences had been flowing out of her. She was more settled in herself, that was part of it, Eleanor knew, still tangled with her grief and shock, but starting, sometimes, to feel a little distance from it too. That Howard, her once aloof and distant brother-in-law, was in the thick of this process with her, calling regularly now to check she was all right, working on a plan for bringing the children to London and taking her out to dinner, was wonderfully strengthening too, adding to the new sense of no longer facing all her troubles alone.

But, crucially, Eleanor was aware of having at last found the right 'voice' to tell Trevor's story; not how Trevor spoke, but how he wished to be heard, the breakthrough being the recognition that the two were entirely different.

Megan blew into the café as Eleanor was putting away her laptop, turning heads with the ripples of cold January air from outside. She fought her way through the tables, several sales shopping bags bouncing on her arms, her square sturdy face, ruddy these days from her outdoor life, creased with sympathy and affection long before she reached the table.

Standing up to greet her, Eleanor's heart flared with an ache, for the message now winging its way to Nick, and for the dear familiar figure fighting to reach her. It had to be two years since they had met, Eleanor realised in amazement as they fell to hugging, both talking at once through tears.

'Oh god, you poor thing... and poor Kat... unspeakable...' Megan choked, winning out in the fight to be heard and scrutinising Eleanor's face anxiously. 'And going so quiet on me for so long... not a line, not a word, *nothing*. But you look... okay... *good*, in fact. Are you okay?'

'Yes... no... I don't know... a lot better, anyway.'

They ate bowls of soup and crusty bread while Megan fired questions with her customary directness, wanting to know all the details of Kat's illness and what Eleanor had been through. As they talked, Eleanor could feel herself warming under the rare and relaxing pleasure of being liked for oneself. Megan's face had grown more drawn over the years, and her hair, cropped into a new boyishly short style, glinted with the occasional premature thread of silver, but they were the same people they had always been; the same two girls who had forged a friendship two decades before. But as the lunch progressed Eleanor could feel the guilt of her betrayal with Billy sitting inside her like a hot coal, making everything still not quite as good as it should have been.

When she got to Kat and her father, Megan went very still. 'Are you going to tell anyone… authorities?'

'Oh no. I am certain Kat wouldn't have wanted that. Nor Howard, for that matter.'

'What about counselling then? For you?' urged Megan.

Eleanor managed a grateful smile and then tried to explain about Trevor and the reviving effect of his kindness. 'I hit a sort of rock bottom, but he arrived on the doorstep – literally – and nursed me through. It's like I was sick, and now I am getting better. And Howard has been brilliant too, like a proper friend. So much makes sense now, you see, and I am sure that's why. Like how Kat used to be, back in the day… do you remember? So hostile and difficult and—'

'She took Nick Wharton from you,' Megan blurted. 'That's why you two fell out.'

Eleanor eyed her old friend ruefully. 'Yes, but by then there was already a lot of…' She faltered, wanting with her new hindsight to find exactly the right word. '…distance between her and me. A terrible distance. Kat put it there, for reasons I am at least starting to understand. But yes,' she conceded, sighing, 'the Nick business didn't exactly help matters.'

'She knew you liked him and she took him – that's what you said,' Megan insisted stoutly, clearly recalling Eleanor's desolation on returning to college after this act of sisterly treachery, how hard she and Billy and their small band of friends had fought to get her spirits back up. 'You spent the next two years avoiding him. Till he left. Then you started the Igor thing.'

'I did,' Eleanor admitted ruefully, privately resolving not to bring Megan up to date on the Nick Wharton front. 'But, actually, Meg, no one "takes" anyone. It's one of the big things I've recently got my head around. Feelings aren't commodities. Nick Wharton fell in love with my little sister. End of. Love happens like that. Boom.

Choice doesn't come into it. Kat just went with the flow... the wrong flow, as it turned out... I never knew the details of their relationship, as you know – I never wanted to...' Eleanor hesitated, remembering some of the recent insights inadvertently granted her by Nick. 'But Kat was shitty to him, I know that much. So the poor man got his comeuppance. The point being,' she concluded in a rush, wanting to close the subject, 'I don't blame Kat a jot. Not any more.'

Megan was watching her tenderly. 'The two of you obviously had time to straighten a lot out. I'm so pleased.'

'I miss her beyond words,' said Eleanor quietly. 'She was my baby sister and I failed to take care of her...'

'No, you are not doing that,' Megan interjected fiercely, grabbing her hand and squeezing it. 'I forbid it. Kat made her decisions. You cannot blame yourself for them. Okay?'

Eleanor nodded meekly. 'Okay.' She took a deep breath, swallowing away the urge to cry, still never far from any conversation about her sister. 'Tell me about these blooming cows of yours instead then, and who in London wanted to talk to you about them.'

Megan launched into an energetic account of the joys of rearing Red Highlands on the Welsh–Shropshire borders and the TV programme featuring specialist cattle that had summoned her to town for a meeting that morning. She then began pulling out her trophies from the January sales, all items of clothing for her sons, apart from a dark green fleece size XL which was for Billy. She held it up for Eleanor's full appreciation. 'Good colour on Bill, don't you think? He's got a bit of a tum these days.' She pulled a goofy face.

'Fantastic.' Eleanor was fighting a fresh yearning to come clean. She and Billy had been so drunk. Everyone knew people did stupid things when they were drunk. Maybe Megan would understand. Truth might matter, Eleanor reflected frantically, but did that justify causing unnecessary pain? Kat clearly hadn't thought so. Kat had thought protecting Eleanor mattered more than anything. Eleanor blinked slowly. Her sister might be gone, but she was understanding her better and that felt good.

Megan was still talking, about underwear now. She had bought a thong and matching skimpy bra – gleefully flashed over the top of a little bag – which she hoped would make Billy happy. She was giggling, mischievous, content.

Eleanor grinned at her. Shattering that contentment was beyond her. It would not be the act of a true friend.

* * *

A huge blue velvet butterfly had somehow got trapped in Doctor Wharton's room. It bounced along the wide polished panes of the glass that framed the even wider seascape of Cape Town sky outside and then flew at the Monet print hanging by the door, coming to settle on the bridge spanning the water lilies.

Pat Driscoll watched it over the rim of her glasses before returning her attention to the desk computer. She had come in to look for a couple of files and have a general sort-out. There had been a lot of stuff to deal with since the accident, reassigning patients, collating letters for files, checking post, but it was mostly done with now. The consulting room was starting to feel empty. Even the thank-you letters from past happy patients, pinned to the cork board behind the door, seemed to hang with a new listlessness, like petals ready to fall.

Swimming, who would have thought it? Pat shuddered, thinking of the stairs down to the shared pool at the new development where she lived and how many times she had told her two young children never to venture there alone.

The emails arriving for Dr Wharton were usually advertisements of various kinds now – drug companies mainly. Pat worked her way through the latest batch with quick, practised fingers, aware of a certain guilty pleasure at sitting in her erstwhile employer's big comfortable rotating chair. Only when she came across what turned out to be a personal email, from someone called Eleanor Keating, did she hesitate. There had been a couple of other pieces of private correspondence in recent weeks which she had forwarded to Mrs Wharton without a thought. But this one was clearly different, not just because of its hint of real hidden drama, but because of the unequivocal suggestion that it was a matter for Dr Wharton's eyes alone.

Pat swung the big chair round in circles, trying to think. Dr Wharton was such a nice man that she couldn't imagine him ever doing anything untoward. From the start he had been so sweet with her, never taking her or her time for granted in the way the previous doctor she had worked for had done.

She looked over at Dr Wharton's most recent desk photograph of the stunning wife and the two still gawky daughters, legs like gazelles and with their big, full-lipped smiles. They were a family that had everything, but there was little to be envious of now, Pat thought sadly. An indicator, if one needed it, that the most solid-looking things could be snatched away in an instant.

Pat glanced again at Eleanor's email and then picked up the desk phone. She dialled the mobile number it gave, first forgetting to add the UK code and then a second time with all the correct digits. She braced herself as it rang. But no one answered and after a while it cut out without even going to an answering machine. Pat sat still for a few moments before, in a quick rash movement, stabbing the delete button. She had had a go at telephoning, after all. And what did any of it matter now, when there was no question of Dr Wharton going to England, or anywhere else for that matter.

26

MARCH 2014 - LONDON

January came and went, taking the notion of Nick's visit to England with it. Eleanor's hopes of hearing back from him receded like a pinpoint on a horizon, bringing relief as well as an underlying sense of let-down. She had geared herself up to do a difficult thing and it felt tantamount to failure to turn her back on it. Yet he had clearly decided he had had enough of the Keating sisters and she could hardly blame him. As a pair, they hadn't exactly wrought him much luck or happiness.

Eleanor drummed the matter out of her mind with her new, feverish work ethic, tutoring her pupils to keep her meagre finances afloat and focusing on a final drive on Trevor's memoirs. By mid-March the manuscript was ready for copy-editing under the agreed title 'For My Sins', with a publication date set for mid-autumn. Despite Eleanor's protestations, Trevor was sufficiently thrilled to insist on taking her out for a pub lunch to celebrate. The one on Clapham Common, he declared, so that we can have a nice walk first.

He was going to be at something of a loss with the book done, Eleanor realised, agreeing to the idea even though she didn't really have the time, and then showing as much interest as she could, while Trevor talked non-stop about new plans for building permission to extend his only recently finished conservatory.

Once in the pub, they settled into a corner seat and ordered two rounds of scampi and chips and a couple of glasses of white wine. Eleanor took herself off to the Ladies, returning to find Trevor absorbed in a newspaper that someone had left behind. She delivered a playful finger-flick to its outer pages as she sat down. Trevor gave the paper a shake and peered over the top of it, pretending to look affronted. He had reached the obituaries. Trevor liked the obituaries: the frisson of gratitude that one's own heart was still beating, the unexpectedly gripping details of a life, emerging usually from under the most unpromising of names and job specifications. He was even daring to wonder if he might not occupy a paragraph or two of national press-space himself one day: *A man who knew how to command an audience, both on and off the stage...* Yes, that would be nice. And with *For My Sins* all set for national release, maybe such hopes weren't so wide of the mark. Thanks to Eleanor, the book was beautifully written, as well as containing all his best stories and some serious gossip. It might make quite the splash.

Trevor's gratitude towards Eleanor sat like a warmth in his gut, along with a certain mystification. Just when he had been prepared to give up on the girl, she had come good. How unpredictable life was.

Trevor glanced again round the side of his paper at his ghost-writer, now studiously ignoring him and checking her phone. She had taken some getting to know, he mused fondly; such a sensitive and buttoned-up soul, endearingly old-fashioned in many ways, and so brave, too, with all that she had been through. It was time to put the paper down and stop teasing her, he decided, but in the same instant his eye was caught by one of the smaller notices on the obituary page, a couple of paragraphs under a smudgy passport-sized photo of man with a Clark Gable moustache: *...born in Moscow in 1948... significant contribution to the polemics dominating twentieth-century moral philosophy... Igor...*

'Okay, so now you are just being rude,' Eleanor quipped, flicking the paper again. 'What?' she asked, noticing suddenly how his expression had changed.

'What do you mean, what?' Trevor slapped the newspaper shut and tried to put it under the bench, but she grabbed his arms mid-movement.

'You're being odd. Why are you being odd?'

'No, I'm not. I just...' Trevor pressed the paper to his chest. She was staring at him in the way he had come to know well, her dark eyes glinting with challenge and a readiness to be hurt. Yes, that was what stirred him most about her, Trevor decided, the hovering expectation of being let down. He sighed. 'That Oxford ex of yours... I am afraid he... he has died.'

'Died?' The word caught in Eleanor's throat. 'How do you mean, *died*?'

'Unless I have got the name wrong,' Trevor faltered, genuinely alarmed by the look on her face. 'That Russian academic you told me about...'

'Igor?' For one despicable moment Eleanor felt relieved. Her heart was performing leapfrogs. She had thought he meant Nick. She snatched the paper from Trevor and found the page. 'And no need to go into panic-mode, Trevor, because I'm fine.'

'I had no intention—'

'It was a very long time ago. Igor had a good life. A successful life. My time with him was... a rite of passage, for both of us.' Eleanor looked at the photo, struggling to see the man she had known, her lover for eight years, in the blurred young face. 'A couple of inches in a national newspaper is impressive though, isn't it,' she murmured, carefully closing the paper and slotting it into her handbag. 'I really am okay, Trevor,' she added, 'I just want to look at it later, that's all. Can we toast your book now?' She grinned, picking up her wine.

'*Your* book,' Trevor corrected her, beaming as they chinked glasses.

* * *

'I had an affair with a dinosaur,' Eleanor cried, on the phone to Megan a few hours later. 'For *years*. He was so *old*. Why did no one stop me? Why didn't *you* stop me?'

'You were still rebounding from one Nick Wharton, as I recall, and wouldn't listen to a soul,' declared Megan, adding rather more sombrely, 'So, are you all right instead of just pretending to be?'

'So all right. You're sweet to ask. Trevor was sweet too. Everyone is so kind to me. Honestly, the only annoyance is that there was no mention of my bloody book. A last chance for some sales totally squandered. I am sure Igor would have been outraged on my behalf.'

After the call, Eleanor nonetheless cut out the obituary and gave the photo a little kiss, before placing it between the pages of the book she had written about Igor's life. She hadn't lied to Trevor or Megan – it had been fun and important to laugh with them – but there was a thread of sadness running through her jollity. Relationships were like stepping stones, she mused, each one leading inexorably to the next. The thought made her rummage for a writing pad and her fountain pen. Nick had not replied to the email, so, short of getting on a plane to South Africa, only the option of pigeon post remained. She would google the address of the Queen Elizabeth Hospital and send it there. Nick might not want to hear the truth, but she needed to tell it to him. People died. One never knew how much time there was, for anything.

Dear Nick…

Eleanor paused, aware that she was about to alienate a man who had once meant so much to her, for good. There would be no going back, not when he knew everything, about her, about Kat, from the very beginning to the very end.

She began writing slowly, aware that what she was going to say would cause Nick abhorrence as well as pain.

This is the hardest letter I have ever had to write. If you are not sitting down, then please do so now...

But soon her pen began to move more fluently and freely. The words she chose thrummed with their truthful power, so that even as Eleanor hated what she was doing, a part of her loved it too.

27

Pat pulled up under the trellis of yellow trumpet-shaped flowers positioned along one side of the car park. The tarmac gleamed in the March sunshine. The building served by the car park looked more like a grand private home than a convalescent unit for neurological patients; which of course was exactly what it must have been once upon a time – one of thousands of big gated properties all over the Cape, designed to keep the privileged safe.

Pat crossed the car park briskly, checking Eleanor Keating's letter was still safely zipped inside her handbag and bracing herself for what would be the first face-to-face encounter with Dr Wharton since his accident. With the initial coma – the result of several minutes under water – the outlook had seemed bleak, but now, three months on, the reports filtering out were all about astonishing strides in his recovery. The turnaround had set Pat reading up about near-drowning cases on the internet, discovering in the process that, while the first six months were always crucial, recovery could in fact continue for years. Health, age, fitness, intelligence, as well as luck, played a part in it. 'It's also a hell of a battle,' one of the Queen Elizabeth doctors had remarked grimly, 'some patients simply aren't up for it.'

Eleanor's letter had arrived the previous week. A plump envelope, studded with English stamps and with the name of the sender on the back, it had stood out at once among the thinning pile of mostly junk mail. Recognising the name, Pat's fingers had itched with curiosity. Yet there had been no doubting her conscience this time. The neurological centre was quite a drive away, but she had resolved at once to take an afternoon off to deliver the letter in person.

Inside the centre, the high-ceilinged circular reception area exuded the air of a luxury hotel. Tall terracotta vases of dried flowers stood in alcoves, skirting a ring of elegant curve-backed chairs set round a low glass table laid out with orderly lines of magazines and a bowl of polished red apples. Overhead, ceiling fans whirred quietly, rustling the fronds in the vases.

Pat signed in and was directed down a long corridor. Dr Wharton's room was on the ground floor and easy to find since there was a name on the door. When there was no reply to her knock, Pat tried the handle and put her head inside. Double doors onto the garden were half open, the long white curtains at their corners lifting in the breeze. Through their folds, Pat glimpsed an empty private square of decking and a wheelchair ramp leading down to the terraced lawns.

'Hello?'

Her voice echoed back at her. She guessed he was enjoying some afternoon sun, but it didn't seem right to go through his room uninvited, so Pat withdrew into the corridor and made her way outside via a fire exit a few yards further on. If she was Dr Wharton she would have been in the gardens every chance she got, with the sun on her face. To have fought for his life in that cold sea, while his wife and friends took so long to appreciate what was going on, made her shudder every time she thought of it.

Pat found herself on a narrow path which snaked down the side of the building towards the main gardens. She set off at a quick walk but stopped abruptly as two voices came into range, very close by, one shrill and female, the other male, and harder to make out. Pat peered round the corner of the building, only to pull back again sharply. Not more than ten feet away, seated on a garden bench with their backs towards her, were Dr Wharton and his wife, Donna, arrestingly elegant in a long blue silk dress with panels that billowed round her slim legs. Dr Wharton looked painfully frail in comparison, a coat-hanger of a man compared to what he had been. His hair had got very long, Pat observed with a stab of tenderness, curling over the collar of his shirt in a way that would have been impossible to imagine when he was the spruce, smart doctor she had once worked for. What had to be his wheel-chair was parked several yards away under a tree; which Pat hoped meant he had been able to walk unaided to the bench.

It took only a moment to realise they were arguing. Pat knew this meant she should retreat back up the path, leave them to their troubles. But the conversation was so compelling that she found herself pressing back against the wall instead, listening in mounting disbelief.

'Of course I'm glad you are better. How could you accuse me of not being glad?'

'I am not accusing you of anything,' Dr Wharton replied, in a weary voice. 'Though I do wish that over these last few months you had brought the girls more...'

'It upset them to see you.'

A silence followed. Pat held her breath, her heart pounding on Dr Wharton's behalf. There were so many possible responses to so terrible a statement.

'And they have been staying with your parents,' was all he said. 'All this time. And only now you tell me.'

'Well, yes. Daddy – and Mum – have been fantastic. I have needed their support... and I have been there a lot too. Look, Nick,' she blurted, '*your* accident, it has happened to me too, you know. None of this has been easy for me.'

Pat shovelled her knuckles into her mouth, to stifle her gasp.

'Yes,' he said quietly, 'yes, I see that.'

'And Daddy has had to help out with money,' Donna went on with some energy, 'because paying for this place has got way beyond what was covered under our health scheme. And when not getting your full salary kicks in, it is going to be a real stretch... I mean, Christ, Nick, why did you never tell me we owed so much?'

'I did tell you. Maybe you didn't listen. And, anyway, it is not a question of "owing so much". It's just that we have a very high standard of living, substantial outgoings, all of which I have often tried to explain—'

'You should have done more of the cosmetic clinic work that Dad got you, that's the truth of it. Started it earlier, taken on more hours...'

'You don't love me.'

The sentence seemed to slice the air. Pat gripped the stone behind her with her fingernails.

Donna barely hesitated, countering, 'Oh, don't be so dramatic, Nick, and, if I may say so, in spite of what you have been through, a little bit childish. Of course I love you, you are my *husband.*'

'That doesn't mean you love me.' His voice had gone hard and solid; a battering ram beating on a closed door.

'Oh for god's sake, Nick, now is not the time for this. We have some serious things to sort out.'

'Love is serious.'

There was a whistle of what sounded to Pat's straining ears like impatient disbelief.

'Love between two people changes, okay?' came Donna's brittle voice. 'Frankly, it would be weird if it didn't. In the meantime, here's the thing. Of *course* I am pleased you are getting better at last. Properly better. But going forwards, there are certain big issues that we have to get our heads round.'

'You mean, money.'

'Yes, Nick, I mean money.' She sounded impatient now. Dr Wharton, in contrast, was sounding increasingly calm.

'In the end money doesn't matter, Donna. Not really.'

There was a whoop of exasperation. 'Oh my god, that is just... so typical.' And then a softening in the quietness that followed. At least Pat imagined it was softening. It had to be, surely. Love or no love, this was such a fragile man whom she was addressing, a man whose five minutes under water might well, by the uncharitable, be attributed to Donna's own extraordinary tardiness in summoning help. 'Nick, I am sorry. You have been through so much. None of this is fair on you.'

Pat exhaled. So there was softening. She readied herself to tiptoe away, but then Donna reverted to her theme.

'This place costs the earth. It is the best there is. Which you deserve, obviously, but...' Donna hesitated, adding in a tone that still sounded like one trying for patience rather than achieving it, 'like I said, we are already well beyond the claim limit and I still can't get a straight answer from the doctors. Have they said anything to you about when you can leave, when you might reasonably think about going back to work?'

A silence followed. Somewhere, a lone cicada clacked.

'I'm not going back to work,' he said at last. 'The hospital, the clinic, I'm not going back to any of it. I am not up to it. Mentally or physically.'

There was an uncertain laugh. 'But you're already so much better. Surely... you can't mean that, you simply can't.'

'I do mean it.'

'Well, in that case, how do you propose we will manage?' Her voice was growing shrill again.

'We are going to have to rethink our lives—'

'Give up, you mean.' There was a clap of hands. 'Oh, I get it. Yes, I should have seen this coming.' She was sing-song now, full of scorn. 'Instead of fighting back and trying properly to get better, you are going to use everything that's happened as an excuse to carry out that crazy plan you had. Sure. Great. You want to drag us all off to England, sell our home, put the girls into some crap old-fashioned school—'

'I have no intention... Donna... Hang on, what are you doing? Where are you going?'

'I need to leave.'

'Now?'

'I need to be somewhere. And, frankly, I can't take any more of this today – your negativity, your refusal to think properly about what is best for me and the girls. Maybe it is just too early for us to be having this conversation. Maybe you are just not ready. And trust me, Nick, when I say that upsets me on so many levels.' Her voice receded during the course of the sentence, to the accompaniment of swishing and retreating footsteps.

'Donna...'

There was more rustling and then her voice came back into focus, meeker-toned. 'Would you like help getting back to your chair?'

'No,' he snapped, sounding properly angry for the first time. 'I would not like your help getting back to my chair. In fact...' An audible intake of breath fell into the hesitation. 'In fact all I would like from you is a divorce.'

There was a short, harsh laugh. 'Okay. I am going to pretend I didn't hear that.'

'You do not love me.'

'I've told you, I do—'

'You are not faithful to me.'

'What? How *dare* you?' The sentence began as a screech but was reined in, perhaps for fear of other patients out using the garden.

Pat pressed harder against the wall. Its gritty surface was starting to hurt the back of her head and her skin through her clothes.

'Oh, I dare, Donna. I dare.' There seemed to be real exhaustion in his voice now.

'You have no right to talk to me like this. No right.' The shrillness sounded close to tears. 'Wait till I tell Daddy what you have just said to me.'

To Pat's astonishment, Nick laughed. 'Is that supposed to be a threat? Because threats only work if the party being threatened is afraid. And I have no fear left, Donna. Of anything. Not even death.' He laughed again, more bitterly. 'And certainly not your father either, who is a bully. Because if I have learnt anything from the last few months it is that life is brief and fragile. In the end not a lot matters. Trying to stay afloat in that fucking sea, all I could think about was... love... the girls. How I hope they know that I love them. Which I believe they do, in spite of your efforts.'

She tried to protest, but he bulldozed on. 'And whatever happens between you and me, *whatever* you try, I will make damned sure they continue to know it. So go ahead, run along and tell that father of yours that I want to divorce you. He is the one you have always answered to anyway. While you're at it why not mention that you have been having sex with Mike Scammell? That might make him sit up a bit...'

Pat had heard enough. She hurried away on trembling ankles, going straight back via a circuitous route to the car park. She crossed the tarmac swiftly, her head hung, her mind numb. It seemed that nothing in the world was as one wanted it to be.

'Hi.' It was a nurse, appearing from behind the cascades of yellow flowers. She waggled a cigarette packet by way of an explanation, smiling ruefully. 'Good visit I hope?'

'Yes... that is... I came to see Dr Wharton...'

'How great is he? We are all of us so proud. It's like... well, let's just say it's patients like him that make the job worthwhile.'

Pat nodded heavily in agreement, fumbling in her bag as she suddenly remembered Eleanor Keating's letter. 'I forgot to give him this. Would you mind?' She handed the envelope over and hastily got into her car. Good intentions had been her starting point. She had wanted to keep Dr Wharton – his life, his beautiful family – on a pedestal; but it turned out brains, money, looks were no defence against anything.

* * *

A few hundred yards away, Nick floated in the space inside his head, a space that seemed to contract and expand, sometimes clear, sometimes dark. Donna had stormed off and he was glad. He could feel the sun beating against his eyelids. It brought vivid, flickering memories of being in the sea, the dryness in his mouth, the pulsing in his temples.

Nick brought the garden back into focus. He shivered with pleasure at the kiss of the light breeze and afternoon warmth on his bare skin, tingling the hairs on his arms and legs. It could be an English summer's day, Nick mused, floating again, with no thoughts this time other than a sense of being. He had said what had to be said, done what had to be done. There would be consequences, waves and waves of them, but for now he was safe back on dry land. For he had been drowning anyway, long before he nearly died.

28

APRIL 2014

'If you feel giddy, then don't look down. Fix your eyes on those trees over there instead. See those two squirrels on that branch?' Eleanor pointed through the foliage spread around them like the panoply of a rainforest. 'They're playing tag, I think.'

Evie giggled. She was holding one of her aunt's hands in both of hers, squeezing so hard the blood was pumping in Eleanor's knuckles. Through the gaps in the planks under their feet were broken glimpses of Hannah and the puppy, christened Bart and at four months old still filling out like a toddler growing into a romper suit.

'Barty-Bart. Silly Bart. I'm *here,*' shrieked Evie, forgetting her fear in delight at the puppy's cock-eared puzzlement.

Hannah waved up at them, laughing, her thick brown pony-tail swinging, glossy as toffee in the April sun. The sight of the nanny, as well as the rest of her sister's family, tumbling out of the car that morning had been a shock, until Howard's quick reassurance that his employee and the dog would be staying with an old school-friend of Hannah's who lived in Tooting. She was keen to see the friend, but it also meant that she could babysit, Howard had explained cheerfully, while he took Eleanor out for dinner. After a whole day with his lot she would be only too glad of the break, he warned her amiably, directing operations to get the luggage out of the car and into her flat, where the children had hurled themselves onto her blow-up mattresses with the glee of penguins plunging into a pool.

They had gone out for a pizza lunch and were now – at Howard's request – in Kew Gardens, which Kat, apparently, had always held dear. Having visited the orchid house, they were exploring the tree-line walk, an elevated wooden corridor set among the highest reaches of some of the park's great trees. After the steamy heat of the greenhouse, the creamy spring air was a joy. Even so, having looked downwards for the exchanges with Hannah and the dog, Eleanor found herself gripping the balustrade with her free hand.

'Vertigo is actually a fear of throwing oneself off a high place rather than fear of the height itself,' remarked Howard, eyeing her with interest as he arrived at her side.

Behind him, the two elder children, clearly unperturbed by the height of the walkway or the glories of the view, were playing a vigorous game of tag, dodging other visitors in a manner that Eleanor couldn't help thinking was a little over exuberant. Since January the changes in them all were striking; thanks to time, counselling, puppies, the entire family was like an algorithm reconfigured. Evie especially, so much taller and fuller faced, her green eyes sparkling with mischief, was hard to link to the pale, tight-faced elfin creature whose fierce, uncomprehending misery had cracked the hearts of a packed congregation five months before.

Most touching of all to Eleanor was how her sister had clearly been absorbed into this new equation; mentioned frequently, easily, Kat seemed already to have become a point of affectionate reference for them all rather than a source of pain. So noticeable was this change that Eleanor had for the first time found herself properly contemplating the strain of living with a wife and mother who was sick, the toll it must have taken.

'If you are strapped in, say, or held tightly, the feeling goes away,' Howard continued, shifting close enough for Eleanor to feel faintly disconcerted. 'Are you all right, sweetheart?' Howard asked suddenly, crouching down to Evie, who whispered something breathily in his ear. 'A pee, of course. I am sure that can be arranged.' Howard stood up, hoicking the child onto his hip and giving Eleanor a what-can-you-do face over the top of her frizzy blonde mop – so like Kat's hair at a similar age that Eleanor had spent all day drinking it in in wonder.

Eleanor immediately volunteered to help, but then stood, digging for patience, while yet another reshuffle of child and dog-care arrangements was undertaken between Howard and Hannah. It made her think Howard's remark about needing a break during the course of the visit was not so wide of the mark.

'God, it's like keeping plates spinning,' she murmured, once they were back on the ground and the new arrangements were in place at last with Hannah to be left in charge of the elder two while she and Howard tracked back to the toilets at the main entrance. Evie skipped ahead of them with Bart, who lolloped and tripped like a cheerful drunk. 'For what it's worth, I think you are doing brilliantly.'

'Thanks.' Howard shot her a grin. He walked purposefully, with a loose easy gait that matched her own naturally long stride, one hand thrust into a trouser pocket, jangling change. 'And so are you, come to that,' he said warmly. 'You look good, Eleanor. Tremendous in fact.'

'Do I? Goodness.' Eleanor dropped her gaze to let the blush work its course. She had bought a new pair of white flip-flops that made her feet look faintly tanned. She watched them crush a path through the lush spring grass, thinking of how carefully she had trodden on the ground by the swing during her Christmas visit to Sussex. Kat was everywhere anyway, she mused, marvelling at how her grief seemed to be turning into something more akin to pure love. She thought too of the quiet thud of her letter to Nick landing in the postbox three weeks before, the sense of a weight lifted. She had told him everything, asking him not to reply, and he hadn't. It had left her feeling free in a new way. The dress she had bought on the same day as the flip-flops swirled round her ankles with each stride. She had spotted it through a charity-shop window, sporting the princely price tag of ten pounds. It was made of black cheesecloth, trimmed with pink stitching – sleeveless, tight across the chest and then flaring out from her ribcage. It was a fantastic dress, flattering, comfortable. The clement spring weather had warranted the purchase, but she would have bought it anyway for how good it made her feel.

'So, the book's going well, I take it?'

'The book?' Eleanor squinted at her brother-in-law. They had emerged from the canopy of trees and the sun was high and blinding. Since finishing Trevor's memoir, she had a new writing project on the go which she had not mentioned to anyone. It was about two little girls, sisters, raised in a home full of adult secrets. Her ambitions for it were growing so fast that all her instincts told her to keep a lid on them. Falling asleep after a recent late-night work session, she had, rather to her surprise, found Jane Eyre tiptoeing into her mind, wanting to play a part.

'The life of that actor-chap – I thought you said it needed editing?'

'Oh, yes, that's all done...'

They were interrupted by a shout from behind. They turned to see Hannah sprinting towards them, her long slim legs in their dark blue skinny jeans at full stretch as she emerged from the cluster of trees. She was waving both arms, clearly panic-stricken. Eleanor saw Howard's face go taut, the jawbone clamp, the marshalling of inner strength.

'Keep an eye on Evie, could you?' he ordered quietly, setting off at a jog to meet her halfway.

Eleanor swivelled back to check the main tarmac path some twenty yards away, where Bart was receiving attention from an elderly woman in a purple coat. Evie was chattering and patting the puppy, the urgency of her call of nature clearly forgotten.

Within a couple of minutes, Howard was back at her side. He was out of breath, grim-faced. Hannah had taken off again, back through the trees.

'What is it? Has something happened?' Eleanor was aware of a strange metallic taste spreading inside her mouth, a taste she dimly recognised as fear.

'Yes. Not good, but not a disaster. Luke's done something to his ankle. Fallen on the steps chasing his sister. Bloody boy. It's blown up like a balloon, Hannah said. We're going to have to get him to a hospital.'

'Oh dear, oh dear,' said Eleanor, but her heart hammered with relief. They could all deal with that. A broken ankle was easy.

* * *

Eight hours later she and Howard were nonetheless seated opposite each other across a sea of crisp white damask and gleaming tableware, awaiting the arrival of their starters.

'This should be quite nice,' Howard murmured, twirling the stem of his wine glass with the confidence of one secure in his own tastes. He stuck his small nose deep into the balloon and then took a sip, taking his time before nodding approval to the sommelier, who had been hovering throughout the ritual, sporting an expression of professional concern.

Eleanor watched in something of a trance as her own glass was filled.

'Aren't you going to try it?

'I will soon.' She took a swig of water. The gin and tonic aperitif Howard had insisted on was still pumping in her head – much needed after the dramas of the day, but she wanted to pace herself. Luke's ankle had been sprained rather than broken, but the diagnosis had taken several long hours in Richmond Hospital, during which time there had been the needs of the other children to attend to, as well as much bolstering of

Hannah, who, for once, had shown some flakiness, repeatedly blaming the mishap on her own lack of vigilance.

Eleanor had assumed their dinner would be called off, but Howard had insisted on going ahead with it, taking care to cheer Hannah with lots of warm reassurances and giving her a wad of money to cover a Chinese takeaway. They had left the entire crew encamped among the mattresses and sleeping bags in front of Eleanor's small telly, awaiting the delivery of their meal; Luke and his bandaged ankle and crutches occupying prime position on the sofa and Bart stretched across the laps of the two girls.

Out in the street, a taxi had been waiting, ordered by Howard while Eleanor had showered, swiping a brush through her ragged hair and dabbing some concealer across her nose and cheeks in an attempt to quieten the pink left by the morning sunshine. They had swept across Chelsea Bridge to a restaurant tucked away in a cobbled mews, where Howard was greeted like a lost friend, and the dining area had the air of a private sitting room, so hushed and salubrious that for the first few minutes Eleanor had found herself speaking in a whisper. To be brought to such a place reminded her with something of a jolt that Howard was a wealthy city banker. Not a bad-looking wealthy city banker either, she told herself. If it was security they were all after in this Kat-less world, then maybe a closeness with her widowed brother-in-law would be one sort of right answer. For one fleeting, despicable moment, Eleanor even allowed herself some hint of poetic justice: two decades on, the Big Sister who was robbed of her first love, levels the score.

Howard seemed troubled by her untouched wine. 'But you might hate it.'

Eleanor smiled wryly. 'Somehow I think that unlikely.' She had glimpsed the wine list, marvelling both at its exorbitant prices and at Howard's willingness to pore over such a relatively short document for quite so long.

'You were fantastic today, Eleanor,' he said quietly, 'bloody brilliant in fact. In the gardens, at the hospital, helping organise and entertain everybody, and then this evening.'

'This evening? Really? What did I do?' Eleanor's mind drifted to the brief ecstasy when it had come to her turn in the bathroom, the respite of being properly alone after the long day.

'All that stuff with Luke about your laptop and phone. Taking his mind off his ankle.'

'Oh that.' She laughed again, starting properly to relax. 'That wasn't me taking your son's mind off his poorly ankle. That was me being a ruthless aunt. I have a new smartphone I don't understand. I want to open a Twitter account and don't know how, and I am thinking of starting a blog. Luke got me further in twenty minutes than I would ever have managed on my own in days. He was fantastic – a mine of information...' She broke off because Howard was giving her one of his new odd looks, as if he was watching her mouth move rather than actually listening to what came out of it.

'What sort of blog?' he asked after a pause.

'Oh I don't know.' Eleanor was aware of striving for a levity she did not feel, both because Howard's intensity was making her nervous and because her blog idea was cherished but still very hazy. 'The challenges of teaching idle teenagers. Why reading matters. Stuff like that. Dull probably.' She took a swig of wine by way of escape, only to find herself gasping out loud. 'Oh wow... that is... my goodness... truly delicious.'

Howard's face lit up. 'So you *do* like it. Good.'

A waiter arrived with their starters, setting down the plates and then proceeding to describe what was on them in such detail that Eleanor had to stifle a childish urge to giggle. With Howard so earnest and the place so grand, she had a sudden uncharitable wish that she was eating out with someone more relaxed and normal – someone like Trevor or Megan, who would have been only too ready to see the funny side.

It was some fifteen minutes later when she had forgotten all about being on her guard, that Howard, chopping at the slithers of pink duck breast he had ordered as a main course, announced solemnly, 'There is something I need to tell you, Eleanor, something I am hoping you might have guessed.'

Under the flap of the tablecloth, Eleanor was all at once vividly conscious of the proximity of her brother-in-law's legs, his knees and shins, inches from hers. She dropped her gaze to her plate, where three scallops, fat as scones, sat on a colourful cocktail of salad and vegetables, surrounded by spirals of a buttery yellow sauce. In spite of everything, her mouth flooded with saliva.

'Hey, are you sure you wouldn't prefer a glass of white with those?' Howard urged, breaking the moment.

Eleanor assured him she didn't, seeking refuge in a hefty swig of the delicious red to demonstrate the point. He was understandably playing for time, she decided, his courage faltering. She must be kind, that was paramount. She sliced off a wedge of scallop and started eating. The taste was sensational; firm on the teeth, but soft as marshmallow, the flavour salty-sweet. She stole a glance at Howard, chewing his duck and looking tormented. All she wanted was a decent friendship, an avenue to her sister's children. Yet sometimes men were drawn to women who didn't overtly need them, as she knew only too well from the wild years after Igor. She swallowed and cleared her throat. 'You were saying?'

Howard threw down his knife and fork. 'You must have noticed something,' he urged softly. 'It's hard to hide. Insane of course. Hopeless.' He shook his head wretchedly. 'And the very last thing I had planned. Or expected.' He pressed his fists to his temples, moaning. 'Eleanor, tell me you must have noticed a certain... closeness—'

'Well I have...' Eleanor swallowed.

'We have to be so careful because of the children,' Howard burst out, all the composure in his face dissolving. 'And I want your blessing on it, Eleanor. I *need* your blessing.'

'My blessing?'

'On me and Hannah.' He held up both hands to stop her speaking. 'I know, I know – it's far too early. And she's young – far too young. But we... there is such...' His face twitched with emotion. 'It's like it was *meant* to be,' he said at length. 'She came through when I needed her. The children adore her, and not surprisingly, because she is brilliant with them...'

'And the dog,' offered Eleanor feebly, groping through her astonishment for something to say.

'Oh yes, Barty too – she's a marvel with him.' Howard laughed the loose easy laugh of one who has divested himself of a great burden. 'She has all of us, the whole gang, eating out of her hand. But...' He shook his head, his expression clouding, 'I am not a complete idiot. I know it is too much too soon. Hannah knows it too. She might be young, but she is no fool.'

Eleanor was tempted to seek clarity on the exact age of the nanny but feared this might appear unfeeling. Amid her own private flood of relief, she also found herself fighting a surge of outrage on Kat's behalf. Six months dead, and her husband had fallen for the au pair.

'It doesn't in any way diminish what I felt for Kat,' said Howard quietly, perhaps having seen more in her expression than intended. 'Like I say, it was not planned. I fought it – we both did. It has just... emerged.'

A look of such sheepish happiness had overtaken him, softening the pointy features of his face, that Eleanor couldn't help smiling. Life did just happen.

'And because of that – because of Kat – I want your approval,' continued Howard doggedly. 'I need your approval, Eleanor.'

Out of the corner of her eye, Eleanor could see their waiter pondering whether to make an approach to clear for the next course. 'Well, I'm not going to give it to you.'

'Because you think it's wrong.' It was a statement not a question, delivered in the grim tone of one hearing what had been expected.

'Oh no, not because of that.' Eleanor hesitated. A small wicked part of her was starting to enjoy herself. The whole situation was indeed insane, as Howard himself had pointed out, but Kat, with her wildness, might even have liked that, she decided suddenly. Most importantly, Hannah would do her best to look after Howard and the children. And love wasn't about choice, she reminded herself. In that sense it could never be 'wrong'. 'What I think,' Eleanor went on carefully, 'is that when two people connect, really connect, in whatever circumstances, it is rare and to be treasured.'

Howard let out a sharp laugh of relief. 'So, you are okay with it?'

'Only you have to be okay with it, Howard. You and Hannah. If you two are happy, then that is all that matters. I'm not going to judge you.' Eleanor sat back smiling. 'I hope that is what you needed to hear.'

In reply he leant across the table and kissed her cheek.

* * *

On the way home in the taxi, Howard suddenly asked if Kat had been faithful to him. 'That you know of.'

'Absolutely. That I know of. Not that she would have told me. We didn't exactly share confidences, remember?' she reminded him dryly. 'Why do you ask anyway?'

Howard absently traced a finger over the red light of the door-lock. 'I found this letter – an email, printed out – from a man called Nick Wharton. It was at the back of her desk drawer, folded up. He was turning forty and wanted to know how she was.' He paused, frowning. 'I remember the name, vaguely, back in the day. One of the many conquests before me.' He chuckled quietly, with what sounded like pride.

Eleanor gripped her knees as her heart rate quickened, glad of the darkness of the cab; one name and still her heart started a stampede. After all that had happened. It was pitiful. She was no better than one of Pavlov's dogs, she decided gloomily, reacting to a bloody bell.

Howard was still talking. 'I checked back in her inbox, but there was no thread that I could find. It just made the fact of printing it out seem a bit odd. It got me wondering whether maybe she had embarked on some sort of correspondence I didn't know about. Everyone's at it now, after all,' he went on cheerily. 'Facebook and Friends Reunited – hooking up with old pals. I've had several old acquaintances get in touch with me in recent years, mostly the ones I didn't want to hear from.' He laughed dryly.

Eleanor's heart had settled back into a normal pace. 'Oh, but I can tell you all about Nick Wharton,' she assured Howard breezily, 'there's no mystery there.' She went on to impart the gist of the Nick history between her and Kat, liking the way it sounded, so distant and over. 'That email arrived when I was visiting Kat that very first time after her op – back in January last year when we... when I... still thought that she was going to get better.' Eleanor faltered as one of the aches of loss ebbed inside her, knowing that, as always, Howard felt it too. 'Kat got me to print it out,' she went on more quietly, 'and then ordered me to help compose a jolly reply. You know how bossy she could be.' She sighed, the sadness still strong. 'It was just a laugh. All very above board.' Howard smiled at her looking somewhat relieved.

The taxi had pulled up outside her flat. Eleanor scrambled out first to beat Howard to the task of paying, only to be told it was on a company account. Upstairs, it was immediately clear that Hannah had known all along the mission behind the dinner date. She avoided Eleanor's eye, fidgeting with her thick curtain of hair, which hung loose for once, and scooping up her belongings as they exchanged pleasantries, hasty and whispered on account of the sleeping children.

'The taxi is waiting to take you on,' Howard told Hannah, smiling at the nanny in a way that blazed his true feelings so clearly that Eleanor wondered at her own dimness in not having noticed. 'I'll come with you. I'll be an hour max,' he promised Eleanor, scooping up the puppy, who blinked sleepily, staying limp with trust in his arms.

Eleanor followed them to the top of the stairs, handing over a set of keys and shooting Howard a look designed to communicate that he could take as long as he liked.

'I'm pleased for both of you, truly,' she whispered, giving Hannah a hug.

The girl muttered a thank you and darted after Howard down the stairwell, only to reappear a moment later, pulling a thick cream-coloured envelope out of her shoulder bag. 'God, I nearly forgot. This came. Your neighbour said it had got into the wrong box downstairs. She was about to put it under the door as the Chinese arrived,' she explained, before racing off again.

Eleanor let the envelope rest in her palm for a moment, feeling its heaviness. Stepping carefully between the sleeping children, she shut herself in her bedroom and sat on the bed. The address was typewritten, the flap sealed so securely it took some ripping to get it open. Inside was another envelope, much smaller and slimmer, with her name on it, and a letter from a firm of London solicitors, grand enough to have a coat of arms under their name. She was the beneficiary of a will, the letter said. The jargon was blinding. Eleanor read it and re-read it, not believing what it seemed to be saying. It appeared she had been left a house. A house on the outskirts of Oxford. A house she had once known intimately because it was where she had worked and made love once or twice a week for almost a decade. A decade of waste and hanging on, as she had always seen it, ended by her lover's return to his wife.

The smaller envelope also contained a line in Igor's spidery hand.

My dear girl, for the best years of my life.

PART IV

2014 - OXFORD

29

It was blissfully cool in the Covered Market. Eleanor stood in line at the flower stall, picking out the colours that would mix well, wanting to be ready when her turn came. She had decided to get enough for two vases, one as a centrepiece for the food and one for the sitting room, something flamboyant and dramatic, so as to give Trevor's guests a lovely shock when they walked in.

At the thought of the evening party, just hours away, her stomach clenched with nerves. Trevor had a signing in an Oxford bookshop and she had offered to play host for a gathering afterwards. It was hardly a big deal. But she did so want it to go well. Megan had promised to come but cried off because of a sick child.

The flower queue was moving slowly. The girl in dungarees attending to customers looked flustered and out of her depth. Over her shoulder, Eleanor could just glimpse the sunlight bouncing off the cobbled stone wall against which she had parked her bicycle, locking it with the new heavy chain that weighed almost as much as the bike itself. Her first bike had been stolen after a few days, from the alleyway that housed the entrance to the small prestigious tutorial college that now employed her. She had emerged from her first teaching session, still reeling at the eagerness of the students, to find her little black padlocked tube in two neat pieces on the pavement, a broken circle.

The girl in dungarees was looking close to tears. She had got some change wrong and her Sellotape machine had jammed, making it impossible to stick the packs of flower food to each bunch. Eleanor was tempted to elbow her way through the crowd to help out, or to cut loose for the deli and come back. The Covered Market was as packed as she had ever known it, thanks to the glorious wave of Indian summer heat and the usual swarms of tourists, combining with long-suffering locals trying to go about their daily lives. It seemed increasingly to Eleanor to be a peculiar miracle of Oxford that the city was able to hang onto itself amid such heaving occupation. The richness of its past hung off every stone, hovered in every particle of air but in a way that buoyed it up instead of dragging it down.

It was in the Covered Market that Eleanor still found her own past echoing back at her most strongly. Snatches were arriving now, as they always did, of Nick cramming forkfuls of beans and toast into his mouth at the café that had once occupied the site between the butchers and the flower stall, talking eagerly about books or dissections, his wide agile lips working to keep up with his brain; and Igor, taking her one quiet birthday many years later to the leather shop that was still on the corner, to buy a handbag.

Some memories never lost their power. It was something she had tried to explain to her Virginia Woolf group that week as they struggled with the author's dense, multi-layered prose, pointing out that it was precisely the shimmering strata of personal history that lay at the heart of being alive. Experiences built up like sediment over the years, no less formative and essential for being invisible and often ignored. The present only derived its shape from what had gone before and what might yet come to pass; every living moment resonated with the oceans of moments that had preceded it and those that were still to arrive. There was memory and there was hope. Life, as something lived, took place between the two. The students had nodded and tapped and scribbled as they tended to when she took flight. But had they understood? What could anyone really understand at eighteen?

A man in a peaked cap came to help the girl and the flower queue began to shift. Eleanor bought carnations, lilies and roses, together with several things she didn't know the name of and a bunch of feathery ferns for filling out. The deli was in a post-lunch lull and had everything she wanted. Soon she was pedalling back down the Woodstock Road, the wind thickening the long bramble of her hair, her loose white shirt billowing over her jeans. She cycled hard, getting overheated in the process but needing to hurry because there was still so much to do.

A text arrived from Trevor while she was waiting at a traffic light. He had checked into The Randolph and would be around soon with the wine. He hoped her fridge had space for the white. He had a speech of thanks prepared but wasn't sure if it was funny enough. She was a star.

Eleanor smiled to herself, grateful as always for Trevor's expressions of appreciation. With *For My Sins* launched earlier in the month and selling very well, she had on occasion found herself musing somewhat darkly on the aptness of the term 'ghostwriter'. She had done her job and received her fee. No one was interested in her. The same had been true of the book she wrote with Igor. Now at least she was directing her spare energies to her own writing project for once. The story was starting to take shape: Two little girls shut out by the strangely intense relationship between their parents. Two little girls who never spoke of the things that mattered because they didn't have the words; who were close beyond measure until events they couldn't share pushed them apart. It had even acquired a working title: *The Habit of Silence*.

The traffic light changed to green. Ten minutes of vigorous cycling later the first glimpse of the pitched roof of what had once been Igor's home still caused Eleanor's heart to skip a beat. One of several properties strung out along the winding approach to Wolvercote, the house was not eye-catching in any conventional sense: a rambling, hybrid of a place, it comprised a stone cottage, added to in an amalgam of questionable styles, with a tumbledown garage at the front and a half-acre of garden at the back. Inside, the general air of dilapidation left by years of letting had initially been a shock, almost erasing at one stroke all Eleanor's memories of the clean, austere warmth under Igor's occupation of the property. The rooms were as numerous and spacious as she remembered them, but in one section an ugly prefab corridor had been constructed to house an extra kitchen and two pokey bathrooms. Few pipes were clear of crusty limescale clinging to their joints, swathes of hairy black mildew forested several walls, doors didn't close, the paint peeled and the carpets were worn to the floorboards; yet Eleanor, taking it all in on her first April visit, her very own set of front door keys dangling in her hand, had still been dazzled.

Five months on, that Igor, of all people, should have presented her with a gift of such magnitude, without warning or strings, was still something of a dream. Pleasingly, it had also lifted the veil on some of the mortification of the tail-end of their affair, allowing her to recall that the Russian had indeed once loved her passionately, as she had him. Eleanor had longed to be able to tell Igor how thankful she was, but by the time the lawyers had made contact, Igor was dead and buried, back in his homeland, beside the wife to whom he had ultimately been true. Eleanor had had to settle instead for paying her own quiet homage, by placing the book containing the newspaper obituary in the middle of the sitting room's main wall of shelves, cocooned among some of her own favourites and where Igor himself had once kept rows of his own treasured scholarly tomes.

Dismounting on the scruffy patch of tarmac in front of the garage, Eleanor noted to her dismay that it was already past three o'clock. She wrestled with the gate latch as usual, propping it open with a flower pot to save a similar inconvenience for guests, before wheeling her bike between the twiggy beds of lavender that bordered the path to the front door.

Inside the hall, grappling with her purchases, Eleanor managed to collide with the stepladder left from the morning painting session that had made her late for the shopping. The ladder toppled with a clatter, only just missing knocking her freshly painted wall. Eleanor stepped over it and hurried into the kitchen, flicking on the radio before settling to the task of unpacking and sorting the fridge for the arrival of Trevor's wine. Twenty guests, tops, he had said. If half of them drank red, that would only mean five bottles to squeeze inside for chilling. Except that Trevor and his friends drank a lot. Ten bottles then. Maybe twelve. Her phone buzzed.

Thinking balloons for the gate? Prevent lost guests. Be there soon. Tx

Eleanor took out one of the cold chicken dishes she had prepared the night before to make some extra room and emptied out her shopping. The wine would get squeezed in somehow. She needed to find vases for the flowers.

A tune she liked came on the radio. She jigged her way into the dining room. A party would be fun. She would travel to the bookshop by bike so as not to have to worry about parking, and wear the charity dress that had seen her through the summer.

She got two vases out of the dining room sideboard, one of the few furniture items to have survived from the Igor days, and then paused to look out onto the garden. The late September sun was hot on her face through the glass. It felt fantastic, like being stroked with big warm hands. Through half-closed eyes she stared out at the square lawn, bushy with moss and daisies, the borders of aged shrubs and various unsightly brambled patches that were clearly hangovers from attempts to grow vegetables. But there were bits that Eleanor remembered fondly and had grown to love again: like the magnolia by the bottom fence, fairly drab in its early autumn guise, but which on her first visit back in April had greeted her like a prima ballerina in full pirouette, its layered skirts of dusky pink flowers in full spin; and the old giant of a weeping ash that arched towards the house, exploding all summer like a great green fountain.

Eleanor was trying to open one of the dining room's lattice windows when the rat-tat-tat of her front door knocker sounded. She kept thumping at the window frame, sticky from more of her own recent efforts with a paintbrush, yelling over her shoulder to Trevor that the door was open. The window gave way suddenly, releasing an angry wasp, which bounced off into the garden like a bullet.

'Trevor, it's open,' she called again, flicking off the radio as she returned to the hall, pausing to pick up the ladder and lean it against the banisters. Having arrived at the door, however, she stopped. The shadow of the figure visible through the mottled glass did not belong to Trevor. It was too tall.

Eleanor stayed motionless, staring. Something wasn't right. She could feel it in her bones, her hackles. She was a great believer in hackles. Animal instincts. Humans ignored them at their peril.

She called out in a firm voice, 'Who is it please?'

There was a muffled answer, which might or might not have been her name.

Eleanor slid the chain into place before turning the handle. A slice of a face greeted her. A face with a broad forehead topped by dusty brown hair, the sides receding; wide, boyish blue eyes, darkly lashed, but heavily crinkled at the corners in the manner of someone over-accustomed to squinting into bright sun. The skin on the face looked rough and pale, the cheeks sunken, leaving the cheekbones like two prominent points of an upturned triangle. It was the third point that saved the face from sadness: the strong jaw, topped by a mouth that was curling up slightly at the corners. It was a face she had thought of perhaps a thousand times, perhaps a million. Such a familiar face and yet so utterly changed.

Eleanor gently closed the door and leant it against it, breathing hard.

'Eleanor,' he called, audibly this time. When she didn't answer, the letterbox flap fluttered open. 'Please.' His voice boomed through the gap, making her jump to one side. 'I got your letter.'

Eleanor looked down at the fingers prised round the metal letter-flap, keeping it open. Unlike Nick's face, they were extraordinarily unchanged, long and strong, the little finger on the left adorned with the signet ring she had forgotten, a lion and sword.

What Eleanor felt most strongly was that there was nothing left to say. She had done all her explaining, written it down in the letter. She had laid herself bare, and then signed off with a final farewell that had come from the innermost point of her heart. The prospect of being forced to go over it all again, and worse, in person felt beyond her capabilities. It had taken a lot to get her life on an even keel. Every atom of her being was poised for the fight to keep it that way.

Besides, there was the shock of seeing him to contend with. He looked old and terrible. She preferred the image she had been carrying round in her head for twenty years; the careless tousled beauty of Nick Wharton at twenty-two, his glory undiminished by baggy home-knitted jumpers, his shoulders broad and proud, his face still full of hope.

Oh god, and now he knew she had loved him, Eleanor remembered, groaning softly. She had told him in the letter. She had told him everything. Loving him. Losing him. Kat. The cancer. The deceit. Vincent's abuse. Everything. She wondered suddenly how much of it he had relayed to the beautiful South African wife; the incredulity and horror they must have shared in the build-up to this latest UK visit. Her guts churned.

'Please go,' she said, the strain making her voice stern. 'I've said everything I have to say. It is done with. All of it is done with. I am so sorry for what I put you through.' She sank to her knees as she spoke because her legs had started feeling curiously unequal to the task of keeping her upright. 'I am sorry, Nick, okay? I've said sorry. Please leave me alone.'

The fingers slowly withdrew and the flap closed with a thwack. Eleanor stared at it. Outside, all had gone quiet. She lifted the letter flap and peered out, seeing a section of the loose path tiles and some straggles of lavender. She got up and picked up the ladder from the banisters. It needed putting away in the cellar. Instead, she set it down again and returned to the front door, opening it quickly.

He was sitting on the wall with his back to her, his long legs stretched out in front of him, crossed at the ankles.

'I thought you had gone.'

'No, I haven't gone.'

Eleanor stayed in the doorway, folding her arms, but only so she could hug herself. He had spoken without turning round. He had a nice voice. She had forgotten that. A light breeze was blowing at his hair, showing thinness over the crown. That his body had grown so stick-like was the fresh shock. It accentuated the length of him, even sitting down, but also made him look oddly angular. He was wearing off-white chinos that seemed far too wide for his legs and a dusty blue jacket through which she could clearly make out the sharp mounds of his shoulder blades.

'Nick, look, I'm sorry—'

'You took some tracking down—'

Having both spoken together, they stopped at the same instant. He was the first to carry on, though still with his back to her.

'Thank you for this.' He plucked an envelope from inside the blue jacket and waved it over his head. Her letter, Eleanor realised with a start. Unbidden, the words that had spilled from her pen began flooding her mind...

I fell in love with you the moment you walked into the college library. Of course I couldn't say. Not at almost-nineteen with a raw heart and no confidence and you with your childhood sweetheart. Tilly. I had just about got my head around that when you fell for Kat. Which you had every right to do, by the way. EVERY RIGHT. Because all really is fair in love and war. You loved my sister and it was up to me to deal with it, which I did, mainly, as you might recall, by avoiding both of you! I am not proud of that now – it was daft, but there you go. Like I say, I was young and had a broken heart. Unfortunately it put the seal on the distance between Kat and me, but as it turned out, there were other reasons for that too, which I fear I will get to in due course...

'Look. Nick...' Eleanor faltered. She wanted, more than anything, to put a stop to the sentences reforming in her head. They were clogging her brain, slowing her down. In retrospect it seemed incredible the detail that had poured out of her that March afternoon. Only the certainty that they would never meet had made it possible.

It was a relief to see him slide the letter back inside his jacket pocket.

'I understand if there is stuff you need to get off your chest,' Eleanor said, feeling calmer, but remaining on the doorstep, an easy decision given that he appeared not even to want to look at her. 'But I really have said everything I have to say. And right now I have to get ready for something. I'm badly behind as it is...' She broke off as he reached for a stick she hadn't noticed, propped on the wall next to him, and used it to lever himself upright and turn round. 'Have you hurt yourself?' It was impossible not to ask.

He prodded at something on the ground with the tip, which had a thick cap of scuffed grey rubber.

'Are you ill?' she demanded next, much more shrilly than she had meant.

'No, not ill. At least...' He seemed about to smile and then sighed. 'It is, as they say, a long story. An accident last December. Some lingering neural damage. But I am much better now.'

'Jesus, I'm so sorry. What sort of accident?'

He looked at her levelly. 'Swimming off the cape. I got swept out too far. Nearly drowned.' He let out a sudden laugh, shaking his head, 'I did drown actually, for five minutes or so, but then I got fished out...'

Eleanor had approached down the path without thinking about it, gawping. 'Christ. How terrifying.'

'It wasn't actually. It was more...' Nick frowned, searching for the right word, trying not to be distracted by the chance to have her near enough to scrutinise properly. She had put a tiny pass-port photo in with the letter, but it did not begin to do justice to the reality of her, so tremendously tall – he had forgotten how tall she was – and so carelessly attired in cut-off jeans and flip-flops, a white, rather grubby shirt half tucked in, her thick tumbling hair the colour of tea, her brown eyes huge and alarmed. '...More simple than terrifying, actually,' he went on. 'What mattered became very clear. Like a voice shouting inside my head.'

Eleanor flinched with surprise but did not say anything.

'There was no fighting it, just acceptance. Just knowing what mattered.'

'And what did matter?'

'Love.' He shrugged.

Eleanor had arrived at the gate and was holding on to it. Through the gaps in the roadside hedge she could see glints of silver which had to be his car. He could drive then, in spite of the stick.

'I am so very sorry about Kat, Eleanor,' he said quietly, 'all of it... just so... cruel. I still can't believe it.'

Eleanor kept her eye on the hedge. 'Thank you. Neither can

I. And I am sorry for having to tell you like that. I can't imagine what you must have felt.' She swallowed, a wave of the old self-mortification coming at her. Justification for what she had done was impossible. She had done her best with that in the letter. 'The worst of it was that we – I – thought she was all right and then she wasn't. It was caught late that was the trouble. There had been things she'd noticed... oddities... for months, but she chose to ignore them. Then she decided she didn't want treatment. Typical bloody obstinate girl. Determined to shoulder everything on her own. Like the other stuff... with Dad.'

Nick groaned softly.

'I am sorry for burdening you with that too. Another shock. It just seemed best to tell you everything, give you the full picture. It all seemed connected.' Eleanor held the silver glints of his car in her gaze, realising that maybe the conversation could be got through after all, if she tackled it head-on and quickly, saying all that he could possibly expect of her, without any fuss. 'It explained so much, you see. How she was back then. With me. With you.' Eleanor took a deep breath. 'And as for what I did, writing to you when she was sick, letting you think I was her – as I have tried to explain, it was never a game. It just somehow started... one decision to do something that led to another... and another. Snowballing. I suppose it took my mind off other things. Did I write that?'

'Yes, you wrote that.'

'I cannot tell you how sorry I am,' Eleanor said softly. 'How ashamed.'

'Yes, you wrote that too.'

A bubble of concentration seemed to have formed round them. Close-to, he looked not only unwell but so deeply sad that Eleanor experienced a rush of guilt worse than any she had hitherto experienced. 'Your feelings for Kat... if I opened those up... I am so...'

The squawk of a car horn made them both start. Trevor's Nissan swung through the gap in the roadside hedge, revving to a stop on the square of tarmac. 'Early guest?' he boomed, leaping out, red-faced, a panama hat sitting at a jaunty angle on the back of his head. 'If that's your car, my friend,' he went on to Nick, jerking a thumb in the direction of the road, 'I have to say that is not the most ideal parking spot – a near-miss, if I am honest. Sweetest, I hope you're feeling strong. We've got a bit to unload in here.' He opened the boot and started tugging at one of several cardboard boxes wedged inside.

'Trevor this is Nick Wharton, Nick this is Trevor Downs,' said Eleanor as evenly as she could, hurrying to Trevor's side so that she could give him a look designed to ward off any unhelpful questions.

Trevor duly limited himself to a brief polite nod in Nick's direction, saying he was delighted to make his acquaintance before hurriedly returning his attentions to the contents of the boot. Trevor was, in fact, beyond curiosity. With just a couple of hours to go, he had entered the blinkered phase of one-track concern that had once characterised his preparation to go on stage and act well. His mind was entirely on himself: his book event, his speech, his reading, and the smooth running of the after-party.

'After all that, I forgot the blooming balloons,' he muttered, trundling off towards the house with a case of wine.

'I better go,' Nick said.

'Yes,' Eleanor muttered, fighting a mad impulse to ask him to stay. She accompanied him to the roadside, trying not to stare as he walked. Both legs worked all right, but the right one stuck out slightly, so that the foot led at an odd angle. She could see at once Trevor's point about how he had parked the car. An attempt to line up with a curve in the road had left it sticking out badly at one end. 'Look, thank you for coming. I hope you don't feel it was a wasted journey. It's just that I've said all I can. There's nothing more I could add to make you understand or forgive me—'

'Of course I forgive you,' he snapped. 'Your letter was...

extraordinary. Life – all our lives – are complicated. Forgiveness is not an issue.'

'Oh,' Eleanor murmured, somewhat stunned. 'Good. Thanks.' She stood by the car, keeping an eye out for traffic as he levered himself into the driver's seat, noting the controls on the steering wheel and the disabled sticker on the windscreen. It impressed her that car-rental firms could be so accommodating. 'Enjoy the rest of your trip,' she said, as he wound the window down.

'Back there...' He nodded in the direction of the house. 'Was that Trevor Downs, the actor?'

'Yes, yes it was.'

'I saw him do *Hamlet* once, decades ago, at the Old Vic. Fantastic.'

'Really? Wow, that's...' Eleanor hopped out of the way as a tractor rumbled into view, bearing a surly-faced farmer and a wide, trembling load of hay bales. Nick needed to reverse to give it room to pass. Eleanor walked backwards behind the bumper offering hand signals to assist during the manoeuvre.

'Thanks. And good luck with everything,' he said, once the tractor had roared off. 'I just felt that, after everything, it was right in the end to try to see you.'

'Yes. Absolutely. So it was. Where are you headed now?'

'My mother. She's in Cheltenham these days.'

'Oh good. Well, best of luck to you too.' Eleanor waved him off. He went slowly, tooting the horn twice.

She raced back to find the Nissan boot closed and Trevor standing in some dismay before the crammed shelves of her small fridge.

'All sorted out there?' He shot her a beady look.

'Yes thanks, all sorted.' Eleanor reached past him and began pulling out more dishes to make room for the wine, gripping them hard to stop the tremor in her hands.

'Tell me later maybe?'

'Maybe.' She rummaged, not looking at him. 'I got some bags

of ice last week, they're in the freezer in the utility room. We could stick them in a bucket now, and put a few bottles in there. What do you think?'

'I think you are a genius.'

'And now I ought to change,' she muttered, pushing straggles of hair out of her eyes and making a mental note to pin it with something for the evening. 'Then I'll be all yours,' she added with a grin, darting off before he could reply.

Only in the privacy of her bedroom, not the one she had shared with Igor, but another, plainer one she had picked out for herself, standing before her wall-mirror in the charity-shop dress, a butterfly-clip in her wild hair, did Eleanor allow herself to pause and breathe and think. It had been good of Nick to come. Good and thoughtful. And very brave. He looked old before his time, and wounded. Nick Wharton had become real again. He nurtured no rancour towards her. It ought to mean she could let him go.

* * *

Nick unclicked his seat belt and pulled out Eleanor's letter. He had got onto the M40 and then off it again, taking the exit to the Oxford Services, where the car park was even vaster than he remembered and a fancy water feature had been added to the front of a building that now resembled an airport terminal. He had deliberately selected a space with nothing on either side, but the moment he turned the engine off, a small dusty black car had pulled up beside him, rap music pulsing from its open roof.

The letter was grubby from handling. The contents, first glimpsed six months before, had ripped at his heart. Shock wave after shock wave, each worse than the last. But they had also offered truth, plainly, beautifully and regretfully expressed. In the heat even of the very first reading, the final showdown with

Donna still ringing in his ears, Nick had recognised the value of this.

He turned his back on the noisy car and scanned the opening lines, in spite of having come to know them by heart.

Dear Nick,

This is the hardest letter I have ever had to write. If you are not sitting down, then please do so now...

Nick jumped as a palm slapped his window. The driver of the black car, waved a cigarette, gesturing a request for a light. Nick shook his head and the man loped off in the direction of the building.

Nick dug inside the envelope for the little photo. He had taken more care of that over the months, held it round the edges, not put smeary fingerprints across her face. She said it was to make up for not having been able to send him one when he asked. Studying it now, dimly aware that the mild tremble in his hands that came and went since the accident was worse than usual, Nick contemplated the candid wide-eyed gaze which he had thought told him so much but which had actually disclosed nothing beyond the very obvious point that Eleanor Keating's always formidable looks had improved with age. It had not, for instance, prepared him for the impact of seeing her; the mesmerising, disarming effect of those looks in the flesh. Nor had it provided any defence against the affecting blend of adult assuredness, so marked in what he now knew to be all her written correspondence, with the apologetic uncertainty that she had displayed that afternoon. He hadn't been prepared for that.

In fact nothing about the encounter had gone as he had envisaged or planned, Nick reflected bitterly. Not one second. For a start, he had felt clumsy and cumbersome with his stick. Maybe that was why he had made such a botch of saying what he had intended to say, failing to ask all the questions he had meant to ask, not offering any of the reassurances he genuinely felt.

With weeks and weeks to come to the decision to track her down, he had believed himself prepared. Steadying himself for the opening of the front door, he had still believed it. But then she had poked her face through the gap, shrieked, slammed the door shut and shouted back at him through the letterbox to leave her alone. All of which had thrown him off course.

He had been outmanoeuvred by his own unforeseen reactions, Nick ruminated bleakly, not to mention the sudden and incongruous appearance of Trevor Downs. Trevor Downs. Of all people. The man who, at the height of his powers as a stage actor, had, virtually single-handedly, shifted Nick's schoolboy perception of Shakespeare as a dull, necessary component of the English GCSE syllabus into a genius capable of evoking a state of awed stupefaction. It had been a school trip. Nick had signed up because his English teacher told him to. He had set off in the coach thinking Hamlet was a verbose, fusty make-believe Danish prince only to find Trevor vividly, convincingly, playing the part as a disoriented student, overwhelmed by life-changing events, as someone, in other words, whom Nick felt he might know. Aged fourteen, he had spent the return journey in an altogether different frame of mind, one that had never left him and which had played a serious part in all the early wavering over medicine. If only he'd had the wherewithal to thank Trevor for this epiphany.

Nick folded the pages of the letter back along its worn creases, wincing at the memory of Eleanor Keating after twenty years, helping him reverse in an Oxford country lane. Eleanor who had written to him for all those months, letting him think she was Kat. While poor dear Kat herself had been dying, holding fast to the unimaginably dark truth about her childhood. Nick had found all the new knowledge converging inside him. It had been deeply disorientating. It had made it hard to concentrate on which way to turn the wheel.

Nick began to slip the letter back into its envelope but then hesitated, glimpsing one of his favourite bits.

Feelings happen. In fact I am astonished that people separate them from facts. They are just as strong, just as solid. They make us do things, not always wise things...

She was such a clever woman, so unflinchingly self-aware, so interesting. He had known that once, a long time ago, and forgotten it. The same warm intelligence had shone out of her emails, so vibrantly that once the initial body blow of shock at the confession about authorship and its tragic circumstances had worn off, Nick had felt almost stupid for not rumbling the duplicity himself. Of course Kat couldn't have written in such a way. She had never had the same intellect, or perspicacity, or patience. As he remembered only too well, Kat's capacity to attend to anything for more than a few minutes had been woeful. It had been one of the most maddening, tantalising aspects of her, the way she flitted from one thing to the next – men, as much as anything – seeking distraction. It all made more sense now, of course, terrible sense. It had been thrilling to be caught in the spotlight of Kat's attention. It was, after all, why he had fallen in love with her. But then it moved on.

And all Eleanor's blessed rules should have rung alarm bells too; the insistence on leaving the past alone, the growing hints of deep distress, the refusal to send a picture, the sudden, panicked closing of the door when he tried to tease her into describing herself. There had been so many hints, but just not enough for him to be able to piece them all together. Little wonder she hadn't been drawn on his suggestion of meeting up either, Nick reflected wryly. The Keating sisters – together – it would have been impossible.

Nick shifted in his car seat, sliding the key back into the ignition and taking it out again. Was there really any point in delaying the journey on up the motorway? Eleanor's letter, now back in its envelope, stared at him from the passenger seat, pale and defiant. Nick shuddered, as Eleanor's brief references to Kat's teenage ordeals floated back into his mind. They had stirred uncomfortable memories of Reverend Keating: a bear of a man who interrogated rather than talked, his voice booming, one hand always busy with his beard or the big wooden cross slung low over his ample torso. What he had done to his daughter, Nick found almost too sickening to contemplate. It filled him with pity, for Kat most obviously, but also for Eleanor, having to come to terms with such information so long after the event, dealing with the inevitable confusion and self-blame it must have caused, and with her father still alive too. The letter had left such matters alone, but Nick could guess them.

Someone else was waving at him through the car window now. A man with a small trolley of cleaning equipment. Did he want a car wash? Nick shook his head. England was still such a shock to the system – his native land, but full of things that kept feeling alien. On bad days he felt like he would never catch up with it. During better times, like that morning, sitting with toast, marmalade and a pot of tea in his mother's tiny back garden, the *Lancet* open at his elbow, the Gloucestershire sky arched overhead, he was overwhelmed by all the joy of a traveller who had returned home.

Nick wound the window down and the car-cleaning man ambled over, abandoning his trolley.

'How much?'

'How long you be?'

'Er... twenty minutes or so.'

'Okay. Five pound.'

Nick manoeuvred himself out of the car and set off towards the water feature. A cup of tea would be a good idea; help him gather his wits before heading back up the motorway. He walked slowly, trying to reduce his dependence on the stick. The self-consciousness in front of Eleanor was still fresh, but more importantly he had a new target in the form of a visit from his daughters at the end of October. He would dearly love the walking support to be gone by then. There were no guarantees of such progress, but already he had come such a long way. That he was still an optimist had been one of the few pleasing discoveries Nick had made about himself that year; a useful piece of flotsam floating out from the wreckage.

Being a Saturday, the A40 Services was busy. Nick queued for a cup of scalding tea and found a seat near the tall glass windows overlooking the water feature and the car park. He tried to FaceTime Sasha, then Natalie, but neither answered. He sent them both messages instead, reflecting with satisfaction on the focus with which he had fought for his rights as a father. In the months building up to his departure from South Africa he had seen them whenever he wanted, as well as securing an agreement to whatever access could be managed in the longer term, once he was back in England. Donna's affair with Mike Scammell had proved a trump card in that respect, any threat by Nick to expose it producing all sorts of handy climbdowns.

As to the financial aspect of the settlement, Nick had asked for so little that it left Donna's exorbitantly priced lawyers nothing left to argue with. At times, he had sensed even his bullish father-in-law looking on in disbelief, wrong-footed by the extent of the surrender.

Dimly, Nick knew his newly decrepit physical state had aided his cause too. Donna put on the occasional demonstration of tearful dismay about the split when it suited her, but when they were talking through matters alone, he often detected flashes of eagerness in her formidable eyes. She had no desire to be hitched to a man with a lopsided shuffle; a man who could offer no guarantee of resuming a full-time career, let alone in the demanding high-profile world which she had been so horrified he might abandon anyway. The prospect of a generous divorce appealed to her far more.

When his phone hummed into life beside his cup of tea, displaying his mother's phone number, Nick had to fight the urge not to pick up. She was so thrilled to have him around, it got too much sometimes.

'That Oxford hospital of yours called. They want to change

the time by half an hour. I think they thought I was your secretary.'

'Oh dear—'

'Which I don't mind. I've made a note in the diary.'

'Thanks Mum.' Nick did his best to sound genuinely grateful, while fighting the usual surge of shame at having his mother so involved with the minutiae of his life

'So it's still a week next Friday but at two not two-thirty.'

'Okay, thanks.'

'How was your friend?'

'Oh fine, thanks. Just fine. I should be home by seven. Seven-thirty at the latest.'

'Good. I've got Bridge, but I've made a shepherd's pie.'

'Super. See you soon,' Nick cut in quickly, seeing that Sasha was trying to get through.

He thanked the miracle of FaceTime as the smiling face of his youngest daughter appeared on his phone screen, her beautiful mouth still bulging with evident discomfort over the recently installed rail-track braces.

'Hey Daddeee, I got your message but I can't talk.'

'Hello Sashkins.'

'Don't *call* me that.'

'Okay Sash-poops, I won't call you that. Sit still or I can't see you.'

'Well, I can see *you*. Where are you anyway? Is it a party?'

Nick laughed, holding up the phone to render a glimpse of his decidedly un-festive surroundings, the queue of weary travellers by the till, the vacant grey plastic seat opposite. 'I've been visiting an old mate from my student days and have stopped in a motorway café. Where are you?'

'Adrienne's. But I've got to go. They're dropping me for riding with Gramps.'

'Fantastic. Say hi to your sister, won't you?'

'Sure. Love you, Dad.'

'And wear your helmets.'

'Of *course.*' She rolled her eyes at the tedium of being worried about.

'And, Sash, I can't wait to show both you and Nat round this place properly when you visit in October. It's the coolest university, I promise. And remember what I said about those things called Rhodes Scholarships?'

'Yeah, yeah, Dad. Gottago. Bye.' She put out her hand, puckering her lips to blow him a noisy kiss.

Nick blew one back, rejoicing at the miraculous resilience of his two astonishing children. Mum and Dad loved them, but not each other, that was the line he and Donna had taken. There had been tears, but not many. They had their friends, their horses, their routines, for solace. Soon their lives were rolling along again, just as Nick had prayed they would. Perhaps his accident had even helped there too, he mused now, since it meant they had got used to not having him around as much. What remained in no doubt was their certainty that he loved them, he had made sure of that, seizing every possible opportunity during the course of the last five months to reinforce the fact. Only his actual departure had been close to unbearable – but Nick did his best never to think about that. Just as he tried not to speculate on what they might really know behind their courage and sweetness. Donna had always reserved her worst behaviour for him, but still, one could never be sure how much they really knew.

Nick could see through the big sloping windows that his car wash had only just started. He checked his emails, seeing confirmation of the changed hospital interview his mother had mentioned and then decided to pass some time by googling Trevor Downs.

* * *

As Trevor stepped up to the front to start his speech, Eleanor found a good perch on the end of a book unit. She flexed her feet and arched her back, easing the stiffness from all her early-morning work up the ladder with a paint roller. The charity-shop dress appeared to be shrinking, she noted absently, observing how it now fell round her shins rather than her ankles. Too much washing, perhaps.

Trevor made a big to-do of asking for a chair to stand on and was soon in full flow. He began with a thank-you to the book-shop, did the joke about a classic being the book everyone owned and no one read and then moved onto the things he always said about Larry.

Eleanor let the bookshop recede, tuning Trevor's voice into white noise. Lots of people had come, including a couple of her work colleagues, which was touching. She wondered how many would pick up on the idea of the after-party and felt glad about all her dishes of chicken. Her gaze drifted from the attentive faces of the guests to the walls of shelves surrounding them, all the rows of spines lined up like regiments on parade, smart, multicoloured, marshalled under their respective headings: Biography. Fiction. Children. Travel. Crime. Historical. They were all stories of lives, she mused, regardless of the headings. The only thing that mattered was that the stories themselves would never stop arriving, never stop being written, never stop being lived. She thought of Kat, and her own trickle of progress on the story about two sisters, and a warmth coursed through her, the sense of being part of something, the sense of belonging.

Lost in the reverie, Eleanor could not have said what she noticed first, Nick Wharton's silver-grey stick, leaning against the central book table beside Nick himself, a copy of *For My Sins* clutched in one hand, a glass of orange juice in the other, or the fact that Trevor was signalling to her to take a turn on the chair.

'It seems only right,' he was declaring grandly, 'that the person too often overlooked, the person who did all the hard work, should have a chance to say a few words...'

Eleanor shook her head, scything a finger across her neck.

But someone in the audience called out the word 'Speech,' which others then took up, turning it into a chant, to the accompaniment of what quickly grew into rhythmic clapping.

'Just a few words, sweetie,' Trevor whispered, having left his perch to take her elbow and escort her to the chair, looking infuriatingly pleased with himself. 'Tell them how awful I was to work with. And your lovely party – you could mention that. Tell them how to get there.'

'What, *all* these people are coming?' Eleanor said weakly, letting herself be led while her brain performed cartwheels about what on earth to say.

* * *

That she did not need to stand on any chair in order to be noticed was Nick's first thought, closing Trevor's book so he could concentrate. His second thought focused on her change of clothes since the afternoon, from jeans and the big white shirt into a charcoal dress which hugged her chest and ribcage and then flared dramatically down to the calves of her long legs. Her shoes had something of the look of old friends about them, flat black pumps, clearly picked for comfort rather than style. And there were bracelets of deep indents in the skin round her ankles, Nick noticed suddenly – sock marks. He struggled to take his eyes off them, distracted by the refreshing notion of a woman too busy to care that they were there. For almost two decades he had lived with a creature who knew every blemish on her body, a creature who used magnifying mirrors to study such outrages as part of a daily, sometimes hourly, crusade for their eradication. It was a battle over which Nick had been expected to express sympathy, while never being allowed to release so much as a hint of even the most complimentary opinion to the effect that the need for such relentless eradications was groundless. It had been one of the minefields. His whole marriage had been made up of minefields.

'It's horrible being a ghost,' Eleanor began, looking both startled and relieved when people laughed. 'I nearly didn't manage it. In fact, Trevor is the only reason I *did* manage it. In fact...' she wrung her hands, accidentally gathering a section of the dress and momentarily revealing the point where one calf muscle narrowed to meet her knee. She had to have become a runner, Nick decided, to have developed legs like that. Or maybe it was just the cycling. He had seen an old bike with a basket propped beside her front door. She probably cycled everywhere. Most people in Oxford did.

'In fact, the last year has been something of a difficult one for me personally, and writing Trevor's wonderful life story – everyone should buy at least *two* copies,' she blurted, interrupting her own flow and holding up two fingers before hastily slapping them back to her side, looking embarrassed. 'The point is, being a ghost, working behind the scenes, *is* hard, but Trevor made it easy and, while he was at it, saved me from falling apart. He knows how and why,' she gabbled, as Trevor shook his head, 'and that is all that matters. And if *For My sins* contains some good juicy bits...' There were more titters from the audience, 'then I can assure you they are all Trevor's doing not mine...'

Someone in the audience yelled, 'Hear hear'. Eleanor looked about her, seeming to lose her train of thought and making Nick angry at whoever had provided so ill-timed a distraction, even if it was well-intentioned. He kept his attention on her face, willing her on as she nervously picked up the thread, delivering a few thank-yous, followed by some fairly incomprehensible instructions for navigating Oxford's one-way system towards Wolvercote.

Eleanor was surrounded as soon as she finished. Nick joined the queue for Trevor to sign his book, trying to focus on what he wanted to say to the actor. A second chance to meet a childhood hero. One didn't get many of those in a life, let alone within the timespan of a single day. Out of the corner of his eye, he kept track of Eleanor, locked now in intense conversation with a group at the drinks table. At one point she caught his eye and he managed to offer a quick thumbs-up of congratulation. Eleanor seemed to smile, but looked away so quickly it was hard to be sure.

* * *

Nick drove at a steady seventy, trying to concentrate on the motorway rather than speculations about the party in Wolvercote, to which Trevor had kindly issued an invitation and which he had refused. Necklaces of headlights streamed in both directions, adding to the deep, visceral sensation of the distance between him and Eleanor growing.

Accepting Trevor's invitation had been out of the question. Eleanor, Nick was certain, would have been horrified. She clearly hadn't wanted him to know of the event that evening. It was only googling Trevor in the services that had put him onto it.

Whether attending the event had in fact been the right thing to do, Nick was now in grave doubt. Getting the chance to speak to Trevor, acquiring his signature in the book, had been a great pleasure. But seeing Eleanor again, first busy talking to other attendees, and then, with that touchingly clumsy reluctance, taking up her stance on the chair, had been deeply unsettling. All the things he had intended and failed to say during the abortive visit to her house that afternoon had started popping back inside his head, together with the growing, dispiriting conviction that she wouldn't have been interested in hearing any of them anyway. The fleeting reference in her speech to what a difficult year it had been for her personally had only made things worse. His heart had wrenched, with a sense of privilege at being party to what those difficulties had entailed and frustration that he could not offer solace and reassurance.

The motorway snaked on towards Cheltenham, a winding river of light through a black sea. Nick shivered, turning up the heating. He felt the cold easily these days. And though southern England was still caught in its pocket of delicious autumnal warmth, the moment darkness fell there was the bite of real chill to the air. A proper winter loomed. His first in almost a decade. Inwardly a part of Nick quailed. It was another indication of the difference between missing his homeland and being immersed back in the reality of it. He had no regrets, yet, but many of his rose-tinted memories – from idyllic images of rural pubs and winding country lanes, to friendly attitudes and good television – were still receiving serious readjustment. England was a busy, overcrowded island with dodgy weather and a population as self-centred as any other. Even without the business of having to rebuild his life, Nick had quickly accepted that it was going to take some time to feel properly integrated again.

When his mobile rang, his first, absurd thought was that it was Eleanor. Instead, Donna's voice came on the line, strident with its new permanent note of righteous indignation.

'Where are you?'

'Hello Donna. Are the girls okay?'

'The girls are fine.'

'Good. Well, I'm driving, so I shouldn't really talk.'

'I tried earlier. Where have you been?'

'Look, if this isn't urgent—'

'I just can't believe that you are going back to it, after everything you said. The whole fucking teaching business was just to wind me up, wasn't it?'

'No... I...'

'Nat told me, and thank God she did, so don't go giving her a hard time—'

'I wouldn't dream of—'

'There is nothing I can do. Obviously. Nothing I *want* to do. Except to tell you that I think it was a pretty cheap way to behave – putting me through all that bull last year about wanting to give up doctoring – when it turns out you had no intention of quitting—'

'But I did—'

'Which makes me see that it was a deliberate ploy all along.'

'Ploy?'

'You have been plotting for years to leave me...'

'No, I—'

'But all I want to say is, don't think that hiding yourself away in the UK means you can wriggle out of increasing maintenance to more decent levels. My lawyers know of the situation and I can assure you...'

Nick held the phone a little away from his ear and let her finish. It made him glad he was on the M40 in England, even if he had made a botch of that particular day. At least he could turn the phone off when he wanted. At least he no longer had to suffer the vibrating air of his wife's anger, tiptoe round it, *manage* it.

When she had run out of steam, he said, 'All those ideas about switching to teaching were genuine, Donna. But plans change. If they didn't we'd be robots not humans. I have an interview for a consultant post and mentioned it to Nat. But I can assure you, that, whatever job I end up getting, whether it does in fact turn out to be back in a hospital or sweeping the streets of Cheltenham, I have no intention of reneging on our agreement as to what portion of my salary should go on maintenance to you and the girls. As I promised, I shall pay their part until they are through university, and yours up until such a time as you remarry, or until your share of my pension kicks in.'

She was silent for a few moments. 'Right. Good. Just so long as we are clear.'

'Oh, we are clear,' echoed Nick bitterly. 'Please kiss the girls for me.'

He tossed the phone onto the passenger seat. That he had started to miss his career had come as much of a surprise to him as anybody. It had been one of the many things he had planned to mention to Eleanor, she knowing better than most all about the early reluctance to follow in his father and sister's footsteps.

She knew too, of course, about the previous year's mid-life career thoughts – the wild idea of returning to England to teach– because she was the one to whom he had, inadvertently, first confessed it. She hadn't pulled any punches in her reply either, Nick remembered, smiling to himself at the recollection of her blunt response which, unlike Donna's bitter and spiteful opposition, clearly stemmed from the desire to protect his interests rather than trash them. *You are hankering after an idyll, nostalgic for something that never actually existed... hold fast to what you have. You never know when it might be taken away.* She may have been writing from her sister's email address, Nick reflected, but it had never prevented Eleanor from speaking her own mind.

His thoughts drifted to the shepherd's pie awaiting him, crusty-topped with cheese, the meat moist and packed with mushrooms and carrots and peppers. Instead of hunger, he experienced a stab of shame. A forty-one-year-old man lodging with his mother, his personal and professional life – not to mention his health – in tatters, was hardly edifying. The ketchup bottle would be ready on the table, he mused grimly, the cutlery neatly aligned with a table mat, the pepper and salt sellers, a glass of water, alongside. The perfectly clean clothes he had left on his bedroom chair would have been laundered, ironed and returned to their drawers. She was pitifully glad to have him – desperate, in spite of his efforts at reassurance, to make up for not having guessed his marital troubles or flown to his bedside after his accident. His plans for moving out were advancing fast, but she didn't like to discuss them. Part of it was sheer mother-love, Nick knew. But mostly it was because she was lonely. His sister, still unmarried and now an eminent neurologist in Sydney, had returned for their father's funeral, but then quickly flown back to her other life.

The truth was, they had never been that close as a family. How he was as a father to Natalie and Sasha could not have been more different. Nick clenched the steering wheel as the memory of the recent airport farewell with his daughters pounced. Nothing in his life had been as hard, not fighting for breath as the cold sea bubbled in his lungs, not forcing his legs to take the first agonising steps in the physio unit. At the security gate even Donna had looked momentarily stricken, her beautiful face convulsing in a fight for composure while Sasha and Natalie clung to him, weeping. Glimpsing her pain, Nick had, for one mad moment, entertained the notion of the pair of them trying again. But then Donna had switched her attention to her phone, and the despair and certainty that had brought them all to such a point washed back over him. Everything would work out, he promised his daughters, placing kiss after kiss on the tops of their heads, his own tears falling in their hair. He loved them. He needed to spend some time in England, but they would speak often and see each other soon. This was an interruption not a separation. They were not to be sad.

Nick took a hand from the steering wheel to swipe the tears off his cheeks. He missed his children. All the time. It was far worse than he had anticipated. There would always be lingering guilt, but the reasons for what he had done remained clear and strong: the need to distance himself from Donna and her controlling father had been important, but paramount was the desire to re-establish roots with his own country, to do what he could to lay the ground for his daughters to follow suit if they chose.

A van shot past, flashing its lights at his occupation of the middle lane. He had slowed to sixty without noticing it. Nick put his good foot down and sped on well above the speed limit, almost missing the slip road for Cheltenham and then having to swerve as something sleek and dark shot across the road in front of him. The car rocked briefly, terrifyingly, onto two wheels before thumping back into balance. Nick checked his mirrors, his heart pounding. By some miracle, the road in both directions had remained clear.

Life hung by such a thread, that was the thing. Bad luck,

good luck, breathing, not breathing, it was always a hair's breadth that separated the two. He crawled the rest of the way home like a learner, the blood still beating in his head, scolding himself that he, of all people, could have allowed himself to forget that, even for an instant.

30

Eleanor rammed her laptop into the front basket and tugged her bike out of the thicket of pedals and handlebars that had grown round it during her spell in the library. It had not been a productive session: three hours, and she had spent most of it fiddling with and then deleting paragraphs that had seemed perfectly acceptable a month before. It was two weeks since Trevor's book party. Her teaching duties at the tutorial college were in full, enjoyable swing, but her treasured writing project seemed to have stalled. Applying for the Bodleian reader's card, earmarking Friday mornings – her one decent slot of free time – had been her big bid to rectify the situation. Instead, if word count was anything to go by, she appeared to be going backwards.

She had woken too early, that was the trouble, Eleanor reflected crossly, bouncing her bike over the cobbles towards the cut-through to the High Street. Knotted in her bedclothes, her hair sticking to her face, she had surfaced before dawn out of a bad dream. The dream itself had been a mangle of things, as they always were, images slithering out of reach as consciousness took hold, although a couple of things had remained very clearly: Nick Wharton, for one, sitting with his back to her in a

handsome winged leather chair, a fire crackling in the grate to
his right, a set of lead-latticed windows to his left, casting a
crossword of sunlit squares across the floor. She had been
standing behind him, happy in the anticipation of being noticed.
But when he turned his head, with a slowness that smacked of
physical difficulty, or reluctance – it was impossible to tell which
– she had felt the first stirrings of anxiety. And with good reason,
since the face, when it presented itself, turned out not to belong
to Nick at all, but instead resembled the blind-eyed, gnarled
features she had always imagined for Jane Eyre's Mr Rochester,
marooned amid his own loneliness and the charred embers of
his once grand home.

'Jane,' he growled, 'is that you?'

In her dream Eleanor had remained rooted to the spot. He
had asked the question again, louder, more angrily, and for one
terrible moment she had been tempted to say yes, that she was
indeed Jane, out of sheer pity, because the poor man was so
wretched and blind, but also because, in his maimed, unseeing
state, there had seemed a fair chance he wouldn't know the
difference.

The bike jumped under her hands over the cobbles. The
reason for such a mishmash of imaginings was laughably
simple, Eleanor reminded herself. She had fallen asleep with
her nose in *Jane Eyre* the night before, re-reading the novel being
a part of her plan for kick-starting some life into that morning's
stint in the library. And though the shock of seeing Nick
Wharton had not dented her resolve to discontinue their correspondence, the man was still, understandably, floating round
her subconscious, causing unwanted and unwarranted mischief.

Being outside offered little immediate respite. The fresh
warmth of early morning had turned muggy. They had edged
into October, but still the Indian summer heatwave hung on, a
foggy sultriness thickening daily between bitingly cold nights.
The sky, murky when she had arrived at the library, was now
filled with oppressive mountains of cloud, billowing round the

city's turrets and spires like thick smoke. A storm was coming, Eleanor decided gloomily, pedalling with her usual speed towards the Cornmarket, calculating that there was just time to grab a sandwich before her first afternoon class.

She went to the sandwich bar in the grid of alleyways near her tutorial college, a porthole of a place manned by two cheerful shouting Italians. A queue of people were snaking out of its entrance. Eleanor padlocked her bike and joined the end of the line, behind a wan little girl licking a blue lolly and clasping the thigh of a man wearing a set of big headphones.

When her phone rang, aware of the little girl staring, Eleanor turned away to answer it.

'Eleanor, it's Howard.'

She relaxed at once, leaning back against the sandwich shop window. 'Howard. How are you? I can't really talk. I'm in queue for lunch, then working all afternoon.'

Howard said something else, but she couldn't make it out. She moved back into the queue checking the bars on her phone.

'Sorry, but I don't seem to have a great signal.' The wan girl had lost interest in her and was batting ineffectually at a wasp busily trying to land on her melting lolly.

'...your father has died.' Howard's voice burst through Eleanor's mobile with sudden clarity. 'Suddenly... this morning. I am sorry, Eleanor.'

'He... This morning? How?'

'The Bressingham just phoned. A member of staff found him in his chair. They are not sure yet of the exact cause, though they think it was a heart attack. They have everything in hand. They are going to get back to me. I said I would tell you.' Eleanor could hear the tenderness in his voice, the recognition that despite everything, Vincent was still her father. He was her father and he had died. 'Eleanor? Are you okay?'

'Yes, I mean... I don't know. I can't really talk now. Thanks for telling me.'

'I'll call later, all right? When I know more.'

Eleanor slipped the phone back into her skirt pocket. She wanted some feelings but none came. She hadn't been to The Bressingham since Howard's kind offer to drive her there on Boxing Day. She had vowed never to go again and stuck to it. Eleanor folded her arms, acutely aware of her heart beating normally. The little girl was still batting at the wasp. The child was getting more frantic, the man ignoring her. It was difficult to watch. So difficult that Eleanor found herself reaching out to flick the insect away herself. She swung at it with the back of her hand, not only making contact but somehow managing to trap the creature between her fingers. Almost at once she felt a fizzing stab of pain. She cried out, shaking the insect free.

The girl squealed and the man removed his headphones. 'What?' He directed the question down at the little girl, making no secret of his irritation.

'The lady got stung.'

'I'm fine.' Eleanor flapped her sore hand dismissively. In truth, the pain in her finger was piercing. She had never been stung in her life before and was stunned that something delivered by such a tiny creature, could have so much kick. Her hand appeared to be reacting badly too, swelling visibly. The finger that had been stung and the two on either side were like sausages. More inexplicably, she felt short of breath suddenly, so much so that she found herself falling against the sandwich shop window. She pressed both palms flat against the pane, staring down in some puzzlement as the colours spilling out of the rows of fat ready-to-go baguettes laid out before her – prosciutto, lettuce, tomatoes, eggs, tuna, cucumber, cheese – merged and ran like wet paint.

Maybe I am in shock, she thought. *Maybe this is grief.* No sooner had the idea formed it felt as if fingers were squeezing round her throat. In the same instant, the ground, hard, cold and smelling faintly metallic, slammed against her face. Under the flutter of her eyelids, a floating, wide, strange face briefly peered into hers, so close she could see the glossy dark tendrils of nostril hair. She wanted to speak but her throat had closed and appeared to be on fire.

If she could have spoken, she would have said, 'I can't see the sky. Please move so I can see the sky.' But then blackness came and everything was gone.

* * *

Nick was almost back at his car when it occurred to him that it would be wise to visit the hospital toilets before embarking on the return drive to Cheltenham. After the interview, he had had lunch in the canteen with Peter Whycliffe, who had been the one to give him a heads-up about the vacancy. It had been a welcome surprise to find how easily they picked up after so much time, exchanging more details of their potted personal histories than their sporadic email contact had allowed and slipping straight back into the vein of relaxed dry humour that had connected them as young men. Nick had insisted on paying for the lunch by way of a minor thank-you and they had agreed to fix a date for a pub supper.

Nick whistled as he retraced his steps across the hospital car park. The interview had gone well. Nothing was certain, of course, and there would be further rounds, but it was a good solid start. The professor in charge of the task of interrogation had appeared genuinely impressed with his CV as well as pleasingly unfazed by his undisguisable, still somewhat limited physical strength. It wasn't a marathon runner they were after but a dermatologist, he had joked, far keener to quiz Nick about interesting cases and the excellent reputation of Queen Elizabeth's, a hospital with which it turned out he was well-acquainted thanks to a stint of working in Cape Town himself.

Crossing the entrance to Accident and Emergency, Nick came to a halt, leaning on his stick as an ambulance swept in. As the doors of the vehicle opened and the crew jumped out to go about their work, a frisson passed through him, but when the stretcher came into view, he began to move on, both out of respect and because the need to pee was growing. Then a wild thatch of dark curly hair caught his eye and he stopped again, staring hard, heedless of anything else. He was a good ten yards away, but from what he could make out, the face, half hidden by an oxygen mask, was severely distorted with bruising and swelling. Nick gripped his stick, trying to process what he was seeing dispassionately. It was certainly a woman. With hair like that it had to be a woman. Lots of women had long thick curly dark brown hair, he reasoned. Not many were that tall, however; from head to toe this one filled almost the entire stretcher. Even then, Nick might have persuaded himself to walk on, had his eyes not alighted upon a foot encased in a scuffed black leather pump.

Nick found himself running, quite effectively, for the first time in ten months. His full bladder seemed to have evaporated. Without thinking, he charged towards the A & E entrance, stopping bewildered, as the jaws of its automatic doors slid shut in front of him, snapping the stretcher and its bearers from view. He then loped back round the side of the building to the main entrance, where he had originally been heading. Once inside, he blinked gormlessly at the array of signs for departments and wards. All he could see was Eleanor flying off her bicycle. Head first, like a human rocket, her rangy limbs thrashing as she landed. It had to be a bike accident.

Nick slumped into one of the big square visitor seats. Eleanor's face, from the snatched glimpse he had had of it, looked in a bad way. She wouldn't have been wearing a helmet. Helmets wouldn't be her style. He groaned quietly, closing his eyes.

'All right, sir?'

'Pardon?'

It was an elderly woman with a soft kind face sporting a large laminated badge saying, 'Volunteer'.

'Oh yes, thanks. Just... taking in some news.'

'I see. If you need somewhere quieter...' She pointed towards the main corridor. 'The chapel is just a little way down there on your right.' She touched his shoulder and moved on.

Nick got out his phone, scrolling to Peter Whycliffe, but then put it away. There was nothing the man could do. Nothing anyone could do that wasn't being done. The ache in his bladder came back with a push of pain, so he got up and stumbled in the direction of the toilets, leaning heavily on his stick with each step. His knees and hip-joints felt shaky and peculiar, as if on the verge of dislocation. The running was to blame, he knew, a ridiculous adrenaline-charged burst well beyond his still cautious limits in the gym.

On the way back, he noticed the chapel, empty, the door open. It was just a room, with a grey carpet, some upright purple chairs and a gaudy gold crucifix on a table beside a vase of flowers. Nick shuffled inside and went to sit on one of the purple chairs. He tried to think about Eleanor but his thoughts kept straying back to her father instead. The Reverend Vincent Keating. Eleanor and Kat's father had given Nick the creeps, but that hadn't changed anything.

More pertinent, Nick decided savagely, was that God, to whom Vincent ostensibly devoted his life, could have been so hoodwinked. Humans could be forgiven for being blind, but not God. Some of the sentences Eleanor had used in her letter swam into his mind; such a bleak, brave attempt to understand what might have gone on that his heart had gone out to her.

Kat was so like Mum. I keep thinking that maybe, in some terrible way, he saw an echo in her of what he missed when Mum died. So maybe it was love that warped him; or what he thought was love.

And where were you today, God, when the bus hit the bike? Nick demanded, as the small square room and its gaudy centre-piece came back into focus. Were you looking the other way then too? And if you were, please could you make sure she pulls through.

31

Eleanor opened her eyes, which felt inordinately heavy. On seeing Nick Wharton sitting in a chair facing her, she allowed them to fall shut again. Presumably she was having another dream. He didn't look anything like Mr Rochester this time. For one thing, his sight was definitely functioning, since he was scanning a newspaper, and though his face had the swarthy hint of evening shadow, he was also noticeably smart and up-to-date-looking, in blue suit trousers and a crisp light blue collared shirt open at the neck. Eleanor considered these details from behind her eyelids.

When the newspaper rustled, she ventured another look, only to find him staring right back at her. The moment seemed to last a long time and for her was not unlike the sensation of falling through space.

'Why are you here?' she said at last, the words coming out in a croak.

'Ah.' He folded the paper shut and dropped it onto the floor beside his chair. 'Now that would be what one might call serendipity.' He threw himself forwards, elbows onto his knees, grinning. 'How are you feeling?'

Eleanor considered the question, taking in the hospital

room, the drip in her arm, the aching stiffness in her body, the memory of the little girl with the lolly. 'I think I may be allergic to wasps.'

Nick chuckled darkly. 'Oh, I think that would be something of an understatement. Severe anaphylaxis, the crash team said. Luckily someone nearby was a doctor. He kept you going until the ambulance got there.'

Eleanor's thoughts fluttered to the man in the headphones with the little girl. Saviours weren't always obvious from the outside. Neither were monsters.

'Since then,' Nick went on, 'you've been pumped with epinephrine, antihistamines, corticosteroids – the works – not to mention getting a fair bit of sleep.' He grinned again. 'You certainly look a lot better than you did. The swelling has started to go down, though there's still quite a hefty bruise, from where you hit the pavement, they reckon.'

Eleanor tried to scowl but her face and throat hurt. It seemed odd, but also not odd, that he knew so much. 'So, there's swelling?'

'Afraid so.' Nick sat back, crossing his arms and chewing his lip in a show of thoughtfulness. 'Er... think, Elephant Man.'

'Elephant...? Oh great. Thanks.'

'Like I said,' he continued cheerfully, 'it's a lot better than it was, and a lot better than I had feared. In fact I thought you had been in a bike accident. Which shows what a rubbish doctor I am.' He looked delighted at the notion. 'Though, in my defence, it was a judgement made from quite some distance, and in a state of slight incredulity. Just don't peek at yourself in a mirror for a while would be my advice,' he teased, clearly not caring whether she was following a word he said or not, but then switching to a tone of sudden, urgent disbelief, to ask, 'Didn't you *know* you were allergic?'

Eleanor shook her head, aware both of the effort this took and the fact that she did not much like the notion of talking to Nick Wharton with a face that resembled the Elephant Man.

The conversation also seemed to be requiring a concentration that she wasn't quite able to give it. She felt light-headed, bruised, not just on her face but over her entire body. As if she had been in a fight. 'Kat was the one who had to be careful,' she murmured. 'We all knew to watch out for Kat. Didn't she ever tell you?'

'Not that I remember.' He frowned. 'But then there was a lot your sister didn't tell me, wasn't there...' Nick faltered, having no desire to lower Eleanor's spirits. A wasp not a bus, he thought suddenly. Did that count as a prayer answered?

'She got stung as a baby,' Eleanor went on. 'Though I was too young to...' She let the sentence hang, arrested by the realisation that the slice of black between the curtains behind Nick's chair was night sky. 'What time is it exactly?'

'Let me see now.' He tugged up his shirt cuff and made a big show of studying his wristwatch. 'Almost half past seven.'

There was a joviality to everything he did, Eleanor noted, everything he said, as if some great happiness or energy was bubbling to get out. It was puzzling, almost more so than the fact of seeing him on the chair. 'But why are you here,' she blurted stupidly. 'I still don't understand why you are here.'

Nick hesitated. Serendipity was indeed the explanation. Yet, during the course of the long afternoon, tracking her progress through A & E, eliciting Peter's assistance, trying not to get in the way while satisfying his own need for answers, it had also dawned on him that in some ways his presence at Eleanor's bedside in an Oxford hospital wasn't chance at all. He was there because, a long time ago, he had known her and turned his back on her. He was there because he had once loved her little sister. He was there because, more recently, he had nearly drowned and got well again; because he had left his wife, left Cape Town, used an old contact to get an interview and then stopped to stare as an ambulance roared across his path. He was there for myriad reasons, all of them interconnected but invisible until one paused to look backwards. Life only made sense in reverse.

Kierkegaard. Nick's heart jumped. It was a truth they had agreed on together.

'Like I said, it was partly luck,' he began, 'I happened to be here this afternoon for a job interview—'

'A *job*?' She tried to lever herself upright but fell back.

Nick started out of his chair, as if to catch her. 'Hey, steady. I'm only here by special permission, so don't go getting me into trouble. I wanted to see you wake up. Trevor came by earlier—'

'Trevor?'

'Yes, I called him. I'm afraid I used your phone. I thought *someone* should be here...' Nick paused.

Trevor had arrived in little over an hour, having belted down the motorway from West London. They had sat side by side in a waiting room while Eleanor received treatment and then slept, sharing their anxiety mostly in silence. Once reports started to indicate that she was going to be all right and Nick had made it clear he was happy to stay, Trevor had withdrawn, accepting an invitation to have a bite of supper and stop over with some Oxford friends, instructing Nick to keep him apprised of developments and saying he would return.

'Trevor is coming in the morning,' Nick reported to Eleanor now, 'hopefully to take you home.' But she didn't appear to be listening.

'A job *here*?' she repeated in a rasp. 'How come?'

Nick couldn't quite think how to start. 'Yes, well... the thing is...' He interlaced his fingers, watching the knuckles whiten. 'I... I have decided to work in England again... for the foreseeable future...'

When the door burst open, he was almost relieved. A petite nurse appeared behind a small trolley.

'Better leave you to it.' Nick leapt to his feet, scrambling for his stick and using one finger to scoop his suit jacket from off the back of the chair and sling it over his shoulder. 'I am well aware it's not official visiting hours.' He directed the comment at the nurse, beaming apologetically as he reached over to intercept the door. She gave him an uncertain nod, edging her trolley past.

Eleanor watched, suppressing the urge to ask when – if – he was coming back. He had already done so much, it didn't seem fair to expect any more. He gave her a quick wave before disappearing into the corridor.

'Apparently he's a great pal of Professor Whycliffe's,' said the nurse, as if this explained everything.

'Is he?' echoed Eleanor faintly. She lay back against her pillows, dimly let down and perplexed, yet still fearing that her own thick-wittedness was to blame. Her head felt as if someone had taken out her brain and stuffed wads of cotton wool between her temples instead. 'So I can go home tomorrow?'

'As long as none of your symptoms flare up again. You were pretty bad, so the doctors wanted to keep an eye.' The girl spoke in a voice that managed to be matter-of-fact as well as gentle. 'You'll be given some tablets to take for a few days – and an epi-pen, I should think, in case it happens again.' She bustled round as she talked, checking Eleanor's chart and pulse and then removing the drip. Eleanor flexed her arm, glad to have it back again. 'Now just the blood pressure and we're done.'

Eleanor held out the other arm to be wrapped, closing her eyes as the band inflated and tightened. She was deeply tired still. Inside the band her pulse bounced like a trapped insect. Her thoughts drifted back to the sting, and it reminded her of the bee buzzing on a warm windy day at her mother's graveside, Kat lolling in the grass with her skirt rucked round her twiggy thighs, their father in his socks and sandals, showing his hairy calves. A jolt of revulsion brought her back to the present. What had he been thinking that day? On any day? When had it started? There was truth. It existed. But all one ever got was glimpses. And now he had died.

Eleanor caught her breath as the memory of this fact rushed back at her. Howard's phone call. Her father was dead. Of a heart attack. She had forgotten. How had she forgotten?

The nurse was holding out some pills and a glass of water and saying something about a supper tray. As Eleanor forced the tablets down, the girl moved round the bed, straightening the sheets and punching air into the pillows, her short thin arms working like pistons. 'Do you want me to stay while you use the toilet?'

'No, I'll be fine thanks.' Eleanor tracked the progress of the trolley back to the door, not looking at the nurse's face, longing for her to be gone.

'The supper will be along soon. Press your button if you need anything.'

'Yup. Thanks.'

The door fell shut with a swish. Eleanor swung her legs out of the bed and sat for a few moments, listening to the quietness. There were feelings now, but not the ones she had expected. Her father was gone. There was relief, but sadness too, like she had lost another piece of Kat.

Gingerly, Eleanor levered herself upright and groped her way across the room, using the edge of the bed and the wall for support. The toilet cubicle had a light switch on a string dangling by the door. Eleanor tugged on it, only to gasp as her face appeared in the small mirror above the washbasin. The bloating made her virtually unrecognisable. Elephant Man had not been wide of the mark. Elephant Man had been kind. She traced her fingers over the new lumpy contours in miserable disbelief. The bruise on her forehead was especially unsightly, a lump like an egg, of veiny blues and yellows, running into the puffy ledge of her eyebrows. She hurriedly finished her ablutions, before stumbling back into bed.

A few minutes later there was a light knock on her door, which she assumed would be her supper, but Nick's face appeared round the edge of it, looking at once hopeful and apologetic.

She threw her hands over her face with an involuntary moan.

'Hey, are you okay?'

'No. Turn the light out.' She spoke through her fingers

'The light?' he repeated, sounding concerned. 'Do you have a headache?' When she didn't answer, he said sternly, 'Eleanor. If you are experiencing severe head pain then—'

'No, no... my head is fine,' she mumbled, widening her fingers to speak through them. 'I looked in the mirror, okay? I looked in the mirror like you told me not to. I am a gargoyle. Worse than a gargoyle. So I'd prefer the light off. *Please.*'

'Right.'

He sounded bemused. Amused. It was hard to be sure without looking. He flicked the wall switch, and for a moment neither of them spoke.

'It's really not that bad,' Nick ventured at length. 'I mean, compared to what it was...' He approached the end of the bed, propping his stick against the frame. 'By tomorrow...' It took him a moment to realise she was crying. Feeling helpless, he gave one of her ankles a squeeze through the bedclothes. 'The swelling is only temporary. By tomorrow you will be almost back to normal. Hey, Eleanor, please don't be upset.' He patted the ankle, the sense of helplessness worsening.

When still she wept, he limped to her side, racking his brain for some more solid reassurances. Donna had always said he was useless when she was upset, that all he did was spout obvious things that made no difference whatsoever. His track record with the girls was better. They always seemed to find his useless words soothing. And his hugs. Those tended to work well.

'Eleanor, stop this at once,' he instructed, trying a harsher tack and perching on the bed. 'The swelling is just part of the anaphylaxis, the reason such an allergic reaction is so danger-ous. Basically, a load of chemicals get released – histamines and so on – from cells in the blood and body tissues. These cause blood pressure to drop to unacceptable levels and also dilate the blood vessels, making them leak fluid. Hence the swelling, especially round the face and throat...'

She had turned on her side, away from him, so he ventured a pat on her back, very lightly.

'Eleanor? I forbid you to be so upset. You are going to be right as rain in a matter of hours. Trust me I'm a...' Nick faltered, partly because faith in his power to say anything helpful was dissolving and partly because his hand had made contact with some of the rivulets of her hair and they were slipping through his fingers, like silk. It took a monumental resolve to pull his hand free and pluck a tissue from her bedside box instead. 'Here.' He dangled the tissue near her face.

'Dad's died,' she said thickly, snatching the tissue and struggling into a sitting position to blow her nose. She had stopped crying, but her body had stiffened, a warning, it seemed to Nick, that in spite of this wretched information no further patting would be welcome. 'Howard had phoned to tell me just before I got stung. Somehow I had forgotten.' She thumped the bedcovers, shaking her poor swollen face, even redder now from her distress. 'Until just now. *How* could I have forgotten?'

Nick started to answer, but she cut across him.

'I loathed him. For how he was with me. For what he did to Kat. I don't even know if he was properly nice to Mum and now I'll never find out. But I've lost all of them. It's just me now. Do you see? I'm the only one left.' More tears were seeping down her cheeks.

'Would you like me to call Trevor?'

'No,' she said crossly, 'I would not.'

'Or perhaps a nurse—'

'A *nurse*?' She managed a withering glance.

Nick stood up with a sigh of defeat. 'Okay. Well, I'm guessing you'd prefer it if I left you in peace, at any rate.'

'No I wouldn't,' she snapped. 'You have been... are being... so unbelievably kind. Thank you. Though I think that might be making things worse.' She plucked out a fresh tissue. 'Kindness makes me cry, you see. So no more of it, do you hear?' She buried her face in the tissue, making small trumpeting noises as she blew.

Nick hovered by the bed, peering at her doubtfully. 'So you don't want me to go?'

Eleanor raised her head, looking at him properly for the first time. She sighed slowly and heavily. When she spoke, it was in a voice softened with tender resignation. 'It isn't a question of what I *want*, Nick.'

'Isn't it?' Nick was aware of all the hairs up and down his arms and on the back of his neck standing upright. 'What is it a question of then, Eleanor?' He folded his arms to steady himself. The room seemed to quiver and then grow very still around them. 'Tell me anything you like, Eleanor. Anything.'

'I still like you.' The words seemed to float out of her mouth. She sounded defeated. 'I mean, *really* like you,' she repeated bitterly. 'A lot. Too much. As bad as before. I thought it was done with, but seeing you again has made me realise that it is not. I can dress up what I did last year – letting you think I was Kat – and, like I said in my letter, it did help distract me from the awfulness of her being so sick, but the bottom line, I can see now, in all its pathetic, despicable glory, is that it was the chance of some contact. With you. I suppose it's in my genes, or something,' she muttered. 'Most people grow out of girly crushes, but not me apparently.' She blew her nose again sharply, before adding, much more matter-of-factly, 'There, at least that's done with. Better that you know. And I can only apologise. But don't worry, just as soon as I'm out of this place I shall steer well clear...' She broke off as quick purposeful footsteps sounded outside the door. Somehow Nick just had time to lunge across the room and put the light on. A moment later Peter Whycliffe, ruddy and bespectacled, blustered in.

'Ah, someone told me that you were still here. Not interrupting, I hope.' He threw Nick a slightly quizzical glance before smiling broadly at Eleanor. 'Hello, I gather from my colleagues

that you are progressing very well indeed. I've just overtaken
Doreen on her way with the late supper trolley, which I can
assure you is good news. Unlike some of our fellow institutions,
we have rather splendid food. Nick, could I have a word? Now? If
it suits?' He held the door wider by way of an invitation.

'Absolutely.' Nick turned in the direction of Eleanor, offering
her a nod of farewell but not really seeing her. What she had
said was still exploding inside his head, each word pinging sepa-
rately, not making sense.

'Arrived this afternoon and we can't get rid of him,' Peter
quipped, pulling a face at Eleanor over the top of Nick's head as
he ushered him outside.

Eleanor had just spotted the stick leaning against the end of
the bed when Nick hobbled back in. He appeared to be breath-
less, as if he had covered a great distance at considerable speed,
instead of just a few yards. 'Don't speak,' he commanded,
pushing out his jaw in a way that she had forgotten he did and
which someone else – not Eleanor – might have interpreted as
hostile. 'I forgot this.' He seized the stick and brandished it like a
sword. 'And to tell you that I like you too. Very much indeed.
And the reason I am job-hunting in England is because my wife
and I are divorcing and I have come back to live here permanently.' He reached behind him as he spoke, hunting for and
missing the door handle.

Eleanor couldn't take her eyes off his face, so familiar, so
longed for. She was glad he had told her not to speak, because
she couldn't think what to say. Her brain was too taken up with
the realisation that this was one of the most tremendous
moments of her life, a moment she had never expected and
which she never wished to end.

32

'So, basically, you are on the rebound.'

'Basically.'

'An ancient forty-year-old—'

'Almost forty-two now.'

'Thank you for the correction. An almost-forty-two-year-old. On the rebound. All single women should beware.'

'They should. Particularly single women with large brains and long legs and fledgling writing projects about two troubled little girls and *Jane Eyre*, which they, understandably, do not wish to discuss because it puts them off.'

Eleanor changed gear, not an entirely straightforward manoeuvre, since Nick's hand was on her knee. He had asked if he could put it there, concerned it would interfere with her ability to concentrate on her driving. It interfered with her ability to concentrate on her own name, let alone driving, but she had vehemently protested otherwise. At the passing reference to her work, she shot him a look of gratitude, marvelling at the balance he seemed to strike, effortlessly, between support and intervention. 'You are trouble, in other words.'

'Major trouble. To be avoided. Like that string of bollards, coming up on the left.'

'I see the string of bollards. I plan to stay to the right of them.'

'Excellent plan.'

'Thank you.'

'I like how you drive, by the way. It makes me feel completely safe, yet slightly excited.'

She giggled, sweeping into the bollarded lane and then out of it, past a short line of cars waiting their turn by a makeshift set of traffic lights. 'That's an interesting combination.'

'It is a fantastic combination. And a surprise. I thought you were purely a cyclist. That day I visited, I only saw your bike.'

'That's because this was in the garage.' Eleanor patted the dashboard of the Corsa, purchased for a rock-bottom price, thanks to its great age and a six-figure mileage, soon after her move to Oxford. 'It was to be part of my new grown-up life, but I barely use it. Don't move your hand, by the way. I like it where it is.'

'So do I. The hand isn't going anywhere.' He slipped his palm a little lower, so that it cupped her kneecap. 'I am so glad you once loved me. Have I mentioned that?'

'You have. Once, I think, or maybe twice.'

'And telling me about it in that letter of yours – that was tremendous of you. Brave. Thank you for doing that.'

'My pleasure. However, as you might recall, you didn't love me back. Not remotely. You loved Tilly, then Kat. You dropped me like a stone.'

'So I did. But I feel bad about that in retrospect, and I certainly liked you. I started to like you twenty years ago and now we are building on it.'

'Building?' Eleanor giggled again. It was ten days since he had left her hospital room and this was how it had been, the conversation buzzing and leaping, playful, serious, utterly delighting. There was so much to say, it was always impossible to remain on one subject for long. It was as if they knew each other, which they did, but also didn't know each other, because in so many ways they didn't. Apart from a couple of phone conversations, they had met just twice, once for a walk round the Parks and once for a greasy-spoon lunch in the Covered Market, a brazen request of hers for a jaunt down memory lane, to which Nick had acquiesced with wry amusement. On this third occasion they were returning from the Sussex coast to Oxford, half lost in a mesh of country roads.

They were driving back from her father's cremation which had been organised with Howard at a crematorium on the outskirts of Lewes. The outward journey had been quite different, with her subdued by nerves and dread, and Nick tactfully silent. But now, with the job done, even the ashes scattered, a brief thin cloud falling into the sea, she felt as if she was floating, a balloon basket free of weights. The presence of Nick was, she knew, integral to this feeling, and yet when he had first come up with the idea of accompanying her to the service, she had said no.

'But why not?' he had retorted. 'It will be an ordeal for you. I would like to think that having me there will make it less of one.'

'Is that so?' she had countered weakly, disarmed both by his determination to be kind and the closeness of his tall angular body. The café table was small. Inches separated their elbows, their fingers, their knees. Each time he gesticulated she had to resist the urge to grab his hand just to hold it. They had agreed during the course of the week to be friends – *good* friends – but whenever they met, the air around them, for her at least, seemed to crackle. Before Nick spoke she had just been watching, transfixed, as he ploughed up the last drizzles of his egg yolk with a piece of fried bread. Fried food of any kind had been 'forbidden' by his wife, he had remarked casually, plunging his knife and fork into a glistening sausage and responding to Eleanor's exclamation of disbelief with a rueful headshake that stopped her enquiring further.

'I did once know him after all,' he had reminded her gently, 'just as I knew your dear sister. Or thought I did.' He paused, looking hollow-eyed for a moment, distracted by some conjured image that Eleanor could only guess at. 'Which means I also have some inkling of why the funeral will be so very hard,' he went on, threading his hand between their plates and mugs and sliding it over hers. 'So let me go through it with you. As a friend,' he added quickly, 'and because you are *not* alone.'

For an instant all Eleanor could feel was relief that he had made some sort of physical contact at last. She had looked down at his hand, loving the vast width of the knuckle span, the way it so easily covered hers. 'You were always ravenous,' she murmured, 'that's what I remember most vividly about coming here when we were students. And full of clever-talk. I used to think you were such a genius, quite the Mr Renaissance, with his doctoring and his literary knowledge.'

'Like your beloved Keats, maybe?'

She nodding, smiling at what he remembered. 'Like Keats.'

'And now what do you think?'

'Now the jury is out.'

'Oh dear. How long does the jury think it's going to need?'

'A very very long time indeed. In fact, the jury may never return.' Eleanor had grinned, aware both that she was blushing and that for once she didn't mind because it was purely from a new brand of happiness that she had no wish to disguise.

'But you were always hungry too,' he had burst out with gleeful indignation. 'I've just remembered. That first time we met – in the college library – your stomach *roared*. Hey, does it still do that?' He peered in the direction of her midriff as if sizing up a dangerous object. 'And you may as well know,' he went on, swiping an abandoned quarter of buttered toast off her plate and chewing it as he talked, 'that way back then, I always thought you were extremely striking. I knew it, but just didn't fully appreciate—'

'No, Nick. Don't,' she had pleaded, serious suddenly.

'Don't what?' He dropped the wedge of toast, his strong blue eyes staring out with a hunger that Eleanor couldn't help thinking had nothing to do with food. He wanted to love and be loved. As did she. As did everyone.

'We must never try and rewrite the past,' she commanded. 'For instance, I don't want you to pretend you liked me more than you did. What happened, happened. We are here now, friends, having this lunch that I am so enjoying. That's all that matters'

'But you were striking and I did like you,' he had insisted, sheepishly.

'Good. Thank you.' She smiled. 'But, with everything that has occurred, including and especially my own heinous, sisterly deceitfulness – which you somehow really do seem to have forgiven...' Eleanor paused. Forgiving herself was going to take longer. 'Because of that, I want – need – us to be absolutely honest with each other. Always. No matter how difficult the subject. Can we agree on that?'

'We can.' He picked up the toast and set it down again. 'But please don't forget I lied to you as well. All that stuff about being happy, you now know it was bollocks. Donna and I had both been the opposite of happy for years. In fact we made each other miserable. And the reason I lied about it when I was writing to you—'

'To Kat.' Her eyes flashed.

'To Kat,' he conceded with a sigh, 'was simply because I wanted you to feel safe enough to continue replying. Though, whatever you say,' he went on quickly, 'it *was* you I was getting to know during those months: your words, your thoughts, your voice. And then you wrote properly anyway... a "real" letter.' He shook his head slowly. 'It was so honest, I couldn't imagine the courage it took. I still can't.'

Eleanor had tried to glare but everything he said made her too happy.

'And as for the Kat imposter business, "what's in a name",' he teased, '"that which we call a rose by any other name would smell as sweet..."'

'Quoting Shakespeare is *not* playing fair,' she had hissed, sitting back and wagging a finger. 'Especially not *Romeo and Juliet*. It's a cheap trick. Corny. We are not in a romcom.'

'No we are not. So let me be at your side for the funeral of your father,' Nick had retorted, suddenly solemn himself, and pinning her with fierce determined eyes until she agreed.

'You were brave today,' he said, a few minutes after the bollards. 'You are always brave.'

'No, I am not, but thank you. And thank you again for coming. You were right, it really helped. And now I feel so relieved, it's almost embarrassing.'

'Good. Don't be embarrassed. Your relief has been well earned.'

Eleanor fell silent, seeing again her father's coffin gliding through the grey silk curtains towards incineration. It had indeed helped having Nick there, filling the space at her side while making no demands on her attention. But the plainness of the surroundings had been strengthening too. In a church she might have wept, for so many reasons, but, somehow, the austerity of the crematorium's so-called chapel, a square modern room, with fresh white walls and pre-taped organ music, had offered a natural bulwark against heavy emotion.

She had feared seeing Howard might set her off, because of Kat, but he had arrived on his own at the last minute, taking a back-row chair in the near-empty room and shooting her look of apology. Afterwards, over the tea and biscuits provided as part of the service package, he had stumbled through some small talk with Nick and then bolted with further apologies, thanking Eleanor again, profusely, for their pre-agreement that she would take charge of the ashes. 'Not near us, or your mother, remember,' he had reminded her grimly, referring to a phone discussion they had had earlier in the week. 'I couldn't bear that. Personally, and no offence, but I hope your father rots in hell.'

'I think he managed to make his own life pretty hellish,'

Eleanor had murmured in reply, finding the thought gave her some solace.

As to the ashes, she was at a loss and had been planning to defer the matter until Nick had suggested the sea, mentioning a perfect cliff-side spot which he had visited several times with his hearty godfather.

'Would that have been the godfather with the dog,' Eleanor had ventured, once they were in the car and on their way.

'The very same.'

'The one you had been visiting when you came to take me out to lunch that time. The day we picked up Kat hitchhiking. The day you first met her. The day you fell in love with her.' Eleanor sighed. 'God she was glorious, wasn't she?'

'Yes, she was,' Nick had replied softly. He was holding the urn on his lap, keeping it wedged between his knees as he issued instructions for when to turn right and left.

'I saw the two of you in bed that night, you know,' Eleanor had admitted, 'the one you wrote about in that last email, when you still thought I was Kat. I had this vague drunken plan of seducing you. I crept along the passageway only to find that Kat had got there first.' She laughed as Nick groaned. 'It's okay. I wanted to die at the time, of course. But it's what happened. In fact, looking back, I honestly think it must have helped Kat enormously, having you in her life. Dad sort of approved because you were mature and decent. And to have you so obviously smitten can only have boosted the confidence she needed to escape properly and make the break for London.' Seeing the set of Nick's face, still faintly pained and studiously staring at the windscreen, she added, 'We agreed straight talking, remember? You have nothing to be sorry for. Besides, Kat wasn't exactly plain sailing, was she, for all her gloriousness? I may have kept my distance, but I always knew she gave you a hard time.'

Nick shot her a rueful smile. 'Your sister was a nightmare,' he had conceded fondly.

There was a small car park and a footpath that ran along a

weather-beaten hedge towards a lookout point on the cliff-side. They went in single file, the wind beating at their clothes, forcing Nick to lean more on his walking stick. After ten minutes they had reached a jutting section furnished with a bench and a telescope. A stretch of fencing replaced the hedge, opening up the view of the cliff drop and the expanse of grey choppy water below.

Nick had stood a little apart from her, fixing his gaze on the horizon, clearly content for her to take however long she needed. He leant against a fence post, clearly lost in his own thoughts as he stared out across the water. Difficult thoughts, quite probably, Eleanor realised. Such an expanse of water. It was a wonder he could even look. She went to stand next to him, placing a tentative hand on his back, and then, in one swift movement, she had unscrewed the lid of the urn and flung the contents as far as she could into the drop below. Nick did not flinch, or speak.

For an instant Eleanor had feared the swirl of ash might blow back at them, like some horrible final ironic twist in a film noire; bits of her unknowable, unforgiving and unforgivable father catching in the creases of her clothes, her hair. But, instead, the wind actually seemed to hold its breath for a few instants, providing a pocket of stillness. The ashes floated and dispersed quickly, a gossamer veil merging into the steely back-drop of water and sky.

When Nick's hand found hers, she had squeezed it hard. 'I don't think he ever loved me. I hate him for what he did to Kat. I'm glad he's gone.'

'So am I. For you.'

'I miss Kat so much.'

'Yes, I know.'

'Like you miss your dad, maybe,' she went on, as they turned back down the path, 'with nothing getting in the way of it, just wanting them back.'

'Yes, I suppose. Though I am not sure my mother would

agree. She's hopeless without my father. The price of love.' He
pulled a face. 'I can't wait to get away. I've started telling letting
agents I'll take anything with a roof. I've not heard back about
the Oxford interview, but I've applied for a couple more jobs,
one in Cheltenham, the other at the Royal Berkshire. I would so
like to have something sorted in time for the girls.'

In the car he had seemed subdued, fighting annoyance with
the stick. But the moment they set off he had brightened.

They were in the thick of the countryside, still an hour off
Oxford, when he rapped the empty urn. 'You know, this might
make a fine plant pot. Geraniums or something.'

'Geraniums?' Eleanor couldn't help laughing.

'I like it when you laugh. Sort of low and throaty.'

'I suppose you're going to say you didn't fully *appreciate* that
either, all those centuries ago.'

'On the contrary, I have no recollection of your laugh whatsoever. In fact, I don't think you did laugh much in your student
days. Maybe that was one of the reasons I didn't pay you as
much attention as I might have.'

Eleanor let out a small whoop of protest. 'Still, he tries to
rewrite history for his own purposes.'

'You're mostly very jolly now though, from what I have been
able to ascertain,' Nick went on, ignoring her. 'Always laughing.
Even today, a bit.' He eyed her shrewdly. 'Anyone could be
forgiven for thinking you were in danger of being happy.'

'Could they? Oh my goodness.'

'By the way, if and when a lay-by comes up, would you mind
pulling into it?'

'Of course. A lay-by. No problem. Nature calls, I assume.'

'It does.'

When a loop of tarmac parallel to the road appeared a few
minutes later, Eleanor steered smoothly onto it, pulling up on its
grass verge. 'Will this do?' She peered through the windscreen.
'A field and a few handy trees.'

'Very handy.'

She turned off the engine and folded her arms. 'No hurry.'

'Good.' But instead of getting out of the car, he shifted in his seat so he was facing her. 'Because I don't like to hurry.'

'Okay. That's fine.' Eleanor swallowed, all the confusion of being in his company rushing back at her. He had made a bad day good. She liked having him nearby, especially when he flirted. But the hand on her leg had been withdrawn and the state of suspension between them was starting to wear her down. Maybe he was playing games. Maybe her stupid, ever-hopeful heart was about to get trampled on again.

'I have to tell you something difficult.' He spoke with sudden gravity, making the confusion no easier to bear.

'Aren't you going to pee?' she asked feebly.

'Nope. I lied. I just wanted you to pull over. You asked for honesty and here I am, already disobeying. You can't trust me for a moment. Trouble, as you have yourself so acutely observed. This thing I have to tell you.' The seriousness was back in his voice. 'It may seem premature. But with this... friendship of ours, I want to take nothing for granted. Straight talking, just like you have said.' He sounded almost cross.

Apprehension was swamping the excitement again. It was like being on a rollercoaster and she was sick of it. Eleanor fixed her eye on one of the trees, a lone silver birch overshadowed by the pines. It looked small and sickly. The ghostly silver birches of her childhood came back at her, the whisper of danger she had heard in their branches. The world, even when it glowed, contained dark places, shadows. She had always known that, long before she understood it. Nothing good was ever plain sailing, least of all love. And she did love him, she realised. 'Get it over with,' she whispered.

He cupped her face and lifted it so that they were nose to nose. 'May I kiss you now? That's the real reason why I asked you to pull over; because of the need to do this.' He brushed his lips against hers. 'It was starting to get in the way. It has been for a while now. Even in the hospital.'

'Really? When I was all bloated?' Eleanor blinked at him.

'I know, bonkers.' He shook his head and started to kiss her.

'The handbrake is sticking into my ribs,' she mumbled.

'That's too bad,' he said, kissing her harder.

A shout outside – loud as a gunshot – made them pull apart, how many minutes later neither could have said.

'Kissing in a car – whatever next,' Eleanor murmured, nestling against Nick, the brake having somehow found a comfortable niche between her thigh and hipbone.

'We should be locked up,' Nick agreed cheerfully, trying and failing to flatten all the wild wisps of her hair tickling his chin. After a moment, he added, 'I may have to start believing in God. Would you be okay with that?'

'Sure.' Eleanor giggled. 'God, Martians, believe what you like.' She wrested herself upright, defeated by the handbrake at last.

'I can't think how to explain it otherwise.'

'Explain what?'

'This. Us. You and me. Now.' He ran a finger down her cheek.

'I don't want to understand it,' Eleanor said quietly, starting the car.

'I'd invite you back to my place if I had one,' said Nick as they re-joined the road. 'Unless you want to meet my mother of course?'

Eleanor shot him a look. 'I would definitely like to meet your mother. But not this afternoon... if you don't mind.'

'Ah. What did you have in mind for this afternoon?'

'My place? A cup of tea?'

'Tea. Fantastic.' He settled back into his seat, folding his arms. 'That sounds ideal.'

At her front-door Eleanor found her capacity to manage the situation in danger of dissolving. There was such anticipation, such joy, but also pressure. Two decades of it. The dashed hopes and dead ends, the shadows of Kat, all the complicated sorrows, for a moment it felt as if the walls of their pasts might cave in on them. Her house keys jumped in her hands as she tried to use them.

'You're not rushing, are you,' Nick murmured, pressing against her and slipping his arms round her waist. 'It would be a shame, would it not, to rush after twenty years.' He shuffled closer, kissing the back of her neck. 'I'd carry you if I could. Over the threshold. But I can't. So you'll have to consider yourself metaphorically carried instead. Will that do?'

'Metaphorically carried?' A laugh of pure joy escaped her. It would have been hard to think of anything she wanted more.

33

Trevor settled deeper into the deckchair, raising the rim of his panama so that the sun could find all of his face and linking his hands across the swell in his belly, the one that contained Eleanor's splendid Sunday lunch and the tumour he had recently been told would kill him. Three months, the oncologist had said. Six at most.

Through half-closed eyes, he let his gaze travel round Eleanor's fine garden, with its high enclosure of greenery and lower tiers of colour. White, yellow, pink, blue, he wasn't good on names, Latin or otherwise, but the colours were a feast, even with autumn getting into its stride at last. The weekend was to offer the last gasp of temperate weather for months, the pundits had warned, news much discussed during the course of Eleanor's delicious lamb tagine and spiced rhubarb crumble, and deployed afterwards by her, quite fiercely, as the reason her guests were to enjoy their coffee and chocolate in the garden. She had opened the kitchen door and shooed them outside, directing Nick and Billy to the lopsided shed that stowed a hotchpotch of rickety folding chairs, leftover from her Russian lover's days, she had explained merrily, and summoning Megan's

assistance in fetching a stack of fleeces and blankets to cover
their knees and shoulders.

As a result, Trevor was as warm and wrapped as a parcel. At
his feet were a cluster of earthenware pots, among them a
doughty geranium he didn't remember seeing before, sprouting
out of a grey ceramic urn in clusters of such vibrant polished red
that he blinked in wonder every time it caught his eye. All the
colours of the world were brighter to him now. It was one of the
upsides of the diagnosis.

Not unlike being in love, Trevor decided, watching Eleanor
and Nick, whose sense of each other was palpable, even when
they were many yards apart. They were, as the adage so aptly put
it, falling in love. They talked and listened to other people, but
really they were only talking and listening to each other. Their
hearts were open and forgiving. No obstacle was too high or
wide to be overcome. They chattered about each other at every
opportunity. He was job-hunting and flat-hunting. She was
teaching and writing. He was soon to meet her nephew and
nieces. In a couple of days she would meet his girls. Their lives
had been stepping stones to each other, Eleanor had gushed
during one rare private moment before lunch, a zig-zag path
towards what was meant to be.

There was no right or wrong to such sentiments. Trevor
knew that from Larry. You found someone and it felt like they
had found you. Then it was a matter of working through whatever came next, none of it easy, none of it guaranteed.

'Sleepyhead.' He opened his eyes as Eleanor tweaked up the
brim of his hat.

'Too much pud.' He grinned.

'Yes, indeed.' She tapped her index finger against the new
bulge of his belly.

'I am glad you are happy, sweetie. I want to say be careful,
but there's no point.'

'No point,' she echoed gleefully, skipping over to flop next to

Megan, who was sitting on a blanket she had laid out as a picnic
rug, one arm slung over Billy, parked in a deckchair alongside.
They had announced during the course of lunch that they were
expecting their fourth child, prompting hoots of congratulations
and much cheerful speculation about how highland cattle, pets,
siblings and busy jobs would be stretched to accommodate
taking care of the new arrival. At one point Billy had left his seat
and walked round the table to hug his wife, saying she was a
marvel and he didn't know where he would be without her.
Trevor had caught Eleanor and Nick exchanging a glance,
sharing some hint of extra knowledge.

Life went on, that was the thing, Trevor mused. His tumour
huge, metastasised, would reap its obvious end. The horrors of
pointless, prolonging treatment had been discussed and abandoned. He was doing what Eleanor's dear sister had done; recognising his time was almost done. Soon it would be painkillers
and difficult conversations. But not that day. That day was lunch
and joy and babies and love. The geranium was blinding.
Bloody. Beautiful. Bloody beautiful. Trevor closed his eyes.

* * *

'Don't move, there's a butterfly on your back.'

'So long as it's not a wasp.'

'It's definitely not a wasp. It's small and blue. I think it likes
your fleece.'

'Everyone's gone.'

'Except me.'

'Except you.'

'It was a great lunch. Great food. Great friends.'

They were lying on the blanket, the afternoon sun flaming
intermittently through the branches of the weeping ash. Eleanor
was on her stomach, one cheek resting sideways on the pillow of
her hands, facing Nick. He was alongside, leaning back on his
elbows, his legs straight out.

'I always liked this garden,' she said, 'even with Igor. I like the way it is enclosed. It makes me feel safe. I know the big bad and wonderful world is out there, but it is nice sometimes, not to have to look at it. When we were little I was happier in London. Broughton had such open views, the sea lurking just behind; I knew it was beautiful but it made me afraid. So huge, so exposed. It was like anything could happen.'

'Which it can.' Nick plucked a blade of grass and tickled her ear. 'The strangest things.'

They smiled at each other.

'Why did you write to Kat after all those years? Was it really just about turning forty, like you said? Don't answer if you don't want to.'

'I do want to. I have wondered myself sometimes. Approaching such a great age was definitely part of it – I got back in touch with several old friends at the same time. But with Kat...' Nick scowled, trying and failing to take himself back to the mindset of soul-searching that had gradually got the better of him. Unhappiness was like being ill, he decided, impossible truly to recollect; a memory of fact rather than feeling. 'Maybe it was also partly to do with wanting to remember what it was like to love some-one. I mean, really to love someone. I wrote to Tilly too, as it happens, perhaps for the same reason, but she didn't reply.'

'And instead of Kat or Tilly you got me.'

'I got you', he said softly.

'Is the butterfly still there?'

'Yes. It's such a delicate dusty blue. Why would anyone want to catch such a thing?'

'Like your Nabokov and Fowles,' she teased.

'I love how clever you are.'

'That's good. Personally, I am only after your body.' She edged nearer him, doing her best to shake her shoulders. 'Fly away, Mr Butterfly, I need to kiss this man.' She shook and shimmied harder, making Nick laugh because she looked funny and because the insect stayed where it was.

'Hang on.' He leant over her and cupped the creature gently between his palms before throwing it at the sky. It fluttered for an instant, regrouping, and then took off, a dark dot merging with the flames of the sunlit ash.

ACKNOWEDGEMENTS

With huge thanks to Amanda Ridout and Boldwood Books for making 'Good Girls' part of its inaugural fiction list, and to Sarah Ritherdon, whose immense editing skills helped me shape the story of sister love that is the heart of the book.

BOOK CLUB QUESTIONS

- What is the real love story at the heart of the book?
- Whose voice did Eleanor hear by the railway line and how was it a turning point in her life?
- Why did Kat really make Eleanor write to Nick for her?
- Was Vincent a thoroughly bad man or a flawed good one?
- What did Connie teach Kat about motherhood?
- What do Kat and Eleanor show us about sister relationships?
- What ultimately troubles Eleanor most about Kat?
- What does the title of the book mean to you in the context of the novel?
- Was Connie a 'good girl' too?
- What would have been different if Kat had told Eleanor her secret?
- How do the men in the book compare to the women?
- Are Nick and Connie both abused spouses?
- Do you think Nick and Eleanor will live happily ever after?

ABOUT THE AUTHOR

Amanda Brookfield is the bestselling author of 15 novels including *Relative Love* and *Before I Knew You*, and a memoir, *For the Love of a Dog* starring her Golden Doodle Mabel. She lives in London and is currently a Visiting Fellow at Univ College Oxford.

Visit Amanda's website: https://www.amandabrookfield.co.uk/

Follow Amanda on social media:

facebook.com/amandabrookfield100

twitter.com/ABrookfield1

instagram.com/amanda_and_mabel_brookfield

ABOUT BOLDWOOD BOOKS

Boldwood Books is a fiction publishing company seeking out the best stories from around the world.

Find out more at www.boldwoodbooks.com

Sign up to the Book and Tonic newsletter for news, offers and competitions from Boldwood Books!

http://www.bit.ly/bookandtonic

We'd love to hear from you, follow us on social media:

 facebook.com/BookandTonic

twitter.com/BoldwoodBooks

 instagram.com/BookandTonic

9 781838 893132